THEATER
IN THE
AMERICAS

A Series from
Southern
Illinois
University
Press
ROBERT A.
SCHANKE,
Series Editor

Other Books in the Theater in the Americas Series

The Theatre of Sabina Berman: The Agony of Ecstasy *and Other Plays*
Translated by Adam Versényi
With an Essay by Jacqueline E. Bixler

Messiah of the New Technique: John Howard Lawson, Communism, and American Theatre, 1923–1937
Jonathan L. Chambers

Composing Ourselves: The Little Theatre Movement and the American Audience
Dorothy Chansky

Women in Turmoil: Six Plays by Mercedes de Acosta
Edited and with an Introduction by Robert A. Schanke

Unfinished Show Business: Broadway Musicals as Works-in-Process
Bruce Kirle

Staging America: Cornerstone and Community-Based Theater
Sonja Kuftinec

Words at Play: Creative Writing and Dramaturgy
Felicia Hardison Londré

Entertaining the Nation: American Drama in the Eighteenth and Nineteenth Centuries
Tice L. Miller

Stage, Page, Scandals, and Vandals: William E. Burton and Nineteenth-Century American Theatre
David L. Rinear

Angels in the American Theater: Patrons, Patronage, and Philanthropy
Edited and with an introduction by Robert A. Schanke

"That Furious Lesbian": The Story of Mercedes de Acosta
Robert A. Schanke

Caffe Cino: The Birthplace of Off-Off-Broadway
Wendell C. Stone

Teaching Performance Studies
Edited by Nathan Stucky and Cynthia Wimmer
With a Foreword by Richard Schechner

Broadway's Bravest Woman: Selected Writings of Sophie Treadwell
Edited and with introductions by Jerry Dickey and Miriam López-Rodríguez

Our Land Is Made of Courage and Glory: Nationalist Performance of Nicaragua and Guatemala
E. J. Westlake

Performing Loss

Performing Loss: Rebuilding Community through Theater and Writing

Jodi Kanter

Southern Illinois University Press
Carbondale

Printed in the United States of America

10 09 08 07 4 3 2 1

Parts of chapters 1 and 2 appeared in earlier form in "Death Becomes Performance: The Reciprocal Usefulness of Death and Performance," *Theatre Annual* 54 (Fall 2001).

"The Five Stages of Grief" from *The Five Stages of Grief* by Linda Pastan. Copyright © 1978 by Linda Pastan. Used by permission of W. W. Norton & Company, Inc.

"One Art" from *The Complete Poems, 1927–1979* by Elizabeth Bishop. Copyright © 1979, 1983 by Alice Helen Methfessel. Reprinted by permission of Farrar, Straus and Giroux, LLC.

Figure 4.2, *Walt Whitman*, by Robert Shetterly from *Americans Who Tell the Truth* by Robert Shetterly, copyright by Robert Shetterly. Used by permission of Dutton Children's Books, A Division of Penguin Young Readers Group, A Member of Penguin Group (USA), Inc., 345 Hudson Street, New York, NY 10014. All rights reserved.

Library of Congress Cataloging-in-Publication Data
Kanter, Jodi, [date]
Performing loss : rebuilding community through theater and writing / Jodi Kanter.
p. cm.—(Theater in the Americas)
Includes bibliographical references and index.
ISBN-13: 978-0-8093-2780-5 (pbk. : alk. paper)
ISBN-10: 0-8093-2780-5 (pbk. : alk. paper)
1. Theater and society. 2. Drama—Social aspects. I. Title.
PN2049.K36 2007
792—dc22 2007009830

The paper used in this publication meets the minimum requirements of American National Standard for Information Sciences—Permanence of Paper for Printed Library Materials, ANSI Z39.48-1992. ♾

Jamaica Kincaid had one perfect reader. I have three.
This book is for my parents and my husband.

Contents

Figures

Acknowledgments

THIS BOOK WOULD NOT EXIST AT ALL WITHOUT JOANNA KLINK, who told me to ask myself what all my favorite books have in common; Della Pollock, who taught me most of what I know about performance studies, gave me permission to write about literature as performance, and helped me understand by her example that scholarship can have its own affective force; Mary Zimmerman, who guided me through a dissertation on a related topic; and David Belcher and Jay Raphael, who supported me in taking a semester's leave from Missouri State University to begin writing.

This book would not exist in its current form without my students at Missouri State University, especially Jill Baker, Meredith Glidden, Sarah Kauffman, and Nicole Trumble; Georgina Ashlock, my collaborator at the U.S. Medical Center for Federal Prisoners; Ginny Smithberg, my collaborator at Hospice Foundation of the Ozarks; my anonymous reviewer at Southern Illinois University Press; and series editor A. Robert Schanke, who saw a shape and patiently helped me to chisel it out.

For generosities and practical assistance great and small, I am grateful to Suzanne Burgoyne, Elizabeth Burton, Sondra Friedman, Derek Goldman, Cheryl Hellmann, Sarah Kauffman, Rob Shetterly, and Vonda Yarberry. For the greatest practical assistance, I am indebted to Kristine Priddy, acquisitions editor at SIU Press, and Mary Lou Kowaleski, my careful and patient copy editor. For the greatest generosity, I am indebted, as always, to my sister, Wendy Snell. And for daily lessons in practicing joy, I am grateful to my stepdaughter, Riley Lewis-Jones.

To the extent that these pages reflect a kind of passionate engagement with their subjects (and I hope they do), it is because my parents, Carol and Arnold Kanter, have always provided extraordinary models of how to be curious about the world, how to work at writing, and how to invest in relationships—with texts and with people. I am grateful for their loving attention to the manuscript, their candor, their encouragement, and the indefatigable joy they take in living.

Finally, I am grateful to my husband, Robert P. Jones, for believing that I had something to say even when I was pretty sure I didn't, for hours of thoughtful reading, for being kinder and more patient on his worst days than I am on my best, for *nachas* till the cows come home, and for being, in all things, my partner.

Performing Loss

Introduction: The Great Holes of History

I STAND BEFORE A GAPING HOLE. It is May, 2004, and I have finally come to lower Manhattan. Although I do not live in New York, I have strong professional and personal ties to the city—I study performance. I have been in the city several times in the last three years, but I have not come to this place. I have not wanted to come. I am not sure that I want to be here now.

The hole is, first of all, fully contained. "I hate to say this," says my partner, "but it's *smaller* than I thought." Its smallness is secured by a mesh wall, through which one must peer at the wreckage. This way, one cannot see what is missing there too clearly. This way, the gaping hole will not spread.

The hole is, second, fully interpreted. Huge signs covered with text mark this side of its perimeter. The signs do not tell of grief; they tell of glory. They tell of the glorious history of this site and the towering city that surrounds it. And they tell of fallen heroes. Not just the firefighters and chaplains and coworkers who risked their lives to save others but everyone who died in lower Manhattan that day is listed here as a hero. This way, they do not have to be—simply, impossibly, unnecessarily—losses. This way, we do not have to be the losers.

The World Trade Center Site, as it is currently known (though surely even this old name will soon be covered up), is exhibit A of our inability to mourn collectively in America. Before the towers were finished falling, it had been transformed from a site of grief into a site of war—indeed, the very center or "ground zero" of global retaliation. The violence has been both personal and communal, both national and transnational. It already shows signs of being insatiable.

In the face of the gaping hole in our cultural, affective, interpersonal, and political lives that this site represents, it is imperative that we look as broadly as we can for models of how better to respond to loss as communities. If we can articulate our losses more honestly, we can create more productive collective responses to tragedy. If we can register and enact our responses to grief more fully, we can negotiate our own losses without begetting others. And if we can diversify the range of responses to loss we are willing to explore, we can devise more creative and more effective strategies for rebuilding the national community.

Performing Loss draws on theories of performance in everyday life, theater for social change, historical narrative, the psychology and sociology of loss, and the speech act. It makes no attempt to combine these theories into a single, unified system for responding to loss through performance; this would be contrary to its goal of expanding the range of possible responses available to individuals and communities. Instead, *Performing Loss* offers a series of perspectives on expanding cultural practices surrounding loss—and, particularly, on finding ways to put these practices into play in public life.

This book began not on September 11, 2001, but many years before, when I became aware of a hole much more personal to me than the one left by the terrorist attacks on the World Trade Center. It was a hole in myself. In my late twenties, I suddenly realized that I had lived nearly three decades without having a single conversation with a family member, friend, or teacher about loss. I knew some strategies for negotiating loss on my own thanks, above all, to Judith Viorst's exceptional book *Necessary Losses*, but I knew nothing about how to talk with others about these experiences, how to affirm their social import, or how to respond to losses at the community, national, or international level in ways that were engaged, creative, and productive. Moreover, I realized that, like so many Americans, I had been protected from loss by a variety of cultural forces, from the distancing mediation of television and other news reporting to the numbing sterilization of technological and medical responses to death.

At the same time, I suddenly became aware that all of my favorite literature and drama dealt in some central way with the problem of representing loss. I loved these books not because I was morbidly fascinated with tragedy but because I needed them. I needed to think about how to respond to this experience that was, in one form or another, everywhere in my community and that would inevitably shape my future. I needed to understand not just how to get through loss but how to *make something of it* as an artist, scholar, educator, and citizen.

Performing Loss, then, is for people who engage, consciously or not, with a variety of losses in their everyday lives, including those that transpire between nations and their citizens; between communities and their histories; between readers and their texts; between parents and their children. It is a book for teachers of performance, theater, literature, cultural studies, psychology, and social work to use in their courses with upper-level undergraduate and graduate students. It is also a book to help health care professionals, social workers, nonprofit directors, and others involved in creating community think creatively about what performance practices might contribute to their work. *Performing Loss* directs readers to the possibilities created by the necessity of responding to loss.

I hope that this book will help readers to become more aware of the range of strategies available to us for negotiating losses of all kinds in our communities. I hope that it may also open space for the rehearsal of new ones. If my opening reading of the World Trade Center Site contains even a kernel of truth, then it is clear that such developments are urgently needed. For Western communities, a greater ability to respond to loss is a matter of political, cultural, and personal survival.

1. Loss, Performance, and Contemporary Culture

I hoped I would cry the right amount.
—Jane Hamilton, *A Map of the World*

CONTEMPORARY WESTERN CULTURE LACKS sophisticated strategies for negotiating loss socially, culturally, and politically—that is to say, collectively. This is not to say that we do not think, talk, and cry about loss. We do so all the time. Since the 1969 publication of *On Death and Dying* made public Elisabeth Kubler-Ross's groundbreaking work with medical students at the University of Chicago, there has been a proliferation of books in psychology and self-help about how individuals do and ought to negotiate loss, death, and mourning. And we have certainly gotten better at many things related to death, dying, mourning, and trauma over the last half century. For example, medical advances have made our lives longer and our dying a more physically comfortable process. Thanks to the pioneering work of Kubler-Ross and her English counterpart physician Dame Cicely Saunders, founder of the hospice movement in both England and the United States, we have even gotten better at listening to the dying and at negotiating our individual dying and mourning processes.

But very little has been written still about how we ought to negotiate these experiences collectively and in public. Despite our advances in understanding individual responses to loss and mourning, in social settings we remain under tremendous, insidious social and cultural pressure, as novelist Jane Hamilton's protagonist puts it, to "cry the right amount." On the one hand, a doctor reprimands a patient in Della Pollock's *Telling Bodies Performing Birth* for her "unnatural grief" one week after losing a three-month pregnancy—she has cried, in his professional estimation, too much.[1] On the other hand, a critic describes the nondemonstrative literary mourning of Jamaica Kincaid's memoir, *My Brother*, as emanating from a "scalded psyche" because she replaces tears with rage, not crying enough.[2]

This dearth of material about negotiating loss is consistent with a culture of individualism that has pervaded American life and been influential in the cultures of our closest political and cultural allies, especially Great Britain. Bellah et al. identify individualism as "the first language in which Americans tend to think about their lives" and describe this language as follows:

> American individualism, then, demands personal effort and stimulates great energy to achieve, yet it provides little encouragement for nurturance, taking a sink-or-swim approach to moral development as well as to economic success. It admires toughness and strength and fears softness and weakness. It adulates winners while showing contempt for losers, a contempt that can descend with crushing weight on those considered, either by others or by themselves, to be moral or social failures.[3]

The culture of individualism, then, works against collective action in general. One of the challenges in creating better responses to loss as communities is that often we must first rebuild a lost sense of the community itself.

The history of collective responses to loss in the West has been articulated by key figures in a number of different fields across three basic realms: cultures and the everyday performances that shape them, language and literature, and history and theory. Although the stories told by scholars in these disparate disciplines naturally vary, each contributing something new to our understanding of how we experience loss, they form an essentially coherent picture of a Western culture for which loss is still too often relegated to the realms of the private and emotional at great cost to our social relationships and our capacity for productive collective action.

Performing Loss in Culture

How do we practice responding to loss in our communities? How can we register loss in national and global contexts? How can we make these responses more diverse, more creative, and more honest?

In *Performance Studies: An Introduction*, Richard Schechner explains the difference between a thing that "is" a performance traditionally conceived (a dance, a play, a song, a juggling routine) and a thing that is considered "as" performance: "Any behavior, event, action, or thing can be studied 'as' performance, can be analyzed in terms of doing, behaving, and showing."[4] To consider a thing as performance, Schechner explains, is to regard it from a performance perspective or in performance terms. As with all cross-disciplinary study, examining through the concepts and practices of performance a thing that is not performance has the potential to yield new insights.

From the earliest days of its formation as a discipline, performance studies was strongly influenced by scholars in the field of anthropology, who increasingly found great value in analyzing everyday behaviors in faraway places as performances of culture. Gradually, these anthropologists began to turn this critical lens on the behaviors of communities closer to home. Today, scholars of culture in various fields continue to find both intellectual and practical value in considering as performance such diverse everyday acts as the gynecological exam, the political protest, and the peeling of potatoes.[5] What might we gain by considering one of the greatest challenges of life—the complex act of negotiating loss—as performance?

Considering our responses to loss as performance has important advantages for better practicing and understanding mourning. Because performance is playful, it enables us to approach a subject whose weight can sometimes be paralyzing. From play comes discovery—in this case, potentially, the discovery of new possibilities for practices surrounding loss, grief, and mourning. In addition, the mode of play encourages an emphasis on experimentation and revision rather than demanding a single, fixed solution. This emphasis encourages community members to entertain diverse perspectives, thereby widening and strengthening community. Because performance is social, it helps us to place experiences and responses that may feel painfully isolated in a cultural context. With the understanding of ourselves as social actors comes a greater power to affect the culture.

The lens of performance also helps us understand the ways in which individual behaviors are constrained by cultural commands. Performances, as Judith Butler cautioned some years ago, cannot accurately be understood as autonomous, progressive acts of the individual will.[6] Rather, they are always shaped and managed by historical and cultural norms. Loss is a shared experience and, therefore, one in which the many institutions that regulate cultures have a stake. Our practices surrounding loss are performative, in Butler's sense, insofar as they are constrained by cultural codes. In order to affect these constraints, we need to understand their history.

From the mid-1970s to the mid-1980s, in a series of books and lectures that were as influential as they were controversial, the French social and cultural historian Phillippe Ariès traced the history of Western attitudes toward death from the early Middle Ages to the present. Ariès identified five broad epochs of attitudes toward death. In the first and longest, death was close, familiar, and "tame," that is to say, normalized. In the second epoch, beginning in the twelfth century, death came to be specified as the death of one's self and was conceived of as a violent and erotic interruption or break; death raped the living[7] and was therefore to be feared. By the eighteenth century, death had acquired a new, dominant meaning as the death of the other. In this epoch, there was a new intolerance of separation between the living and the dead, and mourning was "unfurled with an uncustomary degree of ostentation."[8]

Ariès identifies the fourth period as the epoch of the invisible death. Over the course of the twentieth century (Ariès is imprecise about when this change began, identifying signs of it as early as 1859) and particularly under the influence of a dominant American culture, Western society has banished death:

> In the towns, there is no way of knowing that something has happened: the old black and silver hearse has become an ordinary gray limousine, indistinguishable from the flow of traffic. Society no longer observes a pause; the disappearance of an individual no longer affects its continuity. Everything in town goes on as if nobody died anymore.[9]

Summarizing the Western aversion to the public demonstration of mourning in the second half of the twentieth century, Ariès writes, simply, "Mourning is a malady."[10] Finally, Ariès argues, at the end of the twentieth century, the death that has been evacuated by society "is coming back in through the window, and it is returning just as quickly as it disappeared."[11]

Despite widespread criticism of Ariès's methodology—for example, his indiscriminate blending of evidence from the arts and social sciences—his work retains a certain undeniable explanatory weight. One critic admits that, despite "refusing to bother about the problem of how many examples are needed to prove a trend or justify a general assertion" and dipping "recklessly" into "the mass of disparate evidence thrown up by liturgies, art and literature," Ariès has nonetheless "glimpsed, vividly, some sharply contrasting patterns of human reactions."[12] Further, Ariès's findings with regard to banishment of dying and mourning practices across the twentieth century are supported by a range of subsequent studies in the social sciences.

In the United States, Michael R. Leming and George E. Dickinson note, 70 percent of all deaths take place "offstage" in hospitals and nursing homes.[13] Studies suggest that participation in mourning rituals such as funerals and wakes decreased significantly during the last two decades of the twentieth century[14] and that, to the extent that they still exist, these rituals are now used primarily to hurry the mourner through the grieving process.[15]

Contemporary sociological and cultural studies repeatedly describe mainstream culture in both the U.S. and Britain as suffering from the loss of established death ritual,[16] the privatization of tragedy,[17] the suppression of emotional expression at funerals,[18] and denial as the prevailing coping strategy.[19] Mourning seems to be particularly at odds with American culture—incompatible with the future-oriented values of rugged individualism and the Protestant work ethic.[20]

Not surprisingly, this trend does not apply to American culture wholesale. Contemporary sociologists have noted important divergences from what is generally acknowledged as the prevailing deritualization of death in the West. Donald P. Irish, Kathleen F. Lundquist, and Vivian Jenkins Nelsen note, for example, that African American mourning practices typically diverge from those of mainstream white Americans, especially in their emotional expressivity.[21] The authors further distinguish ethnic variation in the death, dying, and mourning practices of Mexican Americans and American Hmong peoples. Yet, even these exceptions may hold exceptions; the authors note the danger of generalizing about practices across *any* cultural group, warning that there are bound to be differences from community to community and from person to person.

Class seems to be another significant variable in the deritualization of mourning practice. Less affluent groups tend to retain more ritual and greater expressivity, while those who can afford to do so tend to purchase a higher level of containment by way of medical technologies.[22] Still, Howarth notes the danger of romanticizing the death and mourning practices of the economically defined other: "In critiquing what I have defined as the English middle-class way of death, however, there is a danger of romanticizing working-class rituals—where funerals are redolent of meaning and brimming with satisfaction."[23]

Gender is a significant variable as well. Performances of grief and mourning tend to be more frequently enacted by women—at least in aesthetic representations. Elisabeth Bronfen traces the Western representation of the dead body to the present day as an aestheticized female body. She argues that this phenomenon of repression through transference to the female "other" pertains not only to the corpse but to the mourner as well:

> The kinds of power attributed to death are also those associated with the woman, because they are the confounding power of the body. Just as woman *is* the body, she is also the body's caretaker, the nurse, the layer-out of the corpse. If death is a kind of return to her care, then she is also contaminated by it, so that rituals must be found first to enable her care and then to dissociate her from the corpse. Like the decaying body, the feminine is unstable, liminal, disturbing. Both mourning rituals and representations of death may seek strategies to stabilize the body, which

> entails removing it from the feminine and transforming it into a monument, an enduring stone.[24]

Jenny Hockey is at pains, however, to distinguish representations of grieving women from social practice, at least in the English context. In practice, she says, "both sexes are susceptible to the British imperative to conduct their grieving in private. In public, what is required is a display of signs that an appropriate emotional response is taking place, but elsewhere—in the private setting of the home."[25] This socially disciplined emotional reserve is not unique to the English, as American novelist Jane Hamilton's narrator's efforts to "cry the right amount" suggest. And although there may be a particular taboo against masculine mourning, the prevalence of representations of the expressive female mourner in Western culture should not be taken too definitively as a sign of women's freedom to practice mourning in everyday life.

Despite variation, then, it makes sense to speak of a general culture of constraint in American performances of mourning. Although there are significant exceptions to the general rule, even those scholars who highlight these variations warn that these exceptions ought not to be either overgeneralized or overstated.

How *are* death and mourning practiced in the contemporary West? In America, the overwhelming number of dead are embalmed and buried rather than cremated. Jessica Mitford, describing the former process with her characteristic wit, explains that the modern-day "Yorick" is "whisked off to a funeral parlor and is in short order sprayed, sliced, pierced, pickled, trussed, trimmed, creamed, waxed, painted, rouged, and neatly dressed."[26] Although Ariès takes this as a sign of the less radical evacuation of death and mourning rituals in the U.S. as compared with Europe, he also describes the way in which embalming functions not to facilitate contact between the living and dead but to mask this encounter: "It is of paramount importance to create the illusion of life. This illusion enables the visitor to overcome his intolerance, to behave as if the deceased were not dead and there were no reason not to approach him."[27] Mitford, determined to expose the funeral industry, focuses on the high price tag of these mourning practices. In doing so, she cites the industry's comparison between the corpse and a "guest of honor," the eagerness to preserve a "'lifelike naturalness'" through embalming. Such language betrays the industry's collusion with a culture of death denial.

In mainstream practice in America, death and mourning rituals, to the extent that they continue, serve to minimize the encounter between the living and the dead and to suppress the emotional expression of grief over loss, at least in public. "We live," writes Daniel Callahan, "in a society increasingly scant in those cultural resources necessary to sustain our interior life as we struggle to make sense of our endings."[28] We lack cultural resources for finding compensation, expression, and meanings for our private and public losses.

Performing Loss considers everyday behaviors in response to loss as performance. To consider our responses to loss as performances is to consider the power of representation to build on and beyond constraining cultural norms. To imagine performing loss is to enact our responses to these central human experiences despite the longstanding and powerful cultural imperatives not to do so.

Performing Loss in Language and Literature

How do we represent not merely the idea but the full, embodied, affectively overpowering experience of loss in language? What bearings do narrative performances of loss have on our everyday lives?

Despite the "large chorus of thanatologists" Ariès observed in the middle of the twentieth century, representing loss in language remains profoundly difficult. This may be, in part, because of the peculiar relationship between pain and articulation. "Whatever pain achieves," writes literary theorist Elaine Scarry in *The Body in Pain*, "it achieves in part through its unsharability, and it ensures this unsharability through its resistance to language."[29] Scarry distinguishes between physical and emotional pain, reserving the difficulties of representation for the former: "There is virtually no piece of literature that is *not* about suffering."[30] But while it is certainly true that the literature that *talks about* suffering—including the suffering involved in loss—is vast, it is also true that very little of this literature actually *enacts* or *does* loss. The writer Joan Didion experienced the difference between writing that documents loss and writing that performs loss when she adapted *The Year of Magical Thinking*, her memoir about the loss of her husband, for the stage: "I don't even think of it as an adaptation. . . . I think of it as something I wrote—the same way I sat down and wrote the book. You just start from a different place." David Hare, who directed the play, commented that the book was a careful document of the act of grieving, while the play, much less orderly and restrained, would "be that grieving itself."[31]

Renato Rosaldo's critique of death discourse among anthropologists emerged from a painful experience of its failures. Rosaldo conducted anthropological research among the Ilongot headhunters of the Philippines before and after the accidental death of his wife, Michele. His personal encounter with loss radically changed his evaluation of the ethnographic tradition in which he was working: "Ethnographies written in accord with classic norms consider death under the rubric of ritual rather than bereavement."[32] From the perspective of his own catastrophic loss, Rosaldo came to find such descriptions wholly unsatisfying because they masked the emotional force of bereavement, reducing loss and grieving to routines.

Creating a discourse around death, the prototypical experience of loss, is especially difficult, because death is the only subject of which no one, strictly speaking, can know what he/she is talking about. And death is not only difficult to experience; it is difficult to conceive. Perhaps the greatest contributions to the enterprise of conceptualizing the relationship between death and language have been made by Jacques Derrida. Death, for Derrida, is an aporia or "negative form" in three figures or "logics." These logics, Derrida warns, should not be considered mutually exclusive but, on the contrary, mutually informing, mutually "haunting."

In the first figure, death is an impermeable border, "a door that does not open or that only opens according to an unlocatable condition."[33] In the second figure, death is impermeable not because its border cannot be crossed but because its border is not, properly speaking, a border. It is, rather, a threshold whose limit is "porous, permeable, and indeterminate."[34] In the third and final figure, the border of death cannot be crossed because the movement that constitutes a crossing is not possible. The "elementary milieu" of the aporia "does not allow for something that could be called passage, step, walk, gait, displacement, or replacement, a kinesis in general."[35] One of the successes of Derrida's formulation of death in language is that he thwarts traditional narrative structure by insisting on three simultaneous stories. In so doing, he does more than just describe the radical disorientation of death; he begins to enact it.

What can it mean to enact loss in language? In his 1955 lectures at Harvard University, J. L. Austin first proposed the term *performative* to describe utterances that have a more-than-descriptive effect. The name *performative*, which Austin used as a noun, "indicates that the issuing of the utterance is the performing of an action—it is not normally thought of as just saying something."[36] For example, Austin argued, when a person makes a promise or christens a ship, he/she is not merely describing an action but making something happen through these special uses of language. Through performative utterances, Austin argued, we do things with words.

With the advent of the discipline called performance studies in the early 1980s came an explicit disciplinary dedication to transgressing the limits of representation, including the limits of language. Recent scholars in performance studies, building on Austin, have moved beyond categorizing single utterances to describe a general use of language that may be called *performative writing*.

Performative writing is writing that behaves like lived experience. Here, *performative* should not be confused with *dramatic* or *theatrical*. Not all writing for the stage is performative, and some writing that was not intended for the stage is highly performative. Performative writing, like the best live performance, gives the reader a real experience in an imaginary space. Performative writing does not just describe an event or experience—it mirrors, behaves like, *does* its subject. Performative writing asks its reader or audience member to embody the ideas at the center of the text.

Radical loss often finds representation in radical narrative structure. In a more personal register, Derrida performs a discourse of mourning not as a gap in language/ontology, as his use of the word *aporia* suggests but, on the contrary, as a proliferation of language. In the long essay "Circumfession," he mourns his dying mother in endlessly bleeding, weeping sentences that, as they describe her loss of memory, anticipate her death:

> [She is] still alive at the moment I am writing this, but already incapable of memory, in any case of the memory of my name, a name become for her at the very least unpronounceable, *and* I am writing here at the moment when my mother no longer recognizes me, *and* at which, still capable of speaking or articulating, a little, she no longer calls me *and* for her *and* therefore for the rest of her life I no longer have a name, that's what's happening, *and* when she nonetheless seems to reply to me, she is presumably replying to someone who happens to be me without her knowing it, if knowing means anything here, therefore without my knowing henceforth any more clearly myself who will have asked her such and such a question like the other day in Nice . . . [37]

The sentence, of which approximately one fourth is quoted here, performs syntactically the proliferation, the endlessness of Derrida's grief. It also performs the absence of his name, what he calls his mother's "amnesia of me"[38] and the extent to which her loss of the name engenders his own erasure.

The syntactic units of the narrative need not be long to be performative. Consider, for example, the description by French literary theorist Hélène Cixous of her young father's death from tuberculosis:

> I was allowed to go and see him. He no longer speaks. (He spoke no more—cf. Kafka.) I do not want to put a name on my anguish. He addresses me with signs. I respond abundantly, overabundantly. I sense I am playing "completely natural." I put on an act for myself. I saw my father enter into silence while he was alive. Everything held back: smile, held back, breath, held back, life, held back.[39]

Here, the syntactic units are strikingly simple and abrupt. They suggest an urgent telegram: *Father at end, stop. Come at once, stop.* They also perform what they describe: the holding back of the father's speech—and, perhaps, the daughter's tears.

Performative writing is, as Della Pollock specifies in her essay dedicated to the subject, consequential.[40] It has real effects on the shaping of our cultural imagination and with it our cultural practices. It therefore encourages us to think more critically about our roles in the social drama. One consequence of engagement with this kind of writing is a community and, ultimately, a culture better equipped to respond to its most significant losses.

Scholarly biases in the fields of theater, performance, and cultural studies have for decades deemphasized the consequential nature of written texts in general (except, of course, their own) and literary texts in particular. The focus on the cultural context of experiences and artifacts known as the cultural "turn" in the humanities that began in the late 1980s and continues today has been valuable to scholars and readers in many ways. It has made us more aware of the need to examine rigorously the cultural context of every performance we study. It has deepened our investment in the study of performances that were made by people and in places previously ignored by the academy. It has created an explosion of theory in the realm of identity politics that has advanced our knowledge of the often invoked but inadequately understood categories of race, class, gender, and sexuality. And it has encouraged us to take seriously as cultural performances the stuff of our everyday lives—music, advertisements, celebrities, fashion trends, all the little performances that make up what we call popular culture, a realm once eschewed even among anthropologists as being too close to home.

But the cultural turn has also produced its own losses. One such loss in theater and literary studies has been the segregation of the emotional and psychological (the most accessible though certainly not the only domains of literature and drama) from the political and social (the most accessible domains of oral and popular performances), with the latter being the strongly favored objects of study.

According to the paradigm-shifting theories of playwright Bertolt Brecht, the theater had in the first half of the twentieth century to "develop a technique for submitting emotions to the spectator's criticism."[41] Brecht was suspicious of the emotional responses of "pity and fear" to which dramatists since Aristotle had aspired; Brecht believed that an excess of feeling could inhibit thinking and, with it, political action.

Taking its cue from experimental theater and particularly from Brecht, modern performance theory has more than occasionally operated under the assumption that to be emotionally moved by a performance and to be politically moved by a performance are mutually exclusive responses. Studies of contemporary cultural rituals and theater techniques often take great pains to distance themselves from psychology, in which they are not interested, and to ally themselves with sociology and anthropology, in which they are.[42] In so doing, performance studies has often falsely pitted personal transformation against social change. Favoring the latter, it has produced a large body of theory to reassure us about what is social (and therefore political) in individual stories, helpfully redeeming individual experience from the implicit qualifier "mere." In so doing, however, it has often been forced to discard the most highly idiosyncratic individual responses, including those with intense emotional content.

Very recently, performance studies scholars have begun to recognize the costs of this disciplinary break for pedagogy, scholarship, and activism. In 2006, Pollock called for scholars to "integrate more fully methodologies conventionally identified with exteriority and interiority, outer and inner worlds, by working harder to combine social theory and psychoanalytics."[43] Such a call requires recognition of the personal dimensions of social change.

We can better estimate the benefits of attending to the personal dimensions by listening to and observing individuals in our own classrooms, in fieldwork, and in literary texts. *Performing Loss*, therefore, questions theories and practices of social change that value public activism over and against personal transformation. By attending to moments of personal transformation in performance, this book argues for an expanded understanding of the role of the personal in public life.

Another loss of the cultural turn particular to performance studies is the forgotten origin of much of our work in the study of the oral interpretation of literature. To trace this lost origin, we need only look at the evolution of one of the two major academic performance studies programs in the United States—at Northwestern University. Northwestern's department began as the Department of Interpretation, with the foundational belief that embodying literature could be a powerful methodology for understanding others. The department functioned for several decades under this title, becoming the Department of Performance Studies in 1981. The new name signaled the de-emphasis of literature in favor of other kinds of texts.

I am certainly not the first to express the wish that performance studies revalue the interpretation of literature. Performance scholars Beverly Whitaker Long, Mary Frances HopKins, and Paul Edwards have for years been voices in the wilderness on this point.[44] In "Rethinking Elocution," Dwight Conquergood, whose own work focused strongly on ethnography, argued for a more expansive understanding of the eighteenth- and nineteenth-century elocutionary movement "within a wider socio-historical context of racial tension and class struggle"[45] and, therefore, a more complex appreciation of its contributions to performance studies.

More recently, Shannon Jackson has noted that performance studies scholars often associate the category of the literary with elitism and anti-materialism. Jackson argues that it is important to recognize, particularly from a methodological standpoint, that "Literature and English departments have produced some of the most significant and widely circulated critical paradigms in the humanities, models and frameworks that many in drama, theater, and performance studies have adopted despite their own anti-literary rhetoric and institutional location."[46] Jackson labels performance studies' willingness to lose sight of these origins as a "disciplinary blind spot."

Yet, despite these important voices, much contemporary performance studies scholarship treats the study of traditional literary forms (the novel and poetry) as passé. Despite the wide dissemination of contemporary fiction through major motion pictures, talk shows, book clubs, and Internet venues, literature is rarely considered by scholars in the humanities to be part of the popular culture. Therefore, in light of the cultural turn, it often fails to be considered as part of "culture" at all.

But far from being passé, literature is often ahead of popular culture in its ability to enact possible models of human behavior and interaction. As philosopher Martha Nussbaum has written, "If we do not cultivate the imagination in this way [through literature], we lose, I believe, an essential bridge to social justice."[47] Looking particularly at literature about loss, *Performing Loss* recovers the literary as a category situated firmly within, rather than apart from, cultural studies, affirming the power of literature to reflect and, more importantly, to influence cultural practices. By demonstrating how the writing and reading of memoirs, plays, and other texts can help us to negotiate loss, *Performing Loss* values literature as an ally to other forms of cultural expression in our efforts to better articulate and understand this fundamental human experience.

Performing Loss in History and Theory

How can histories engender loss? How can we compensate for such losses? How can theory expand the possibilities for responding to loss productively?

Performing Loss proceeds from Hayden White's observation that loss is the very content of human history. In *The Content of the Form*, White argues that the symbolic content of narrative history is the "universal, human quest for meaning [which] is carried out in the awareness of the corrosive power of time."[48] It is our nature to strive to compensate for this inevitable corrosion. Our narratives arise "out of a desire to have real events display the coherence, integrity, fullness, and closure of an image of life that is and can only be imaginary."[49] According to White, we ought not to regret this appeal to the imaginary. Indeed, "far from being an antithetical opposite of historical narrative, fictional narrative is its complement and ally in the universal human effort to reflect on the mystery of temporality."[50] For White, the content of the form, whether this form is history or fiction, is "the tragic vision itself."[51]

The role of performance in responding to the incoherence of history is a complicated one. Performance may, like narrative, work to compensate, staging unheard voices and unseen bodies. But it is also the nature of performative forms of narrative to trouble narrative coherence, preserving rather than eliding disruption and disorder. While traditional narrative structures move in predictable, linear arcs, performative structures attempt to mark and sometimes account for gaps and ruptures in our experience, persistent failures of historical coherence.

In performance studies, the work of theorizing about the relationships among loss, performance, and history has been taken up significantly in several contexts. In *Cites of the Dead*, Joseph Roach develops a way of thinking about how people compensate for historical losses, which he calls "surrogation." Roach is interested in the role of the performer as a living effigy. He demonstrates how people of differing social classes throughout what he calls the circum-Atlantic world (Europe, Africa, and the Americas) create substitutes or surrogates to fill key social/cultural roles when people vacate those roles through death.

As an example of surrogation, Roach reads two New Orleans Mardi Gras parades, one led by Rex, King of Carnival, the other by King Zulu, originally the leader of the working class African American Zulu Social Aid and Pleasure Club. The first of these parades has been happening in New Orleans since 1872, the other since 1909. "Every year there is a new Rex and a new King Zulu, and every year they are supposed to look and act as they always have."[52] In 1991, when Roach witnessed the simultaneous parades, he noticed two remarkable features. The first was the complex network of racial substitutions visible on the faces of the African American participants, who wore "blackface laid on thick over an underlying layer of clown white."[53] The second was the literal collision of these two parades. Both observations indicate that the repetition of roles during Mardi Gras is far from seamless. No path, either geographical or genealogical, is strictly replicable. Therefore, the process of surrogation is always potentially subversive of normative roles.

Yet, however necessarily imperfect, surrogation is also compensatory. For Roach, performance is our primary cultural tool for responding to loss through "death or other forms of departure."[54] By standing in or acting as surrogate for absent others, we perpetuate their roles in the social drama; we account for their absence by entertaining, in a double sense, their presence. Thus, all our cities are cities of the dead, reproduced and reinvented by the living in an endless recirculation of traditional roles.

Of course, to think about New Orleans as a "city of the dead" is an entirely different enterprise today than it was when Roach's book appeared a decade ago. In 2005, Hurricane Katrina, the worst natural disaster in American history, made New Orleans a city of the dead in previously unfathomable ways. Although Katrina is not a focus of this book, it is worth pausing briefly here to note the extraordinary confluence of types of losses Katrina engendered, many of which are addressed in other contexts in the pages that follow.

Some of the losses of Katrina are well documented and discussed. Katrina killed more than sixteen hundred people, displaced as many as one million, and destroyed hundreds of thousands of homes. Places of business were destroyed, as well as schools, libraries, and other public buildings. During the evacuation, children were separated from their parents and parents from their children.

As a national disaster, Hurricane Katrina also represented the loss of American ideals in ways different from the terrorist attacks of September 11 but no less damning. September 11 represented, for some, the beginning of an era of massive public deception by the U.S. government in order to justify war. Katrina graphically represented the enormous socioeconomic disparities among Americans. Katrina exposed the extent to which, as one analyst wrote, "The floodwaters of poverty are eroding the shores of opportunity."[55] And although economic disparities do not precisely track ethnicity, Katrina made it impossible to ignore that, overwhelmingly, the face of poverty in America is black.

Finally, the erosions of Hurricane Katrina were not only metaphorical. Environmentally, the hurricane was part of an overall doubling of the incidence of category 3 and 4 hurricanes over the last thirty years that, in turn, is a symptom of the devastating effect that human activity is having on a greater history, the history of the Earth. The 2006 documentary *An Inconvenient Truth* projected our already massive environmental losses into the future, suggesting that we have less than a decade to avoid complete catastrophe.

Environmental devastation is not a necessary outcome of human activity. A long historical view suggests that indigenous peoples inhabited the North American continent for at least ten thousand years without severe ecological damage. Yet, in a few centuries of European settlement, notes ecologist David Abram, "much of the native abundance of this continent has been lost—its broad animal populations decimated, its many-voiced forests overcut and its prairies overgrazed, its rich soils depleted, its tumbling waters now undrinkable."[56] Abram argues that our neglect of the natural world springs from a devaluation of all things sensorial. His book *The Spell of the Sensuous* mourns the sensory connections between the human and "more-than-human" worlds.

The mourning for the losses of Hurricane Katrina was summarized for political commentator Donna Brazile in a famous jazz lyric, "Do you know what it means to miss New Orleans?" Brazile writes, "We miss New Orleans—its smell, its weather, its culture, its people, its language, and, most importantly, we miss our neighbors and our homes."[57] Brazile's lament for New Orleans echoes Jamaica Kincaid's lament for Antigua, Suzan-Lori Parks's lament for America, Tony Kushner's lament for Afghanistan, and so many other laments for not only the people but the very ground of home.

Della Pollock's work has focused significantly on loss, both as it troubles historical narrative and as it infuses the experiences that narrative endeavors to give form.[58] Pollock attends to narrative performances, specifically, the stories women tell about their experiences of giving birth. In the introduction to her book, *Telling Bodies Performing Birth*, she explains how the normative expectations that narrative should be orderly, linear, and structured function specifically in the context of birth stories:

> While only a few [narratives] closed with complete satisfaction, most rose out of even the depths of terror and anger to embrace the emerging baby and the norms by which it was deemed healthy and whole. . . . Most stories followed the linear, "progressive" structure inculcated in prenatal classes and pregnancy handbooks by which planning becomes conception becomes pregnancy becomes a ten-fingers-and-toes birth. . . . With all the flourish of a Shakespearean comedy, they delivered order from disorder and pleasure from abandon, transgression, and pain.[59]

Pollock chooses to focus on stories that thwart this received model, that have, following the title of the first chapter, their "origins in absence." These stories include but are not limited to abortion, miscarriage, and stillbirth. Pollock focuses on what is lost, not only in the telling but in the very experience of birthing new life. She argues, against a contemporary culture full of promises that the right exercise, diet, or surgical procedures can make us whole again, that neither our selves nor our stories ever were.

Pollock's personal investment in the stories she writes about is quietly but persistently present throughout her study. She begins the book's second chapter with a five-word story of her own: "My daughter was born blue." Isabel's birth narrative was, in one sense, a story of "origins in absence," because she was rushed off for care, absent from her mother for much of the time during the first days of her life. In a more important sense, though, Pollock and her daughter escaped the serious scars of absence that some of the author's subjects describe.

Margaret is not as fortunate. After her first CVS (choronic villi sampling) test produces inconclusive results as to the health of her baby, Margaret undergoes a series of invasive medical tests that happen "every week for—you know—a couple of months,"[60] again with inconclusive results. Margaret is left with what she repeatedly calls "the not knowing."[61] Eventually, she is forced to make a decision based on this not knowing. And so, Pollock writes, "In the absence of incontestably negative test results, from beneath the rumble of data and medical instruments, and against her own body's advice," Margaret decides to have an abortion. Although Margaret already has two healthy children, it is this third birth story she is most eager to tell the oral historian/performance scholar.

Pollock notes that this story of Margaret's third, abortive birth experience becomes "the 'original' from which the others now took their meaning." The story of the abortion haunts the other children's births with "a sense of what might have been, had they been subject to the same scrutiny with the same inscrutable results." Although she found the conclusive test results in the cases of her other two children comforting, Margaret concludes her story by wondering "if it's really so good sometimes to know" if the results are negative or inconclusive. Furthermore, the loss irrevocably separates Margaret from the promised coherence of the medical narrative, leaving her "bereft of the kind of authority that comes with believing, unequivocally, innocently, in the value of acquiring scientific data and its implications for action."[62] Through the performance of her story, Pollock argues, Margaret not only mourns the loss of her third child, she mourns the losses this "original" loss begets in her relationship to her two, healthy children. She also mourns the loss her story creates in her relationship to narrative itself; within the frame of the narrative, "medicine knows," Margaret's story is fatally incomplete.

Narrative performance, with its socially cultivated promises of wholeness, is frequently aborted or miscarried. And even birth, the archetypal experience of presence, often has its origins tangled up in absence. Babies, for one of several possible reasons, are not born, or they are born and die, or they are born and, through their birth, create losses in other relationships.

But it may be precisely performance's partiality that makes it an appropriate medium for negotiating loss. Elsewhere, Pollock writes that such performance "marks itself an active, material signifying process that is neither a prison house nor a fun house, not a place even, but a boundary space, inviting laughter and transformation."[63] Performance enables and invites us to do something with loss and, in the very means of doing, find some compensation.

By artfully integrating events and imagination, narrative performance in particular offers compensations for the gaps and losses of history. In the introduction to her edited volume *Exceptional Spaces*, Pollock cites scholars from a wide array of disciplines who challenge the clear opposition between truth and the imaginary. Paraphrasing Hayden White, she argues that "what is imaginary is not simply made up in excess of a real and determining social structure. Rather, it derives from the same kind of ideologies, institutions, and social practices that structure the events described."[64] Scholars who understand this are able to "bring the trickster in history onto the stage of history—and challenge us to entertain him for a while."[65]

In reminding us of the incompleteness of our bodies—even at birth—and our stories about the world—even the ones we know by heart—Pollock affirms the need to value the gaps in history. This means that we must value bodies that are not with us and stories that are not "true." Only by embracing what is absent can we hope to approach being whole.

Diana Taylor uses a performance perspective to understand how public memories are transmitted in the face of historical trauma, death, and other kinds of losses, focusing on the peculiar obstinacy with which historical actors refuse to disappear. In her first book, *Disappearing Acts*, she looks at how cultural ideas/ideals of gender and nation were enacted during Argentina's civil war in the late 1970s and early 1980s. In the process, she examines a variety of specific strategies through which the memories of people who were "disappeared" continued to be put in play.

Taylor's second major work, *The Archive and The Repertoire*, examines public memory at a diverse range of sites throughout the Americas, from Latinos' remembrances of Princess Diana, to New Yorkers' remembrances of the World Trade Center towers, to Peruvians' remembrances of centuries of civil conflict across that country. She articulates a central rift between two bodies of knowledge, the archive and the repertoire. The archive is comprised of "supposedly enduring materials (i.e., texts, documents, buildings, bones)," and the purportedly ephemeral repertoire is comprised of "embodied practice/knowledge (i.e., spoken language, dance, sports, ritual)."[66] She examines these two bodies of knowledge together for the purpose of questioning the ephemeral status of the latter.

Her analysis suggests, in a move reminiscent of Mark Twain's famous statement about himself, that the reports of the repertoire's death have been greatly exaggerated. Instead of privileging texts, the products of the archive, as even performance and cultural studies scholars have been so wont to do,

Taylor argues that we ought to look to scenarios for understanding. These products of the repertoire, she argues, are "meaning-making paradigms that structure social environments, behaviors, and potential outcomes."[67] What a performance paradigm makes visible, for Taylor, is a world that operates not primarily by mimesis or duplication, as many forms of representation might encourage us to see it, but by the reactivation of archetypal scenarios that never entirely disappear.

For Taylor, what is gone is never entirely gone. In *Disappearing Acts*, she outlines five categories of representation by which the disappeared in Argentina were, in some sense, made to reappear. These categories include oral and written testimonies of survivors; visual representations of the disappeared by others, especially the hundreds of women witnesses and activists known as the Madres de Plaza de Mayo; fictionalized representations in novels, plays, and other writings; and scholarly representations. In *The Archive and the Repertoire*, she analyzes the myriad ways in which the World Trade Center towers are, paradoxically, more present since their destruction. She also attends to the ways in which Princess Diana's ghost, in Taylor's words, keeps "dancing," keeps itself in play, and even in many ways brings itself more strongly into play following her untimely death.

Not only does the repertoire resist disappearance but, Taylor insists, certain kinds of knowledge live more—and better—in the repertoire than in the archive. In a particularly persuasive chapter, Taylor witnesses and theorizes the performances of Yuyachkani, Peru's leading theater collective. The company has worked together for more than thirty years to transmit that country's most painful memories, what Taylor characterizes as a "history of extermination and resistance"[68] to new publics. The group comprises white, mestizo, and indigenous artists. In order to reflect the diverse concerns of its audiences, the company added members of many rural communities to their group: "[T]he actors learned Quechua; they trained in indigenous and mestizo performance practices that included singing, playing instruments, dancing, movement, and many other forms of popular expression."[69]

Taylor insists on the power of refusing to disappear. Her work on trauma, death, and history in Latin America suggests, in contrast with much other important work in performance and cultural studies, that performance can be a lens through which to notice how people and events *last*. She analyzes and theorizes the ways in which we transmit presence across cultures, across languages, across generations, and across death.

Peggy Phelan's work is significantly animated by "a passion to know our relation to loss more intimately."[70] She pursues this passion by theorizing about a wide range of acts of historical documentation, with a special emphasis on documentary photography and film. Her interest in visual representation notwithstanding, Phelan questions the wisdom of the project of making underrepresented subjects *visible*, a project that has been high on the agenda of many academics, particularly in the fields of performance and cultural studies. Phelan suggests that, on the contrary, the act of refusing visibility, what she calls "*active* vanishing,"[71] may be the most powerful act of all.

For Phelan, the world of visual representation is at least as interesting for what it misses or loses as for what it records. In *Unmarked*, she critiques the assumption, operative in both progressive and conservative politics, that "greater visibility of the hitherto under-represented leads to enhanced political power."[72] Her aim is to "outline, however speculatively, a different way of thinking about the political and psychic relationship between self and other, subject and object, in cultural reproduction."[73] For help in this project, she turns to performance, arguing that we ought to value performance over other forms of representation because it is "the art form which most fully understands the generative possibilities of disappearance."[74] In her second book, *Mourning Sex*, Phelan focuses even more of her analysis on documentary representation, particularly following the onslaught of the AIDS epidemic, and searches for the value that remains when the real bodies it documents are continually lost.

The key sites of Phelan's inquiry into the relationships among loss, performance, and history range from the smallest features of our physiognomy to the largest reaches of our political ambition. At the most intimate level, she argues that the human eye is physically determined by loss. "When Newton discovered the prismatic properties of light," Phelan writes in mournful tones, "the human eye became a poor creature, an organ whose limitations define its properties more precisely than its powers."[75] However hard we may try, we can never see anything completely; our very physiognomy prevents it.

The partiality of the eye has particularly painful ramifications for Phelan, who suffered acute physical and considerable emotional distress as the result of an eye condition, eventually diagnosed as open-angle glaucoma, for five years in early adulthood before her doctor ordered her to have surgery. In "To Suffer a Sea Change," an essay about this period in her life, Phelan draws multiple connections between "the body and the self, between the holes in words and the holes in seeing."[76] Most strongly, she notes the weakness, unreliability, imperfection, and impermanence of both.

Phelan connects the losses of the eye to the losses of the psyche. In both cases, the residue of what was lost remains. "Just as physiologists posited the idea of an 'after-image'—a shadow of an image which remains on the retina . . . so too did psychoanalysts posit that a 'trace' of a psychic event remains in the unconscious, [Sigmund] Freud's mystic writing pad."[77] Of course, most of us do not consciously experience perception as a struggle against blindness. But given her own traumatic experience with sight, the idea of the after-image offers Phelan theoretical and personal, psychic and physical compensation for loss.

Still images are performances of loss insofar as they thwart photography's claims as a documentary form (claims that, for Phelan, are already ontologically inaccurate). The photographs Phelan values intentionally lose or "vanish" their relationship to the real, live subject, either through a purposeful objectification of the original or through the endless proliferation of copies, surfaces beneath which the subject refuses to let her observers see.

Cindy Sherman is one of the photographers in whom Phelan has a significant interest. Sherman's photographs are characterized by a proliferation of subjects or, more accurately, of roles, because each photograph is a self-portrait. They celebrate the subject, according to Phelan, through the replacement of a single subject with many subjects, an endless movement between multiple possible identities. Sherman's oeuvre is, for Phelan, a "performative record of the disappearance of Sherman's body."[78] Her work accrues power by vanishing *with* her subjectivity, leaving only the play of surfaces before the eye of the desiring viewer.

Writing is another documentary technology that Phelan would have scholars and critics use in the service of performing loss. Although she notes that writing about performance fundamentally alters the event, she cautions, "It does no good, however, to simply refuse to write about performance because of this inescapable transformation. The challenge raised by the ontological claims of performance for writing is to re-mark again the performative possibilities of writing itself."[79] These possibilities, whatever they may be, involve writing "toward disappearance" rather than toward the preservation of original events and subjects. Performance theorist Vivian Patraka built on Phelan's idea of writing toward disappearance in the context of representing performances of the Holocaust. In a helpful adaptation of Phelan's language, she writes in *Spectacular Suffering* of the importance of preserving the "goneness" of Holocaust victims' (and even some survivors') experiences and stories.[80]

The challenge, then, is to develop an understanding of representation sufficiently nuanced that one can distinguish those losses that constitute acts of violence against individuals or groups as such from those that hold "the power of a finely calibrated invisibility."[81] Sometimes being lost in the frenzy of representation, both cultural and political, is a travesty; sometimes it is an opportunity. If we can recognize the difference, we can develop our own strategies to save what we love through varied acts of representation and disappearance.

Phelan's work demonstrates that our world is inescapably infused with loss, from the mechanical functions of our eyes to the configuration and reconfiguration of our social identities. Her work also demonstrates how a performance perspective on texts of all kinds can teach us to *value* loss, "to learn not the meaning but the value of what cannot be reproduced or seen (again)."[82] And, finally, her work teaches us how performative practices in a variety of media can help us to act not exactly against but, rather, in spite of the inevitability of loss in representation and in our lives.

Although the texts, methodologies, and conclusions of these scholars differ considerably from each other and from my own, their theoretical articulations, taken together, have created a space in which to think about the multiple relationships between loss and performance. They have also frequently framed questions and articulated possible answers in ways that are both deeply personal and formally experimental. In so doing, they have attempted to preserve the affective force of a subject that, following Rosaldo's critique, is too often objectified and anesthetized by scholarly narratives. Their work opens up productive spaces, spaces toward which the present volume moves.

Consideration of Terms, *Mourning* and *Compensation*

I frequently use the term *mourning* to describe the subject's responses to loss. *Mourning* and *melancholia* have been contested terms in contemporary scholarship in the humanities across the disciplines ever since they were initially defined by Sigmund Freud in his 1917 essay "Mourning and Melancholia." Originally, Freud argued that the two states are clearly distinguishable by doctor and layperson alike. Whereas melancholia is obviously an illness, it "never occurs to us to regard [mourning] as a morbid condition."[83] As the terms have most commonly come to be used, mourning is a grief that moves toward conclusion; melancholia is defined by a refusal to let go of one's losses.

But in his later essay "The Ego and the Id," Freud began to revise his estimation of melancholia as pathological.

> We succeeded in explaining the painful disorder of melancholia by supposing that . . . an object-cathexis has been replaced by an identification. When this explanation was first proposed, however, we did not appreciate the full significance of the process and did not know how common and how typical it is. Since then we have come to understand that this kind of substitution has a great share in determining the form taken on by

> the ego and that it contributes materially towards building up what is called its "character."[84]

This passage is provocative grounding for the present study not only because it seems to open the door toward a depathologization of melancholic mourning but also insofar as it suggests that the incorporation of loss is central to identity formation and transformation.

Today, scholars continue to disagree about whether—and to what extent—mourning constitutes a malady. In contemporary critical theory, we find multiple, conflicting attitudes toward the performance of mourning, broadly conceived. Some would have us practice only that mourning that moves toward a conclusion. In *Mourning Becomes the Law*, Gillian Rose notes that postmodernity "identifies itself as a process of endless mourning, lamenting the loss of securities which, on its own argument, were none such."[85] Rose wants to distinguish between mourning play, an embrace of the postmodern condition as one of mourning, and what she calls inaugurated mourning, in which the mourner "return[s] from devastating inner grief to the law of the everyday and of relationships, old and new, with those who live."[86] The latter is, for Rose, the "law" of mourning, one that she seeks to enforce. For Rose, melancholia is simply the failure of mourning to work. This failure poses a threat to human well-being. If we embrace melancholia as a cornerstone of our postmodern identity, Rose asks, how can we ever mourn effectively, when mourning is constituted as a movement out of grief?

And yet we do. We do, somehow, perform through, with, against, inside, and outside the experience of loss. We give voice to this almost unspeakable experience. We do the very thing that undoes us. And, some suggest, we must. Derrida's later theoretical work on mourning positions ongoing mourning as an act of fidelity toward the dead.[87] Many black feminist scholars in the 1980s and, more recently, scholars in queer studies have advocated a politics of strategic affiliation in which the ongoing mourning of lost connections, under the name of melancholia, plays an integral role. José Esteban Muñoz argues that "melancholia, for blacks, queers, or any queers of color, is not a pathology but an integral part of everyday lives . . . a mechanism that helps us (re)construct identity and take our dead with us to the various battles we must wage in their names—and in ours."[88] To novelist Jane Hamilton's protagonist's acknowledgment "The grief, I knew, wasn't really ever going to go away,"[89] Muñoz's perspective adds an imperative, namely, that the grief *mustn't* go away, that to lose our grief is in a very important sense to lose our historically inflected understanding of who we are and who we might, even should, be.

Following most closely this last group of scholars, I resist what I believe is a narrow equation of mourning and healing, such that genuine mourning can only be said to be taking place if it is "working" or helping the subject to "get better" or "get over it," to disidentify with lost objects. Some of the mourners in the performances, scenes, and texts of this book eventually do get over it (although never through a linear narrative of progress); some do not. For me, the psychic endpoint of mourning is less important than the ability to imagine the mourning process itself as a performance, as a creative and productive act. Still more important is the question of to what end we might create such performances. That is, what does imagining a fully and fittingly expressive performance of mourning enable social actors to then *do*?

I also, however, resist the absolute disavowal of healing that a politics of melancholia suggests to me. Therefore, while I am sympathetic to contemporary scholars who, reacting to cultural sanctions against affective response, favor the term *melancholia*, I wish to retain *mourning* as the more capacious term.

Similarly, I refer to some of the strategies for negotiating loss analyzed in these pages as strategies of compensation. I use the word *compensation* not in its economic sense, as one receives compensation for services rendered, but in its more colloquial sense, where it is often accompanied by words like *small*, *little*, and *paltry*. It has always been curious to me that South Africa's Truth and Reconciliation Commission chose the word *reparations* over *compensation* for its monetary awards to victims of apartheid, because it seems to me that it is even less possible to repair such profound trauma than to compensate for it. The word *compensation*, to me, has connotations of partiality or incompleteness that make it the best, though admittedly imperfect, descriptor of the kind of success that is possible in the face of grave loss.

Consideration of Terms: A Note on *Performance*

In *Performing Loss*, I use the term *performance* in a number of ways. Many of these ways will be familiar to scholars in performance and cultural studies, who are accustomed to what Beverly Whitaker Long and Mary Frances HopKins have called the "essentially contested" nature of the term in academic fields. Yet, even for specialized readers, it may be helpful to know which meanings of the term will be operative here.

I have occasionally wished aloud to the students in my performance of literature classes that we in performance studies might in general replace the term *performance* with the term *rehearsal*. The former term, containing as it does the word *form*, risks overemphasizing presentations and arrivals.

The latter term emphasizes the extent to which the value of performance lies primarily in the safe space it affords one to practice, to experiment, to try things out and try them on, to become more experienced, and in that sense (and perhaps in that sense alone) more proficient.

Bearing in mind this sense of performance as rehearsal, my considerations of contemporary performances surrounding loss will be grounded in several particular categories.

Performance in Everyday Life

The everyday-life behaviors of ordinary people such as hospice patients (see chapter 2) may be considered performances. This is not to suggest that these behaviors are theatrical, though sometimes they are. Rather, it is to suggest that every set of behaviors in response to loss repeats with more or less difference a set of cultural norms as to how such things are done.

Here, everyday performances include ritual practices. Although it is true that these practices may often be defined precisely by their divergence from the everyday, I believe that it is the theoretical and practical separations too often made between ritual and everyday behavior that have left us without ways of responding to loss. By considering them together, I hope to model possibilities for the reintegration of ritual practices into everyday behaviors.

In the case of performing loss in the contemporary West, everyday behaviors are explicitly nontheatrical. They keep bodily and affective displays to a minimum. They "cry the right amount." But, like all performances, everyday practices that respond to loss, even when they wish to, rarely conform to cultural norms. In their difference lies the hope for new norms, for the remaking of culture.

Theatrical Performance

Although much of what contemporary performance scholars do is to consider behaviors and events, particularly cultural rituals, *as* performance, this emphasis, at least to the degree that it has prevailed in recent times, does not sit well with everyone. In her article "Geographies of Learning" (later the title of her book), Jill Dolan laments the extent to which performance studies has moved away from the study of actual theatrical events.

> But as much as performativity seems to capture the academic imagination, and as much as performance captures the political field, theatrical performances, as located, historical sites for interventionist work in social identity constructions, are rarely considered across the disciplines, media, and politics that borrow its terms.[90]

Performing Loss considers a "devised" theatrical performance, created by college students, about hospice patients, staff, and caregivers; a stage adaptation of a novel; a musical composition for chorus commemorating the terrorist attacks of September 11, 2001; and a series of solo performances of historical narratives in response to the same event as sites at which social identities are constructed.

By theatrical performance, I mean here performance that is marked by the characteristics of Schechner's category of "is" performance. These include a prepared presentation (sometimes fully scripted, other times more generally plotted or planned) to an unprepared audience; the use of performance tools such as costumes, props, scenery, lighting, and sound by live performers; and an event structure with a defined beginning, middle, and end.

Improvisational Performance

Improvisational performance, as outlined particularly in the theater games of Viola Spolin and Augusto Boal, is not designed for public display. Rather, it is based on group exploration of movement, sound, and space. This kind of performance depends on the existence of a group of spect-actors, Augusto Boal's term for participants who are both spectators and performers. It occurs whenever a community makes an agreement to make believe. It is important to consider this kind of improvisation as performance in order to properly value both its social and aesthetic elements. Improvisation as performance enables participants to try out and try on identities they might not feel comfortable debuting in everyday life. It also draws from theatrical performance, because, even in an empty room, we have one reliable scenic, costume, and lighting designer: our own imaginations.

Community Dialogue as Performance

The two community-based performance projects described in this book (see chapters 2 and 7) fit Schechner's category of "is" performance, but they also exceed it. The first of these performances, devised from ethnographic research at a community hospice, involved the writing of a performance text, rehearsal, and a formal performance with consciously selected aesthetic elements (props, costumes, music) for a live audience. But the purpose of this "is" performance was to evoke everyday-life performances from audience members, both within and beyond the theatrical space. If this had not been achieved, the performance would not have succeeded.

The second of the two projects, a collaboration between college students and federal prisoners, also involved rehearsal and other preparations on the part of one community, but the second community, the "audience," was involved in the performance event from start to finish. Unlike in most traditional performance events, at least in contemporary Western cultures, there was no division between audience and performers. The performance was itself a dialogue between two communities.

Performative Writing

Finally, in special cases, writing about loss moves beyond merely describing it to become a kind of performance or practice of losing. As with both everyday and theatrical performances, the ability to recognize and participate in such rehearsals through active readings of historical and fictional narratives has the potential to enlarge our individual and collective responses to loss.

Pedagogy as Performance

Although not explicitly discussed, one more kind of performance pervades these pages: the performance of pedagogy. Being directly involved in this unique and symbiotic relationship for many years has served, for me, as a kind of antidote to deep engagement with the study of loss. If working to understand our responses to loss through and as performance can help us to live with it—and each other—better, pedagogical performance provides a unique opportunity to live not merely with or despite but in some real way *against* loss. If the performances of everyday life, the stage, and certain kinds of literature are characterized by their movement toward disappearance, pedagogical performances are characterized by their investment in continuation. We participate in learning as both teachers and students out of the promise that something will remain.

Pedagogy continually rebuilds community. Teachers teach us through their own attachments to people, places, and ideas as well as through the idiosyncrasies of their own modes of inquiry and expression. (I will never forget, for example, how my high school English teacher looked at us with his intense, beady eyes on the first day of class and said in a hushed voice, "I am obsessed with the literature in this course to the degree of mental illness." We all have such stories, if we are lucky.) Students teach us through their efforts to move from a more or less outsider perspective in relation to certain disciplinary practices into a community that teachers, as relative insiders, take for granted. Pedagogy is a way of holding on to the most basic unit of community, the singular, live relationship between two people, in this case a particular teacher and a particular student. Happily, the relationship always troubles both terms, awakening the students to their own expertise and authority, the teachers to the continual process of discovering what they are missing.

2. Practicing Grief: Devising Scenes of Living and Dying

I AM PRODUCING THE SHOW OF A LIFETIME: My own death. It is a homework assignment in my hospice volunteer training. I have before me a lengthy questionnaire overflowing with details and decisions about how the death itself and the funerary rituals will proceed. I feel daunted. I call my sister. "How do you want to be remembered?" I ask her. "Fondly," she replies, and we both laugh. Back to the questionnaire. I begin to make some decisions. Irises, I want irises, even if they don't last. This isn't a time to be practical. Whom do I want to give the eulogy? Without hesitation I write, "Dad." Then I realize that, if the story goes as it is supposed to, he won't be there.

Dying involves the mingling of multiple griefs. At a minimum, during the dying process, the griefs of loved ones and caregivers (who may or may not be the same people) mingle with those of the dying patient. Yet, often these griefs mingle in silence. If our culture is ill equipped to negotiate the expression of grief among mourners, we are even less equipped to make space for conversations between the dying and those they leave behind.

In an era in which ritual practices surrounding loss are fast diminishing, the hospice movement encourages the performance of endings. St. Christopher's Hospice, the first modern hospice, was founded by Dame Cicely M. Saunders at Sydenham, London, in 1967. Its mission was to provide holistic care to terminally ill patients and their families. This included not only palliative medical treatment for the relief of pain associated with terminal diseases but social, psychological, and spiritual care as well. St. Christopher's was founded as a Christian care facility but open to people of all spiritual orientations. Although it sought "to help patients with strong and unfamiliar emotions,"[1] it did so with an emphasis on spirituality rather than on psychology.

In the United States, the opposite emphasis prevailed. Saunders came to speak to the Yale Study Group that, in 1973, began serving dying patients and their families as Hospice Inc. and provided invaluable practical support to the fledgling organization. But it was psychiatrist Elisabeth Kubler-Ross, whose seminars at the University of Chicago, lectures across the country, and writings made hospice a household word in America. Thanks in large part to the influence of her work, America's National Hospice Organization was established in 1977.

Despite differences in the movement between the United Kingdom and the United States and, now, the many other countries on all continents in which hospice care is practiced, many of the core principles of hospice translate across cultures. These include the consideration of the family, however constituted, as opposed to the patient alone as the "unit of care," and the giving of that care by an interdisciplinary team including, at a minimum, a doctor, nurse, social worker, chaplain, and volunteer.

The role of the volunteer in the hospice-care team is unique in the field of health care. "For medical staffers," observe two veteran hospice volunteers, "most of the change [from hospital care] is in degree and emphasis. But the volunteer is introduced to direct patient care and contact in an area that carries an enormous responsibility. The nature of the hospice program not only permits this heightened role for its members, but encourages and capitalizes on it."[2] Key to the nature of this heightened role is a responsibility for witnessing the performance of "strong and unfamiliar emotions," including grief.

> The volunteer, as an unassuming layman, may be perceived by the patient and family as someone outside the normal health care delivery system, someone to whom the patient can convey thoughts and feelings not expressed to medical personnel. The volunteer's freedom from other hospital responsibilities permits talking and listening at length, particularly at a critical juncture when a patient wants to unburden him- or herself.[3]

Hospice staff and volunteers invite patients to narrate their lives, as well as their experiences of dying. Through their attentiveness to the wishes and needs of the dying person—an attentiveness that begins with a shared understanding that the hospice patient is, by definition, terminally ill—the volunteers also often create a stage for encounters with death that the patient directs and designs.

The many processes through which artists and, sometimes, community members create original theatrical events offer similar opportunities in the art world to those that hospice organizations offer patients and caregivers in the medical world. Like the hospice structure, these processes, most commonly called "devising" in the United States and "applied theatre" in Canada and Britain, offer participants an increased sense of ownership over a process that involves them intimately.[4] Like hospice care, devised theater helps to build bridges between groups of people who should but often do not talk to each other—here artists, academics, and community members. In close harmony with the mission of hospice for the dying, devising projects can help artists and community members assuage feelings of "social isolation and spiritual alienation" through "the rigorous and deeply satisfying act of making work together."[5] Consistent with hospice's philosophy of talking openly about death and dying, devising demands a "visceral investigation of content"[6] that the interpretation of already existing texts does not require. While I wasn't consciously aware of all of these affinities at the outset, I had an intuitive sense that the processes of devising performance could offer meaningful tools to address issues related to death, dying, and grief for both patients and caregivers. I also had the sense that a hospice community would be particularly receptive to this work.

At the beginning of 1999, I began training as a volunteer at Evanston Northwestern Hospice in the Chicago area. The decision to volunteer was both personally and professionally motivated. As I was doing preliminary research for a dissertation on loss in contemporary fiction, I realized that, at age twenty-nine, I knew almost nothing about death and dying. I had lost a grandfather to cancer and a beloved childhood caretaker to a heart attack, but both had been old people who lived far away from me, and, in both cases, I was away at college when the death occurred. I flew in for the funeral, wept, and flew back to college.

Like so many young people in the contemporary, English-speaking West, I had been shielded from the end of life.[7] Although I hadn't yet intimately known anyone facing death, I knew that, as I entered my thirties, the odds were against this trend continuing much longer. I felt completely unequipped to handle this eventuality. Gaining experience with the dying seemed suddenly imperative, both for my work and for my life.

Hospice Volunteer Training as Performance

Hospice volunteer programs vary greatly in length and depth. I was fortunate that the one I found provided extensive preparation. Two hours every Monday night for nine weeks, I met with a group of nine adults, mostly women in their fifties and sixties, to prepare psychologically and intellectually to meet dying patients. (I have since participated in shorter volunteer-training programs, but this was the best and most thorough training I received.) Each session consisted of a presentation by the hospice volunteer coordinator, a question-and-answer session with a member of the hospice team, and an activity aimed at encouraging us to reflect on our personal relationship to the subject of dying.

And not merely reflect. In hospice training, I was asked to actively rehearse my own death. One of the most dramatic exercises in this regard was a lengthy questionnaire volunteers were asked to complete at home between their first two training sessions. Many of the questions encourage volunteers to rehearse their own death scenes in great detail. They are asked to consider, for example, to whom they would want to say goodbye, what extraordinary measures they would want taken to prolong their lives, whether they would want music at their funerals and, if so, what kind, and what they would want done with their bodies/remains.

Perhaps surprisingly, this activity is not unduly depressing for most volunteers. It can even be, in the words of one veteran volunteer, "kind of *fun*!" It is pleasurable to be the creator of a performance, perhaps especially when that performance is the one over which we are taught to expect the least control. Having consciously rehearsed their own deaths, hospice volunteers are then better prepared to be empathic participants in others' dying.

I worked with the Evanston hospice for a year before my volunteer activities were interrupted by a move to a new city. In that time, I served as a companion and helper for four dying women. I have since met other hospice patients and their caregivers, but I believe I can best indicate the range of performances of dying in everyday life by describing the rehearsals of two of those four women.

Performing Dying in Everyday Life

For Mrs. Greenbaum,[8] the first hospice patient for whom I volunteered, dying was the occasion for some of life's most dramatic performances. Mrs. Greenbaum relished the power her new role afforded her. I was forewarned that she could be difficult; she complained a great deal, and it was often hard to tell how much of what she said was true. Although much of this description turned out to be accurate, I never found Mrs. Greenbaum difficult. Rather, I very much enjoyed the pleasure she found in making scenes around her dying. Indeed, to a student of the theater, the theatricality of Mrs. Greenbaum's performance was recognizable, familiar, and even comforting.

On my first visit to her retirement home, Mrs. Greenbaum, who had been diagnosed with terminal cancer of the liver, still appeared quite healthy. A heavy-set woman in her early seventies, she walked through the hallways of her apartment building at a steady clip. Shortly after I arrived, she led me down to the ground floor to show me the laundry facilities, as she had asked for a volunteer specifically to help with this task. As we walked down the hall, we encountered two more elderly looking women, friends of Mrs. Greenbaum. They asked her, politely and casually, how she was doing today.

"Not so good," Mrs. Greenbaum said, looking around and then leaning in toward her friends for dramatic effect. When they asked, on cue, what was wrong, she continued in a stage whisper, "I've got CANCER." Then, without pausing for their response, she lifted her head and marched on. Through this performance, Mrs. Greenbaum demonstrated her understanding that one of life's greatest dramas was about to unfold, with her in the leading role.

On my second visit, Mrs. Greenbaum asked me if I would mind doing some light housework. I told her that I would be happy to; my hospice training had prepared me for the range of reasons patients request a volunteer. Some have major logistical tasks with which they need assistance, some want minor daily help around the house, and many simply want companionship. Although occasionally a volunteer task requires special abilities—for example, the physical strength to transfer a bedridden patient from bed to bath—the overwhelming majority of patients' needs can be met by any volunteer who is willing to help in diverse ways.

Mrs. Greenbaum gave me a rag and asked me to dust the credenza in her living room. When I was finished, I asked if there were other things she wanted me to dust. Yes, she said, there were.

Pause.

As it was clearly my line, I asked what she would like me to dust next. Mrs. Greenbaum extended her stout arm and made a grand sweep across the air in front of her body. "The house!" she said. Here, still in the early stages of dying, Mrs. Greenbaum, who had raised not only two children of her own but two of her grandchildren, theatrically relinquished her domestic tasks.

Mrs. Greenbaum's illness progressed quickly, and her strategies for commanding attention in performance became correspondingly more limited. In my last few visits to her apartment, her performance of dying was restricted first to moving back and forth continuously between the bed and a living room chair, then to moaning as loudly and as consistently as she could and then, finally, to the silence and stillness of a coma. But while she still could, Mrs. Greenbaum clearly enjoyed the various kinds of authority that her role as a dying patient afforded her. And what, as she might have asked, was so wrong with that?

Dottie, another hospice patient for whom I volunteered, flourished in the months before her death in a very different way from Mrs. Greenbaum. While Mrs. Greenbaum used death as an occasion for theatrical performance, Dottie's performance of dying followed the model of organizational performance, evaluated not on aesthetic grounds but in terms of "such things as productivity, tardiness, motivation, innovation, and the ability to establish and fulfill goals which support the organization's own goals."[9] To Dottie, performance at the end of life was not about flair but about efficiency.

In her discussion of the AIDS documentary, *Silverlake Life*, Peggy Phelan notes that death, like the camera and, implicitly, like all performance, heightens our awareness of the ordinary. "The things that are routine and assumed—eating, sleeping, going to the grocery store—are, from the heightened point of view shared by the movie camera and the dying, returned to their original intensity."[10] Deaths, both aesthetic and real, may become performance by teaching us, as performance does, to value the present.

While Mrs. Greenbaum spent her energy lavishly, Dottie conserved hers. Acutely aware of her limited time, she wanted to spend it talking about and, when possible, to those who mattered most: her two daughters and their children.

More than once when I visited her, Dottie was wearing a shirt she had sewn many years before, embroidered with the names of her grandchildren. Our relationship blossomed early when, through this fortuitously marked garment, we discovered that I knew two of her grandchildren and had been in school with one of them for many years. "Was he always a shining star?" she asked me, and I was able to tell her with complete honesty that her grandson, who excelled in nearly everything, including affability, had indeed always been a shining star.

When I first met Dottie, she was playing a game of trivia with other residents of the nursing home in which she was living. I was there to visit her, as was her daughter Tina. The game was being led by a young staff member, and at first Dottie participated. After about a half dozen questions, though, her enthusiasm abruptly waned:

YOUNG WOMAN STAFF MEMBER: Who was the first president to ride in a motor car? [*Silence. No one knows the answer to this question.*] Buchanan.

DOTTIE: Who writes these questions, and why do we need them? Why are they important?

OLDER MAN: Does everything have to be so important?

DOTTIE: In a sense.

OLDER MAN: Can't we have a little fun? Everything has to be significant?

DOTTIE: President Buchanan, why is he important?

OLDER MAN: He wasn't so important. But it's interesting how some people's minds remember things, and others don't.

DOTTIE: I don't remember President Buchanan.
OLDER MAN: This lady is against trivia!
YOUNG WOMAN: No, she's good at trivia. She answered a lot of questions.
OLDER MAN: She's good at it, but she's against it.
YOUNG WOMAN: I just think maybe we've been playing a little too long.
DOTTIE: Maybe.

As this scene of playing trivia dramatized, imminent death did not make life trivial for Dottie. On the contrary, it made it critical to distinguish between what was important to remember and what was not. Dottie's insistence that she does not remember President Buchanan is most importantly a refusal to spend any of her remaining time on unimportant things. On the stage of her dying, every act had to be made "in a sense" significant. Otherwise, for Dottie, it simply made no sense at all.

Adapting and Performing Voices of Grief

In the summer of 2001, now living and teaching in Springfield, Missouri, I received a phone call from Virginia Holtmann, the vice president for patient services at Hospice Foundation of the Ozarks. Ginny had just been made the head of the "arts and education" committee for the umbrella organization to which the foundation belonged, Community Alliance for Compassionate Care at the End of Life. She told me that although she knew a good deal about education, she knew nothing about the arts. She was looking, she said, for a creative way to help educate medical professionals and caregivers about living with dying patients.

For the last two years, I had been working with a group of very talented and unusually mature student actors on small projects relating to theater and social change. Most of them were now seniors. Here, I thought, was a perfect opportunity to respond to a real community need by attending to performances in everyday life and turning them into what Richard Schechner would call "is" performances—that is, theatrical presentations intended for an invited audience. In our case, the performance, entitled *Not Quite Through*, was a series of short monologues, scenes, and text-and-movement pieces that offered a series of perspectives on end-of-life issues. I eagerly accepted Ginny's invitation to meet.

There was, as there so often is, very little time. At the beginning of the fall semester, the students completed a two-week volunteer-training program and the necessary medical preparation (hospice volunteers must have a current tuberculosis test). They then had less than three months to begin working with patients, generate writing and other performance ideas based on those encounters, and create a performance for public viewing.[11] If this seems a ridiculously short time, it is; but because patients are typically admitted to hospice when a doctor has confirmed that they have six months or less to live (of course, doctors are occasionally wrong),[12] three months represented a significant portion of the total time any volunteer has to get to know a dying patient.

My plan was to help the students create a performance by applying a variety of scripting techniques (see appendix A) to a variety of sources including interviews, personal narratives, nonfiction materials (in this case from the psychological literature on death and dying), and the adaptation of literature. I had come to believe. with many of my colleagues who work to produce maximally dialogic performances,[13] that more voices are usually better and for many reasons: formally, to provide variation in the piece and as one way to open space for that key dramatic element, surprise; structurally, insofar as the alternation of voices can provide a pattern and, therefore, a shape to the work; and, politically, insofar as a model of many voices within the performance can help to encourage a multivocal dialogue in the discussion, formal or informal, that follows the performance. I set the due date for the students' first major writing assignment, an interview with a hospice patient, for one month into the semester.

Interview material has become a common source for performance texts since Anna Deavere Smith's watershed solo work, *Fires in the Mirror*, premiered in the mid-1990s.[14] Some performance artists, like Smith and playwright Moises Kaufman, excerpt interview material verbatim. Other artists such as Heather Woodbury, Danny Hoch, and Rhodessa Jones take a more interpretive approach to these texts, forming composite and/or fictionalized characters from interviews and ethnographic material.

To prepare for their interviews, the students read material on interviewing techniques and practiced interviewing each other. They wrote informed-consent forms in order to secure permission from interviewees to include their words, without attribution, in the performance. And they reflected in their journals about their relationship to the subject matter with which we would be dealing. Most of them had not had to do this before with respect to death and dying. They were visibly stressed by the task but determined to press on. Ultimately, they would find many ways of connecting the subject to their own experiences, and some of these would be incorporated in the final script.

After their first individual meetings with patients, the students informed me that the one-month deadline would be too soon for them to conduct even an informal interview with the patients. They weren't ready. They were just getting to know them.

Of course, it was not really too soon to conduct an interview; after all, an interview, I reminded them, was simply an exchange between two people, something that happened naturally all the time and frequently between strangers. But the students' fear was appropriate both to the cultural climate in which they were living—a climate that both the hospice movement and, in a modest way, this book, are striving to change—and to the demands of hospice volunteer work. As Lucy B. McBee and Maureen Mason observe, "These are large demands for an individual: to meet a stranger whose life is ebbing away and to summon up the necessary patience, compassion, and sensitivity to sustain that person."[15] The students worried, as I did in my initial experience as a volunteer, that they were not up to these demands.

To their great credit, however, the students were also trying to tell me something in this first negotiation over the course of our project: the needs of these patients were far more important than mine as their teacher or theirs as my students or even those of the health care community in the Ozarks. Getting to know these individuals and attending to their needs were the students' first priorities.

Instead of conducting initial interviews with patients, we decided to begin our work with interviews of hospice staff members. This was not only a nonthreatening way to begin but proved for the students a very useful one. As what anthropologists call key informants, the staff members served as links from outside the hospice community, where the students began, to deep inside the community, where the patients were firmly positioned.

With the staff, the students felt free to indulge their deepest curiosities and anxieties: What did it feel like to watch another person die? What do dying people like to talk about? In a professional life devoted to giving and grieving, what did the hospice staff do to keep themselves sane?

Ethical Considerations

Some of the staff interviews yielded material that raised questions about the ethical responsibilities of performing material from everyday life. One interviewee, a chaplain, expressed ambivalence to a student about the entire performance project as we had conceived it.

> I don't feel comfortable with this performance of such a private and difficult experience. If you want spirituality, to join someone's spirit in this time of change, to walk with them on this journey, to experience a person's soul and be there for *them*, not their drama. If what you want is spirit and love, not a spectacle. If you are saying, "Here's an armload of my spirit I'm giving to you." If you are embracing the patients on the inside for them, not grasping them on the outside for you, that is moving. And I'm joyful that you are here. Just be careful. Please. People's lives are to be experienced, not exposed. Just be careful.

Devisors of performance often worry about which voices they are excluding when they select material, and they should; thoughtless exclusions can easily reify cultural norms about both who is allowed to speak and what they are allowed to say.[16] This interviewee, however, underscores the point that inclusion, too, is an ethical act that carries significant responsibility. His concern echoes what Dwight Conquergood has called the "custodian's rip-off."

> A strong attraction to the other coupled with extreme detachment, results in acquisitiveness instead of genuine inquiry, plunder more than performance. [. . .] The immorality of such performances is unambiguous and can be compared to theft and rape.
>
> Potential performers of ethnographic materials should not enter the field with the overriding motive of "finding some good performance material."[17]

Although Conquergood's warning and its echo in the chaplain's words bear remembering, I have never encountered a college student with an interest in performance ethnography whose overriding motive was to find good material. For one thing, good material is attainable at the library or bookstore with far less trouble. For another, a genuine interest in learning about difference tends to bring with it a humility that raises sensitivity to issues of power.

Nonetheless, students should be encouraged to think in detail about the implications of specific choices in scripting and performing. For example, is the material they are including fairly and maximally representative of the interviewee? To what extent should the circumstances of the original interview be included in the performance, and why might this, in some cases, be important? Should the interviewee's voice be included in the performance, and why might this, in some cases, be important?

In the case of this project, we spent one full rehearsal period deliberating about how to respond to this early interviewee's concerns. Did we need to abandon our work? Abandon this voice? Reconceive the project? After much discussion about the value and risks of our enterprise, we incorporated the interviewee's critique into the performance as the first piece, under the title "Warning." It served as a valuable ethical touchstone to us throughout the creative process: these were people's lives we were encountering and trying to represent. Despite my experience, in general and with this project in particular, of college students' vigilance on this point, a reminder embedded in the performance was useful to us and, I suspect, to our audience members, particularly those most intimately connected to the project.

Listening for Spoken Metaphors

As we search for meaning, we instinctively search for comparisons: What is this like? It's like . . . Sometimes, as in dreams, the metaphor even precedes the understanding. And, if we recall the metaphors of our dreams, it is a short step to understanding performance as metaphor.[18] We tend to think of metaphor as a literary conceit. But, as Anna Deavere Smith has often pointed out, metaphor is a natural feature of human speech: "[E]veryone, in a given amount of time, will say something that sounds like poetry."[19] Smith capitalizes on this feature of speech regularly in her work. For example, *Twilight*, the title of one of Smith's major works, uses an interviewee's words about dusk as a metaphor for interracial dialogue.

In the students' interviews with staff members, we found metaphors that seemed ripe for staging. One hospice staff interviewee spoke about the widely observed ability of terminally ill people to wait for the completion of some unfinished personal (often interpersonal) business before dying.[20] She described some of her patients as "not quite through." We adopted this phrase as a metaphor for the position of the terminally ill, and it became the title of our performance.

Other interviews yielded metaphors that in the acts of extending and embodying required the students to move from observation of to active participation in the hospice community. One staff member discussed the effort many people make in their everyday lives to hide from death. This discussion turned into a comic piece in which, to the tune of the Pink Panther theme song, an actor tried to hide—behind some flowers, by posing as a Greek statue, by wearing a wig and dark glasses—from another actor in a black cape playing Death.

Betty, the volunteer coordinator at the hospice, answered a student's question about how she sustains herself in this difficult work with the metaphor of a psychic cup.

> Talk about things I do to heal myself?
> [. . .]
> I spend time with myself
> um,
> just reviving myself, just kind of putting back what I give out.
> You just give a lot when you do that.
> Sometimes it's really, um, painful for the person,
> they may cry the whole time
> and, um,
> you can't help but feel down
> I mean you do

So
I have to give back to myself, so that I can give back out again.
Fill myself back up.
I empty the cup, and I have to fill it back up.
But I have learned that,
that it's very important to do that,
because if you don't
I think you'll just totally burn out.

Building on the metaphor provided by this speaker, I asked each of the students to come up with a list of approximately half a dozen things they do or experience to fill their own cups. Not surprisingly, perhaps, the most commonly recurring items on the combined list were food items. The second most recurring items, again not surprisingly for this group, were related to performance. We played with this list and with a set of colored, plastic cups filled with water that were passed around in a variety of formations to create the penultimate piece for our performance.

What follows is an excerpt from that piece. The numbers designate which of the six student actors spoke each line. I purposefully did not assign students to speak their own "cup fillers," partly to protect their anonymity among each other and partly for the performative exercise of having them share in each other's comforts.

2: Church campgrounds
3: The dinner table
6: Cranberry juice and grapefruit juice mixed together
5: Music
4: Jumbo scallops
3: Moo Shu vegetables
4: Hot showers
3: Spirituality
2: Coffee shops
2: A dark theater
ALL: Fill my cup.
1: My mom's conditioner
5: Food
6: Crossword puzzles
1: Strawberry shakes
5: Barbados
4: Family
6: The park
1: The Fox Theater

6: Comic books
2: Friends
    ALL: Fill my cup.
3: Butterflies
4: Laughter
5: Literature
6: Music
5: Traveling
4: Partying
3: Education
2: Spirituality
1: Theater
6: Nature
    ALL: Fill my cup.

Although this was the second-to-last piece in the performance, it was important to the process that we constructed it early on. The proliferation of concrete images of replenishment helped the students to feel safe treading into some unfamiliar and emotionally risky waters.

Staging Metaphors of Time and Space

The students would be responsible not only for generating the material but for staging it. I wanted to give them flexible tools for doing so, tools that had been demonstrated to be useful in working with original material. During our first few weeks together, therefore, the students studied the Viewpoints, a technique for creating stage movement developed by experimental director Anne Bogart in the 1980s and 1990s. I provided the students with some basic staging exercises through which they learned to explore individual elements of time and space as well as selected combinations of these elements.

The Viewpoints are a language and technique for creating movement on stage. More specifically, they are nine "points of awareness" for performers and directors.[21] In her explanation of the Viewpoints, director Tina Landau, a longtime collaborator of Bogart, divides them into four Viewpoints of time and five Viewpoints of space. The Viewpoints of time are tempo, duration, kinesthetic response, and repetition. The Viewpoints of space are shape, gesture, architecture, spatial relationship, and topography.[22]

I am not an expert in the use of the Viewpoints, and many directors have written about them better than I can.[23] What is important for the present discussion is that the text the students were working with and their own sensibilities helped them to focus on actions among the Viewpoints that were particularly germane to the subject of grief.

The students' second assignment was to use Bogart's Viewpoints to direct a performance of an already existing text, Linda Pastan's poem "The Five Stages of Grief." Dividing them into pairs, I gave each duo a different combination of Viewpoints on which to focus, and the best results were combined in the second stage of our work.

Pastan's poem appears to be an elaboration of the five stages of mourning articulated in Kubler-Ross's *On Death and Dying*:

> The night I lost you
> Someone pointed me towards
> the Five Stages of Grief
> Go that way, they said,
> it's easy, like learning to climb
> stairs after the amputation.
> And so I climbed.
> *Denial* was first.
> I sat down at breakfast
> carefully setting the table
> for two. I passed you the toast—
> you sat there. I passed
> you the paper. You hid
> behind it.
> *Anger* seemed more familiar.
> I burned the toast, snatched
> the paper and read the headlines myself.
> But they mentioned your departure,
> and so I moved on to
> *Bargaining*. What could I exchange
> for you? The silence
> after storms? My typing fingers?
> Before I could decide, *Depression*
> came puffing up, a poor relation,
> its suitcase tied together
> with string. In the suitcase
> were bandages for the eyes
> and bottles of sleep. I slid
> all the way down the stairs
> feeling nothing.
> And all the time Hope
> flashed on and off
> in defective neon
> Hope was a signpost pointing

straight in the air.
Hope was my uncle's middle name,
he died of it.
After a year I am still climbing, though my feet slip
on your stone face.
The treeline
has long since disappeared;
green is a color
I have forgotten.

In its final lines, however, the poem becomes a critique of *On Death and Dying* (at least as that classic text is usually misread), performing the nonlinearity of the grieving process.

But now I see what I am climbing
towards: *Acceptance*
written in capital letters,
a special headline:
Acceptance,
its name in lights.
I struggle on,
waving and shouting.
Below, my whole life spreads its surf,
all the landscapes I've ever known
or dreamed of. Below
a fish jumps: the pulse
in your neck.
Acceptance. I finally
reach it.
But something is wrong.
Grief is a circular staircase.

I have lost you.

Beginning with the first of Kubler-Ross's five stages, the poem seems to proceed in an orderly fashion toward the last stage, acceptance, until in its last two stanzas, the orderliness of the process comes undone.

If the interview process attuned the students to metaphor in everyday speech, working with the Viewpoints attuned them to action as metaphor. The performance text they created was primarily marked by two characteristics of movement, one that Landau places in the category of Viewpoints of Time and one that is a Viewpoint of Space.

The Viewpoint of Time most closely associated with loss and the one to which the students naturally gravitated is repetition. The students instinctively built on Pastan's critique of received grieving narratives by emphasizing, both through speech and through gesture—each of the repeated phrases below was accompanied by a repeated body movement—the traumatic repetitions of grief.

Adapted for performance,[24] the poem read as follows:

Wanda, Elaine, Sue, Laura, and Jacob all standing in a line on stage left tied together with rope. The audience can't see the rope. All move center.

ELAINE: The night I lost you / someone pointed me towards / the Five Stages of Grief.

ALL: Go that way,

ELAINE: They said,

ALL: it's easy,

LAURA: like learning to climb stairs after an amputation.

ELAINE: And so I climbed.

They take off in different directions. It becomes obvious when they start to move that they are tied. Elaine stops first. Elaine sits.

ELAINE: Denial was first. I sat down at breakfast carefully setting the table for two. I passed you the toast

She makes a sweeping motion to suggest this. Each time she repeats the words, she repeats the gesture.

I passed you the toast.

Repeat.

Repeat.

Repeat.

She continues to repeat the line. All keep tugging on rope.

WANDA: Anger seemed more familiar. I burned the toast and snatched the paper and read the headlines for myself, but they mentioned your departure so I moved on.

Wanda starts pulling on rope violently.

WANDA: and so I moved on.

Moved on

Repeat,

Repeat,

Repeat.

Sue and Jacob are now face-to-face center, pulling each other back and forth with the rope.

SUE AND JACOB TOGETHER: to Bargaining
SUE: what could I exchange
JACOB: for you
SUE: the silence after storms?
JACOB: My typing fingers?

During their conversation, Sue and Jacob repeat the motion of pulling each other across the space.

SUE: Exchange
JACOB: For you
SUE: Exchange
JACOB: For you
SUE: Exchange
JACOB: For you

Laura is moving around the stage. Soon she starts to get tangled up.

LAURA: Depression came puffing up, a poor relation, its suitcase tied together with string. I slid all the way down, feeling nothing.

Laura slides down into a sitting position. All pulling on rope now.

ELAINE: Feeling nothing
WANDA: All the time Hope flashed on and off
SUE: Hope was a signpost pointing straight in the air
JACOB: straight in the air

All stop.

ELAINE: After a year I am still climbing.
But now I see what I am climbing
towards.

All stand except Elaine.

WANDA: Acceptance, written in capital letters

Wanda unties herself.

SUE: A special headline

Sue unties herself.

JACOB: Acceptance, its name in lights

Jacob unties himself.

LAURA: I struggle on waving, shouting

Laura unties herself.

ALL EXCEPT ELAINE: Acceptance I finally reach it

LAURA: But something is wrong; grief is a circular staircase

All except Elaine walk to stage right. As they speak, they repeat their earlier gestures.

ELAINE (still sitting): I passed you the toast.
LAURA: I am still climbing

Laura repeats "I am still climbing" *through what follows.*

ELAINE: I passed you the toast
WANDA: I burned the toast
JACOB: What could I exchange
SUE: What could I exchange
JACOB: What could I exchange
SUE: What could I exchange

All voices stop.

ELAINE: I have lost you.

As Cathy Caruth explains in her reading of psychoanalytic theory, repetition is the most salient characteristic of traumatic experience: "In its general definition, trauma is described as the response to an unexpected or overwhelming violent event or events that are not fully grasped as they occur, but return later in repeated flashbacks, nightmares, and other repetitive phenomena."[25] Through their adaptation of Pastan's poem, the students performed a central feature of coming to terms with traumatic loss over time.

Further, the students extended Pastan's critique. Although the poem says that the movement of grief is circular, the students created a much more complex pattern involving repetition, overlap, regression, and simultaneity. Performance made this possible.

In addition to repetition, the performance text emphasizes spatial relationships. Landau defines the Viewpoint of spatial relationship as "the distance between things on stage, especially one body to another, one body to a group of bodies, or the body to the playing space."[26] Of course, the relationship between one body and another has everything to do with loss. That the players in the above scene are literally tied together with string can be read, like the patterns of spoken and gestural repetition, as a metaphor for the interdependence (and nonlinearity) of the five stages of grief. But it can also be read as a metaphor for melancholia, the mourner's attachment to the lost object.

In the performance, different subjects have different responses to this attachment. Some embrace it, some struggle to find their way within it, some struggle violently against it, and others (acceptance) release themselves from it. But this release is troubled in performance, as in Pastan's poem. Even when they are released from physical tethering to the lost object, the mourners repeat the gestures and behaviors that bind them to loss.

Worth noting here, too, is that through a further metaphor embedded in performance practice, the six different mourners in this performance can be read as aspects of a single, complex, and conflicted self. This brings me to the students' next assignment, an exercise in bifurcation.

Bifurcation

While the Viewpoints are a relatively new theatrical language, bifurcation is one of the original strategies of *chamber theater*, a special technique for the oral interpretation of literature developed in the 1940s and named by Northwestern University's Robert S. Breen. Breen developed chamber theater in order to "take full advantage of all the theatrical devices of the stage without sacrificing the narrative elements of the literature."[27] Today, the term *chamber theater* is seldom used, but Breen's practices have become the foundation of much work in literary adaptation and performance, both in the classroom and on the professional stage.

Chamber theater embodies the idea that narrative prose is dialogic, as the Russian literary theorist Mikhail Bakhtin has argued.[28] In addition to the novel's many dialogues between characters, there are dialogues within characters. Multiple voices or, as Bakhtin called them, languages, are embedded in a single speaker. Adaptation to performance allows the differences among these multiple selves to be fully represented through the technique of having more than one actor portray a single character. Breen describes the chamber-theater approach to J. P. Donleavy's *The Ginger Man* this way:

> A Chamber Theatre production of *The Ginger Man* might do well to feature two actors in the role of Sebastian Dangerfield with the intention of dramatizing for the audience the bifurcation of his character, the unredeemed and the unredeemable, the natural and the unnatural man. One actor would speak the external dialogue, the other would speak the internal monologue. A third actor should then be used to speak the objective narration. The picture we now have of the novel is that there is a Dangerfield who lives an internal life with its memories and fantasies while a second Dangerfield lives an external life with O'Keefe, Mary, Miss Frost, etc., and still another Dangerfield who tells his own story in the third person with an artist's objectivity and control.[29]

Bifurcation is also common in the solo performance tradition. And while here it is usually used to allow one performer to play multiple roles, it nonetheless reminds the audience member of the diversity of voices within a single subject. It reminds us, too, that human beings are storytellers, naturally taking on different roles as we narrate our lives.

After showing them some examples of bifurcation in performance, I asked the students to listen for multiple voices in the hospice patient or caregiver with whom they were working. In their next written assignment, they were to choose two or more aspects of the character they were studying and dramatize them in a solo performance.

The exercise resulted in what I believe—and what postperformance interviews indicate—was one of the strongest pieces in *Not Quite Through*, performed by a young woman who was both a keen observer and an outstanding actor. It is reproduced here in slightly abbreviated form.

DENIAL: I guess you could say I'm happy here. I really like the workers. They're very personable, and keep me company when I need it. I'm finally starting to feel like this is home . . .

TRUTH: I miss my home. Do you want to know the truth? I can't tell you the name of one worker here. One lady sticks her head in every once in a while and leaves, and I guess she considers that a visit. I know I'll never really be able to call this place home. . . . I miss my home . . .

DENIAL: You know, the one thing I definitely don't miss is cleaning house. I don't have to worry about washing the dishes or vacuuming or any of those type of things—it's all done for me here, so I don't have to worry about that . . .

TRUTH: I actually miss doing little chores around my house. I used to love keeping a clean house—washing dishes, dusting—I would give anything for someone to put a pile of dishes here in front of me so that I could just clean them—I would give anything to do that.

DENIAL: People always ask me if I get lonely, and I would have to say . . .

TRUTH: Yes. I'm lonely all the time. You know, when you leave here today, I'm going to be as lonely as can be. I'll just want to go to sleep, and I probably will, but don't worry yourself about that.

In performance, the shifts the actor made between these two voices were extraordinarily subtle—and perfectly clear. Denial and Truth both sat in the same straight-back chair, and for both characters, the actor's hands were folded gently in her lap. When she shifted from Truth to Denial, the actor took a moment to curve her spine slightly, no more than an inch. She also flattened her vocal inflection almost imperceptibly, and her facial expressions became less animated. In performance, then, these two voices were intimately intertwined by a shared physicality.

They were also intertwined by temporal proximity. The most powerful moment in the performance was the penultimate one in which the character rehearses her response to the question about loneliness. Here, breaking an established pattern of small, complete speeches by each voice, we watch the speaker's optimistic persona crumble and give way under the weight of a particularly painful question.

In performance the audience did not know that the student had entitled the voices Denial and Truth; the voices appeared as conflicting aspects of the same character. Had we had more time, or had we been intending to publish the play script, I would have encouraged the student to rename these voices in accordance with this experience. If we actually heard one of these voices as true and the other as false, we would quickly dismiss or ignore half of the performance. The speaker here is compelling because we can hear each of her two conflicting voices as faithfully representing her on different days, at different times, or in different moods. Key to the power of the piece, I believe, is that *both* voices speak the truth.

Performance as Community Dialogue

The most successful piece in *Not Quite Through* happened by accident. From another writing assignment, several of the students had created monologues about an object connected to someone they loved—a seashell necklace, a box of crayons, a bottle of conditioner (see appendix A for fuller description of the object-narrative exercise). Some of these loved ones were living, some were dead; the important thing was the connection to a person through an object. I made this assignment thinking that we might use one of the pieces as a monologue, or if there were a number of good ones, use the idea of attachment to lost loved ones through objects as a structuring trope in the performance.

Three of the pieces ended up in the first draft of our performance script, but they gave too much weight to intentionally idiosyncratic memories and made the performance as a whole too long. We edited the monologues down to a fraction of their original length and put them together in a scene in which three women, perhaps sisters, perhaps friends, dug through an old trunk and shared object memories. Still, the piece seemed to emphasize the particularity of these objects and their relationships rather than something that was transferable, shareable. The students said that they felt silly performing it.

We decided that we would try having the three women take the objects and their stories into the audience. Each student would bring her object to a particular audience member. After telling her own personal story,[30] the student would invite that audience member to tell about an object that was strongly connected to someone important in her life. The students were skeptical about this approach, partly because they were not used to making direct contact with an audience, partly because they feared they would make audience members uncomfortable, and partly because they worried that each of their individual stories would be lost to all but a single listener. Still, they agreed to try this version of the piece during dress rehearsal.

The dress rehearsal took place in our college classroom and was attended by about half a dozen people including a couple whose family had received hospice care, two or three hospice staff members, and Andrea, the coordinator of service learning on the university campus, who had made the initial contact between hospice and my student group.

Andrea came to the dress rehearsal to do her job. "I didn't go for a performance," she told me in a conversation several years later, "I went as part of my responsibility, and then, you know, it just . . . " Her voice trailed off.

As I remember it, it was the object piece that made Andrea weep. A student approached her, offered an object story, and asked for one in return. Andrea broke down into quick, quiet tears, managing to explain that her grandmother was ill.

But in our conversation, Andrea remembered the incident differently.

ANDREA: I don't think the students approached me. I think they knew to stay away. My grandmother, she . . . [measured, fighting back tears] she has a lot of stuff.

JODI: Objects?

ANDREA: [Nods silently, then softly] Yeah.

Whether or not it was this piece that evoked Andrea's original emotional reaction, her recollection in an interview two years later of objects belonging to her dying grandmother confirms the power of objects as metonymic expressions of loss.

In every performance of *Not Quite Through*, the object piece received the strongest response. Each student's object story was heard by at least half a dozen people per performance. Audience members seated near the person the student selected as primary listener leaned in to hear the story, and sometimes the student had time to approach a second person/group before the time ended.

But it quickly became more important for the students to hear stories than to tell them. Although the students simply asked audience members to talk about an object that reminded them of a person they cared about, many spoke of the dead. Almost always, there were tears. And almost always, there were expressions of gratitude for the opportunity to share their memories. With this piece, then, the performance moved from theatrical "is" to performance as community dialogue, where the goal is not to give but to exchange, to open up a genuine conversation about a shared experience or concern.

Bradley Fisher first attended *Not Quite Through* in his role as a member of the Community Alliance for Compassionate Care at the End of Life. Seeing how the object-catalyzed dialogue worked in one of the early performances, Fisher asked us to give an additional performance at the church where he was a member. His community, he told us, was struggling with the recent loss of several important members, and they hadn't really been able to have a conversation about these losses. I asked the students, who were days away from graduation, if they wanted to do an extra performance and all but one of them said that they did. The students gave a slightly abbreviated version of the performance that excluded the pieces featuring this performer.

What drew Fisher into the performance was exactly what pulled Andrea out of it, namely, the breaking down of barriers between the professional and the personal. Fisher described this effect in explicitly theatrical terms: "Here we are all these committee members [of the Community Alliance] in our front stage roles and this asked us to go into our backstage roles." I asked Fisher about the value of going "backstage." He responded,

> When you get people emoting about their concerns, we begin to see people like ourselves. And whenever you humanize people who meet professionally, it makes it easier to be more patient. I like people more when I know who they are. I can't box people in because I start to see some of their complexity. And maybe I'm hoping people see some of my complexity. When I see people moved by the same things that move me, I begin to realize that maybe we have more in common than we have differences.

When I asked Fisher what difference it made that the event was a performance, he said that performance creates a "general mood of interest and openness." He also spoke of the vital role that creativity plays in aging, both directly through the new opportunities the elderly often have in their retirement to participate in the making and contemplating of art and indirectly by modeling artful adaptation to life's changes.[31]

Impact

Not Quite Through did not magically transform the cultural context in which it was made and in which it intervened. It did not make it easy to talk about death or to give care to the dying. But it did provide a model for productive action. Some audience members expressed the idea that the performance offered a number of different ways to begin conversations about death. The director of nursing at a local hospital asked for permission to use the videotape of the performance as part of her employee training, as a way of suggesting a range of approaches that health care professionals could use to relate to dying patients. Others began sharing their own stories for the first time during the performance itself.

The composition process also had a complex effect on the student performers. Devising *Not Quite Through* was hard on the students. Very hard. There were logistical problems with some of the volunteer assignments, mostly in coordinating the students' schedules with those of the hospice staff. And then, of course, there were the emotional demands of the project, the work of being present with the dying, and therefore the necessity of reflecting on one's relationship to that experience (see appendix D for some suggestions about pedagogy and the performer's grief).

Because script material had to be generated quickly and because some of the early assignments had to be delayed in order to allow relationships between students and hospice patients to develop, the students ended up having more writing due per week than the course syllabus outlined.

This work came, of course, as is all too tempting for teachers to forget, as part of a full course load including, in this case, performances that needed to be prepared and presented for other classes. The students expressed outrage when, on top of all of this, I stuck to my original plan of giving them a final exam through which they analyzed and reflected upon their experiences in the project. They expressed further outrage when I assigned them a *grade* for this exam, as well as a grade for their journals, and another for their portfolio of writing.

For all these reasons, the students felt that I was asking too much of them. But the performances went a long way toward dispelling these feelings. After our first performance, I wrote:

> Yesterday we performed an abbreviated version of *Not Quite Through* at the monthly meeting of the Community Alliance for Compassionate Care at the End of Life for 30-40 visibly tired health care professionals, religious leaders, etc. Half of them cried. They gave the students applause between every piece, and at the end of the 30 minute performance (the full show is an hour long), a standing ovation. A number of them came up to us afterwards and asked about whether we could do additional performances, distribute a videotape of the performance to hospitals and nursing homes for staff training, do the performance again in the fall. The students were clearly impressed by the strength of the audience reaction.

The program for *Not Quite Through* included a blank page for feedback on the performance. Over what became an eight-performance run (originally six), the students received numerous positive comments from audience members. The following comment is representative.

> I wish my family and I had seen this presentation while we were coping with my father's death. It would have gotten us into and through the difficult conversations, phases, and experiences with more compassion for ourselves, our father, and each other. I now understand better both how to love the living and how to love and grieve those dying.

In turn, reflecting on the project in their final evaluations, students demonstrated a keen awareness of how their work had affected others and themselves. Four of the six students said that the most valuable aspect of the project was meeting the dying patients and caregivers they served. Two said that the most valuable part of the project was seeing the impact of the performance on audience members. And one noted that the project gave her hope "that I can use my theater training in meaningful ways away from the stage."

Perhaps even more tellingly, two of the students maintained contact with their hospice families well beyond their graduation from college, and a third maintained contact with her staff mentor. Although one or two of the students still harbored resentments about the demands of the process, they clearly knew that they had created a space for grief in the lives of people who needed such a space—even themselves.

And, if the performance provided a space for learning to practice grief, engagement with grief also provided a space for learning about performance. When I asked Andrea how it felt to have her feelings about her grandmother "pushed up front" (as she described it), she responded without hesitation, "Oh, I did not like it. I did not like that. If I went again, I'd have my guard up so that it wouldn't happen again." At the same time, like Dr. Fisher, she theorized about the value of the performance frame for effective community work: "Maybe it's a good thing for people who would be very anti-therapy to go thinking this is just a performance." She went on to answer a question I hadn't asked, about the very nature of performance.

> What I'm learning is that theatre is so much a part of life, church, other community organizations, fundraising. I don't know if counseling is theatre or not but I just think that theatre is a part of what most people don't consider. They probably have more intersection with theatre than they ever realize.

This is not to say, of course, that everyone welcomes "what most people don't consider" into their lives. As Bradley Fisher explains,

> Grief demands that we deal with our own mortality. That we hurt. . . . Grief demands that we confront our pain. We don't like to suffer at all. The way we act suggests that we have a low threshold for pain. I don't

> think that's true. But we act as if it's true. Kinda like Sergeant Friday, just the facts, ma'am. We're comfortable with facts. We have a harder time with emotion.

Andrea would certainly concur. She concluded our interview, "I still like visual arts more. It's much more comfortable for me. I went to see the Ansel Adams exhibit yesterday, and I was very comfortable with the trees."

3. Practicing Adaptation: Losses and Gains in Staging *Blindness*

> *Above all, when you get to the new home, you should adapt yourself.*
> —Olga, an elderly Jewish woman advising a friend, in Barbara Myerhoff, *Number Our Days*

THE PROCESS OF ADAPTATION ALWAYS ENTAILS SOME MEASURE OF LOSS. Even when, as in scientific adaptation, there is little question that the value added outweighs the value lost, there is always a mourning of the old form to be negotiated. The question, then, for those embarking on a conscious process of adaptation, theatrical or otherwise, is not whether loss will occur but how to anticipate which losses will be sustainable—at best, most productive, at worst, least detrimental.

The process of adapting literature to the stage has been the subject of remarkably little scholarship since it was recognized as a legitimate academic undertaking some time in the middle of the twentieth century. At Northwestern University, Wallace Bacon and Robert S. Breen were exploring "literature as experience" in their classrooms as early as the mid-1940s, though it was not until 1978 that Breen, at his colleagues' urging, published *Chamber Theatre*, which remains the most comprehensive monograph about a particular method of literary adaptation for the stage.

The journal *Text and Performance Quarterly*, originally established in 1980 as *Literature in Performance*, has for decades documented the efforts of dedicated professors who have educated their students about both the study of literature and effective communication strategies through theatrical adaptation and performance. A small handful of books on literature and performance, including Beverly Whitaker Long and Mary Frances

HopKins's *Performing Literature: An Introduction*, Bruce Henderson and Carol Simpson Stern's *Performance: Texts and Contexts* (1993), and Paul H. Gray and James Van Oosting's *Performance in Life and Literature* analyze literary texts on the page and suggest how these texts provide clues to their more-or-less faithful performance (Long and HopKins use the language of possibility and probability).

These writings constitute a valuable archive of methods for appreciating both literature and performance. They describe reading, rehearsal, and performance in productive detail, although they often skip the actual process of moving from literary text to theatrical adaptation. Even articles such as Michael S. Bowman's wonderful and provocative "Novelizing the Stage" (1995) provide a *theory* of productive adaptation rather than a method. Considering this body of literature as a whole, one might conclude that the methodology of adaptation is intractably local, too specific to any given text to be analyzed and described in general terms.

Having worked on and taught the adaptation of literature for many years, I have found that there are some transferable lessons about how to successfully adapt a text from literary to dramatic form. Some of these lessons involve techniques that can be practiced through targeted exercises and assignments (see appendix B). Others depend more on the particular story for their articulation. Adapting Jose Saramago's novel *Blindness* for the stage crystallized for me some ideas about adaptation in general and about the adaptation of stories of loss in particular.

Selecting the Text

We like to think that we choose our largest projects in great moments of inspiration or, at least, from a place of intense artistic investment. I chose *Blindness* because it had sixteen chapters.

I had not read *Blindnes*s until I found it on a table at a bookstore a few weeks before my course on the adaptation and performance of literature was to begin. In the fall of 1999, my first semester of teaching as a full-time university faculty member, fourteen students enrolled in the course. (My department, I am happy to say, offered performing literature as an advanced course. In many university programs where the course is offered, it is only offered at an introductory level.) For the final assignment of the semester, my students were to perform adapted excerpts from a novel. I had to find a novel long enough to offer each of my advanced students a substantial final project assignment, and ideally short enough that we as a class could cover it in its entirely. *Blindness* was divided into sixteen chapters, each roughly fifteen pages long. I could assign each student to adapt one chapter, leaving two of the least optimal assignment chapters out.

The novel also met certain other basic criteria. It met the criterion of having ample narration for the students to work with, a requirement most novels fulfill, although occasionally a novel relies so heavily on dialogue that it doesn't make for a good adaptation assignment. It met the criterion of having many major characters, so that in performance, the students would need to make a wide range of physical and vocal choices.

Finally and most substantively, the novel provided a compelling representational challenge, namely, how to tell a story in a visual medium about people who cannot see. I told the students that the one thing they could not do was to perform in the dark. Like many in the field of performance studies, I am always seduced by the challenge of representing what seems unrepresentable.

I was astonished and inspired by the work my students did on the novel that semester and in the two subsequent semesters in which I assigned it. One student created a tissue-paper rainstorm. Another managed to make us all feel absolutely disoriented in the small, black-box theater that was the classroom where we met twice a week. A third played all seven major characters in a virtuoso solo performance. I was so inspired that I decided to try to adapt the novel myself. My adaptation went through a staged reading at the university and, later, a full production. It also had a professional and public staged reading at Chicago's Piven Theatre Workshop. I saw the story, then, in many incarnations, some of which I scripted and/or directed and others which I did not.

Blindness is a story about a state or nation in which the entire citizenry suddenly and spontaneously loses vision. The entire citizenry, that is, except for one character, designated "the doctor's wife," who is randomly blessed/cursed with the ability to see in a sightless world. *Blindness* is the story of how through the negotiation of collective trauma a group of strangers becomes a community.

The novel is written in the form of a fable. The characters are referred to by physical characteristics, vocations, or relationships rather than names, and the narrative is nearly devoid of clues as to the time, place, scope, and duration of events. Unlike a fable, however, the narrator's voice in the novel is strange and complex, sometimes seeming to emanate from a single character, sometimes from the citizenry as a whole, and sometimes from a perverse God who stands apart from the story but observes it all with wry wit. It is unclear whose story *Blindness* is. Although the character whose thoughts and actions it tracks most closely is the Doctor's Wife, each of the story's seven major characters becomes the central figure at some point in the novel, as do several characters outside this cast.

Blindness is a story of loss on many levels. The loss of eyesight begets the loss of home for each character as the government herds them into a former mental hospital in a futile effort to quarantine the city. Many of the characters indeed come close to losing their minds as they struggle to preserve relationships, identities, and most of all, a sense of dignity. The tenuous, new community they form in the institution is threatened several times through infidelity, rape, and death. Finally, as always, the characters in the narrative lose time; when they are finally free, one remarks that they have lost an entire season.

In retelling the story of *Blindness*, I would eventually confront questions about how to represent these various losses on stage. First, though, I would need to confront the more basic question of loss embedded in every process of adaptation: Which pieces of the story, which words, sentences, passages, characters, and plots could I bear to lose?

The Question of Coherence: Killing the Darlings

The phrase "kill your darlings" has been attributed to a number of great American writers including Mark Twain, William Faulkner, and Ernest Hemingway and has been invoked by nearly everyone who has ever written a book about how to write, regardless of genre. The idea behind the popular dictum is that writers are susceptible to falling in love with the details of their work, whether or not these details serve the creation as a whole. No matter how much he/she cherishes a phrase, a paragraph, a character, even a plot line, if it is not necessary to the tale, a good writer will be able to recognize this and excise it.

In *Chamber Theatre*, Breen warned against applying this dictum to the adaptor: "The admonition that should govern the adapter's decisions is 'don't': don't cut anything unless, for the sake of the 'two hour traffic of the stage,' you must abbreviate the original text."[1] Breen cautioned that if a great deal of cutting and other alterations proved necessary, "the story is likely a faulty one."[2] In other words, by the time the prospective adaptor has a work of literature by a highly skilled writer in hand, it is likely that the darlings have already been killed.

But I would argue that the adaptor must kill them again. He/she must do so for reasons of time, because literature is much more patient with and hospitable to the narrative strategy of description than theater.[3] Literature, after all, is not in a hurry. It has the luxury of unlimited time and space. It can linger in the field, noticing a patch of particularly thick grass, homing in on an individual blade, and even waiting for a particular drop of dew to swell and roll from the tip of that blade to the ground. The same is true when a writer describes a character's interior landscape on the page. If the description is done well, we are fascinated and have all the time in the world to entertain it.

But a stage adaptation of a novel that preserves all description would be interminable. Dublin's annual verbatim relay reading of James Joyce's *Ulysses* takes twenty-four hours to complete. The Royal Shakespeare Company found that to tell the full story of Charles Dickens's *Life and Adventures of Nicholas Nickleby*, as they were determined to do, required eight and a half hours of stage time, and this was with a full awareness of the different demands of the genre. "Dickens can introduce characters with lengthy descriptions," explained assistant director Leon Rubin in his account of the production process, "but on stage there is only a little time for the audience to become familiar with each character."[4] The novel is far more capacious than the drama.

Time is not the only practical constraint on a literary adaptation. While a novel, like a film, is free to move endlessly from location to location, on the stage "the physical realities of a set and furniture limit the amount of continual geographic transposition" that can be achieved even with the most simplified setting.[5]

Most importantly, coherence works differently in the two media. What is absolutely necessary to a narrative in one medium may be extraneous in another; different forms generate different necessities. While written works cohere in large part through a sense of development, either of character or of plot, oral and embodied events also cohere in part through economy. In his *Poetics*, Aristotle prescribed what he called the "three unities" of drama—time, place, and action. And although these unities are today more often violated than observed, there is nonetheless an economy to much dramatic writing that gives it its energy and shape. Even for a production with no practical constraints on budget or space, "continual geographic transposition" is likely to trouble the sense of coherence in what directors call the world of the play. And while a novel can usually afford enriching narrative digressions that serve the development of character or plot, every element of the drama, from the characters to the plot to the mise en scene, must serve the central story or purpose. Playwright Anton Chekhov once noted that if there was a gun on the mantel in the first act of the play, someone had better get shot by the last. In other words, everything that appears must have a purpose.

In adapting a novel for the stage, one must first decide what parts of the story *not* to tell. I killed a number of little "darlings" early on in the process of adapting *Blindness*, including several minor but vivid characters and several minor but colorful digressions in the narrative. The most important excision, though, and the only truly painful one, was an event that takes up the better part of two chapters of the novel, the homecoming of a central character called "the girl with dark glasses." Several times throughout the first three-fourths of the novel, the girl, who is by turns crass, violent, and tender toward the other characters, openly grieves her separation from her parents and anticipates a family reunion. When she is finally able to return home, the place is grotesque, the primary character she encounters there is both horrible and strangely compelling, and the entire scene is one of the saddest in the novel.

In the first version of my adaptation, which was read before an audience, I retained this episode. A playwright friend who attended the reading told me it should come out. (You can't kill your darlings if you can't identify them, and almost everyone needs help doing this at some point.) Based on the following criteria, I decided that she was right:

1. Practical considerations. For a variety of reasons, from the cost of the space after hours to the estimated attention span of our audience, the running time had to come in well under two hours. The running time of the reading was slightly more than two hours, and staging would add time to the piece. Something fairly significant had to be cut.

2. Unity of narrative and place. The story of *Blindness* is very much a collective story. This is reflected in its placement. Most of the first half of the adaptation takes place at the institution, and most of the shorter second half takes place at the home of the doctor and his wife, where the central characters eventually congregate following their escape. Excursions to other places are extremely brief. The substantial digression and relocation required to communicate this part of the story, in which only the girl is involved, would have disturbed the sense that this was a collective story and would have undermined the forward movement of that story.

3. Unity of character. The new character introduced in the episode of the girl's homecoming, while fabulous in both senses of the word, does not interact with any of the other central characters and does not reappear in the rest of the novel.

To evaluate the question of coherence in an adaptation, it may be helpful for the adaptor to formulate a one-sentence summary of the story she is trying to tell as a kind of test. If, for example, I tested the chapters in question against one of the sentences I used above to summarize the story, "*Blindness* is the story of how, through negotiating collective trauma, a group of strangers becomes a community," the subject of this sentence would clearly suggest that the material of the girl's homecoming should be cut because it does not concern the community that is the novel's subject.

Narrative Adaptation: Losses and Gains

The killing of darlings may or may not be as painful for an adaptor who loves a work of literature as it is for a writer who loves his own words. David Edgar, in conversation with RSC director Trevor Nunn about the possibility of adapting *Nicholas Nickleby*, "wrote a long letter about the whole question of adaptation, about the immense responsibility that he felt to the work of a dead writer, and how he suffered over having to make the changes that were necessary for adaptation."[6] It was this reverence for the work in its original form that both earned Edgar the job and made the job so difficult. Anthony Minghella, by contrast, literally left the novel at home when he went off to work on his adaptation of Michael Ondaatje's *The English Patient*, and produced an enormously successful film, though one that retained almost none of the verbal lyricism of the original.[7]

These two adaptors represent two basic approaches to the process, approaches that I will call *narrative adaptation* and *autonomous adaptation*. Narrative adaptations are as Breen advocated "in the service of literature."[8] They seek to provide a different kind of access to the novel than reading does, but one that nonetheless evokes in some way the experience of the original. These adaptations retain the strategies of narration of the original. That is, they excise neither the descriptions of the physical world nor the insights into characters' interior worlds the novel provides. They also preserve the novel's first-, second-, or third-person narrative perspective. In the United States, this kind of adaptation is far less common in the professional theater than it is in the classroom. Only a very few prominent stage directors have made adaptations of this variety commercially viable.[9]

Autonomous adaptations transform works of literature by essentially turning them into dramas. The adaptor excises all verbal description; everything that is not communicated through dialogue is communicated visually. The narrator, if there is one, is relegated to the frame (often represented in film by a voice-over) and, when applicable, translates his/her narrative perspective from the third into the first person, eliminating special access to the thoughts, feelings, and motivations of other characters. The autonomous adaptor is free to radically change the structure and emphasis of the story so as to create the most compelling work possible in the new medium.

But does the narrative adaptor always serve the text? And does the autonomous adaptor always somehow betray it? The very notion of what it means to be "faithful" to a text is a fundamentally contested one. Adaptor and director Derek Goldman invokes theorist Michael Taussig's notion of "sensuous fidelity"[10] to navigate his course between service and autonomy.

> We're working on something. And if we're working on it in a spirit of sensuous fidelity, say, of caring about what was there to begin with and

> thinking seriously about why it matters now and what it means to translate it into this new form, to adapt it, then yeah we're going to lose stuff we're going to gain stuff but there's a way to worry productively about that by working at it really hard. By taking really seriously the choices that the writer already made.[11]

Like Goldman, I am interested in situations in which the adaptor wants to give the audience an experience that honors "what was there to begin with." For me, that means creating something closer to the narrative end of the continuum than the fully autonomous. This choice is dictated by both limitation and desire. While I admire many autonomous adaptations, I could not begin to do one myself, nor do I know of any helpful set of guidelines for success in the realm of autonomous invention. I also prefer narrative adaptations because I was drawn to the process of adaptation as a lover of literature.

Yet often, adaptors, performers, and audience members alike seem to find narrative adaptation unpalatable. In my performing literature classroom, my students so often eliminated every description and changed every "she" and "he" to an "I" in their adaptations that I had to make rules against doing so in order to ensure that they would get to explore the challenges of narrative adaptation. Bowman reports a similar and widespread distaste among theater audiences, at least for traditional recital-style readers' theater productions in which the text is simply read aloud. He attributes this distaste to a number of factors, "either because 'nothing happens,' or because of the seemingly endless chatter of 'The Narrator,' or because of the 'boring' simplicity of the mise en scene."[12] But most of these problems have disappeared as the practice of adaptation has evolved, because most contemporary adaptors break the minimalist staging conventions of this style. (This does not solve the problem of adapting narration, which is discussed separately below.) Contemporary adaptations are rarely lacking in movement or dramatic action. In performance, they nearly always feature a theatrical mise en scene and embodiment, representational or otherwise, of the narrative.

Why, then, this ongoing aversion to narrative adaptation? Perhaps it can be explained by obsessive concern, particularly in America, with the style of realism, a preference that the wild popularity of "reality TV" in the early twenty-first century has confirmed in spades. In narrative adaptation, as Frank Galati plainly explains, "The stage is always a stage and the story is always a story."[13] Perhaps it is our appetite for speed and action that makes us devalue the narrator's unique ability to linger on intricate details.

Or perhaps, at least for some, it is something deeper. The audience member in the traditional drama, like the jailor in Michel Foucault's panopticon, can see the entire scene without ever himself being seen. But the narrator sees us, addresses us. In narrative adaptation, we lose the unassailable position of seeing without being seen. We also lose the illusion that we are directly observing the world of the story. Narration constantly reminds us that our knowledge of the characters is mediated and, therefore, partial. In narrative adaptations, we are banished to the outside, where we must rely on the mediating narrator, more knowledgeable and more powerful than we are, to give us partial access to the characters' interior worlds. Perhaps it is this visibility to and reliance on the narrator that some audiences find unacceptable.

But narrative adaptation offers several compensations for this banishment. First, it enables us to avoid other losses that some, myself included, find less tolerable—the loss, for example, of descriptive writing. No matter how brilliant the staging (or cinematography), I know of no way to compensate visually, for example, for this description by Welsh writer Leslie Norris in her short story "Blackberries."

> His father reached up and chose a blackberry for him. Its skin was plump and shining, each of its purple globes held a point of reflected light.
>
> "You can eat it," his father said.
>
> The boy put the blackberry in his mouth. He rolled it with his tongue, feeling its irregularity, and crushed it against the roof of his mouth. Released juice, sweet and warm as summer, ran down his throat, hard seeds cracked between his teeth.[14]

Nor do I know of any way to compensate in dialogue for Chekhov's descriptive foray into the psyches of both protagonists near the close of his short story "The Lady with the Pet Dog."

> Anna Sergeyevna and he loved each other as people do who are very close and intimate, like man and wife, like tender friends; it seemed to them that Fate itself had meant them for one another, and they could not understand why he had a wife and she a husband; and it was as though they were a pair of migratory birds, male and female, caught and forced to live in different cages. They forgave each other what they were ashamed of in their past, they forgave everything in the present, and felt that this love of theirs had altered them both.[15]

Similarly, in adapting *Blindness*, I knew of no way to compensate for the strange, powerful, and anonymous voice of the narrator.

> There being no witnesses, and if there were there is no evidence that they were summoned to the post-mortems to tell us what happened, it is understandable that someone should ask how it was possible to know that these

> things happened so and not in some other manner, the reply to be given is that all stories are like those about the creation of the universe, no one was there, no one witnessed anything, yet everyone knows what happened.[16]

Without such passages of the narrator, the experience of these pieces of writing would, for me, be drastically diminished.

Second, the direct address of the narrator offers a kind of intimacy with the story that no traditional drama can provide. Goldman explains:

> To me losing the narration has always been . . . you lose the author and implied author speaking to you, you lose the intimacy of contact between the narrator and characters and the kind of interiority of consciousness and the beauty that the narrator can go into this person's head but not into this person's head.[17]

Here, Goldman is pointing to two different kinds of intimacy, that between audience and narrator and that between audience and character. But because the latter relies on reports of a character's unspoken thoughts and feelings, both kinds of intimacy are only possible through the presence of a mediating narrator.

A third argument for retaining the narrative perspective of the text is that this very distance between character and audience can be productive, that it can help us retain a critical stance that ultimately enables us to engage more productively with all of the characters in the world of the novel and not just those to whom we have privileged access. This argument is familiar to students of the theater in its resemblance to Bertolt Brecht's "alienation effect,"[18] which privileges critical appraisal and action over aesthetic immersion in the theatrical experience. Brecht's theories served as inspiration for both the avant-garde theater movement and much contemporary experimental theater, including narrative adaptation.

Some critics are deeply skeptical of such an argument as it applies to adaptation. Bowman cautions that narrative adaptation is not necessarily politically grounded at all and is certainly not necessarily grounded in an ideology as radical as Brecht's. Rather, it is only reliably useful in revealing "the reflexive character of the modern, alienated self in its struggle to know itself."[19] And although Bowman does not argue that the two projects are mutually exclusive, he is at best skeptical that they could be related.

Other artists and critics in both theater and literature believe strongly in the potential social efficacy of all literature and in the interrelatedness of personal and social change. Robert E. Scholes, for example, argues that an orientation of critical distance can produce ethical readings that are valuable precisely to the extent that they lead to ethical action.

> No matter how strongly we feel about Bulstrode, Asaubon, Dorothea Brooke, or any other character in *Middlemarch*, we cannot act in that world. We can only read, interpret, and criticize. When we connect the text of the book to the text of our lives, however, the world of choice and action opens before us.[20]

I would add that narration, more than any other element of fiction, facilitates this work. It is the narrator's role, too, after all, to connect the text of the book to the text of our lives. The narrator's address on the page—and live on the stage—is a constant reminder of the need to make such connections. More than either autonomous adaptations or traditional dramas, narrative adaptations encourage audiences to search more actively for connections between the action of the novel and "the text of our lives."

Finally, retaining the narrator in a stage adaptation "restores to the narrator his/her power of directing and, indeed, creating the story."[21] To preserve the narrator's function is to underscore the transformative power of storytelling. It is easy enough to get lost in the world of the drama when the fourth wall is up, and one is acting as a voyeur in another world, compellingly created. But when one is constantly being reminded that a story is being crafted, the transformation assumes the wonder of a magic trick; no matter how diligently one watches the cane, it becomes, before one's eyes, a bouquet of flowers.

The Problem of the Narrator: Conceptual Solutions

Performative Structures

The central problem for narrative adaptations is the problem of the narrator: He talks too much. He never shuts up. How is the adaptor to manage what Bowman calls his "seemingly endless chatter"? One place to begin to answer this question is by thinking performatively about the role of the narrator in the text. It is a paradox of the genres that writers of literature do this regularly, while playwrights almost never do.

Narrators in the conventional theater often play a minor or primarily functional role, conveying critical information to the audience or, somewhat more substantively, centering the story—usually unsuccessfully—in a single character's journey. This is true even in a play like *The Glass Menagerie*, where the narrator also plays a major role in the drama and where, in his narrator capacity, he delivers the play's most indelible speeches. Despite Tom's major role as both teller and actor, the tone of the play and the affect it produces from scene to scene are largely determined by the actions of the characters inside the frame. Our experience of the play is affected as much by Amanda's hysterics, Laura's fearfulness, and even Tom's anger with his mother as it is by the narrative frame. Indeed, that each character contributes so strongly to our affective response is one of the marks of its success as a more or less conventional drama. (Imagine what a different experience it would be to read *The Glass Menagerie* as a short story narrated by Tom.) By contrast, narrators in literature almost always play a major role in one's experience of the narrative, even when, as in *The Great Gatsby*, they play a minor role in the story itself. That role is not merely to provide the reader with information or even to provide the reader with a particular perspective on the story. More than any other element of prose fiction, narration shapes one's affective experience of the text. This is why the loss of the narrator is always a significant loss.

It is therefore helpful for adaptors to think more about what the narrator *does* to one's experience of the narrative than what the narrator says and to try to translate that doing into the new medium. Specifically, the adaptor might ask, what tone or affective environment does the narrative voice create? In some cases, the function of creating this tone in adaptation will continue to fall to a narrator, although the identity of the narrator may change. In others, it may be relocated to other elements of the performance.

In *Blindness*, the narrator creates two sharply contrasting tones, one grim and antagonistic, the other sensuous and sympathetic. Sometimes, the narrator evokes the authoritarian regime under which the characters are living. At these times, he seems to stand coldly apart from the characters and their situations, suggesting the sinister force that is clearly at work in the frightening and often brutal events of the novel. At the beginning of the novel, for example, the narrator offers a detached and technical description of the first man being struck by blindness: "The eyes wide open, the wrinkled skin of the face, his eyebrows suddenly screwed up, all this, as anyone can see, signifies that he is distraught with anguish."[22] Later, in a description of the institution, he says, "Now, with all the beds occupied, all two hundred and forty, not counting the blind inmates who have to sleep on the floor, no imagination, however fertile and creative in making comparisons, images, and metaphors, could aptly describe the filth here."[23] In such passages, the narrator seems to refuse to identify with the characters' distress.

Sometimes, the narrator almost seems to *be* the sinister force, as, for example, in a series of wry aphorisms about the behavior of men and women in general such as "A consenting cuckold is a cuckold twice over."[24] Even more sinister is a series of statements that seem to include the reader as conspirator, whether in sympathy with the main characters' physical discomfort—"we know how pressing our bodily needs can be"[25]—or in the perverse joy of watching the worst villains be destroyed—"let's see what happens when he runs out of ammunition"[26]—or, perhaps most eerily, in seeming to control the end of the torment: "Say to a blind man, you're free, open the door that was separating him from the world, Go, you are free, we tell him once more, and he does not go."[27] The primary function of this narrator is to evoke or perform the controlling environment into which the characters are thrust.

How can this antagonistic function of the narrator be translated into performance? In my adaptation, I used several different strategies. Because performance offers more diverse tools for creating the affective environment than literature does, I delegated some of the narrative function to the mise en scene. Though the production was a modest one, this included a row of hard, heavy, metal bunk beds made where the inmates slept; bright lighting; bland, uniform clothing (light-blue medical scrubs); dissonant music; and a large video screen on which the minister of the fictitious government was periodically projected. The rest of the controlling function I delegated to two guard figures, composite characters played by two actors on stilts (see fig. 3.1). These figures were responsible for incarcerating the rest of the characters, watching over them, and narrating the activities of the commission of logistics and security that is set up when the epidemic begins. In other words, they performed the roles of all official representatives of the government. They also doubled as the "thugs," ordinary inmates from another ward of the hospital who turn violent and perpetrate a series of crimes against the other characters. Although the narrator in the novel is an anonymous and mysterious presence, I assigned that presence, at least in part, to two minor characters in the drama.

These strategies were moderately successful in evoking the controlling narrator's voice in performance. If I revised the adaptation today, however, I would expand the role of the two guards. Although their physical presence was strong both because they towered above the stage and because they were on stage a great deal, I wish that they had been on stage continuously and that I had placed them farther downstage where their presence would have been impossible to ignore. More importantly, I wish I had expanded their narrative role beyond representing specific characters in the novel. For example, none of the passages I quote above are assigned to any specific figure in the novel, but all could have been fittingly articulated by the two most sinister characters on stage. It was also easy to see in retrospect that the strange narrator's aphorisms, which are anachronistic in the novel but unsettlingly so and which I largely chose to eliminate, would have been at home in the guards' mouths.

Figure 3.1. Guards (Jenn Tosatto, at left, and Matt Reese) interrogate the Doctor's Wife (Sarah Kauffman) in *Blindness*. Photo courtesy of Missouri State University.

Dissemination

Another way to embody or perform the narrator's function is to disseminate narration among two or more characters on stage. How widely the narration is disseminated depends upon its functions. If the narration aligns the reader strongly with a certain character or characters, dissemination will tend to be narrower than if the narration aligns the reader with multiple characters or, as in *Blindness*, with the novel's entire community.

The model of narrow dissemination is central to Breen's style of chamber theater. He called his technique *bifurcation*, referring, as the word suggests, to a split of the central narrator's voice between two actors (see also chapter 2 of the current volume). In the most traditional form of bifurcation, the central character is performed by two actors: one assumes the narrative function for the story, the other acts as the central character within the scenes. The actor playing the narrator might, for example, represent the character as an old man reflecting on the events of the story, while the actor within the scene represents the character as he was during the events of the story. This technique is used frequently in film adaptations of novels, with the older version of the narrator located off-screen, as a voice-over. It is used in a more sophisticated and theatrical manner in places like the HBO television series *Six Feet Under*, in which a dead person frequently returns to the scene to represent a voice in the head of one of several central characters.

Bifurcation enables the adaptation to retain some of the psychological insights of the novel, particularly when, as in the works Breen considered, the narrator's omniscience is limited to the thoughts and feelings of a single character. And, as later adaptations have shown, there is no limit to the number of refractions of self the technique can accommodate. In Mary Zimmerman's *Notebooks of Leonardo da Vinci*, the script indicates the role for each of the eight cast members (four men and four women) as "Leonardo." Because the piece is entirely nonnarrative in structure, this is in part just an extra-theatrical joke for the audience to enjoy when reading the playbill. But in part, naming each of the characters Leonardo reminds us that the range of voices represented here belongs, remarkably, to a single remarkable man.

Bifurcation does, however, restrict the number of characters into whose thoughts and feelings the story can enter, at least on stage. Breen conceived of the single narrator, and although one could imagine the technique of bifurcation extended to two central characters, each with a narrator double, for example, an adaptation of Chekhov's "Lady with the Pet Dog" for four actors (two Annas and two Gurovs), it is likely that having more than these two doubles on stage would make the staging unwieldy and difficult to follow.

The other dissemination model is called *story theater*. Viola Spolin, a contemporary of Breen, developed this technique, in which the narration is disseminated through the performance ensemble. Sometimes, an actor-narrator transforms into a character, but he/she often does so only briefly, releasing that character when the scene is over to adopt another role in the story. Moreover, as one actor-narrator becomes a character, that character's thoughts and feelings might be narrated by the character him/herself or by any other combination of actors on stage. The narrator in story theater, then, is not a specific character split in two; rather, the function of narrator is disseminated more widely throughout the ensemble. This broader dissemination enabled the narration to move from one perspective to another with lightning speed and created a strong sense of relatedness among the characters, as well as between the characters and the narrator. But because character locations were unstable, story theater sometimes sacrificed character for tone or plot. Although this technique produced a great deal of momentum in the telling, the individual characters were rarely as differentiated or as compelling as they were in the original work.

In locating the narrator of an adaptation, it is important to ask not only what the narrator does in the story but whether the story's narration favors breadth or depth. Narration that favors breadth might suggest a wide dissemination of the narrative function as in traditional story theater, while narration that favors depth might suggest a narrower dissemination as in traditional chamber theater.

Many contemporary adaptations blend the two techniques in an effort to hedge against losses accumulating too much on either side of the ledger. In Zimmerman's *Arabian Nights*, an adaptation of the Persian classic, there are both a central character/narrator across the piece and a plethora of minor narrators within individual stories. As Zimmerman describes the fluid relationship between these two strategies of narration, "Scheherezade moves easily between narrating the stories and taking on small parts in them, and she may also shadow the various narrators of the stories within the stories."[28] In *Nicholas Nickleby*, the company discovered that "we had to employ many different styles and techniques in order to capture and communicate Dickens's multitudinously varied work."[29] These techniques included using all of the characters in the company as narrators as well as having the actors assigned to central characters speak to the audience from within the scene itself. Both adaptations combine the depth and stability of character afforded by chamber theater's casting with story theater's ability to disseminate the narration widely and among all the characters on stage.

In addition, the most effective adaptations complicate the use of story theater such that even the least-central characters narrate from distinct and stable perspectives; every narrator is, in effect, cast. *Nickleby* assistant director Rubin reports the important discovery in the rehearsal process that "the strength of narrative comment came from a basis in character and emotional involvement in the scene."[30] Merely disseminating the narration widely, even with a stable distribution of roles, did not make for compelling storytelling. Rather, each narrator has to have a specific relationship to the story, a reason for telling it. The stronger each narrator's investment in the events of the story, the more effective he/she can be as a narrator. This is particularly evident in Zimmerman's published scripts, in which characters are rarely referred to as "narrator" but, instead, as "laundress," "jester," "sleep," and "perfect love."

If the first function of the narrator's voice in *Blindness* is to evoke the oppressive authority of the government that controls the characters' world, the second, contrasting function of the narrator's voice is to generate a feeling of solidarity with and among the characters. This narrator moves into the thoughts and feelings of the characters with great sympathy, not only for the diverse emotional burdens of the ironically blind eye doctor, the seeing Doctor's Wife, and the worldly Girl with Dark Glasses but even for a character named "the thief," who, at the beginning of the novel, steals the First Blind Man's car.

> In the end, disoriented as he was, tense beyond endurance, he drove the car into a minor road where he knew there were no traffic lights, and parked almost without looking, he was such a good driver. He felt as if his nerves were about to explode . . . [31]

In addition to frequent forays into specific characters' thoughts and feelings, this narrator also delves sympathetically into the shared feelings of the inmates in a way that emphasizes the collective nature of their experience. In one of the periodic luminous passages in this extraordinarily dark novel, the narrator says:

> Everyone in the ward thought that it was nothing more than an act of charity that the girl with dark glasses should have offered herself to the old man with the black eyepatch, but there were men there, sensitive and dreamers, who having already enjoyed her favours, began to allow their thoughts to wander, to think there could be no greater prize in this world than for a man to find himself stretched out on his bed all alone, thinking the impossible, only to realize that a woman is gently lifting the covers and slipping under them, slowly rubbing her body against his body, and then lying still, waiting for the heat of their blood to calm the sudden tremor of their startled skin.[32]

The narrator of this passage contrasts sharply with the narrator who routinely greets the characters' suffering with empty aphorisms. This narrator's function is to create community of feeling among the central characters and between the central characters and the reader.

The empathic function of this narrator was translated into performance through a strategic blending of the two dissemination techniques. In my adaptation of *Blindness*, there was a one-to-one relationship between actors and characters, as in both traditional theater and autonomous adaptation.

The focus, however, was on the breadth of the story and its effect on an entire community. Therefore, the narration was disseminated among all of the characters, as in story theater, with narration of common experiences moving from one actor to another. For example, when the Man with the Black Eyepatch enters the ward carrying a radio, the characters pass it hungrily among themselves.

MAN WITH THE BLACK EYEPATCH: And so from bed to bed
DOCTOR'S WIFE: the news slowly circulated around the ward
DOCTOR: increasingly distorted as it was passed
BOY WITH THE SQUINT: from one inmate to the next
GIRL WITH DARK GLASSES: in this way diminishing or exaggerating the details
FIRST BLIND MAN'S WIFE: according to the personal optimism
FIRST BLIND MAN: or pessimism
MAN WITH THE BLACK EYEPATCH: of those relaying the information.

Here, the sharing of the storytelling mirrors their efforts to share a treasured vessel of messages from the outside world.

Widely disseminating the narration facilitates more complex theatrical choices as well. In *Blindness*, there is a particular solidarity among the women in the novel, born perhaps of the more severe trauma they suffer. In a scene late in the story in which one of the women gives the Man with the Black Eyepatch a bath, the wide dissemination of narration allows the washer to remain anonymous:

MAN WITH THE BLACK EYEPATCH: He wanted to ask, who are you, but he couldn't speak. Now he was shivering, but not from the cold.
GIRL WITH DARK GLASSES: The hands continued to wash him gently. The woman did not say
DOCTOR'S WIFE: I am the doctor's wife
FIRST BLIND MAN'S WIFE: I am the wife of the first blind man
GIRL WITH DARK GLASSES: I am the girl with dark glasses
DOCTOR'S WIFE: They simply continued their work.

In a traditional staging of this scene, the real identity of the washer (about which the reader has a strong hunch but which is never finally revealed) would need to be decided by the director or at least reduced to one anonymous body. Here, the mystery can be preserved.

Because it was so critical that the story be and feel shared, we also used other techniques to disseminate the focus. With the help and at the instigation of a talented choreographer, E. E. Balcos, the actors developed a kind of sign language that they used at moments of intense anxiety to stand in for their names. Each character had his or her own distinct gesture or set of gestures with which to communicate. Although these gestures were abstract and at the beginning foreign, the audience came to recognize them over the course of the performance, effectively learning the characters' shared language. In this way, too, we preserved the sense, critical to the original parable, that this story was everyone's story—potentially, even the reader's.

The Problem of the Narrator: Technical Solutions

Performative structures must be created in relation to the function of the narrator in a given work, and decisions about the dissemination of narration depend on the depth or breadth of the relationship between the reader and the characters, but a number of generalizable techniques are available for scripting passages of narration so as to maximize variety, color, and texture. I have come to call these *orchestration techniques*, because they are ways of distributing narration among voices, much like a composer does when creating an orchestral score. Many of these techniques will be intuitively familiar to those who have adapted literature. Nonetheless, it may be helpful to catalog them here in order to ensure a common vocabulary for talking about what we are doing.

Although I describe them as technical solutions, the effective use of these strategies is never purely technical. Rather, each one can help dramatize certain kinds of moments, experiences, and relationships. The experienced adaptor will be able to select and use a particular technique not only to generally enrich the texture of the staged work but because, at a given moment, a particular technique best illuminates the drama.

Choral Speech

Choral speech can mean simply two or more actors speaking in unison. Although the idea of choral speech is as old as Western theater itself, in adaptations, this speech need not be delivered by a discrete group of actors designated the chorus. Rather, any combination of characters may speak together at any moment in the story, and the composition of this impromptu chorus can change every time choral speech occurs. This speech creates at least two different effects.

Choral speech may suggest shared experience. For example, the first instance of choral speech in my adaptation of *Blindness* occurs early in the inmates' incarceration when, in the middle of a quarrel-ridden discussion about their predicament, the Boy with the Squint makes an abrupt and inconvenient announcement:

BOY: I want to do a wee wee!
ALL: On hearing him, all of them felt an urgent desire to urinate.

This instance of choral speech has the fringe benefit of also producing a comic effect; the Boy with the Squint's statement is so powerful that it produces the same bodily urge in all seven characters simultaneously.

The other effect of choral speech is one of emphasis. Consider this passage, in which the Thief, having been wounded by the Girl with Dark Glasses, attempts to escape from the institution.

THIEF: It was after four in the morning. The thief raised his body to a sitting position. He rolled over on to the side of his healthy leg and then, with both hands under his thigh, he tried to move his injured leg.

ALL: Like a pack of wolves suddenly aroused

THIEF: The pain went through his entire body. After several minutes, his breathing became more regular and he got to his feet slowly, putting his weight on his good leg. He knew that the other one would be no good to him, that he would have to drag it behind him wherever he went. He thought,

ALL: I can't go on rotting in this hole.

THIEF: When they see me in this state, they'll put me in an ambulance. They'll take me to a hospital. They'll treat my wound. They'll cure me. This is just like stealing a car. Ways and means can always be found.

FIRST BLIND MAN: Suddenly, his conscience awoke and censured him bitterly for having allowed himself to steal a car from an unfortunate blind man.

THIEF: But his conscience was in no mood for casuistic discussions now. He was outside the main door . . .

In staging this passage, I also directed the ensemble members to mirror the Thief's movements. This choral speech and mirrored movement, in addition to creating aural and visual variation, intensified the sense of the Thief's desperate physical pain, as well as the urgency with which his inner voice is speaking to him. (Note that the bifurcation later in the excerpt creates another type of variation and also produces a comic effect as the Thief in effect tells his conscience to shut up.)

The effectiveness of choral speech depends on how economically it is used. In Mary Zimmerman's *Metamorphoses*, for example, there are few instances of choral speech by two characters and only one instance toward the end of the play where the ensemble speaks as a single chorus. Choral speech is the italics of group performance and must be used with similar judiciousness.

Serial Speech

Serial speech is a technique in which multiple characters speak the same set of words, but instead of speaking in unison, they begin in a staggered, overlapping fashion, as in a round. If choral speech creates unity, serial speech creates disorder. The disorder may be of a character happily overcome by his senses, as in this passage of narration from adaptor and director Matthew Spangler's adaptation of Thomas Wolfe's novella *The Lost Boy*:

A: Behind the counter were great bins for coffee, grits and rice. Then up to the ceiling were the loaded shelves—jellies and preserves, relish, pickles, ketchup, sardines, canned salmon, canned tomatoes, corn and peas, pork and beans.
B (*overlapping*): coffee, grits, and rice, jellies and preserves, relish, pickles, ketchup, sardines, canned tomatoes, corn and peas, pork and beans.
C (*overlapping*): coffee, grits, and rice, jellies and preserves, relish, pickles, ketchup, sardines, canned tomatoes, corn and peas, pork and beans.
A: Enough, thought Grover, for a city. Enough, it seemed to him, to feed everyone in town.

Alternatively, the disorder may be an unhappy one, as in this scene from *Blindness* when the inmates' tenuous connection to the outside world falls apart:

Man with the Black Eyepatch: Throughout this first day, the old man listened to the radio. He passed on the real news, and rejected the patent falseness of the optimistic prophecies being officially communicated. Then, suddenly, he heard the announcer call out
Voice: I'm blind.
Girl with Dark Glasses: Then the noise of something striking the microphone, a hasty sequence of confused sounds and then . . .
Doctor (*He begins as Girl reaches the word* striking): Then the noise of something striking the microphone, a hasty sequence of confused sounds and then . . .
First Blind Man's Wife (*She begins as Doctor reaches the word* something): Then the noise of something (*etc.*)
First Blind Man (*He begins as Wife reaches the word* noise): Then the noise (etc.)
Boy (Begins as FBM reaches the word *noise*): Then the noise (etc.)
Doctor's Wife (*She begins at* noise): Then the noise (*etc.*)
(*Long silence.*)

Following the cacophony of voices above, the silence performs what need not be said: blindness has shut down the radio station.

Echo

Echo is serial speech without the overlap of voices. While serial speech offers the illusion of time run-amok, echo slows time down. Here, for example, is a postproduction rewrite of the scene in *Blindness* in which the three central female characters finally bathe for the first time since their incarceration (see fig. 3.2). I added echo to the scene in order to extend the time and pleasure of this intensely sensual moment in the story.

Doctor's Wife: Help me with the washing.
First Blind Man's Wife: But we can't see.
Girl with Dark Glasses: It doesn't matter. We shall do what we can . . .
First Blind Man's Wife: My God, how the rain is pouring down on us.
Girl with Dark Glasses: My God, how the rain is pouring down on us.
Doctor's Wife: How it trickles between my breasts
Girl with Dark Glasses: How it trickles between my breasts
First Blind Man's Wife: How it lingers between my thighs
Girl with Dark Glasses: How it lingers between my thighs
First Blind Man's Wife: Only God sees us.

The scene continues for another page, with the Doctor's Wife serving as mirror for the two blind women and then, ultimately, with the blind women serving as mirrors for the Doctor's Wife. Slowing down the beginning helps the audience to enter the intimate, vulnerable, and even sacred space in which a true witnessing of each other is possible.

Figure 3.2. The Girl with Dark Glasses, the Doctor's Wife, and the First Blind Man's Wife bathe. Photo courtesy of Missouri State University.

Refrain

A *refrain* is a phrase or line that, like the refrain in a song, is repeated at more or less regular intervals throughout a performance text. While it is desirable to generate variation in the way narrators speak, it is also desirable to create a sense of structure. In a nonlinear narrative, one of the simplest ways to provide this structure is through repetition within the text. (Other internal repetition devices include a recurring minor character, movement sequence, setting, or sound cue. A number of external devices also create structure, for example, thematic scene titles that are announced or displayed.) The refrain is a kind of "you are here" on the map of the performance text, telling the audience that a segment of the piece has concluded, and another is beginning.

Refrains work best when they accrue meaning through repetition. In Zimmerman's retelling of the Orpheus story in *Metamorphoses*, Eurydice repeats the single word "farewell" five times across the second half of the piece, performing the growing extent to which Orpheus is haunted by his final encounter with her. Spalding Gray's *Swimming to Cambodia* begins with the words "It was the first day off in a long time." In the torrents of language that follow, the line "and it was the first day off in a long time" is repeated periodically. This repetition serves several functions. First, it helps to return the reader to the present scene from Gray's often long digressions. Second, it creates, as it accrues, a deep sense of the main character's exhaustion. And third, because it refers to Gray's work as an actor in a Hollywood movie, it underscores the distance between those creating the film and those the film is about, who never have a "day off."

In *Blindness*, the sense of order, when it comes, is oppressive. When the inmates enter the institution, the Minister recites a series of rules:

> First, the lights will be kept on at all times, any attempt to tamper with the switches will be useless, they don't work. Second, leaving the building without authorization will mean instant death. Third, three times daily containers with food will be deposited at the main door on the right and left. Fourth, the internees cannot count on any outside intervention should there be any outbreaks of illness, nor in the event of any disorder or aggression. Fifth, in the case of death, whatever the cause, the internees will bury the corpses in the yard without any formalities. Sixth . . . this communication will be relayed three times daily for the benefit of new arrivals.[33]

This passage, cut here to one-third its original length, is partially repeated multiple times in the adaptation (fading in and out) to create both the sense of time passing and the sense of dehumanizing monotony in the ward. Five scenes later, the refrain ends with the announcement, "Attention, attention. There is no more room in the asylum. All of the wards are now full."

As these examples suggest, refrains in full-length scripts usually work best to structure a given segment, rather than the piece in its entirety.

The use of orchestration techniques can help the adaptor diversify the narrative voice and emphasize both particular dramatic moments and important themes in the story. These techniques can also help to provide a structure to the story. The structure can enhance the sense of dramatic coherence discussed earlier. It can also pave the way for structural deviation and, therefore, for surprise.

Representing Loss: Theatrical Strategies

Beyond methodological questions of how to negotiate losses (and gains) in the process of adaptation generally, I discovered in working with students and colleagues on adapting *Blindness* several theatrical strategies for negotiating the substantive challenges of rehearsing and staging loss. My students and I did not invent any of these strategies, but it may be useful to collect them here as a toolbox of techniques for representing loss in performance.

The Scale of Loss

Manipulation of the scale of objects on stage is a powerful way to represent emotions, ideas, and experiences that otherwise seem either too large or too abstract to perform. In 1989 at Carleton College (where I was a student at the time), Lee Breuer showed a series of slides of designs for the Mabou Mines production of *King Lear*, which he was in the process of directing. In this production, the genders of the main characters, including Lear, were reversed, but this was not what fascinated me. The set design did. For the beginning of the performance, the set pieces were made to scale. But they grew gradually larger over every act as Lear's mind deteriorated. By the final act, Lear's throne was too big for him (or, in this case, her) to mount. This upward manipulation of the scale of Lear's environment was a brilliant way of performing the king's loss of control over his kingdom.

A decade later, in my performing literature classroom, a student did another memorable performance about loss by manipulating scale, this time downward. Because she was a particularly sophisticated student, I assigned her one of the most emotionally and intellectually challenging chapters in the novel, the one in which the blind thugs in the next ward demand sex from the blind women in exchange for the food they have hoarded. The mass rape is preceded by a visit to the main ward by three of the blind thugs. At this point, the coldness of the narrative tone reaches its most numbing level. When the men determine that only seven women are in the ward,

> The blind thugs laughed, Too bad, said one of them, you'll just have to work all the harder tonight, and another suggested, Perhaps we'd better go and look for reinforcements in the next ward, It isn't worth it, said the third blind man who knew his sums, it works out at three men for each woman, they can stand it.[34]

How would the student adequately evoke the magnitude and horror of this loss in performance?

She did it with paper dolls. She sat on the bare stage floor and began slowly and methodically to cut out the shape of a figure from a folded piece of paper. As she cut, she began to sing.

> Three blind mice
> Three blind mice
> See how they run
> See how they run
> They all ran after the farmer's wife
> She cut off their tails with a carving knife
> Have you ever seen such a sight in your life as
> Three blind mice
> Three blind mice.

She sang the song through several times and calmly finished her cutting. Then, she unfolded a delicate strand of white paper silhouettes, all holding hands.

I do not need to look at my notes to describe this performance that happened in my classroom six years ago. Its efficacy was amplified by the audience having read the story ahead of time, including chapters subsequent to the one she was performing. Without this exposure to the story, an audience would not know the exact nature of the violence the performance represented nor appreciate the foreshadowing of a pair of scissors, which plays a major role in a later scene. For any audience, though, the performance was a chilling representation of dehumanizing violence and the catastrophic loss that can ensue.

Light, Sound, and Space as Metaphors of Experience

Midway through the rehearsal process, I was interviewed by a local television station about our production of *Blindness*. The interviewer had one burning question: How did I get the seeing actors to act blind?

"Well, the story is a parable, so what we're trying to do is to figure out not so much what it actually feels like to be blind, but what is the experience of totally losing one's moorings—"

"Yeah, but how do they act blind? Do you get them to close their eyes?"

"These characters have suddenly lost all independence, all sense of who they are as individuals. They are totally dependent on each other—"

"And they're all blind, right?"

The interviewer was interested in the technical challenge of the students representing people with a different bodily experience than their own. But the real challenge in representing these characters was not to demonstrate convincingly to an audience what their losses might look like but to evoke what they might *feel* like. In this case, an important part of what loss felt like was to have nowhere to turn for comfort.

Some of the ways in which space, lighting, and sound represent loss in our production of *Blindness* worked against common associations with loss. For example, one might expect the lighting of loss to be dark, and this might be effective in dramatic situations in which loss results in loneliness. Instead, unnaturally bright lighting better evoked more public or shared losses as well as losses of personal autonomy. This is certainly not a new idea. Jean-Paul Sartre's *No Exit* takes place in a room where the lights can never be turned off. Similarly, for us, bright lighting best evoked the sense that for the inmates, even more than for Tony Kushner's Homebody (see chapter 6), the realm of the private was gone. Late in the story, when the characters regained autonomy and the possibility of privacy, the lighting became darker and more soothing.

One might also expect the sounds of loss to be slow, sad sounds. In our production, I worked against this expectation by asking the composer to create music that was "carnivalesque." He created a modern variation on the traditional carnival tightrope melody, the playful mood of which, when juxtaposed with the blind community's forced incarceration, was grotesque. The music became slightly more dissonant each time it played until it was strident. Just as nothing was empathic about the government's treatment of these characters, nothing was hospitable about the production's music. The exception to this was the radio scene, for which the composer wrote a lovely, melancholy melody that was recorded for the production by one female vocalist.

Finally, one might expect the space of loss to be big and empty. But in our production, the stage space was terribly crowded. Because of the large, institutional bunk beds, characters had to literally crawl on top of each other and often through other characters' beds to get to their own spaces. There was little room to walk on solid ground.

Our production, then, did not seek to evoke the characters' losses. On the contrary, by making design choices that worked against conventional expectations about what loss looks and feels like (dark, slow, and empty), our production created an environment in which there seemed to be no room for negotiating loss. The effort was not to demonstrate grief but to evoke the pressure of a world in which grief is restrained, gagged, and, as banished feelings do, longing for a home. Creating this space was, for us, far more valuable than showing how sad—or how blind—the characters were. Only in such a space would this group of strangers be forced to find community in each other.

The process of adapting *Blindness*, like any adaptation process, was a rehearsal of loss. In both the scripting and the staging, we had to try on or practice different losses to discover what could be transferred from the novel, what could be translated through conceptual and technical strategies, and what had to be excised in order to retain the coherence of the text in a different medium. All this practice was in the interest of avoiding what for narrative adaptors are unacceptable losses: the loss of descriptive language and the loss of the narrator's presence as a guiding force in the making and telling of the story.

Because *Blindness* is a text about loss, it also afforded more particular insights about the rehearsal of private and public grief. Grief could be expressed in performance through the manipulation of scale, space, lighting, and sound. These elements proved most effective when they evoked an outside perspective or force (in this case, the sinister environment sometimes represented by the narrator's voice) and not the characters' interior landscapes. In this way, design served to dramatize the distance between the cultural milieu of the novel that, like our own, would have us "cry the right amount" and the expressive and reflective capacity of individual actors, fictional or real, lesser or greater than ourselves, from whose lives we have so much to learn.

4. Practicing Community: Representing National Tragedy

In the face of the great evil of September 11, one ought to speak in hushed tones, humbly and graciously, as before a mystery.
—Nicholas Wolterstorff on Rowan Williams's *Writing in the Dust*

"THE SECOND TOWER COLLAPSED, GUYS."

Kyle, lanky with sandy, shoulder-length hair, is standing among the clutter of desks, full of his own importance in the empty classroom. He is reporting with breathless excitement to a few stragglers after class on his ongoing cell-phone conversation with his dad, who works in the Missouri state government. It's the cell phone I've asked him repeatedly not to bring to class. Kyle will eventually have to withdraw from the class, a class on the adaptation and performance of literature, because of excessive absence. But here he is at his most fully present, relaying the up-to-the-minute information from his father in Jefferson City to his classmates in Springfield. They are not nearly as excited as he is; they are confused. I am confused, too. I don't understand why the building is falling. And I don't understand why it is important that the building is falling.

Not until late that afternoon, when I come home from my full day of teaching, turn on my television, and see the charred suits of firefighters with their backs to me will the absurdly obvious occur to me: *there are people in the buildings.*

For the next two and a half days, I cry. I stop to teach, and then I cry some more. I cry as I have never cried for strangers. I begin to have an almost Pavlovian response to turning on the television: press, picture, weep. Press, picture, weep. I cry when my father calls to tell me that a friend of a friend was on the Pennsylvania plane and that the mutual friend said he just knew this man was the sort of person who would have tried to do something. I cry over cereal. I cry at bedtime.

On Friday, I race home from my morning class to watch the service at the National Cathedral. I could watch it at school, of course, but I don't want to. I want to be alone.

Billy Graham appears at the podium. I grit my teeth. I know nothing about Billy Graham, I couldn't pick him out of a line-up. I know nothing except the word *evangelist* that floats around him in my hazy memory.

"President and Mrs. Bush, I want to say a personal word on behalf of many people. Thank you, Mr. President, for calling this Day of Prayer and Remembrance. We needed it at this time."[1]

I am surprised by his manner. His voice is not tremulous or lilting; it is dusty, almost a whisper. His eyes are not ablaze with zeal; his head is bowed. His arms do not flail; they stay quietly by his sides. He is old and gentle. I am still waiting for the other shoe to drop.

"But how do we understand something like this? Why does God allow evil like this to take place? Perhaps that is what you are asking now. You may even be angry at God. I want to assure you that God understands those feelings that you may have."

How. Why. Perhaps. May. This is not what I thought the language of an evangelist sounded like. I am still waiting.

"But what are some of the lessons we can learn? First, we are reminded of the mystery and reality of evil. I've been asked hundreds of times in my life why God allows tragedy and suffering."

The next few seconds seem to last an hour or more. This is it, I think to myself quite consciously. This. Not the planes crashing into the towers. Not anthrax in the mail. Not homelessness or disease. This is the moment that the world I have lived in will fail me, and I will not know what to do. I see the next sentence in front of me, like a truck in the oncoming lane. I can't see it all, it's too far away, but I see two words. The words are "His Plan." When that truck comes into full view, I do not know what I will do to save myself.

The sound of Graham's voice wafts from the television. "I have to confess that I really do not know the answer totally, even to my own satisfaction."

Grateful, again, I weep.

Mystery

In her book *Unmarked*, Peggy Phelan argues that performance is, in its very being, "unmarked"; that is, performance "cannot be saved, recorded, documented" but rather, "becomes itself through disappearance."[2] If it is true that performance is unmarked, it is also true that performance is uncharted—it admits no strictly enactable plan. Thus, though practitioner-scholars like to talk about performance as a "way of knowing," to truly perform is to enter a space of radical *un*knowing. To write (or speak) performatively is to preserve a space for that unknowing.

A sacred space. For, if evil is, as Graham said, a mystery and reality, so, too, is goodness. In his essay "Speaking of God," Richard F. Ward writes, "The preacher as an actor in a holy ritual seeks the emptiness of 'holes' that liturgical performance aims to open up."[3] Only a hole, only a mystery can make room for the possibility of presence—call it God, call it meaning, call it knowing.

Two principal dangers exist in representing history's losses through performance. First, there is the danger of reducing them through mastery. Any attempt to wholly answer the question of why historical atrocities occur is bound, as Graham knew, to fail. An integral part of the fabric of historical atrocity is what performance scholar Vivian Patraka, writing about the Holocaust, called its "goneness." But it is the responsibility of the writer/performer to mark this goneness as such.

The graver danger for the writer/performer is refusing to engage with the questions that atrocities raise. Dwight Conquergood, in a different context, called this the "skeptic's cop out": I cannot possibly understand, says the skeptic, and therefore I will not represent. Such an erasure is what is most intolerable to those affected by historical traumas. If Theodor Adorno was right in his famous proclamation that there can be no poetry after Auschwitz, he was also wrong: there cannot *not* be poetry after trauma, if for no other reason than to mark our own failure to understand.

In May of 2002, Michael Murray, a composer and colleague, asked me to write the text for a choral piece that was to be performed at a university memorial service on September 11, 2002. Because I am always drawn to represent what seems to me unrepresentable and because I was still eager for an opportunity to better understand that moment in history, I agreed. Beginning work on the text, I knew that I wanted to create for others the same kind of space that Graham's words had created for me at the National Cathedral. I wanted to create a space for mystery in the face of historical trauma.

THE WEIGHT OF LOSS: THE *NEW YORK TIMES* PORTRAITS

I began my research with the *New York Times*'s collected *Portraits of Grief*. When it arrived in the mail, I couldn't imagine what the package contained. It must have weighed five pounds. Six. Could it have been seven? When I opened the large, heavy box, I was holding a hardcover book with a glossy, white, paper cover. I had to hold it with both hands. I tried to open it on the living room table, but the glass top was rickety, and with the weight of the book on it, I couldn't lean in. I moved to the couch and sat for a few minutes, just dumbfounded by the weight.

I opened the cover. *Aha*, I thought, *a preface*. I quickly imagined all the possible filler—preface, introduction, and several long, commemorative essays. The tragedy would need to be placed in its historical context. Official responses from the nation, the city, and its institutions would need to be documented. Momentarily relieved, I decided to flip through the preface.

The preface was one page long. It was immediately followed by portraits of lives. Each portrait, typeset, was no longer or wider than my hand. Each had a photograph of the victim's head the size of a postage stamp and a headline of four or five words. The portraits came one after another in columns, sometimes running over on to the next column or the next page. There was no white space. The *A*s ended on one page. The *B*s began on the next. There was no white space.

Flipping the pages, I came across a full-page picture of a group of children, hands pressed together, singing for a group of firefighters. *Aha, I thought, pictures.* I kept flipping through. There were, perhaps, five of these in the book, sandwiched in between hundreds of pages of hand-sized narrative portraits. The entire weight of this book, then, was comprised of paragraphs of memorial text. It was hard to understand that these brief, glancing, obviously miniature portraits could come to weigh so much. And what was more, this was an unfinished volume. Still, not every life had been accounted for.

I had ordered *Portraits of Grief* as a way in to writing the text for the choral piece. I thought being steeped in the specificity of these losses would help orient me. But quickly this accumulation of details began to have the opposite effect. Docile reader that I am (at least at first), I began with the *A*s. I wrote on a piece of paper the page numbers of portraits I found particularly striking for one reason or another. Soon I had a page of page numbers. Two weeks later, at the *E*s, it became clear that reading through the portraits was too great a task. But how to skim such material?

I tried various strategies. I looked for a particularly striking headline or face. One day, I decided I would read all the portraits that memorialized two people at once—a father and son, sisters, spouses, best friends. This strategy, too, crumbled under the weight of the book. Finally, there was nothing for it but to close the book of portraits and begin to try and write for myself.

From Particularity to Abstraction: Bad Greeting Cards

Everything kept rhyming.

"It doesn't have to rhyme," said Mike. "In fact, it's better if it doesn't."

"I know, I know," I said. "For some reason it just keeps coming out that way. Listen to this one: If I ever thought a star was a hero / If I ever thought life was long / If I ever thought gratitude was simple / I was wrong."

"That's awful."

"Wait, there's a second verse. If I ever thought people were selfish—"

"Stop, stop!"

"I just keep writing bad greeting cards."

"You'll run out of them eventually."

Della Pollock identifies one of the key characteristics of performative writing as metonymy. Performative writing "is a self-consciously partial or incomplete rendering that takes its pulse from the *difference* rather than the *identity* between the linguistic symbol and the thing it is meant to represent"[4] (emphasis original). In its very refusal to master a subject or experience, performative writing makes room for what Graham called the "mystery and reality" of that subject.

The opposite of this self-conscious metonymy of expression is sentimental writing. In response to an essay by James Baldwin, poet and essayist Alan Shapiro observes that in sentimentality, "the irreducibly unique and tangled nature of reality is exchanged for some manageable abstraction that tricks us into thinking that everything is figured out, understood, and therefore no longer needs to be examined, considered, looked at freshly, or attended to."[5] Shapiro encourages us to think generously about sentimentality, to consider it not, as Baldwin did, the expression of an arid heart but the expression of a heart that is too full.

My bad greeting cards were bad because they were sentimental. What made them so was their invocation of nouns such as "life" and "gratitude." Even as the content of these lyrics sought to trouble the nouns as manageable abstractions, the parallel, rhyming, repetitious, and familiar structure reinforced the sense that these ideas no longer needed to be examined, considered, or looked at freshly. In order to move from sentimental writing to performative writing, I decided, one would need to move from manageable abstractions to overwhelming details.

From Abstraction to Particularity: The Failure of Metonymy

A name tag that says "Emilio"
Two coins from her trip to Japan
Her three-year-old daughter

Her father's ring
And a watch that was still keeping time.[6]

The very incompleteness of Graham's rhetoric at the National Cathedral had moved me. But while Graham's response was partial, it was not metonymic. In it was—in the classic example from film theory—no red balloon to stand in for the loss of a little girl protagonist.

Turning away from the big, abstract nouns that produced my bad greeting cards, I began to try to write metonymically about the tragedy. But as in the excerpt above from one three-verse poem, the results felt paltry, pathetic. Here was yet another failed attempt to write performatively about the historical losses of September 11. And this time the problem was not abstraction; the items in this list were taken directly from *New York Times* portraits and news stories. It was, rather, the failure of these parts to stand in for the whole.

For one thing, the list represented only those whose losses were particular and tangible. But the piece was to be performed in Springfield, Missouri, where relatively few of us had experienced direct losses; most of us experienced the tragedy through our televisions. As with most witnesses to historical losses, we did not have tokens to make the losses tangible. The choral piece, in fact, was an effort to mark that very absence.

But this was not the heart of the problem. The problem was that these lists and samplings of memorial objects were purely aesthetic objects, displayed as in a museum. They were interesting enough as images and ideas, but they didn't *do* anything. They didn't perform their own weight, as the collection of *New York Times* portraits did. They described loss but did nothing to enact it.

In retrospect, one way to have made such details act would have been to let them accrue much more exhaustively. Three verses are too elegant and too simple a number. What if the list above was expanded to several hundred items? Twenty minutes of listed objects would have begun to act upon the listener in a way that a mere three verses of metonymy would not have. But such a strategy would also have severely limited the audience for the piece. As commemorations of national tragedies, lists, usually lists of names, are read once a year. Mike and I hoped our piece could be performed more frequently. But if big abstractions and small metonymies had both failed, what was left?

Lost Syntax

Syntax, defined simply as the order of words in a sentence, is the structural center of language. When it is lost or broken, other things feel lost or broken, too. For me, some of the most powerful performative writing is syntactically mimetic. On the level of the sentence, it enacts what it describes. In my performing literature classes, I use part of a poem by E. E. Cummings to help students understand what syntax means and then, later, to help them understand the idea of performative writing:

> since feeling is first
> who pays too much attention
> to the syntax of things
> will never wholly kiss you.

Here, Cummings both advocates and performs a willful disregard for the rules of syntax. Pure feeling, he suggests, defies orderliness and rules of grammar.

The approach I finally hit upon for the first section of what became a three-part choral piece (only two parts are discussed here) was an example of disordered syntax. It had at its center an adverb without a verb.

> September
> After the fall
> Just after the fall
> Not one day later
> When the praying started
> Or three months later
> When the burning ended
> Or two years later
> When the stone was erected
> But then, just after the fall
>
> Somebody spoke it
> For we who were speechless
> A single word
> Impossible as spring
> And yet someone spoke it
> An electric whisper
> Like wind on your neck
> More suggestion than sound:
> *Again.*

It's important to be clear about my writing process here. I did not arrive at this piece of text in the way the analysis above might suggest. I did not sit down and work to create a poem that was syntactically mimetic. Rather, the impulse came from my own brokenness of feeling and my sense that this was the idea we were all trying to speak, trying to perform, trying to believe in the immediate wake of September 11: again. We could not say, or certainly *I* could not say, just what it was that we would do (or be) again, but somehow we needed to assure ourselves that things were not utterly transformed. We needed to preserve the possibility of repeating something from our life before that morning.

Of course, I mean our collective, national life, our American community. Many of our individual everyday lives in places like Springfield, Missouri, were not altered by the events of 9/11, at least on a practical level. Fredric Jameson rightly questions the "vast tidal wave of identical reactions" the media coverage in the wake of the disaster suggested.[7] In the days that followed the attacks, we struggled differently to understand our relationship to the events than those who lost loved ones on that day. Would this experience divide us from them? Did "we" mean the same thing it had meant when we went to sleep the night before? If not, would it mean the same thing again, and if so, how soon?

Because the text ends in effect with the promise of performance (of doing something "again"), it is worth reconsidering the concept of performativity in the context of this writing. Performativity, as articulated by Judith Butler,[8] is about both constraint and agency. The constraint in performativity lies in the necessity of repeating established norms, particularly with respect to identity categories. I cannot make up a radically free performance of "woman"—I am constrained by my cultural inheritance and all the performances that have come before mine. To think otherwise is to delude myself about the possibility of being outside of law, that is, outside of culture.

The agency in performativity comes through the constraint that even if I try, I can never repeat culturally mandated performance completely faithfully. Try as I might through exercise, surgery, self-help, or study, I can never perfectly enact the category of woman. In the necessary difference of my performed repetition comes its political power and promise. Robert N. Bellah et al. noted that not even major changes in public policy are as important to the rebuilding of social trust as is "a sense of agency that can come only from the participation that enables people to belong and contribute to the larger society."[9]

But what "September" offers is precisely the possibility of repetition as agency. Certainly not repetition without difference, as this is all the more impossible in the case of historical ruptures. Yet, repetition, nonetheless, with an emphasis on similarity, on a recognizable resemblance to an original action. In this sense, the various command performances of patriotism that the government tried, with some success, to enforce after September 11 were false performances, as they were not repetitions of our former identities.

What we wanted to do "again" in the days after September 11 is precisely what we had done before: to dissent, to meet a friend at the airport, to practice our religions. At its most ambitious, what the piece endeavors to do is to make "again" a performative utterance which, like the word promise, does what it says.

Repetition has gotten a bad name in the realm of performance scholarship. It is the law of repetition that forces us to adhere to cultural norms of what it means to be white, black, male, female, Western, Eastern. But some feminist scholars have noted that not all repetition is bad. Nancy Fraser criticizes Butler along these lines, asking, "Why is resignification good? Can't there be bad (oppressive reactionary) resignifications? In opting for the epistemically neutral 'resignification' as opposed to the epistemically positive 'critique,' Butler seems to valorize change for its own sake and thereby to disempower feminist judgment."[10] In the wake of historical atrocity, it can be an act of agency to repeat old performances of self, of community without (much) difference. Through repetition, we may reaffirm our identities as actors in and makers of our culture.

One matter of live interpretation is worth noting. As the piece was scored, the choir sings the word *again* twice. Although they sing in unison both times, the dynamic changes dramatically; the first time the word is sung softly, the second time quite loudly with a sharp, clean cutoff. I am ambivalent about this performance of the language. At its worst, this dynamic suggests a false, neat narrative of triumph over atrocity. At its best, the louder version of the word *again* is a dream, a premonition of a better, stronger day in our national life, a day that has not yet arrived.

Lost Objects

October

We stood.

We heard. We watched. We wept.
We hoped. We wept. We prayed.
We fell. We embraced. We wept.
We raged. We stormed. We sang.
We trembled. We sang. We guarded.
We remembered. We return. We sang.

We stood.

We . . .

Nine days after the terrorist attacks, President George W. Bush spoke to a joint session of the U.S. Congress. His speech forged an American "we" in two ways: by opposition to a hostile "they" and by proscribing certain performances for grieving citizens.

Bush's short speech was interrupted by applause twenty-nine times. One of the biggest applause lines was his declaration to foreign nations, "Either you are with us, or you are with the terrorists." Later in his speech, he elaborated on this choice. "Freedom and fear are at war. The advance of human freedom . . . now depends on us."[11] In the wake of this historical atrocity, then, Bush defined a community, a "we" by opposition to a common enemy. Such polarizing language, as theologian Martin Marty warned in a *Newsweek* article, "can inhibit self-examination and repentant action."[12] Moreover, the imperative of being, as Diana Taylor writes in another context, "united in tragedy"[13] threatens to squelch political dissent, as occurred so dramatically with the profusion of pro-American symbols and sentiment in the months after the attacks. The violence of this forced unity redoubled in the weeks that followed, as we were urged to display the flag, travel, and most of all shop, or risk being labeled a traitor to the national "we."

An even more tremendous chorus of applause came when Bush described how this "we" would act—or, more precisely, how "we" would not act, in the future. "We will rally the world to this cause by our efforts, by our courage," Bush told the nation and the world. "We will not tire, we will not falter, and we will not fail." Here was Bush's earliest performance of what Taylor, writing about September 11, calls the "masculinist rush to save the day."[14] Even more troubling than the hasty machismo of this statement is its enactment of what has been called a culture of certitude that characterizes the administration.

What seemed vital to me, as it did to many others, in the aftermath of the attacks was to preserve the diversity of the national "we." At first, I thought I would try to do this by highlighting, in different sections of the chorale, different key perspectives, including that of victim, survivor, and witness. In the end, though, rather than separating out these perspectives, I did the opposite, consolidating them into a single pronoun, "we."

If the first section of my text for the choral piece offered an adverb, the second section offered verb and subject. Many verbs, one subject. But this subject, this "we," was different from the "we" of President Bush's speech.

This "we" was, instead, more like the image a colleague designed for the 2002 program of the university's memorial event. In it, two candles stand in for the World Trade Center towers and, as symbols of mourning, for the victims of the tragedy (see fig. 4.1). Like this image, the "we" of the chorale text does not exclude any perspectives mentioned. It does not exclude my students and colleagues in Springfield, Missouri. It does not exclude those who displayed flags in their windows in response to the tragedy, and it does not exclude those who did not display flags. It does not even exclude the writers and consumers of bad greeting cards.

Figure 4.1. "Candles," created in the week after September 11, 2001, by Roman Duszek. Courtesy of Roman Duszek.

Yet, it need not make a claim on any of these subjects. It invites listeners in and also allows them to remain outside, should they so choose. It answers the question posed by the "somebody" in the first section—who spoke it? We did—and yet it is not a particular or masterful answer.

If the first section of the chorale enacts the possibility of continued action, the second section enacts a diverse yet recoverable "we." This is particularly true in performance, where the variability of this "we" is enacted by the orchestration of voices, sometimes in unison, sometimes overlapping, and sometimes a single voice to a single action. What did we do? We watched. We wept. We spoke. We remembered. Some of us did some of these things. Some of us did all of them. Some of us did none but wished we had or could have.

Pollock writes that performative writing is "nervous," "neither willing nor able to stop moving, restless, transient and transitive."[15] Such writing moves. It does not simply occupy multiple locations but *affects* transitions or transformations in locale. Slowly. The text above offers some sense of movement from one place to another but not a simple one. There is repetition and relapse. And there is the final "we" that, not incidentally, was arrived at collaboratively, an idea of the composer to which I enthusiastically agreed. Against the bravado of post–September 11 presidential speeches, the final "we" marks a lack of finality to the process of repairing our ability to act. And, unlike the ending of the first section, this "we" trails off in performance on a soft, elongated note, fading into silence.

In nature, mysteries are beautiful. In literature, they are fun. In history, they are sometimes horrific. In the first two instances, it is not difficult to honor mystery; in the third, it is difficult indeed.

Westerners are accustomed to knowing history. We are continually assured that this is the way to avoid repeating its mistakes. But in the rush to master facts and figures, we miss the incomplete, the inexplicable, the incomprehensible, and everything that exceeds the capacity of the human mind.

Westerners are accustomed to making history, both as economic powers and as the authors of history's texts. But in the rush to make history, we often act without fully processing the events to which we are responding. In so doing, we not only risk grave political and moral error, we also miss what H. Richard Niebuhr called "the grace of doing nothing." We miss the opportunity to accrue strength through a collective pause.

Clarity

This is what we did. How did it happen? How could we?
—Dorothea Lange, photographer

On a clear morning in late September of 2002, surrealist painter Robert Shetterly is pacing furiously around his small studio in Brooksville, Maine. He feels that, at any moment, a network of veins might rise to the surface of his skin, and he might actually explode—from anger, from shame, from grief, from the almost unbearable pressure he feels welling up inside of him to do something.

But what can he do?

He keeps pacing, fists clenched, streams of sweat crossing his temples, until suddenly he notices another stream, a torrent of words writ large on his wall, there for so long now he rarely notices them. They are the words of Walt Whitman. Shetterly thinks, *Man, if I paint his portrait and scratch his words into it, I might feel a little better.* Through painting, Shetterly considers, he could address his own overwhelming feelings of grief. *I was thinking, "First, save yourself."*

Shetterly's feelings were based in a different sense of American history than the one most frequently articulated in the aftermath of September 11. At that time, many commented on the singularity of this event in American history. Those who recognized precedence were able to identify a single model in our past, arguing that the attack was most like the 1941 attack on Pearl Harbor. In 2001, the American government was characterizing the September 11 attacks as the start of a "new kind of war," and President Bush, addressing the nation on September 20, said that on September 11, "night fell on a different world."

But to Shetterly, the tragedy was neither unique nor the primary object of mourning. "When I talk about 9/11 [as an inspiration for my work], it certainly isn't 9/11 itself, because I see that as part of a continuum of American policy and other people's policies, and they're all conflated. It was an extraordinary event but not really off the continuum."[16] Shetterly was able to do what so many of us failed to do—to place it in history.

For Shetterly, the real loss marked on September 11 was not the loss of human life, terrible though it was, but the loss of "real values, of the ideals that I had taken as, you know, the centerpiece of what it means to be American." These ideals included courage, integrity, humility, fairness, and, above all, honesty. They also included the ideal of a national community bound by these qualities.

A central outcome of the terrorist attacks was the creation of a new kind of American community, one falsely unified by a common enemy and a common goal of defiance. When President Bush divided the world into two camps, he was clear that those who were with "us" would seek retribution, understanding that "if this terror goes unpunished, their own cities, their own citizens may be next."[17] Taylor described the federal responses as a "show of national unity and directionality that by-passed the public itself."[18] This false unification of the American community was achieved through "the downright prohibition of seeing and knowing imposed by the government."[19] The epitome of this prohibition, for some, was the satellite photograph of purportedly active chemical-munitions bunkers[20] used as the centerpiece of Secretary of State Colin Powell's February 2003 testimony before the United Nations, supposedly based on eyewitness accounts and later exposed as false evidence of nuclear proliferation in Iraq. For Shetterly, who "knew sitting at my little computer in Brooksville, Maine that it was based on lies,"[21] the false rationale for going to war in Afghanistan more than a year earlier was already emblematic of the prohibition.

But it was not only the Bush administration that, by September 11, had lost track of American ideals. "This has nothing to do, absolutely nothing to do with Democrats and Republicans," Shetterly stressed. "They're equally up to their eyeballs in this stuff. It has only to do with complicity with a system which is unsustainable." Indeed, the painter himself felt complicit:

> The other major feeling besides grief which I think often accompanies it especially when you feel that you are complicit with the causing of the grief is shame. I felt an enormous shame. And, well, like most people, you don't want to be sad, angry and shameful all at once.[22]

So, to relieve his own feelings of sorrow, anger and shame, Shetterly painted Walt Whitman (see fig. 4.2). The portrait, thirty-six inches long and thirty inches wide, features the torso of the old poet, with a full beard and mustache, his entire face framed by a thick mane of wild, grey and white hair. Beneath a brown hat, Whitman's eyes look deeply tired, and a shadow falls over the right side of his face. His dark clothes fade into the black background, and he looks like a floating head. He is surely very near the end of his seventy-one years—or perhaps even older, a haggard spirit. Just below the beard, covering nearly half the canvas, are these words:

> This is what you shall do: Love the earth and sun and the animals, despise riches, give alms to every one that asks, stand up for the stupid and crazy, devote your income and labor to others, hate tyrants, argue not concerning God, have patience and indulgence toward the people, take off your hat to nothing known or unknown.[23]

The quotation is etched in thin lines and small print with imperfect spacing, the word "unknown" by itself on the bottom line.

Why Whitman, I asked Shetterly many years later. He replied that there was "no more essential democrat" than Whitman. To Whitman, as the above quotation demonstrates, democracy meant believing in the equality

Figure 4.2. *Walt Whitman*, created in January 2002 by Robert Shetterly. Used by permission of Dutton Children's Books.

not only of all people but of all living things. In Whitman's world, Shetterly explained, "All created life is essentially equal and has to be treated that way, with that same respect . . . he's talking about butterflies and bugs and leaves and grass and everything. We have to think about them all as essentially equal."[24]

A few days later, Shetterly painted a second portrait at the urging of his partner, Gail. ("For Chrissakes," he recalls her saying, "paint some more portraits! You were a nicer person to live with for a couple of days!") The idea of a series then came to him.

> I thought, I'm gonna surround myself with people I feel proud of so I don't feel so goddamned ashamed all the time of who I am and what I represent. And that was the beginning of the painting of the portraits was this desperate move to say, wait a minute, there's a community here which I want to ally myself with.[25]

He decided to paint fifty portraits. They would not be for sale. And they would be called, "Americans Who Tell the Truth."

This was a radically different sort of response to loss than the one I tried to produce following the attacks, not just because of its broad historical approach and not just because of a difference in medium or scope but because of a fundamental difference in purpose. In my effort to respond to the loss of life on September 11, it had felt critical to me to refuse any definitive interpretations, to reject the idea that one could say what such an event meant. In his effort to respond to the loss of "what it meant to be American," Shetterly felt the opposite impulse, an impulse toward simplicity, clarity, and directness.

It was a major shift in Shetterly's own style of painting. Before the portraits, he had been a self-described "champion of ambiguity and mystery as the place where one goes when one wants to understand human motivation." He still admires this kind of work, calling it "redemptive" because it shows how fine the gradations are between our own behaviors and others. "We look at it and we say, wow, I could have done that, anybody could do these things," Shetterly said. "We all do these things . . . and we can forgive."[26]

But the present moment, he felt, called for something different. It called for "trying to turn from facing an audience about being sort of mysterious, to facing an audience and saying, 'These are critical issues, and I'm using my art to come to grips with them. And I'm not just telling you what has been but I'm telling you what is and also a way out.'"

The new style had to be direct, almost transparent: "The pictures aren't about the way they're painted. It becomes a teaching tool, it becomes a conversation tool, it becomes a healing tool, it becomes a tool to do what William Sloan Coffin says, 'Improve the quality of your suffering.' Take all that grief that you're feeling personally and reach out—with a lot of other people's help—to heal other people who are also suffering."[27]

This transparency mirrored the directness of the style of many of the portraits' subjects. "What I tell," Whitman wrote in his preface to *Leaves of Grass*, "I tell for precisely what it is."[28] In order to create this transparency in his painting, Shetterly combined more representational images than he had produced in the past with messages in the subjects' own words. He was careful to choose the most challenging words he could find.

> Our culture really tries to neuter, castrate really, the most important statements and the most important things that a lot of these people lived and died for. You get the celebrity stuff and the feel good stuff like Martin Luther King and I have a dream, but you don't get their guts and their analysis of what the problem is. And I come in with that. So I'm talking about Martin Luther King but I'm not talking about I have a dream. I'm talking about him equating racism and imperialism in the Vietnam war . . . and then when he says my country is the greatest purveyor of violence in the world today, I come in with what they said when they were talking from their gut.[29]

In recovering the "guts" of important figures in American history, Shetterly attempted to compensate for the "castration" of American ideals. According to the description on the back of the note cards later made of the portraits, the series "celebrates Americans who sacrificed much to insure that the promise of America is fulfilled—simply, that it does what it says." Shetterly performs this promise by reconstituting an American community where dissenting voices are valued.

Not everyone appreciated the version of the American community Shetterly was constructing. In a scathing review of a book version of the portraits, lawyer Alan Dershowitz called the book "revolting" and accused it of being "child propaganda." He argued that the subjects of the portraits "hate the United States and its allies."[30] Shetterly responded to Dershowitz's attack with another American value—dissent: "All of them [the portrait subjects] have been very angry at the forces in American culture and economics that have often kept the country from fulfilling its own promise, but their principled opposition reflects their love for American ideals and their insistence on equal opportunities for all individuals."[31] Dershowitz, in return, named seven other Americans he called truthtellers and complained that they had been "disqualified" from Shetterly's list. Speaking from his studio a year after this public debate, Shetterly laughs, "But that's because I'm doing this, and they aren't. People challenge me on that, and I say, 'Hey, paint your own series!'"

About two and a half years after the project began, the portraits number ninety-eight and still counting. They continue to tour throughout the United States, often to middle schools, high schools, and colleges, often with Shetterly accompanying them to foster a dialogue about democracy, community, honesty, and other American ideals.

I first encountered Shetterly's portraits in August of 2004 on his "Americans Who Tell the Truth" Web site, after a colleague told me that they would be coming to our campus late that academic year. (Or that some of them would be coming. By this point, there were upwards of seventy large canvases.) The series fit very neatly with a course that I would be teaching both semesters that year, in which students created solo performances of historical figures. I decided to structure the course around the portraits. Each student could pick one of the seventy subjects to research, script, and perform. I would select the four strongest performances to be produced at the gallery opening of the show in May.

For my students, this project of performing the portraits had nothing to do with either the grief or the historical events that had inspired Shetterly to paint them. Nonetheless, the performances did literally bring to life certain American ideals, ideals that the students may or may not have perceived as lost or threatened but to which, in any case, they were strongly drawn. One of the strongest performances, interestingly, was of Whitman and was a testament to the poet's honesty, both inside and outside his work. It was performed very simply with no costume, no set, and very few props. It included the voices of several of Whitman's critic contemporaries, who had little to say about the substance of his work and whose characterizations of the poet as a cult figure and egomaniac were indirectly but definitively refuted by excerpts from the poet's own words.

Another performance was a collage of speeches by Sojourner Truth calling plainly and forcefully for gender and race equality, its refrain her timeless question, "Ain't I a woman?" When asked why she chose Truth as a subject, the student, Jacqueline Siemann, replied,

> There was no question in my mind that I wanted to do Sojourner Truth. Her words are worth doing. . . . Her feelings when she speaks are elemental. She wants equity and respect, and she has suffered, and that's so universal that that was where I was able to really connect. Especially in the "Ain't I a woman" speech. She's talking about stuff that I feel like anyone in America or anywhere else could say well yes, of course.[32]

Siemann's comment reveals her own awareness of the performative potential of language. Truth's words were not only worth doing in the narrow sense of performing her speeches, they were worth realizing in action.

Perhaps the clearest example of a piece that dealt with the loss of the American ideal of community came from a student who performed New York police detective Frank Serpico. Serpico encountered a broken American community in his early years with the NYPD when it became clear to him that the police department did not take seriously its role in keeping America safe. His account of the corruption he discovered and his efforts to expose and reform the system were made famous by the 1972 film *Serpico* starring Al Pacino and are also documented in the book of the same title by Peter Maas.

Serpico's story is a long one, including several years of accumulating evidence of corruption, several years of attempting to expose it, and several years of recovery and then retirement. The student's original adaptation of the story, inspired by a great admiration for the man he encountered in his research, was long and lacking in structure. It proceeded from incident to incident in a linear way, and by the time it reached some of the story's most important events, the audience was tired. At my suggestion, the student decided to use a key incident in Serpico's professional life as the organizing episode of the piece, a scenario in Taylor's sense of the word that would accrue different meanings in different historical repetitions.

The revised adaptation began with a mysterious scene. In it, an elderly man hunched over an invisible crime victim and, with a clear sense of panic, told him, "No worry—I call police—police help you." The piece quickly moved to a more conventional beginning, in which Maas, the biographer, meets Serpico for the first time and hears his story. In the first half of the piece, we learn that the victim in the inaugural scene is Serpico himself and that his fellow cops ran away from the crime scene when he was shot. Serpico very nearly died in the incident that left him permanently injured. When the complete scene is played in context, and the actor repeats the old man's worried assurance, "No worry—I call police—police help you," we understand the bitter irony that it is precisely the police who are responsible for this man lying alone on the floor, bleeding profusely. The very police in whom the old man is placing his confidence are corrupt and care more for their own safety than for their responsibility to the community and even to each other.

In the second half of the piece, we learn about Serpico's efforts, at least partially successful, to reform the New York Police Department. The piece ends with a third rehearsal of the crime scene in which the old man, now calmer and more confident, concludes, "No worry. I call police. Police help you." This repetition of the scenario enacts a different American community, one in which a person can say with assurance that the police will indeed help those in need.

Another student performed the photographer Dorothea Lange, who so forcefully documented the inequalities between classes and races within the American community that more fortunate Americans refused to see. If the Serpico performance enacted the process of repairing community through a scenario, the Lange performance enacted this process by encompassing a wide range of subjects and by giving each of these subjects a powerful voice in the performance. Although the assignment guidelines strongly encouraged students to incorporate other characters into the subject's story (see appendix A) and although most of my students did this in some way, few found a way to make the subject's community such a central and living part of the story.

The student performed not only Lange herself but the subjects of several of Lange's photographs, including an image of her assistant, Ron Partridge; her most famous image, which came to visually represent the entire Great Depression, "Migrant Mother;" and "Japanese Grandfather," an image from Lange's lesser-known efforts to expose the suffering inflicted on Japanese Americans through World War II interment camps. The student placed reproductions of these images and many others on a black backdrop behind her. When it was time to shift to a new voice, she would begin by physically imitating the still image behind her and then animate this image. In this way, she echoed her fellow student's sense that the subject's work (in this case visual rather than spoken) was "worth doing." In addition, through one of the unique privileges of solo performance, the subjects of Lange's work were brought into community by inhabiting a single body.

The students' work had a strong effect on Shetterly:

> When you actually try to be somebody else, somebody with courage and integrity, it tells you for a moment that you could do that, too. It isn't Sojourner Truth, oh my God, she's on a huge pedestal, she's in a pantheon of great Americans, and we should all admire her but none of us could ever be like her. You act her out for a while and, by God, I could do that. I can say these words. Maybe I could do the things she did, too. And that's the thing that's so incredible about those performances . . . that's why as soon as I saw it, I was just blown away. I thought, wow, this is something that I've got to spread around and would love to have other people do.[33]

Despite Shetterly's insistence on transparency, it was the metaphor provided by the performer's body (a young college student as the self-educated, eighty-year old Sojourner Truth, for example) that extended the possibilities of his message. If a college student could "be" Sojourner Truth, so could an elementary school student. So could a president. So could anyone.

Shetterly invited the students to travel with the portraits to the New York opening, where they performed for school groups and for a large public reception. As a group of white college students from Missouri entered into dialogue with hundreds of elementary school children from Harlem, community was again reconstituted.

For Shetterly, one of the greatest benefits of public interest in his portraits was that it enabled him to travel more and to see community making in action across the country.

> We will find our way out of the problems we're in only through community. One of the wonderful things that I see as I travel so much now

> is community. Lots of communities coming together, some people in great depression and despair feeling that they don't have any voice, but at least they're together.[34]

Making community, making a real and meaningful and diverse "we," can be a significant step toward collective healing.

5. Practicing Responsibility: Race, Class, and Specters of Justice

> *No justice . . . seems possible or thinkable without the principle of some responsibility . . . before the ghosts of those who are not yet born or who are already dead, be they victims of wars, political or other kinds of violence, nationalist, racist, colonialist, sexist, or other kinds of exterminations, victims of the oppressions of capitalist imperialism or any of the forms of totalitarianism.*
>
> —Jacques Derrida, *Specters of Marx*

> *To hell with dying.*
>
> —Alice Walker, "To Hell with Dying"

IN THE ANCIENT GREEK CITY-STATES, women presided over dying and mourning rites and, particularly, over the singing of laments. Their laments were not only sad; they were also angry. The mourners raged at the dead, at the vanquishers, and at the world. When citizens heard these angry, mourning voices, they sometimes took to the streets with revenge in their hearts. So afraid were the state's leaders of these grieving women's anger that, beginning in the sixth century B.C., they introduced legislation to restrict women's ability to mourn in public.[1]

Today, we also fear grief's rage. We acknowledge anger as a "stage" of mourning but one of the earliest and, therefore, least mature. We associate prolonged, repeated, or especially pronounced anger over loss with children. Judith Viorst, author of *Necessary Losses*, asked an eight-year-old boy to provide a comment about living with loss. He replied, concisely, "losing sucks."[2] Though we recognize and perhaps even admire the honesty of such a response, we consider it age appropriate. As adults, we have learned to be "good sports" in every game, including the game of life.

We associate anger, too—though we are less likely to admit this—with low socioeconomic status. About her own college experience, bell hooks recalls,

> Loudness, anger, emotional outbursts, and even something as seemingly innocent as unrestrained laughter were deemed unacceptable, vulgar disruptions of classroom social order. These traits were also associated with being a member of the lower classes. If one was not from a privileged class group, adopting a demeanor similar to that of the group could help one to advance.[3]

Bourgeois values eschew anger.

Jamaica Kincaid is an adult and a member of the upper-middle class. She is also the angriest writer I know. She has no shortage of good reasons to be angry; as a child growing up in Antigua, Kincaid was alternately neglected and emotionally abused by the overbearing mother, who is the subject of many of her works, most famously her widely anthologized short story, "Girl," and her later novel, *The Autobiography of My Mother.* She also witnessed the short- and long-term effects on both her family and her country of a racially inflected poverty, both under British rule and under a government of Antiguan natives, largely people of African descent. One effect of this systemic poverty was the lack of decent medical care for Antiguans, including Kincaid's brother, whose illness and death from AIDS she chronicles in her memoir *My Brother.* Another effect was a lack of formal education that might have helped to end the debilitating cycle of poverty. Kincaid managed to escape this cycle by emigrating to the United States as a young girl. But her adult grief over her brother's death must be read in the context of the sustained and multifaceted trauma of her Antiguan childhood.

This trauma must not be read in isolation or as the result of Kincaid's particular set of unfortunate circumstances. Rather, following Diana Taylor's directive, it must be read in dialogue with the experiences of many other populations in the Americas that have experienced sustained social violence: "Approaches to memory and trauma that privilege the individual subject fail to do justice to the cumulative and collective nature of the trauma suffered by illiterate and literate communities alike."[4] Kincaid's memoir affirms the value of an approach to loss that emphasizes community. Specifically, it affirms the value of anger in helping us enact our collective responsibility for the dead. Anger helps deprivatize grief by refusing to be quiet, by insisting on the relationship between personal and political losses. This relationship between private grief and the public sphere is important to all of us. To those whose experiences have been denied collective expression or whose collective expression has been systematically ignored, it is indispensable.

For Taylor, it is through embodied performance that traumatic experience becomes transmittable. For Kincaid, however, who traces her history to an illiterate community, it is particularly critical that this performance be enacted as literacy/literature. Kincaid's memoir *My Brother* affirms the value of literature as performance, as not merely a description, prescription, chronicle, or cultural artifact but a rehearsal of transformations both social and political. This affirmation is important for performance studies because it calls into question the hierarchy of objects of study that have, for the last quarter century or more, so strongly favored "low" cultural objects over "high" ones, performances generated by everyday behaviors over those generated by the literary imagination. Kincaid's writing serves as a reminder that the two realms are often indistinguishable and that in their very intermingling, the possibility of social change is nascent. Further, Kincaid's memoir demonstrates the unique value of literacy as a performance of social power.

My Brother works for *historical* justice. It widens the circle of responsibility for the loss of her brother to include the culture that suppressed his story; the governments, indigenous and otherwise, that ignored his suffering; and the privileged people, including herself, who purchased their survival at his expense. It also troubles normative narratives of historical progress by returning to its beginning again and again.

My Brother insists upon *narrative* justice, both in terms of the imperative to narrate unwritten histories of loss in colonized countries and in terms of the need to tell these stories differently. Through the regeneration of key words, phrases, and images, the memoir haunts both writer and reader and refuses to disappear.

My Brother demands *emotional* justice vis-à-vis the performance of mourning. It refuses to simplify, minimize, abbreviate, or inflate the sometimes complex, sometimes ugly, and sometimes even vacant work of practicing our responses to loss. Through relentless repetition, the memoir performs the emotional complexity it discursively disavows.

Finally, *My Brother* is a stage upon which these three kinds of justice related to loss are uniquely intertwined. Oral historian Samuel Schraeger has argued that there is always something social in the account of a single life. Kincaid's memoir suggests that there is always something political in the account of a personal loss, no matter how much we may prefer to minimize its impact by relegating the loss to the realm of the "merely" personal.

Critical response to *My Brother* reflects the salience of these multiple levels of justice. As a work of historical narrative, Kincaid's book was considered a success. Her prose was hailed as amazing, unforgettable, stinging, and perfect. As a work of mourning, however,[5] it was considered a failure. Specifically, Kincaid was criticized for not sticking closely enough to her subject and, as she usually is, for being too angry: "What is off-putting about *My Brother* is that it is only glancingly a portrait of her younger half brother. . . . Its real subject is Kincaid's scalded psyche. . . . The underlying, overflowing theme, as always, is anger."[6] In addition to suggesting, as several others have, that Kincaid's mourning work fails because its subject is too diffuse, this critique suggests that it fails because its emotional content is inappropriate. But *My Brother* gains its power precisely from its insistence on forging a relationship between private grief and public anger.

Historical Justice: Trauma as Continual Inauguration

The time of historical narrative is the time of progress; beginnings move us toward middles that develop into ends that produce new beginnings. History, Hayden White explains, demands that "events must be not only registered within the chronological framework of their original occurrence but narrated as well, that is to say, revealed as possessing a structure, an order of meaning, that they do not possess as mere sequence."[7] Similarly, normative psychological narratives demand a progressive movement from sickness through struggle and back to wellness.

Not all events, however, conform to the demands of narrative time. As noted in chapter 1, one of the most salient psychological characteristics of traumatic experience is its failure to progress. The repetition of traumatic events and themes is equally characteristic of collective experience. As Taylor summarizes in the context of social trauma, there is "'no over' in situations of social violence."[8]

It is not surprising, then, that Jamaica Kincaid is fundamentally cynical about the model of narrative time as either historical or psychological progress. She creates a parable of this cynicism in her description of an Antiguan slave monument:

> We walked up a road, past a monument to commemorate a slave who had led a revolt. The monument was surrounded by a steel fence and the gate was locked; the fence made of steel and the locked gate weren't meant to be a part of this particular commemoration to this slave's heroism.[9]

Here, with biting wit, Kincaid uncovers the lies perpetuated in the name of narrative conclusions. Time has not moved forward for the slave represented in the monument; he remains imprisoned, locked in. If the middle of a story can be defined, as White defines it, as transition, as a kind of forward movement, then Antigua's history is perpetually trying to get started. It has not moved forward in time from its broken beginning.

Nor has North America's history moved forward. Although "for very convenient reasons [America] insists on this status, 'New World'" and although even "people from everywhere else, for myriad reasons, need it to be a 'New World,'"[10] it is not only subjugated peoples who have been held back by the delusion of progress. If the steel fence holds the slave in, it also holds the white master out, still imprisoned in his inability to move toward common ground. North American narrative time continues to be thwarted by abuses of power in the name of progress, mistakes we have repeated from our earliest recorded history.

The progress of Kincaid's brother's history is similarly stalled. Just as the monument to the heroic slave would tack a conclusion onto a story that has not yet been successfully inaugurated, so Kincaid's mother tries to write a narrative in which her son ends up sounder than he departed. At the end of the first section of the book, Kincaid's mother tells her that her brother "was very well, so well he might go to work; he found a job, but the person who had employed him ran out of money. He was better beyond anyone's expectation, he had gained quite a bit of weight, he was staying out all night, he was drinking beer."[11] Here, Kincaid's mother unwittingly demonstrates the lack of progress in the narrative of her brother's illness. At the midpoint of his story, her brother's story seems to be progressing. It is only returning to the same old beginning again.

Nor, it would seem, does Kincaid's own story progress. Kincaid ends her book with the assertion that she is still consumed with inauguration, with the beginning of her writing life. In so doing, she rehearses that beginning again:

> It was because I had neglected my brother when he was two years old and instead read a book that my mother gathered up all the books I owned and put them on a pile on her stone heap, sprinkling them with kerosene and then setting them alight; I cannot remember the titles of these books, I cannot remember what they were about (they would have been novels, at fifteen I read only novels), but it would not be so strange if I spent the rest of my life trying to bring those books back to my life by writing them again and again until they were perfect, unscathed by fire of any kind.[12]

Here, Kincaid rehearses a kind of resurrection, a return, through the act of narrating, of what she once lost. But it is difficult to know where—or whether—to locate hope in this passage. The phrase "until they were perfect" suggests at once a possible end time—"until"—and an impossible end state—"perfect." The book ends, then, with the imperative to begin writing. This imperative, like so many others—the imperative to live, to remember, to love—is never concluded, never done once and for all. But this is no reason not to keep writing. That there is "no over," as Taylor argues, "offers survivors the opportunity to reassert their capacity for intervention, no matter how overdue."[13]

The difference between Kincaid's repetition of her traumatic beginning and the other false inaugurations of which she writes is that she does not suffer from the delusion of narrative progress. On the contrary, for Kincaid, to practice beginning is precisely to let go of closure in favor of the continual struggle to come to terms with the violent and violated places and people she is from. Like Derrida's ghosts, these places and people return again and again. They are, to use Derrida's French and most precise term *revenants*—returning presences. Kincaid can never finish mourning the aborted stories of her brother, her country, her childhood. And it is because she can never conclude that Kincaid devotes herself to the only act in which she can ever find meaning: beginning again and again and again.

It is not only for her own good that Kincaid keeps returning to the beginning and refusing progress; it is also for the good of white readers. Kincaid is determined, in Toni Morrison's words, to demonstrate "the impact of racism on those who perpetuate it."[14] Kincaid challenges us not to build false monuments to progress but to hold a mirror up to the slave and, in doing so, to see ourselves.

Narrative Justice: The Regeneration of Language

What happens to a performer when the performance is over? For Peggy Phelan, the performer's body disappears—this is the very basis of performance's usefulness in understanding our relationship to loss. For Jacques Derrida, the body never completely disappears. Rather, it returns as a ghost, a revenant that continually haunts the living.

In *My Brother*, the body is neither permanently gone nor permanently present. Instead, it *grows back*. Jamaica Kincaid performs both death and mourning as regenerative phenomena, their reappearance mirroring most precisely the behavior of a weed in a garden that, no matter how many times it is uprooted, comes to the surface again.

In *AIDS and Its Metaphors*, Susan Sontag notes in passing the use of botanical metaphors in the description of AIDS. HIV is the "budding" stage of the disease, and it may be years before the patient develops "full-blown" AIDS. Her analysis suggests that this metaphor is inaccurate. It is cancer that makes cells proliferate, "bloom" out of control; in AIDS, cells die off.[15] But what is more important for Kincaid is that in both cases, the course of the plant's growth slips beyond the gardener's control.

Kincaid's lifelong interest in gardening began to occupy a central place in her writing around the time of her brother's dying. In a speech at Smith College in October 1995 that anticipated her 1999 collection of writings, *My Garden (Book)*, she described the botanical garden of her childhood as being associated "with our dominators, the English people, and their need to isolate, name, objectify, and possess various parts, people, and things in the world."[16] Against this imagery, Kincaid figures her brother's death as a weed, impossible to control or possess, unceasingly reproducing itself.

Kincaid's brother, ironically, had a facility with flowers, with living things; he might have been a gardener himself, she speculates. Now, though, his body itself is bitter, poisoned soil. Thrush flowers in his throat. His penis looks "like a bruised flower that had been cut short on the stem."[17] And deep inside his body "a death lives, flowering upon flowering, with a voraciousness that nothing seems able to satisfy and stop."[18] It is not cells per se but death itself that flowers, unstoppable, in Kincaid's brother. And so, Kincaid, a gardener herself, does what any good gardener does with any growth that threatens the garden's health: She weeds out her brother's death.

The first section of the book begins with her brother on his deathbed. It describes Kincaid's emergency visit to Antigua, where her brother is dying, her acquisition of the drug AZT from the United States, and the improvement of his condition "beyond anyone's expectation."[19] At the end of the first section, her brother seems to have made a full recovery. He is seeing friends, staying out all night. The flower of imminent death within him seems to have been uprooted, and Kincaid returns to America.

But the second section begins with the three-word sentence, "My brother died."[20] In this narrative moment immediately following his recovery, his death has grown back and has grown back with a vengeance. The language of his death reappears continuously throughout the second part of the book. "And my brother *died*," she writes again in the center of the second section, "for he kept *dying*; each time I remembered that he had *died* it was as if he had just at that moment *died*, and the whole experience of it would begin again"[21] (emphasis added). Here, Kincaid moves almost imperceptibly from performing her brother's death to performing her experience of that death and her mourning. Through the continual reiteration of his death, Kincaid performs mourning as that which, like death, grows back, re-members itself.

It grows back not only phenomenologically but historically:

> This way of behaving, this way of feeling, so hysterical, so sad, when someone has died, I don't like at all and would like to avoid. It's not as if the whole thing has not happened before; it's not as if people have not been dying all along and each person left behind is the first person ever left behind in the world. What to make of it? Why can't everybody just get used to it?[22]

Here, Kincaid figures mourning not only as an individual trauma but as a collective one. As Kincaid would like to weed out the regeneration of her own experience of mourning, so she would like to weed out the historical regeneration of mourning as the necessary and emotionally painful response to death across time ("all along") and across cultures ("everybody"). But she knows she cannot. The very absurdity of the question "Why can't everybody just get used to it?" underscores the power of the figures of death and mourning as regenerating phenomena.

> . . . if it is so certain, death, why is it such a surprise, why is everybody who is left behind, who is not dead, in a state of such shock, as if this thing, death, this losing forever of someone who means something to you, has never happened before. Why is it so new, why is this worn-out thing, death, so new, so new?[23]

Here, fifty pages after she first excised it through articulation, even Kincaid's question about the historical regeneration of death grows back.

This growing back of language about loss in *My Brother* acts upon us as readers and causes us to re-act in a fundamentally different way than would a single, discursive statement about mourning as regeneration. Through her rehearsals of writing about loss, Kincaid invites us to practice a losing that returns each time we weed/read it out. As the mourner must respond to death again and again as if it were new, so in Kincaid's regenerating narrative, we are asked to respond to her recurring description of the experience of loss anew.

As a response to the regeneration of bodies, both writing and reading regenerate themselves in the memoir. *My Brother* is at least as much the story of Kincaid's saving herself as it is the story of her brother's death. These two processes, her brother's dying and her own living, are linked, metaphorically, by a single act: reading. From an early age, her mother demands that Kincaid "forgo something or other that had previously occupied my leisure time, and then something or other that was essential (my schooling), to take care of these small children who were not mine."[24] But she disobeys this command. Forced one day in her youth to make the unnatural choice between nurturing herself and providing care for her baby brother, Kincaid chooses the former; she reads a book instead of changing his diaper as she has been instructed to do by her absent mother. By reading, she is training herself, even here, to stand outside the fate of her family, whose "prospects were not more than the contents of my brother's diaper, and the contents were only shit."[25] The young Kincaid, then, disobeys her mother by reading, thereby mothering herself instead of her brother.

Kincaid's mother cannot abide such a choice. Upon returning to her reading/living daughter and her soiled/dying son, she turns her wrath against Jamaica and, in the passage quoted earlier, burns her books. Kincaid returns to this act several times in the memoir, always linking it to the image of her brother's dirty diaper. The passage resonates strongly with her description, in *A Small Place*, of the destruction of the national library:

> It's a good thing that you brought your own books with you, for you couldn't just go to the library and borrow some. Antigua used to have a splendid library, but in The Earthquake . . . the library building was damaged. This was in 1974, and soon after that a sign was placed on the front of the building saying, THIS BUILDING WAS DAMAGED IN THE EARTHQUAKE OF 1974. REPAIRS ARE PENDING. The sign hangs there, and hangs there more than a decade later, with its unfulfilled promise of repair . . . [26]

Later in *A Small Place*, Kincaid explains that, had the reader seen the old library, "you would see why my heart would break at the dung heap that now passes for a library in Antigua."[27] In both texts, Kincaid condemns the destruction of books through a metaphor of excrement.

Kincaid describes the whole of her writing life as a response to her mother's early attempts to decimate her relationship to language. As death grows back in her brother's body, words grow back in her own. Kincaid reads, and later writes, against the violences of forgetting. She performs her writing as the only *revenant* rivaling death, the only other thing that has the power to return once gone: "The source of the books has not died, it only comes alive again and again in different forms and other segments."[28] By writing her lost books again and again, Kincaid raises the dead. In so doing, she saves herself, avenges herself against a family, a nation, and a global community that would have let the source and sustenance of her life go up in flames.

My Brother ends, somewhat anachronistically, with the abbreviated story of another death entirely, the death of Kincaid's "perfect reader," her longtime editor, William Shawn:

> For a very long time I had the perfect reader for what I would write and place in the unscathed books. . . . The perfect reader has died, but I cannot see any reason not to write for him anyway, for I can sooner get used

> to never hearing from him—the perfect reader—than to not being able to write for him at all.[29]

It may seem odd that Kincaid ends her memoir of her brother's death with a reference to someone from her professional life in North America who appears nowhere else in the story. But through this ending, Kincaid calls us to our responsibility as readers. If writing is the living revenant, this ending suggests, reading is the productive force behind its perpetual return. The act of witnessing lost bodies in language itself requires an audience, and if the perfect audience has died then we, her current readers, must serve as surrogates, reading in his place. Indeed, through a simple substitution in the story of Kincaid's childhood trauma cited earlier, it is easy to understand reading, like writing, as an ongoing attempt to recover a sense of wholeness:

> I cannot remember the titles of these books, I cannot remember what they were about (they would have been novels, at fifteen I read only novels), but it would not be so strange if I spent the rest of my life trying to bring those books back to my life by *reading* them again and again until they were perfect, unscathed by fire of any kind. (emphasis added)[30]

In reading, we, too, participate in regenerating language. We share the responsibility for its survival.

Emotional Justice: Deconstructing Grief

My Brother is not a tender story of dedication and transformation at the end of a life. It is true that Kincaid is performing the role of a good sister, flying home to take care of her dying brother. But make no mistake: She is not happy about it. Now that she has, after many years as an au pair and many more as a struggling journalist, attained success and comfort as a writer in North America, she is not eager to return to her homeland to help her sick and dying brother. On top of it all, her brother wants her shorts:

> [E]arlier he [her brother] had taken me aside to ask me for the pair of shorts that I was wearing; they were a pair of khaki shorts I usually wear when I go hiking in the mountains. I gave them to him, and even though I could easily replace them, I did not like giving them to him at all. I did not want them back, I wanted not to have had to give them to him in the first place.[31]

This emotional and material stinginess on Kincaid's part gives me hope. When I read Mitch Albom's bestseller *Tuesdays with Morrie*, I think, *I will never mourn this reflectively.* When I read John Bayley's *Elegy for Iris*, I think, *I will never mourn this peacefully.* But Kincaid's bitter, generous, conflicted, combustible mourning is a mourning I can reach. Kincaid cannot be understood as a "good" mourner by conventional North American standards. Yet, her anger is startling in its honesty and power. Her writing demands a reimagining of what it means to mourn well.

In Della Pollock's influential essay on the subject, she characterizes performative writing as evocative, conjuring "worlds that are other-wise intangible, unlocatable: worlds of memory, pleasure, sensation, imagination, affect, and in-sight."[32] Insofar as performative writing aims to evoke the affective force of its subject, Kincaid's writing seems absolutely unperformative. She names her feelings, but she specifically refuses to "do" them. She even speaks about valuing writing not for its ability to make her feel the experience of her brother's death but for its ability to distance her, to help her "think about him in a purposeful way,"[33] to "make an attempt at understanding his dying,"[34] to withstand and stand apart from it.

The writing seems unperformative, but it isn't. Part of what Kincaid is performing is the inseparability of an individual act of mourning from issues of race and class, specifically, the extent to which a youth of poverty and powerlessness in Antigua has hardened her fellow Antiguans against feeling empathy for others.

What mitigates the cruelty in Kincaid's mourning voice is its other salient characteristic: repetition. Repetition is, as we have already seen, critical to the process of negotiating catastrophic loss. Describing the psychoanalytic dialogue around Sigmund Freud's classic case of the father's recurring dream of his burning child, Cathy Caruth explains that the survivor of trauma must "receive the very gap between the other's death and his own life, the one who, in awakening, *does not see but enacts* the impact of the very difference between death and life"[35] (emphasis added). To survive is, therefore, to return again and again to others whose absence one does not "see" (understand) but nonetheless "does" (performs): "To awaken is thus to bear the imperative to survive: to survive no longer simply as the father of a child, but as the one who must tell *what it means not to see*"[36] (emphasis original). Kincaid enacts this imperative to survive in her repeated witnessing of her brother's death.

In *My Brother*, Kincaid explains that she uses repetition to make difficult-to-know things known to herself. She insists on naming, without allusion, her brother's disease: "It was for my own peace of mind that I said it; I wanted it to be real to me, that my brother was suffering and dying from AIDS; hearing that he was sick and dying was new to me and so every opportunity I got I would say it out loud: 'my brother is sick from and dying of AIDS.'"[37] Similarly, when Kincaid sees her brother's dead body, her description is riddled with repetition:

> [H]is hair was nicely combed and dyed black—for how else could it have gotten to such a color—his lips were clamped tightly together and they made a shape that did not amount to his mouth as I had known it; and his eyes had been sewn shut, sewn shut, and I have to say it again, sewn shut.[38]

As she repeats not once but twice this final detail of her brother's physical appearance, Kincaid forces herself to do what her brother cannot do: see.

If repetition helps us to comprehend trauma, it also troubles easy answers. Reiteration is the means by which, in classical theories of deconstruction, the aporias or gaps in language are laid bare. As Kincaid's use of repetition underscores her need for rehearsal, it demonstrates the emotional complexity of death and mourning, deconstructing concepts we recall and rehearse too easily in our practices, especially death, grief, and love.

Death

Kincaid's repetitions deconstruct the binary separation between life and death. In Kincaid's descriptions of an AIDS death, life and death repeatedly infect one another until it becomes difficult to tell exactly which is which. Of course, Kincaid suggests, all lives and deaths infect each other. Death is always present in life in "the usual ways": "the airplane on which I flew from place to place might fall out of the sky, a vessel in my brain might suddenly burst, my heart might be stilled as if someone had reached in and stopped it."[39]

But this is very different from the life and death of the person with AIDS: "On one side, there is life, and the thin shadow of death hovers over it; and on the other, there is death with a small patch of life attached to it. This latter is the life of AIDS."[40] In the body of a person with AIDS, then, death is unusually present. This is true for Kincaid's brother and, indeed, seems always to have been true. Kincaid repeatedly represents her brother's living and dying as unstable terms, one continually threatening to overturn the other.

Death appeared in Kincaid's brother's life only hours after his birth. The day after he was born, when he lay against his mother's body sleeping, "an army of red ants came in through the window and attacked him. My mother heard her child crying, and when she awoke, she found him covered with red ants. If he had been alone, it is believed they would have killed him."[41] Kincaid compares this early near-death experience of her brother's with his ultimate death from AIDS, and this infuriates her mother: "But I was only wondering if it had any meaning that some small red things had almost killed him from the outside shortly after he was born and that now some small things were killing him from the inside."[42]

What links this first "death" of Kincaid's brother's to his ultimate death and what distinguishes it from the ordinary sense in which death is always within us are death's visibility: "Perhaps everyone is living in death, I actually do believe that, but usually it can't be seen; in his case it was a death I could see."[43] In this way, Kincaid insists on the specificity of AIDS death: "to have the HIV virus is to have crossed the line between life and death."[44] But in her memoir, Kincaid's brother seems to cross and recross this line.

Death always infects her brother's life. Even when, at the end of the first section of the book, he seems to have recovered, Kincaid concludes the section by harkening to her first glimpse of his face following his diagnosis, a face "full of deep suffering, beyond regrets or pleadings for a second chance."[45] He is "living while being dead,"[46] having "been dead for at least a year before the breath left his body."[47] No matter how alive her brother may seem, he is always already dead and gone.

At the same time, Kincaid's relentless repetition of the central fact of the book, "My brother died," gives her brother a curious, forceful presence in the narrative. Through this repetition of the words "My brother died," it is not just her brother's death but her brother's life that become real to Kincaid, more real than it has ever been. Through these repetitive deconstructions of the terms *life* and *death*, Kincaid wants to distinguish AIDS as a particularly liminal death, one that thwarts our attempts to distinguish—as it were, to quarantine—these states.

Grief

Kincaid's repetitions also deconstruct normative concepts of grief as a sorrowful display. Against the overwhelming cultural expectation that a death—any death but certainly the death of a family member—will produce sadness, Kincaid insists, watching a child's funeral in her country, on the irreducible complexity and particularity of feelings surrounding loss:

> [A]ll this made me *not sad* then, only now when I think of it am I sad, at the time when I was taking in the whole spectacle, at some moments I felt disdain, at some moments I felt triumphant, at some moments I felt awe, at some moments I felt bewilderment, at some moments I had a revelation; but *never did I feel sad* then. (emphasis added)[48]

Here, in discursive miniature and by way of a funeral that is not his, Kincaid represents her response to her brother's death, a death that arouses a plethora of feelings (add to the list in his case anger and guilt) but repeatedly refuses the ones we most expect and even demand of those in mourning. When she sees her brother for the last time, for example, Kincaid repeats not her sadness but her distaste for her dying brother:

> I was so *tired of him* being in this state, not alive, not dead, but constantly with his demands, in want, constantly with his necessities, weighing on my sympathy, at times preying on my sympathy, whichever way it fell, I was *sick of him* and wanted him to go away, and I *didn't care* if he got better and I *didn't care* if he died. That was just the way I felt, that was the only thing I felt just at that moment when he would not die and when he would not live; I only wanted him to do one or the other and then *leave me alone.* (emphasis added)[49]

Similarly, when her husband tells her of her brother's death, Kincaid feels not sadness but a mixture of relief and surprise—relief that this is not a death her husband will have to mourn—"I was so glad about that, so glad at the thought, the feeling that this death, this look of sadness in his face, had to do with someone who was not related to him"[50]—and surprise "even though I had been expecting it."[51]

And tears? Well, yes, there are tears, but these have a very brief place in the story. In the second to last sentence of the narrative, Kincaid describes the eulogy for her brother given by their other brother. "His voice broke as he spoke of his brother; I cried when I heard him speak of his brother, but why did he and I do that."[52] This reaction that we most expect, a sister crying at her brother's funeral, is least explicable and in many ways least valuable to the mourner herself. Even if, in the end, Kincaid does manage to cry a little (if not quite "the right amount"), she does not do so for the right reason or, as she would have it, for any reason at all. If Kincaid shrinks from the tears she finally sheds at the end of the book, perhaps it is because she recognizes the danger that the complexities of her narrative could be wiped out by this single normative display.

Love

Kincaid's repetitions also complicate assumptions of love between a dying man and his sister. "I did not love him," Kincaid asserts early in her tale. "What I felt might have been love, but I still, even now, would not call it so."[53] And yet, even earlier in the story, "It surprised me that I loved him; I could see that was what I was feeling, love for him, and it surprised me because I did not know him at all."[54] But, of course, we love our brothers and sisters. Or we are expected to.

Once we know more of the history of the relationship between this brother and sister, we, too, might be surprised that she feels love for him. It is not only that when Kincaid leaves home for good, he is three years of age. It is not only that she wishes he had never been born, as any jealous, older child wishes a newer sibling had not been born. It is that the material circumstances of Kincaid's life are dramatically and adversely affected by his birth, because "it was his birth that plunged our family into financial despair."[55] How can she love this person whose only contribution to her home life was to destroy it?

Still, she does love him . . . doesn't she? No, she insists, "I did not love my brother, I did not like my brother."[56] What she feels for her brother is "not love, but a powerful feeling all the same, only not love."[57] And yet, so many of Kincaid's sentences admit the fact—and then, backing off, the possibility—of her love: "I did not love him or did not recognize my feelings for him as being love."[58] And "someone I did not know I loved had died, someone I did not want to love had died."[59] In meaningfully contorted syntax, she allows for the possibility of discovering love for her brother in the distant future: "One day something may happen and I will understand that all the things I now feel, which do not at all seem like love, . . . are in fact love."[60]

But she does love him . . . doesn't she? Kincaid explains that the reason we are so hung up on love is not that it is good, but that it is simple: "*Love* always feels much better than not-love, and that is why everybody always talks about *love* and that is why everybody always wants to have *love*: because it feels so much better, so much better" (emphasis added).[61] Real feeling, Kincaid suggests, is not so simple. "I love the people I am from and I do not love the people I am from, and I do not really know what it means to say so, only that such a thing as no love now and much love now, these feelings are not permanent, or possibly not permanent."[62] Here Kincaid deconstructs not only the singularity and the comprehensibility of love but the myth of love's constancy. In doing so, she removes it from the realm of the nameable and knowable.

As the repetition in Kincaid's narrative voice always threatens to overshadow or outdo its angry tone, so does the narrative content. However removed or indifferent she may sound, Kincaid does not act coldly or cruelly. She is, on the contrary, extraordinarily generous. She acts like someone who cares deeply or, to use her word, "powerfully," about her brother. Kincaid, however, vigilantly contextualizes this narrative, articulating an economy of feeling; to the extent that she as a North American is both more empathic and more sentimental, making more of a display of support than her Antiguan counterparts. It is only because her position of economic and social privilege enables her to be so.

Mourning in Antigua: The Local Economy of Feeling

By devoting significant space in her memoir to the physical and cultural landscape of Antigua, Kincaid articulates the importance of locating mourning on a particular ground, even as she illuminates the ways in which that ground can and must be shifted. In so doing, she responds to the call of race theorist Paul Gilroy, who urges attention to "the relationship of identity and non-identity in black political culture."[63] Although the uniqueness of Antigua should not be used to excuse "the pursuit of any unifying dynamic or underlying structure of feeling in contemporary black culture,"[64] its particularity matters and must be addressed.

The climate of the narrative in *My Brother* is one of protracted decay. Like her brother's body, Antigua has fallen into disrepair. On the first night of her visit, Kincaid takes a hired car from the hospital to her hotel and describes, as she passes them, sign after sign of deterioration. The stoplight at the major crosswalk is broken. The Happy Acres Hotel is no more. Even the Dead House, a temporary storage place for dead bodies not yet claimed by their families, has been torn down. Such details continue to accrue throughout the book as Kincaid travels back and forth, takes a walk with her brother, or sits in the unsanitary hospital room. "Antigua," Kincaid tells us, "is a place like that: parts for everything are no longer being made anywhere in the world."[65] Most of all, however, Antigua does not have the power to repair itself; "in Antigua itself nothing is made."[66] In this ground, nothing grows but death.

In the context of her brother's dying, Kincaid places the blame for the landscape's decay differently than she otherwise might. In *A Small Place*, Kincaid asks the presumed white, North American or European reader,

> Have you ever wondered to yourself why it is that all people like me seem to have learned from you is how to imprison and murder each other, how to govern badly, and how to take the wealth of our country and place it in Swiss bank accounts? Have you ever wondered why it is that all we seem to have learned from you is how to corrupt our societies and how to be tyrants? You will have to accept that this is mostly your fault.[67]

In *My Brother*, however, Kincaid insists that the cause of the deterioration is not external: it is native neglect. Antigua belongs to "the self-destructive of the world."[68] Its hospital, which was "never a great hospital" under the English colonial government, "is a terrible hospital now" under self-rule.[69] Its government, which was never a good government, now "made up of people with his [her brother's] own complexion, his own race," is "corrupt and did not care whether he or other people like him lived or died."[70] When a British woman suggests to Kincaid that racism is to blame for her brother's continued illness, Kincaid responds, "[I]t must be, in some way, very nice to have the all too real evil of racism to blame. But it was not racism that made my brother lie dying of an incurable disease in a hospital in the country in which he was born; it was the sheer accident of life, it was his own fault."[71] Antigua, Kincaid insists, is a political and cultural body that refuses to take care of itself.

Kincaid continually reasserts the idea that the Antiguan people are neglectful of their bodies and lives. An HIV–prevention effort fails on the island because, as the young men tell the native doctor, "[T]hey would rather die than leave the butter women alone."[72] So, Kincaid's brother, newly released from the hospital, immediately begins to drink, stay out all night, and have unprotected sex.

There is no helping these bodies, no enriching a soil that will not nurture itself. Even if the landscape of his body were to be repaired by the acquisition of some foreign "part," Kincaid insists that her brother would not become productive, more responsible: "[S]o many times we used to say that if by some miracle Devon could be cured of his disease he would not change his ways; he would not become industrious, holding three jobs at once to make ends meet; he would not become faithful to one woman or one man."[73] Similarly, the Antiguan landscape never changes:

> And that day that he was buried was not at all unlike the day on which I first saw him lying almost dead in a bed in the Gweneth O'Reilly ward of the Holberton Hospital. All days in Antigua must be the same, people count on it, it is for this reason they go there, it is for this reason they leave there; the days are the same, the sun shines, no rain will fall, the sun rises at around six in the morning, the sun sets at around six in the evening.[74]

Kincaid's brother's death is as predictable as the Antiguan sun.

The emotional landscape of Antigua mirrors its physical atmosphere. The psychological climate of the narrative is one of indifference, from the midwife who tells Kincaid's mother that she will not come and assist with Kincaid's brother's birth until she has finished her supper, to the simultaneous funerals at the end of the book in which "[t]he other dead man's family did not say a sympathetic word to us and we did not say a sympathetic word to them."[75]

Kincaid says of Antiguans, "We are not an instinctively empathetic people."[76] And specifically, in the treatment and care of people with AIDS, she notes, "[P]ublic concern, obsession with the treatment and care of members of the AIDS–suffering community by groups in the larger non–AIDS-suffering community, does not exist" in Antigua.[77] So that when Kincaid attends an AIDS workshop given by her brother's doctor, Dr. Ramsey, she comments, "This was something very new to me: ordinary people in Antigua expressing sympathy and love for one another at a time of personal tragedy and pain, not scorn or rejection or some other form of cruelty."[78] Ordinary Antiguans, Kincaid insists, are indifferent to each other's pain.

This emphasis on her country's self-neglect is curious and uncharacteristic on Kincaid's part because, of course, racism *is* a part of this body politic and certainly not an insignificant part. This ground is not only a ground of internal neglect; it is also a ground of violence and neglect by the developed world. In his opening remarks at the AIDS in Context Conference in Johannesburg, South Africa, South African Supreme Court of Appeals Judge Edwin Cameron said with sorrow, "Of all the desolate figures and statistics in this epidemic, none is more awesome than this—that two thirds of all those living with HIV and AIDS in the world are in Sub-Saharan Africa; and that *90% of them are in the developing world*" (emphasis added).[79] Cameron argues that the use of the lack of infrastructure within these countries as an argument for keeping life-saving medications inaccessible is morally indefensible.

More broadly, that the Antiguans fail at self-rule cannot be separated from their long history of subjugation, the history for which Kincaid so viciously blames the white reader in *A Small Place*. Kincaid's brother knows this as well as she does: "[H]e thought (as do I) that this history of ours was primarily an account of theft and murder ('Dem tief, dem a dam tief')."[80] Despite her emphasis on the nation's self-neglect, Kincaid hints at Antigua's inheritance of violence throughout *My Brother*.

Echoing her description of the Antiguan slave monument, Kincaid describes her brother as a would-be extraordinary thinker: "He was not meant to be silent. He was a brilliant boy, he was a brilliant man. Locked up inside him was someone who would have spoken to the world in an important way. I believe this."[81] As the revolutionary slave was not meant to be fenced in by his own monument, so Kincaid's brother was not meant to be silenced by his own identity. As Antigua has continually reenslaved itself by perpetuating a legacy of violence, corruption, and inequality, so the developed world's neglect of the AIDS epidemic continues to erect silencing, steel fences around our most beloved, most brilliant young bodies.

Yet, we should not allow ourselves to think that our governments are more culpable than ourselves. The stigma attached to AIDS death, dying, and mourning has been widely documented. Kenneth Doka's work has been devoted to developing an understanding of griefs that are culturally disenfranchised for a variety of reasons: "In few other areas of care for the dying and their loved ones is the concept of disenfranchised grief likely to be more powerfully demonstrated than with AIDS."[82] Neil Small elaborates: "The public presentation of the disease had continually to be tempered with the realization that elaborate stigmatization was attached to those with the virus and, indeed, to those identified with what were considered high-risk life-styles, those of gay men in particular."[83] Small notes that this stigmatization does not end with the AIDS victim's death but is perpetuated by practices of inaccurate reporting on death certificates. "It may be that the doctor considers that they have fulfilled . . . their duty to the patients and family by omitting the diagnosis from the certificate."[84]

Although it is the context of homophobia that is most often cited in the stigmatization of the AIDS victim, other axes of discrimination are also operative. These include "the wealth and power inequalities between the first world and the rest, poverty within countries as well as between, racism, the oppression of women and prejudice against gay men and women."[85] Despite the cliché of AIDS as a global epidemic, there are also, as Small argues, meaningful differences between and within nations.

In parentheses amidst the retelling of a conversation with her mother, Kincaid describes her "now privileged North American way" of speaking: "(my voice full of pity at the thought of any kind of destruction, as long as my great desires do not go unmet in any way)."[86] Reading this parenthetical statement backwards, it is only that her "great desires do not go unmet" that allows Kincaid's voice to be "full of pity," full of concern for someone else. If ordinary Antiguans, conversely, do not express sympathy for someone else's pain, it is because their own pain is too great; their "great desires," and even their most basic ones—an attentive mother, a sanitary hospital, access to books—have gone unmet. They literally cannot afford to be empathic.

Kincaid's performance of mourning in *My Brother* defies Western cultural norms about both emotional and historical progress following traumatic loss, complicates traditional understandings of concepts such as death, grief and love, and illustrates an economy of feeling in which only the materially privileged can afford to be emotionally free.

Losses in Representation

Kincaid does not perform the lost story of her brother's life so much as she repeatedly marks the loss of his story. She can no more fill, by writing, the absence of his story than she can bring him back to life. And, like Suzan-Lori Parks (see chapter 6), she is careful to mark this necessary incompleteness of her narrative. She makes it clear that it is the loss of her brother's ability to represent himself more than the loss of his living body that she mourns:

> A great sadness overcame me, and the source of the sadness was the deep feeling I had always had about him: that he had died without ever understanding or knowing, or being able to let the world in which he lived know, who he was; that who he really was—not a single sense of identity but all the complexities of who he was—he could not express fully.[87]

To write the story of losing her brother, then, is not only to write what his story does—ends, disappears—but what that story is: an absence. A silence. Perhaps this absence, too, contributes to Kincaid's sometimes detached tone. After all, how can one mourn what was never really there?

Kincaid marks not only the absence of his story but the absence of a language in which to tell it:

> But the feeling that his life with its metaphor of the bud of a flower firmly set, blooming, and then the blossom fading, the flower setting a seed which bore inside another set of buds, leading to flowers, and so on and so on into eternity—this feeling that his life actually should have provided such a metaphor, so ordinary an image, so common and so welcoming had it been just so, could not leave me.[88]

Here, her own silence mirrors and echoes her brother's.

Kincaid does not fully understand this suppression of her brother's story until very near the conclusion of the book when at a reading in Chicago following her brother's death, a stranger informs her of a central fact of her brother's life: he was a homosexual. Then, what she fully understands is how much she will never know of her brother, how much he never allowed himself to know of himself. And this not because of time, not because her brother died young but because of oppression and fear.

At the same time, as Kincaid discursively marks the loss of her brother's story, she marks the loss of a story of her own. For all of the details of her childhood that Kincaid remembers, it is this memory that haunts her, rising to the surface of its own accord: the memory of *what did not happen.* The memory of the life she did not lead. This, above all, is the importance of her brother's life for Kincaid:

> I shall never forget him, my brother, but this was not because of his smile, or the way he crossed a swelling river and saved a dog, or his sense of humor, or his love of John Milton . . . I shall never forget him because his life is the one I did not have, the life that, *for reasons I hope shall never be too clear to me*, I avoided or escaped. (emphasis added)[89]

More than any neglected act of caretaking, it is her refusal to live in her brother's locked-up place that haunts Kincaid.

It haunts her every word. Kincaid evades not only her family's life but their language. She distinguishes between the kind of English her family speaks and "de kind of English that I now immediately understand."[90] Her text is sprinkled with small segments of her family's language, relegated to—locked up in—parentheses, that she translates for us in the main body of the text. Sometimes, her family's expressions would likely be readable without translation—("Me hear you a come but me no tink you a come fo' true")—sometimes they would indeed be incomprehensible—("Me no get dat chupidness, man")—but Kincaid always decodes her family's words for the reader, always acting as mediator between their language and ours.

Except for its purest, most emotional appeals, Kincaid's brother's voice is always surrounded, locked up, outspoken by the more refined English of his self-described privileged, North American sister, who has made a profession of using her voice. The presence of native expressions underscores the extent to which it is her absence from her family and country that enable Kincaid to be present to us. Only because she did not live her brother's life can Kincaid write about it.

And if the story of Kincaid's adult life in Antigua is missing from her narrative, so, too, is the story of her premature death. Although Kincaid is, to some extent, the hero of her brother's story, the North American sister who flies in to supply order, love, and AZT, the book is haunted by questions of her own evasions concerning the care of her brother. Kincaid performs her guilt concerning her failures in meeting the moral claim—a claim of Biblical proportions—of the person to whom she refers in the title and throughout the book as "my brother." (Her brother's name appears only a handful of times late in the text.) Like Cain, Kincaid is haunted by her brother's death, a death that might have been hers and for which, therefore, she feels herself in some elusive but profound way responsible.

Kincaid writes *My Brother* against a group of cultural expectations concerning mourning, race, and history. She writes against that most powerful imperative that our historical narratives progress, against the expectation that mature and civilized mourning is comprised of sadness and love, and against the pernicious cultural habit in America of ignoring the racial and national particularity of certain kinds of grief, loss, and violence. Further, the memoir's very existence as writing is a subversive performance; Kincaid writes against the expectation that a person of her race, class, and nationality would ever write at all. By writing *My Brother*, Kincaid acts upon her own responsibility to work for an end to illiteracy and, with it, poverty, racism, classism, and colonialism. She enacts her responsibility to work for justice—and not just for her brother.

Kincaid insists on the critical relationships between neglected bodies and neglected countries; fenced-in slaves and fenced-out masters; reading, writing, and staying alive. She refuses to relegate mourning to the hypocritical position of the fenced-in monument to liberation. A liberated mourning is neither isolated nor comfortable. It is meticulously historically, geographically, economically, and racially contextualized. Kincaid's angry and reiterative mourning insists on practicing responsibility for the losses of our dying brothers and sisters by all who continue to live well at their expense.

6. Practicing Compensation: Filling the Great Holes of History

A MAN STANDS ALONE ON STAGE. He is standing in a large hole. The hole is not the first hole; it is a copy of another hole, a very old one. He tells the audience a story of a man who loses his life. Sometimes, the man in the hole speaks his own words; sometimes, he speaks someone else's.

A woman sits alone on stage. Next to her is a table, on which rest a small lamp and a book—a history book, a very old one. Beneath her feet lies a rug, and on top of the rug sits a brown paper shopping bag. She tells the audience the story of a man who lost a part of his body. Sometimes, the woman in the chair speaks her own words; sometimes, she speaks someone else's.

These are key scenes from two contemporary American plays. They are scenes about history, about how to account for the pieces of history that have been lost without anyone mourning their passing. The scenes differ in culture, style, and subject matter. But they echo each other across these differences, animated by a similar yearning, a similar impulse to compensate for something that has too long been missing.

In *The Archive and The Repertoire*, Diana Taylor urges scholars in performance and cultural studies to attend to what she calls scenarios (rather than texts) in order to articulate cultural, social, and historical meanings. The scenario as a methodological tool "includes features well theorized in literary analysis, such as narrative and plot" but is also broader, demanding "that we also pay attention to milieux and corporeal behaviors such as gestures, attitudes, and tones not reducible to language."[1] The scenario is situated in time, space, and bodies (both the "actors'" bodies and the relationship between the actors and the witnesses or audience), but it is not necessarily mimetic. It is characterized by and derives its power from its ability to reactivate, rather than duplicate, past situations. As an example, Taylor offers the scenario of conquest, which has been replayed and subverted throughout the Americas for many centuries: "Scenarios change and adapt, but they don't seem to go away."[2] Rather, they are reactivated over periods of years and sometimes decades by a wide variety of social and political situations.

I want to use the analytical category of the scenario but make two disciplinary corrections in the process. First, I employ the scenario in a way that Taylor might consider anachronistic: to read texts. Although I have seen and refer to multiple stagings of one of these texts,[3] I am most interested here in focusing on the losses they mark most permanently, as indicated by their archival or written forms. Second, I focus not on scenarios activated in history and everyday life, as Taylor primarily does, but on dramatic scenarios. In focusing on the scenario as it appears in drama as opposed to other cultural forms, I am responding to theater scholar Jill Dolan's plea that we return the insights of performance studies scholarship to theater studies, her desire to "see theatre studies acknowledged and visited, rather than raided and discarded, as part of the proliferation of the performative."[4] In Suzan-Lori Parks's *The America Play* and Tony Kushner's *Homebody/Kabul*, performance does not merely raid material from culture but provides culture with tools for responding better to its most persistent absences.

The scenario I want to forward as being of major importance in contemporary drama and, therefore, in contemporary culture is that of *filling a hole*, whether in discourse, human relations, or history itself. Parks deliberately and playfully places the action of her play around—and sometimes in—a hole. She joins other major twentieth-century playwrights who have staged holes, from Samuel Beckett, whose *Happy Days* features a character progressively swallowed up by one, to Arthur Miller whose *Crucible* can only be filled with human scapegoats. Della Pollock observes that the historical hole has been of interest to theorists of culture for some time, from the early deconstructionist project to uncover the essential instability of meanings to a postmodern historicity adrift in "radical contingency and partiality."[5] The desire to fill the great holes of history is intimately related to the desire to account for and, sometimes, to compensate for loss.

On the surface, it may seem misguided to look to a medium that scholars and practitioners alike have long valued for its ephemeral nature to fill in for anything. However, it is precisely the precariousness of its ontology that makes performance a uniquely powerful tool for addressing the most cavernous holes in our cultural stories. This is not to say that performance always succeeds in filling historical holes. Indeed, its success is always partial.

Race and *The America Play*

In the beginning, all the world was America.
—John Locke, quoted in *The America Play*

Arguably the deepest hole in American history is the absence of the African American experience from the public archive. The historicity of this hole, its existence over so many centuries of American life, makes it uniquely difficult to fill. Toni Morrison notes that it was "in the absence of real knowledge or open-minded inquiry about Africans and African-Americans" that early American attitudes toward these peoples emerged.[6] Writing about the silence surrounding matters of race in contemporary literary discourse, Morrison argues that the historical problem is further compounded by "the fact that the habit of ignoring race is understood to be a graceful, even generous liberal gesture."[7] We have made the historical hole deeper through the practice of an insidious new cultural habit.

For playwright Suzan-Lori Parks, the solution to this problem is to write literature for the theater. Parks criticizes literary critics such as Henry Louis Gates Jr. for getting mired in discussions about "how the African-American literary contribution should be incorporated into the canon."[8] She sees theater as a powerful tool for creating new canons:

> Since history is a recorded or remembered event, theatre, for me, is the perfect place to "make" history—that is, because so much of African-American history has been unrecorded, dismembered, washed out, one of my tasks as a playwright is to—through literature and the special strange relationship between theatre and real-life—locate the ancestral burial ground, dig for bones, find bones, hear the bones sing, write it down.
>
> The bones tell us what was, is, will be; and because their song is a play—something that through a production *actually happens*—I'm working theatre like an incubator to create "new" historical events. I'm re-membering and staging historical events which, through their happening on stage, are ripe for inclusion in the canon of history. Theatre is an incubator for the creation of historical events—and, as in the case of artificial insemination, the baby is no less human. (emphasis original)[9]

Parks aims to fill the holes of history, not with literature alone but with the creation, through theater, of more history.

In some of Parks's plays, this new history seems entirely original, born of an extraordinary theatrical imagination that gives birth to characters with names such as Lots of Grease and Lots of Pork, who participate in events such as *The Death of the Last Black Man in the Whole Entire World*, and use words such as "do in diddly dip didded thuh drop," which she defines in her essay "Elements of Style" as "meaning unclear."[10] In other plays, however, Parks seems very consciously to be reworking or reactivating the elements of a received history to create something new. One discrete example of this is the history-teasing title of her contemporary riff on *The Scarlet Letter*, *Fucking A*. But nowhere is Parks's project to make "new" history more energetically animated than in her 1993 *The America Play*.

The America Play takes place astride—and sometimes inside—a hole. The dramatis personae, the stage directions at the beginning of the first act, and the stage directions at the beginning of the second act all place us at "A great hole. In the middle of nowhere. The hole is an exact replica of The Great Hole of History."[11] Before the hole stands another replica, a man "who was told that he bore a strong resemblance to Abraham Lincoln."[12] Through this man, Parks will work to fill the great hole.

The man is a gravedigger by trade but has made his livelihood as a Lincoln impersonator. He is named the Foundling Father and is also referred to as the Lesser Known. In the first act of the play, we watch him try, through direct speech to the audience and, to a lesser extent, through his assumed role of Abraham Lincoln, to fill various great holes in American history, including the hole in the head of the assassinated president and the hole between the "real" Lincoln and the imitation. We also learn of his wife and son, whom he left when the son was a child, in order to go "out West."[13] In the second act, we see the Foundling Father's wife, Lucy, and son, Brazil, still working to fill the hole he left in their lives when he abandoned them thirty years earlier (see fig. 6.1). In the final scene of the play, the Foundling Father, "dead but not really,"[14] returns to his wife and grown child to perform the death of Lincoln one final time.

Parks and her characters use a range of strategies to fill the holes their collective and individual histories have left them. Yet, even as she proliferates these strategies of compensation, Parks refuses to let the hole be completely covered up or forgotten.

Digging Up Difference

In her introduction to *Exceptional Spaces*, Della Pollock traces the important role that the idea of difference has had in the making of cultural theory over the last four decades and more, including Marxist, deconstructionist, and feminist perspectives. Summarizing a common question posed by each of these critical perspectives, Pollock asks how our stories about culture have "suppressed its historicity and so suppressed difference and the volcanic power of heterogeneity."[15] It has been the project of many influential cultural

Figure 6.1. The Foundling Father (left, Reggie Montgomery), Brazil (Michael Potts), and Lucy (Gail Grate) are atop the Great Hole of History in *The America Play.* Photo by Martha Swope, courtesy of Photofest.

theories—and many important artists—to expose particular differences that history has kept buried.

The America Play fills the great holes of history by uncovering and highlighting difference, especially the difference of the African American presence in American history. Parks's central character, the Foundling Father, underscores the differences between the historical power of whiteness and the powerlessness of blackness. People tell the Foundling Father that he is a "dead ringer" for Abraham Lincoln, that he "played Lincoln so well that he ought to be shot," and that he has a "virtual twinship with greatness."[16] And yet there is one critical difference between the Lesser Known and the Great Man: race. The Foundling Father never mentions this difference directly. Instead, he quotes strangers who remark upon "[h]ow, in a limited sort of way, taking into account of course his natural God-given limitations, how he was identical to the Great Man in gait and manner how his legs were long and torso short."[17] Through the event of digging up this difference and through the language she uses to enact it, Parks underscores how in America race can create the space between freedom and limitation, a foundling and a founder, a "great man" and a "lesser known."

One key difference between the two "fathers" lies in how they are mourned. Historically, the death of Lincoln was considered so important that the mourning words of his wife, son, and close associates were all documented in the historical archive. The Foundling Father quotes Mary Todd Lincoln's words, "*Emergency* oh, *Emergency*, please put the Great Man in the ground"[18] no fewer than five times. Of course, the Great Man was not only put in the ground but memorialized by one of the largest and most stately monuments ever to be built on American soil. Dramatically, the entire first act of *The America Play* revolves around the reenactment of Lincoln's death, suggesting American fascination, even obsession, with the assassination.

The death of the Foundling Father, by contrast, is unmarked. Lucy tells Brazil, "His lonely death and lack of proper burial is our embarrassment."[19] When, in his digging at the Great Hole of History—Brazil and Lucy are gravediggers by trade—Brazil uncovers an artifact that might have belonged to his father (a "medal for fakin"), he erupts into uncontrollable sobbing. A few moments later, he and Lucy have the following exchange that ends the scene:

BRAZIL: Mama Lucy?
LUCY: Whut.
BRAZIL:—Imissim—.
LUCY: Hhh. (*dig.*)[20]

Brazil's mourning for his father must be condensed into a single, halting word, to which his mother hardly responds before returning to the work of mourning (presumed white) strangers. Thirty years after his disappearance, there is still scant space for the mourning of the black man's life, even within his own family.

Joking with History

The America Play fills the great hole of history with cultural criticism delivered through the powerful vessel of humor. In addition to being one of her most strongly historical plays, *The America Play* is also one of Parks's funniest. "I can get more out of history if I joke with it than if I shake my finger at it and stomp my feet," Parks told Michele Pearce for *American Theatre* in 1994.[21] In *The America Play*, Parks repeats and revises two essential jokes: one about our insatiable appetite for violence, the other about our selective appetite for truth.

In the first act of *The America Play*, the Foundling Father tells us that, as an ordinary Lincoln impersonator, he was "a curiosity at best."[22] It took a more sensational idea to make this repetition of history sell. And a more violent one:

> The Lesser Known returned to his hole and, instead of speeching, his act would now consist of a single chair, a rocker, in a dark box. The public was invited to pay a penny, choose from the selection of provided pistols, enter the darkened box and "Shoot Mr. Lincoln." The Lesser Known became famous overnight.[23]

Here, Parks satirizes not only our general cultural preference for violence over visionary "speeching" but our more particular desire to scapegoat the "lesser-knowns," especially those of color.

From this moment on, the Foundling Father's monologue is regularly interrupted by the appearance of "visitors," customers who pay him for the privilege of participating in the reenactment of Abraham Lincoln's murder:

THE FOUNDLING FATHER: What interested the Lesser Known most was the murder and what was most captivating about the murder was the twenty feet—

(A Woman, as Booth, enters.)

A WOMAN: Excuse me.

THE FOUNDLING FATHER: Not at all.

(A Woman, as Booth, "stands in position.")

THE FOUNDLING FATHER: Haw Haw Haw Haw.

(rest)

HAW HAW HAW HAW

(Booth shoots. Lincoln "slumps in his chair." Booth jumps.)

A WOMAN: "Strike the tent." (*Exits.*)

THE FOUNDLING FATHER: What interested the Lesser Known most about the Great Mans murder was the 20 feet which separated the presidents box from the stage.[24]

This small scene is repeated with revision six more times over the course of the first act. Sometimes, the visitor playing Booth is a man, sometimes a woman, once a newlywed couple. Sometimes, as above, the visitor shouts the words of Robert E. Lee, sometimes the words of Mary Todd Lincoln, sometimes "The South is avenged," Booth's alleged murdering words. Through the repetition and revision of this scene, Parks humorously criticizes the banality of contemporary scenes of racial violence[25]—Booth always interrupts politely, and the "murder" does not even cause the Foundling Father to lose the train of his sentence. Through the repeated sequence of unobtrusive murders, Parks also demonstrates the ineffectiveness of violence as a strategy for avenging anything at all.

If Parks jokes with our historical appetite for violence because it is insatiable, she jokes with our appetite for truth because it is selective. More than they like the real thing, Americans like copies. The copies may be exaggerated—indeed, it is preferable that they be a little larger than life. But the exaggeration is bound by rules: it must not be so large as to completely discredit the replica; we like our truth and fictions mixed just so.

The Foundling Father has, through trial and error, arrived at the right proportion of truth to exaggeration in his replication of Lincoln's appearance. Showing the audience one of the beards in his collection, he says, "This beard I wear for the holidays. I got shoes to match. Rarely wear em together. It's a little *much*."[26] Explaining why he rarely wears his yellow beard, The Foundling Father says, "If you deviate too much they wont get their pleasure. Thats my experience. Some inconsistencies are perpetuatable because theyre good for business. But not the yellow beard."[27] It is not deviation from the truth per se that bothers us; it is only any deviation that interrupts the fantasy of authenticity.

The Founding Father's son, Brazil, has not yet learned the subtleties of effective repetition and revision. He describes for visitors to his replica of the Great Hole of History how his parents honeymooned at the original Great Hole:

> He and Her would sit on thuh lip and watch everybody who was ever anybody parade on by. Daily parades! Just like thuh Tee Vee. Mr. George Washington, for example, thuh Fathuh of our Country hisself, would rise up from thuh dead and walk uhround and cross thuh Delaware and say stuff! Right before their very eyes!!![28]

But Lucy corrects him, explaining that the Washington they saw on their honeymoon was a look-alike of the original and admonishing him, "Keep your story to scale."[29] For Brazil and Lucy's public, even the wildest improbabilities are acceptable as long as they remain in proportion to the hole.

One more category of "perpetuatable inconsistency" has to do with the size of the historical replica. The Foundling Father explains that he wears a stovepipe hat, although Lincoln never wore one indoors, because "people don't like their Lincoln hatless."[30] A Lincoln who was several inches shorter than the familiar icon would be an unbearable disappointment, even if it offered greater authenticity. This is not only true for visitors to the historical reenactment but was probably true for visitors of the real Mr. Lincoln, whose trademark hat enhanced his already great height.

"I mean, humor's a great way of getting to the deep shit, isn't it?" Parks asked one interviewer rhetorically in 1995.[31] In *The America Play*, the playwright uses humor to get to deep issues of scapegoating and violence, lying and truth.

Supplying Agency through Repetition

Parks very consciously repeats old histories in order to diverge from them. Of her own use of repetition, she emphasizes, "[I]t's not just repetition but repetition with revision. And in drama change, revision, is the thing. Characters refigure their words and through a refiguring of language show us that they are experiencing their situation anew."[32]

Repetition has been recognized in cultural theory, most notably in the work of Jacques Derrida and Judith Butler, as a strategy for social and political empowerment. In order for cultural norms to hold, notes Butler, they must be repeated. But in this very necessity lies the possibility of doing things differently: "The resignification of norms is thus a function of their inefficacy, and so the question of subversion, of working the weakness in the norm, becomes a matter of inhabiting the practices of its rearticulations."[33] Both in its substance and in its cultural milieu, *The America Play* fills the great holes of history by repeating the American drama with black people at its center. In the world of this play, African Americans are actors in more senses than one.

As a new American history, *The America Play* celebrates the wit and ingenuity of African Americans. The Foundling Father does not merely imitate one of the most important figures in American history; he *replaces* him. If a founder is by definition an original, a foundling, too, is a figure of unknown or unrecorded ancestry. The "lesser known" holds center stage in place of Lincoln throughout the first act of the play, with visitors coming, some of them weekly, to see him. The second act is animated by discussion of the Foundling Father's absence, the search for signs of him, and his penultimate return. It is also interrupted regularly by scenes from *Our American Cousin*, the play the Lincolns were watching at Ford's Theater on April 14, 1865, when the president was shot. In this revision of the play, a cousin of the original, the Foundling Father plays, alternately, a character in the drama and himself.

Importantly, none of this drama requires the Foundling Father to be persecuted or oppressed by white people. As Parks asserts in her essay "An Equation for Black People on Stage," "The Klan does not always have to be outside the door for Black people to have lives worthy of dramatic literature."[34] Connecting this element of Parks's politics to her humor, Shawn-Marie Garrett observes that Parks, more than any other recent writer, shows "exactly how and why trying to make black history a minor subplot of a white story is laughable."[35] Although the overwhelming majority of stage relationships in which black people are represented are relationships between black and white, Parks's plays deliberately explore the history, present, and future of blackness on its own terms.

The America Play makes only the most oblique references to race or racial injustice, either past or present. The Foundling Father is said to resemble Lincoln uncannily, "taking into account of course his natural God-given limitations."[36] In one speech, he wishes to say "something about the freeing of the slaves" not to directly imitate his doppelganger but only in order to "make a great impression as he understood Mr. Lincoln to have made."[37] If anything, it is the Foundling Father who exploits white history in *The America Play*, besting the Great Man by making a handsome and pleasurable living off Lincoln's death.

Nor is the Lesser Known, finally, less celebrated here. Although Lucy and Brazil have never been able to mourn the Foundling Father's departure, in the play's final moments, he becomes his own memorial, introduced by Brazil as "our newest Wonder: One of thuh greats Hisself! . . . Note: thuh last words.—And thuh last breaths.—And how thuh nation mourns—."[38] Having witnessed the Foundling Father's wit, ingenuity, and occasional wisdom, it is not difficult to regret his leave-taking. By the play's end, when, in the final reenactment of Lincoln's death, the Foundling Father "really" dies, he has indeed become "one of the greats hisself," more real to us than Lincoln. We, a newly constituted nation, mourn his passing.

The Great Holes of History

The very nature of history's greatest holes is that they are too wide and too deep to ever be completely filled. Those directly involved in any mourning process know this but struggle against powerful cultural imperatives to forget. One of the greatest anxieties about "successful" mourning, both personal and historical, is that in letting go of our grief, we will relinquish our responsibilities to our most important ghosts.[39] It is appropriate, therefore, to view any solution to the problem of loss that purports to be total as suspicious, even pernicious.

Despite its prodigious inventiveness and brilliant humor, *The America Play* is structured to retain the very holes it fills. Through her restless repetitions and revisions, Parks undertakes a process of supplementation and compensation that is always necessarily and consciously partial. Even as Parks fills the great holes of history, she takes care not to hide them, not to erase our memory of them, and not to pretend that they have disappeared.

The America Play proliferates stories of holes, reminding us again and again of the central and varied role they play in our national mythology. The published play begins with the epigraph from John Locke cited at the beginning of this section, a reference to the myth of America as the great uncharted frontier. Brazil reminds us that this myth did not begin with America but with our most cherished story of how life itself began. "In thuh beginning there was one of those voids here and then 'bang' and then *voila*! And here we is."[40] "This Hole," he goes on to say, "is our inheritance of sorts. My Daddy died and left it to me and Her. And when She goes, Shes gonna give it all to me!!"[41] The inherited hole here is at once the Big Bang, the hole Brazil and Lucy are digging, and the hole left by the Foundling Father's abandonment of his family thirty years before the play begins. It also resonates with "thuh great black hole that thuh fatal bullet bored"[42] in Lincoln's head, with which the Foundling Father's customers are so fascinated and which is, in some sense, the hole on which *The America Play* is founded.

Early in his monologue, the Foundling Father explains how his life was shaped by a hole:

> The Lesser Known had a favorite hole. . . . . The Hole and its historicity and the part he played in it all gave a shape to the life and posterity of the Lesser Known that he could never shake.[43]

The Foundling Father, like the subjects of Pollock's birth narratives, has his origins in absence, not only because his life bears the shape of a hole but because that hole itself is a replica, the marker of an absent original.

Parks also leaves the great holes of history open by demonstrating the undesirability of essentializing any community's experience. The structure of repetition and revision empowers her to do this. Cultural theorist Paul Gilroy describes the ethical content of black musical structures in general and jazz structures in particular:

> [There is] a democratic, communitarian moment enshrined in the practice of antiphony which symbolizes and anticipates (but does not guarantee) new, non-dominating social relationships. Lines between self and other are blurred and special forms of pleasure are created as a result of the meetings and conversations that are established between one fractured, incomplete, and unfinished racial self and others. Antiphony is the structure that hosts these essential encounters.[44]

Although this antiphony is even more pronounced in other plays of Parks in which the cast of characters is less spare, the repetition and revision of words and ideas between the Foundling Father, Lucy, and Brazil are sufficient to remind audiences that no totalized "black" version of history, even a Foundling Father's, can ever fill the great hole.

And even as the play's reconstituted nation laughs, it is meant, in the final speech of the play, to "Note the death wound."[45] Even in the act of making new history, the playwright reminds us of the need to take note of the holes still to be excavated and filled. It is Parks's peculiar mastery that enables her to create so many new stories without erasing the gaping hole.

The hole of African American absence from the public archive/repertoire is by no means the only hole into which Parks is writing. While she embraces her identity as an African American woman, Parks resists any readings that reduce her plays to racial issues. "It is insulting when people say my plays are about what it's like to be black—as if that's all we think about, as if our life is about that. My life is not about race. It's about being alive."[46] While *The America Play* is certainly about the staging of a hole in the history of race in America, it is also about restaging nationhood itself in a way that calls into question our heroes and, with them, our values. Brazil's "Hall of Wonders," for example, houses not only Lincoln's medals for bravery and honesty but awards for those deeds and qualities that never make their way into the annals of history:

> For advancing and retreating. For makin do. For skills in whittling, for skills in painting and drawing, for uh knowledge of sewin, of handicrafts, and building things, for leather tannin, blacksmithery, lacemakin, horseback riding, swimming, croquet and badminton. Community Service. For cookin and for cleanin. For bowin and scrapin. Uh medal for fakin?[47]

The list suggests other holes to be filled, among them the history of work traditionally assigned to women such as sewing and cooking, the history of work traditionally assigned to the lower classes such as blacksmithing and cleaning, and the history of the theater itself, which may surely be included under the rubric of "fakin." It also suggests Parks's interest in women's sexuality, another historical hole at which some of her later plays (most notably *Fucking A* and *Venus*) are more directly aimed. In her essay on style, Parks suggests that she is engaging this issue in *The America Play* as well: "People have asked me why I don't put any sex in my plays. 'The Great Hole of History'—like, duh."[48]

Nationality and *Homebody/Kabul*

> *Look, look at my country, look at my Kabul, my city, what is left of my city?*
> —Tony Kushner, *Homebody/Kabul*

Many of the most important scholarly monographs that have emerged in the field of cultural studies over the last fifteen years, as well as many important books in other fields ranging from economics to business to science and technology, have been animated, at least in part, by a growing awareness of another great hole in history. Unlike the holes of discourse around race and sexuality, which it makes some sense to speak of within the context of American history,[49] this other great hole by definition extends beyond the geographical boundaries of America, the Americas, and even the more broadly constituted West. It is the hole left by the unacknowledged bonds of responsibility between nation-states. The very title of the play *Homebody/Kabul* makes this hole visible.

"'Our story begins,'" reads the Homebody, alone on stage, "'at the very dawn of history, circa 3,000 B.C.'" (see fig. 6.2). She is reading from an outdated guidebook to the city of Kabul, "A guidebook to a city which as we all know has . . . undergone change."[50] The change the Homebody articulates here has no agent, no relationship with the Western nation (England) in which she is so comfortably situated. Throughout her long monologue (originally the entire first act of the play), Tony Kushner's Homebody rehearses the history of a distant and ravaged city, trying to fill the enormous hole between the ancient wealth and present day decimation of Afghanistan and, in the process, to account for the role of the West in making and deepening this hole. She also rehearses, through an everyday narrative performance, the story of a wounded Afghan hat merchant, actively imagining the merchant's speech, thoughts, and feelings in the face of unimaginable personal loss. In so doing, she tries to fill the great hole in his body, the great holes in his life, the great holes between his life and hers, and, most of all, the great holes in the relationship between Kabul and the Western nation she calls home.

In *Homebody/Kabul,* Kushner decries the great holes in history left by our allegiance to the arbitrary borders of nationhood. Early in her monologue, the Homebody laments, "We all romp about, grieving, wondering, but with rare exception we mostly remain suspended in the Rhetorical Colloidal Forever that agglutinates between Might and Do."[51] In her own seductively colorful words, she suggests that we live suspended in a hole made of talk, a hole between Might and Do, between seriously contemplating our world and taking certain kinds of action.

What we ought to be both contemplating and doing, as the Homebody does and as the play as a whole does, is our relationship to the ethnic and cultural Other, of whom the Islamic world has become so strongly and painfully symbolic in the last decade. But we are, as we have been since "the very dawn of history," unwilling to take the energy to contemplate or the responsibility to act. Kushner fills this hole in our evolving history not with new stories, as Parks does, but with a repertoire of four essential practices aimed at moving us out of sticky suspension.

Figure 6.2. The Homebody (Amy Morton) in her Afghan hat reads from the Kabul guidebook in *Homebody/Kabul*. Photo by Michael Brosilow, courtesy of the photographer.

Homebody/Kabul fills the great holes of history with *contemplation*. This is a practice that is rarely modeled in contemporary American culture. It is absent in our theaters, which have succumbed to the demand for action and to the short attention span our supermediated lives help cultivate. It is increasingly absent in our increasingly market-driven classrooms. And it is woefully absent in our political life, where, as suggested in chapter 4, we have become so concerned with appearing strong, certain, and unified that we no longer care if we are smart, honest, or just. By opening up private spaces in which its principal character can explore the history and culture of Afghanistan, the play imagines what it might mean to reflect seriously upon Western responsibility for the losses of non-Western nations.

The play fills the great holes of history with *interpretation*. If Parks's repetition and revision happens before the play begins (e.g., by conceiving of a character like the Foundling Father) and while the play transpires (e.g., through the continuous revisiting of Lincoln's assassination), Kushner's interpretation and ensuing revision happen during the play and afterward. By opening up an interpretive space *between* contemplation and action, between what the Homebody calls "Might" and "Do," *Homebody/Kabul* imagines how we might make meaning in response to loss on a global scale. And by framing even our most public actions as rehearsals subject to revision, *Homebody/Kabul* imagines how we might "do" better in the future.

And the play fills the great holes of history with *action*. Kushner's is not, by and large, the highly fanciful and occasionally abstract action of Parks's *The America Play* (although his most celebrated play, *Angels in America*, features a winged angel and several fabulous ghosts). If Parks's action is animated by the exercise of critique and the desire to remake the world, Kushner's is animated by the exercise of empathy and the desire to remake human beings. By staging a dream in which the Homebody becomes the devastated Afghan man, *Homebody/Kabul* imagines ways that we might more fully enact our responsibility to those outside our national borders.

Contemplation

We cannot act responsibly toward others if we do not even think about them. In the afterword to *Homebody/Kabul*, Kushner laments the loss of a space for contemplation in contemporary public life. He relates that on September 12, 2001, several newspapers contacted him, along with "anyone who'd ever written anything," with a request to write about the terrorist attacks on America of the preceding day. Kushner refused to accommodate the newspapers' requests: "I've never been shy about offering opinions, but opining felt hasty, unseemly, and unwise."[52] In the aftermath of the attacks, when the press and the United States government were already grasping for ways to act, Kushner demanded time for contemplation.

The Homebody explains that in the twentieth century, Western or "civilized" society has historically demonstrated contempt for "those who merely contemplate" without moving to action.[53] In her monologue, the Homebody explicitly mourns the loss of a space for contemplation, a private space: "Ours is a time of connection, the private, and we must accept this, and it's a hard thing to accept, the private is *gone*"[54] (emphasis original). In several deliberate and important ways, the Homebody works to reconstruct a private space.

In the isolation of her barren reading room, the Homebody would seem to have nothing but privacy. But for the Homebody, a private space seems, somewhat paradoxically, to mean a space in which she can meaningfully connect with others both absent and present, an intimate space. Her home is no such place. The Homebody's home is populated by a husband with whom she rarely speaks and a daughter who is starving for her attention. She has aloneness but without intimacy and therefore nothing she can meaningfully call privacy. In this space, she attempts to make room for contemplation through the reading of an outdated guidebook. But her reading about the ancient city of Kabul is, by her own admission, doomed.[55] Although she will cling to her reading throughout her monologue, she will also be perpetually distracted from it. Ultimately, it is not through the outdated guidebook that she will be able to see why Kabul should matter to her but through private contemplation.

Resigned to her public life, the Homebody decides to have a party in her home: "Several months ago, I was feeling low and decided to throw a party and a party needs festive hats. So I took the tube to ________."[56] In a prefatory note to the script, Kushner explains how this omitted name is to be performed: "Where the name would fall in the sentence, she makes a wide, sweeping gesture in the air with her right hand, almost as if to say, 'I know the name but I will not tell you.'"[57] It is in this unnamed, borderless locale that the Homebody performs her most striking effort to recover a private space.

The shop at "________" to which her journey takes her belongs to an Afghan merchant. As the Homebody narrates the event of purchasing the hats—which we take to be a real event as evidenced by the presence of the hats, later removed from a paper bag on stage—she moves almost imperceptibly into fantasy. Through her fantastic contemplation, the Homebody finds compensation for personal and global losses.

The Homebody notices, in purchasing the hats, that the merchant is missing several fingers on his right hand. Her transaction complete, the merchant offers her this incomplete hand, and she takes it, "and we go out of the shop but no longer on ________ *(Gesture)*, we are standing on a road, a road in Kabul."[58] Through the physical connection of their hands, the Homebody magically enters the private space she has long been trying to locate through her guidebook.

Once in Kabul, "demurely hidden from the sight of the ailing and the destitute and the war-ravaged we, the hat merchant and I, make love." During this lovemaking, another miraculous transformation occurs. "We kiss, his breath is very bitter, he places his hand inside me, it seems to me his whole hand inside me, and *it seems to me a whole hand*"[59] (emphasis added). In that most private place, the inside of her body, the hat merchant recovers his lost hand. In that other most private place, the inside of her mind, the Homebody recovers her desire. For the Homebody, it is only in the most private places that we can contemplate our connectedness to others and, in doing so, find compensation for our losses, make ourselves whole.

A month after the terrorist attacks of September 11, 2001, Kushner was asked to prepare a statement for the press, because the play had turned out to be more timely than he ever anticipated, and "it was assumed that, given the subject of the play, there might be controversy."[60] In his statement, Kushner noted that *Homebody/Kabul* was, among other things, a play about grief. We had been plunged into grief by action: "by 9/11 first and foremost, by the incomprehensible yet inescapable fact that we are under attack by an unknown enemy using biochemical weapons, and by the actions, both here and abroad, of our own government."[61] Amidst all this action, Kushner said, "My greatest hope for a play is always that it might prove generative of thought, contemplation."[62] The theater, Kushner suggests, is a privileged space for contemplation.

Interpretation

The space between contemplation and action is the space of interpretation. It is the space where meanings are made and, therefore, the space on which all the power of action depends.

Perhaps no one has delineated the space of interpretation more rigorously than the literary critic Robert Scholes. In *Textual Power*, Scholes outlines the three processes that make up the act of reading: small-*r* reading, interpretation, and criticism. Small-*r* reading, for Scholes, is a passive activity that enables the reader simply to follow a narrative. It is an even more primitive process than Kushner's contemplation, because it does not require the reader to entertain perspectives outside the text. Although reading is not a sufficient activity for making meaning, it is a necessary one.

Insufficiencies or, as Scholes calls them "hitches," in the reading process force the reader to move from reading to interpretation. Interpretation "depends upon the failures of reading," on a reader's perception that the text is incomplete without an active or conscious effort of making meaning: "The move from a summary of events to a *discussion of the meaning* or theme of a work of fiction is usually a move from reading to interpretation"[63] (emphasis added). As Scholes points out, many of the complex texts that we call literature are designed to force exactly this shift.

Recognizing interpretation as a discrete site between contemplation and action allows us to understand the constructedness of meanings. Just as meanings do not simply inhere in any text, whether that text is a guidebook, a city, or another human being, so they do not inhere in any loss. They are not simply waiting to be read and then acted upon. Rather, we make meanings, prompted to do so from a sense that the text is insufficient without them.

Making meaning responsibly means taking outside perspectives seriously. Perhaps the most damning criticism of George W. Bush's administration at the time that *Homebody/Kabul* premiered was that it evaluated the Muslim world without taking the time to interpret it. Despite Bush's moves in the aftermath of September 11, 2001, to distance himself from claims by his friends that Islam was "a very evil religion," Christian theologian Martin Marty argued, "Regular appearances by the president at meetings of certain evangelical groups . . . make it hard for friendly Muslims not to hear the word 'Islam' whenever Bush portrays terrorists as absolute evils."[64] The problem with such hasty evaluation, Marty suggested, is precisely that it short-circuits the interpretive process, inhibiting "self-examination and repentant action."

Responsible action requires both contemplation, a private space of reflection on the relationship between self and other, and interpretation, a careful construction of the meanings of a cultural, social, or political "text" that prompt this action. The need for interpretation is particularly great in negotiating experiences of loss, which can have such volatile effects on us as individuals and communities. It is important, too, to recognize that action is rarely the endpoint of any interpretation of loss. Rather, our responses must continually be redone through an ongoing process of re-interpretation and revision.

Action

Alone in her reading room, the Homebody notes our society's propensity for preventing us from feeling each other's losses. Describing her relationship with her husband, she explains that he "cannot bear my . . . the sound of me and has threatened to leave on this account and so I rarely speak to him anymore. We both take powerful antidepressants. His pills have one name and mine another. I frequently take his pills instead of mine so I can know what he's feeling."[65] Although the Homebody's solution is hilarious, her critique is real: Our culture "injects" us with powerful messages to discourage our incorporating certain kinds of others into our actions.

Homebody/Kabul rejects these medicines with respect to the relationship between Afghanistan and the West. If the play imagines a space for contemplation in the face of personal, national, and global losses and a space for making and remaking meanings, it also imagines a space for compensatory action.

One of the most important ways in which the Homebody acts is to perform the losses of a complete stranger, the Afghan hat merchant. By taking on the speech, thought, history, and imagination of a person so culturally, historically, and geographically distant from herself, the Homebody takes on the responsibility of creating a fuller response to the losses engendered by Western nationalism.

Inside the shop on ________, the Homebody asks the hat merchant what happened to his hand. As I cannot excerpt the reply she reports without compromising its integrity, it is here in its lengthy entirety:

> And he says: I was with the Mujahideen, and the Russians did this. I was with the Mujahideen, and an enemy faction of Mujahideen did this. I was with the Russians, I was known to have assisted the Russians, I did informer's work for Babrak Karmal, my name is in the files if they haven't been destroyed, the names I gave are in the files, there are no more files, I stole bread for my starving family, I stole bread *from* a starving family, I profaned, betrayed, according to some stricture I erred and they chopped off the fingers of my hand. *Look, look at my country, look at my Kabul, my city, what is left of my city? The streets are as bare as the mountains now, the buildings are as ragged as mountains and as bare and empty of life, there is no life here only fear, we do not live in the buildings now, we live in terror in the cellars in the caves in the mountains, only God can save us now, only order can save us now, only God's Law harsh and strictly administered can save us now, only The Department for the Promotion of Virtue and the Prevention of Vice can save us now, only terror can save us from ruin, only neverending war, save us from terror and neverending war, save my wife they are stoning my wife, they are chasing her with sticks, save my wife save my daughter from punishment by God, save us from God, from war, from exile, from oil exploration, from no oil exploration, from the West, from the children with rifles, carrying stones, only children with rifles, carrying stones, can save us now.* You will never understand. It is hard, it was hard work to get into the U.K. I am happy here in the U.K. I am terrified I will

> be made to leave the U.K. I cannot wait to leave the U.K. I despise the U.K. I voted for John Major. I voted for Tony Blair. I did not, I cannot vote, I do not believe in voting, the people who ruined my hand were right to do so, they were wrong to do so, my hand is most certainly ruined, you will never understand, why are you buying so many hats? (emphasis original)[66]

Here, the Homebody performs the role of the hat merchant. The performance moves from a confession of the merchant's offenses, to a lament for the city of Kabul, to a prayer for salvation, and back to the confessional mode. Yet, none of these forms can account for the merchant's losses.

The hat merchant's losses are unaccountable as confession because the facts are complex, contradictory, and, ultimately, not constitutive of the truth—what does it matter, really, if the merchant stole bread for or from a starving family? Would either version satisfactorily explain the loss of his hand? His losses are unaccountable as lament, because once the lamenting starts, it has no end—a hand, a city, a country, a part of the world, a world. And they are unaccountable as prayer because threat and refuge are now indistinguishable. It is even unclear whether God himself is a threat or a refuge, a savior or something to be saved from. Only two things are certain. First, personal loss. "My hand is most certainly ruined." And second, lost connections. "You will never understand," the hat merchant tells the Homebody and just a few moments later, again, "You will never understand."

Yet, the Homebody's performance puts at least this second loss into question. As Kushner explains in his essay "Some Questions about Tolerance," to recover lost connections is the very role of the theater artist:

> The artist embraces or expresses difference, spends her or his time imagining it with as powerful and graceful empathic leaps as the limitations of human consciousness permit. . . . This process is doomed to at least partial failure—if the Other is to stay truly Other then failure is axiomatic. But when an audience watches an artist in this process it is exhilarated, because a miracle of sorts is taking place, in which the Self's isolation is being discarded but not at the cost of its integrity. It is in moments like these, when art is most successful, that it may perhaps teach useful gestures to society, to political action.[67]

Through the rigorous and embodied exercise of empathy, the radically isolated Homebody performs her connection to another part of the world. Her rehearsal of the hat merchant's multiple perspectives is a form of ethical action in the face of loss. Through performance, she actively incorporates another person and, through him, another nation.

This action becomes a rehearsal for an even bolder one, the departure of the Homebody for Afghanistan. We will never see her again and will therefore never know for what purpose she traveled to Kabul or what she hoped to do there. Nonetheless, we know that the act of exercising empathy has moved the most intractable Homebody to a place of deep engagement.

Reinterpretation and Revision

The process of writing *Homebody/Kabul* demonstrates the power of revision. Indeed, few plays have been as publicly revised. Kushner has redone the play from its original form as a monologue in 1997 to what he called an "unproduceable 250-page script,"[68] to a three-act play with thirteen characters that premiered at the New York Theater Workshop two months after September 11, 2001, to a revised script, published in August, 2004. That the revised script is still four hours long suggests that the need for revision may still not be fully satisfied.

Kushner's willingness to revise the script so publicly is a rare and a hopeful sign for contemporary drama, as well as for the rehearsal of productive responses to loss. Although the classroom and the rehearsal room have long been recognized sites of performance practice, the history of *Homebody/Kabul* opens the possibility that the professional theater might also become a place to revise and "redo." The promise of *Homebody/Kabul* is that contemplation, interpretation, and action can all become places of connection, where the meanings we make of loss are neither private nor permanent.

Recognizing revision as an integral part of any full response to loss allows us to understand that even actions are provisional, subject to being revised over time. Understanding the provisional nature of action can work, on the one hand, to encourage doing against the temptation to contemplate endlessly. Valuing revision can mitigate the anxiety that might forestall a public response to loss burdened by a perception of finality. Valuing revision reminds us that all such responses can be and probably should be redone over time.

But if valuing revision encourages us to act, understanding its provisional nature should also infuse us with an appropriate attitude of humility about our actions. Not only do our actions need to be based on careful interpretations, they also need to be themselves reevaluated on an ongoing basis in light of the new reality that follows, sooner or later, every response. World leaders would do well to cultivate such a humility in responding to catastrophic losses among their citizens and allies.

Performance texts can uniquely compensate for history's losses in a number of important ways. Although we can read key scenarios as they are reenacted in diverse cultural forms, performance allows us to compensate for the problems of these scenarios with great economy. In Parks's *The America Play*, for example, key historical "holes" may be filled multiple times in minutes or hours, creating new history that would, in everyday life, require decades to make. Performance texts also benefit from the playfulness of their frames; we can often, as Parks suggests, get more out of history by joking with it. And, as the Homebody demonstrates, performance texts frame the exercise of empathy as meaningful action, action that can lead to renewed engagement with the losses beyond our national borders for which we are rightly held responsible.

Finally, performance texts provide a space in which to recognize and even celebrate the tenuousness of our answers to history's most urgent questions. The necessity of continually reanimating the performance text forces us to recognize that our responses to loss are always partial. They fill the hole but never completely and never permanently. This should make us humble as we recognize the overwhelming temptation to act without contemplation or interpretation. It should also make us bold as we increasingly understand that action is not the end but a necessary beginning.

7. Practicing Joy: Improvisation in a Federal Prison

I've never had fun fun.
—Danny, a federal inmate

THE BUILDING LOOKS SO SMALL. *This always surprises me. It isn't really small at all, I have to remind myself; it's just that it is set way back on the property, separated from the busy Kansas Expressway by an enormous lawn. The lawn is green, well manicured, and completely vacant. It is surrounded by short white posts connected with iron link chains. I drive up to the squat, brick tower where there is a wire mesh microphone. I always feel like I am ordering from some very austere take-out restaurant until a look to my right reminds me that the microphone is connected to a much taller tower, a lighthouse of sorts, from which a man in a white shirt looks down and speaks to me.*

"Purpose of your visit?"

He never says hello.

"I am here to see Dr. Ashlock."

(I've learned that this is the simplest answer.)

"Do you have in your possession any knives, guns, radio or video equipment, cellular phones, or pagers?"

"I have a cell phone. I'll keep it in my glove compartment."

"Good idea. Drive through, and park to your left."

I walk up the stone steps to the glass door of the huge, brick building and into the shabby lobby, where there is just room enough for the check-in desk, lockers, and, to the left, three plastic chairs for waiting visitors. It has a faded yellow linoleum floor and a restroom with a rickety wooden door. I always use the restroom before I go through security; otherwise, I'll just have to do everything over again. I fill out both sign-in forms (finally, after several weeks of running back to my car, I know my license plate number by heart) and walk through the open frame of the metal detector. I put my purse in a locker, pocket the key, take an identity tag to wear around my neck, and get my hand stamped with the invisible entry stamp. Now I just wait.

Keith, Dr. Ashlock's assistant, arrives from downstairs in his dress pants, white shirt, and tie. Tom, the guard, arrives soon afterward in his vaguely nautical uniform. When the students arrive, I follow them, Keith, and Tom in through the first electronic door, which opens slowly, mechanically, like a bank vault. It must close all the way behind the eleven of us crammed into the tight space before the second one, not more than four feet ahead, will move. When it does, I shine my hand under the ultraviolet light and see what the stamp is: Today, it's a bunny.

I follow the group through the long path of hallways and stairs that everyone has memorized by now except for me. Each hallway has a different paint design, color scheme, ceiling texture. It reminds me of my elementary school gym. I've asked Tom at least twice if it didn't used to be a school, but he assures me that it was built in 1933 as a prison. It used to have its own morgue, he adds. Down the hall, I see the familiar array of beige jumpsuits, the familiar range of shaved and shaggy heads. I take another breath and say hello.

Prison inmates are steeped in loss. They often have their origins in absence, a kind of absence that never goes away. One man says to me, after I have described my grandmother's house in a theater exercise, "I got a very strong sense of home from what you said. And I've never had that before." Another, a young man, after describing a place that is meaningful to him, says, "I haven't been there in twenty years." For many, the prison is the first community of any kind to which they have belonged.

And, whether or not they have come from loss, they are certainly steeped in it now. Because they have often been the perpetrators of loss, they live with the burden of other people's grief. During the prisoners' long years in prison, they have lost their connections with the outside world and, therefore, any opportunity to practice interacting with it. Many have been abandoned by friends and family, who never visit, rarely call. The longer this is true, the deeper their sense of fear about the outside world and how it will act upon and against them. Most of all, they are condemned to what psychologist and concentration-camp survivor Viktor Emil Frankl calls a "provisional existence"; without the prospect of a different future, prisoners lose "their hold on life."[1] These experiences of suffering received and, especially, of suffering inflicted are precisely what constitutes these men as a community.[2]

Inmates have also lost something that many of us take for granted: the opportunity to be seen as fully human. Many prisoners talk about being viewed as animals by the outside world. As playwright Eve Ensler writes, many are forced to "*become* their mistake," and, through these losses, they have often lost their sense of themselves: "They're not allowed to really exist any more in the culture, and so very often they don't exist to themselves." They have lost their physical freedom and with it much of their ability to manage stress. (There are some limited opportunities for physical exercise in prison but not for physical play.) Most of all, many have lost contact with their imaginations, too mired in what is to think about what might be.

When I began to work with prisoners, I remembered the writing of Michel Foucault. In 1975, Foucault's *Discipline and Punish*, a history of the modern prison, was published. In writing this history, Foucault traced the development over the first half of the nineteenth century of "new tactics of power, among which are to be included the new penal mechanisms."[3] Such mechanisms included, most importantly, hierarchical observation; the power of social norms; and the medical examination. This new kind of punishment, Foucault said, pretended to be more scientific, more egalitarian, and more humane than earlier methods. However, it was merely more insidious. Through humble and often invisible means, it created a new kind of body, one that was both docile and useful, a body characterized, above all, by the loss of liberty.

The antithesis of the disciplined body is the body at play. A body at play is neither docile nor useful. It does not obey rules. It does not get things done. It barks like a dog. It laughs. It takes real tours of imaginary places. Would it be possible to make a space for this kind of body in the very institution designed to eliminate it?

In 2003, I trained two small groups of college students to lead theater workshops at the U.S. Medical Center for Federal Prisoners, or the "Fed Med," as it is known. The Fed Med, the only facility of its kind, is located in Springfield, Missouri. Inmates at the Fed Med negotiate loss even more intensely than those at other prison facilities. The institution houses prisoners at every level of security and from every geographical location who suffer from mental or physical health conditions too serious to be treated at a standard prison infirmary. Therefore, in addition to the typical, if extreme, psychic losses inmates experience, these inmates are all experiencing physiological losses of some kind.

In the case of our workshops, the prisoners were coping with mental illness. The participants were ten to twelve male prisoners in "Axis 2," a life-enhancement program for inmates with a diagnosis of borderline personality disorder (BPD). The program involved ongoing group and individual behavioral therapy. If inmates successfully completed the program (a process that takes twelve months), they could be moved to lower-security facilities nearer to their homes. This program was the first of its kind in the federal prison system.[4]

The students, eight advanced theater students, were all white, college-age men and women. The inmates were men, black and white, ranging in age from early twenties to late forties. I participated in each session. A guard and at least one therapist were present at all times.

We led eight, ninety-minute workshops for inmates over eight weeks. The workshops were based largely on Viola Spolin's theater games and Augusto Boal's image theater, as distilled for the students in rehearsal workshops with me and in Michael Rohd's handbook *Theatre for Community, Conflict, and Dialogue.*

In addition to developing story theater as a mode of performance, Spolin developed improvisational theater games through the WPA Recreational Project in Chicago during the 1930s for use with young people, educators, and social workers. These games, as described in her book *Improvisation for the Theatre,* were designed to help professional actors and young children cultivate basic performance skills, such as concentration, listening, and creative impulse. The games are now widely used in the United States to encourage people—especially young people—to be active participants in their artistic and educational communities.

Boal developed his image theater, largely silent group work, for use with economically and socially disenfranchised populations all over the world, particularly in Latin America. His aim was to spark dialogue about pressing community issues and, ultimately, to facilitate action by oppressed communities on their own behalf. His *Theatre of the Oppressed* was inspired by the work of educational reformer Paulo Freire, whose *Pedagogy of the Oppressed* envisioned a liberating classroom practice.

My own training is more strongly rooted in Spolin's exercises than Boal's. As a teenager, I learned and practiced Spolin's theater games at the Piven Theater Workshop in Evanston, Illinois. I have incorporated this work into my classroom teaching for many years. It was only much later, as a graduate student and then college teacher, that I was exposed to and experimented with Boal's work.

The theater workshop sessions were highly structured and rehearsed. I provided the students with a written plan for each session and designated two leaders charged with special authority for facilitating the games each time. The plan included time for the prisoners and students to process each game after it was played through a brief discussion of the experience and its value to participants. We met several days before each session to review the plan, to assign specific students to lead each exercise, and to review, sometimes in discussion and sometimes on our feet, how each game was played.

Over the course of two semesters, spring and fall 2003, the project was completed twice with two different sets of participants, both inmates and students. In the second incarnation, students received a more thorough orientation to the prison community. These students also received written materials outlining behavioral guidelines, and these helped them feel more secure.

Rule 1: Inmates should address you by your last name.
Rule 2: Do not wear low-cut or tightly fitting clothing.
Rule 3: Do not give anything to or accept anything from the inmates.
Rule 4: In the unlikely event of a fight, get up against the nearest wall, and let the staff step in.
Rule 5: Do not leave gum in the prison. It can be used to lock a door or to make an imprint of a key.

In addition, a more thorough introduction to the particular prison facility, how it operated, and typical clinical profiles was helpful in orienting them. The second time, too, the workshop sessions were lengthened to two hours at the suggestion of the first group of participants.

The idea for the project came from students in a performance ensemble that I direct at the university. The ensemble's mission is to create theater for social change. At the beginning of the school year, a guest speaker from the university's service-learning office talked with the students about community partners who might be interested in working with them. She listed at least a dozen possibilities from churches to after-school groups to health care organizations. The students unanimously chose the Fed Med.

Part of the reason why they chose the prison is, undeniably, the glamour of working in such a mysterious and dramatic environment. There's something cool about telling friends that you're working on the "inside." It's a privileged space. Less cynically, as one student noted, the other volunteer sites suggested by the guest speaker are places to which the students could gain access on their own. The prison project was something they couldn't do without institutional support.

Part of the attraction, too, possibly, is the similarity of the two populations. Though their situations are obviously radically different, the college students nonetheless have an intuitive (if almost certainly unconscious) feeling of kinship with a population that is isolated from the rest of society. Even if the isolation is voluntary and aimed at growth rather than punishment, students, especially in a place like Springfield, Missouri, know that they are cut off from a significant part of the real world during their college years.

As theater students in particular, they feel a kinship with a population that is looked at as peculiar or, worse, as radically other. "In nine years I've never had anything like this," said one prisoner, "where people didn't view us as animals behind a wall." One student told the prisoners, "I've never had anyone look forward to my presence before." Another student said it was precious to her "to come here and be accepted as who we are, which is *nuts*." Perhaps most keenly, they feel a kinship with people who are trying to figure out who they are.

What the students didn't know was that in choosing the prison as the site for their performance work, they were becoming part of a community of artists across the country who do visual, literary, and performing arts workshops in prisons. Many of these artists come to the prison individually to work with inmates, who often are women. Their work emphasizes different skills, different avenues toward creative work.

Jean Trounstine spent a decade working in the Framingham Women's Prison in Massachusetts beginning in 1988. She taught acting and directed eight plays there, including *The Merchant of Venice*. Her experiences with women inmates are chronicled in her book *Shakespeare behind Bars*.

The performance artist Rhodessa Jones has also worked with women prisoners for many years, helping them through writing and improvisation to create their own texts for public performance. Because of the lower security level of the population with whom she works, Jones has been able to create public performances of the women's work. Her extraordinary leadership and successes are beautifully documented and evoked in Rena Fraden's *Imagining Medea*.

For more than five years, playwright Eve Ensler has been leading writing workshops in New York's Bedford Hills Correctional Facility. Here, the women do not perform the material themselves; rather, their work is affirmed by the participation, as performers, of five of the nation's leading actresses: Mary Alice, Glenn Close, Hazelle Goodman, Rosie Perez, and Marisa Tomei. Ensler's experiences and those of the women with whom she works were documented in the 2003 film *What I Want My Words to Do to You*.

Indeed, as one colleague put it, performance-related work in prisons has become "a thing." I was taken aback when another colleague I ran into at a national conference said to me, "Hey, I hear you're doing prison stuff, too." Although I am encouraged by the presence of a community of artists doing this kind of work, I don't like to think of my work or my students' work with federal inmates in Springfield, Missouri, as "prison stuff." It is much more important to us than that.

It is also much more personal. Although outside the workshop, we are aware of our desire to participate in a larger, cultural transformation in the prison system—including a greater commitment to true rehabilitation of inmates in prison communities—inside the workshop, we are concerned with individual voices and stories, bodies and breath. In the cold, overheated, crowded, lonely room of the prison workshops, we do not think about social change; we think about the eyes into which we are looking, which are looking back at us.

Our work differed from the work of the performance artists who have brought their talents to prison populations in the past in a number of ways. First, there was no end-product, no public or even semi-public performance. For security reasons, a public performance would be impossible at the Fed Med. But beyond logistics, the inmates' time in the program is too short, too tenuous, and the inmates themselves too impatient to work toward a final performance that they might or might not be around to see. As inmates with borderline personality disorder, their ability to regulate their emotions and, therefore, their behavior is impaired—and they know this. They know that they may or may not be able to hang on in the privileged space of the treatment program for another week, another day. They live for and in the present; they are, in this respect, natural performers.

Second, the focus of our workshops was on performing bodies and not on written text. Using improvisational games, the inmates themselves produced the text, not on paper but in motion, in living time. The second time through the workshops, I experimented some with scripted scenes from Samuel Beckett's *Waiting for Godot*, pairing students and inmates to build relationships around the idea of waiting—an activity the inmates know much about. A few of the inmates were excited by this challenge. On balance, however, no matter how freely they were allowed to adapt this text, they strongly preferred unencumbered movement through space and spontaneous interaction with the students.

Third, although many of the artists mentioned above work with the prisoners alone, a partnership with the prison staff is central to our work. The indispensable key to the efficacy of our theater workshops was finding a partner at the prison who not only theoretically but actively supported our work. Dr. Georgina Ashlock, who also taught an occasional course in the psychology department at the university, prepared both students and prisoners for the project. She discussed what she saw as its potential values, and its potential risks, both considerable. She gave the students a brief orientation (later expanded), including both basic prison rules and an overview of borderline personality disorder. She took them on a tour of the institution, during which she introduced the students to some of the inmates with whom they would be working.

Even more importantly, Dr. Ashlock monitored the sessions, occasionally interjecting to make explicit connections between the theater curriculum and her own therapeutic work. She pointed out to the inmates how through the theater workshops they were regulating their own moods, something they had enormous difficulty doing in other contexts. She underscored the lessons in empathy that came from simple role-playing. When things went wrong, she was there to correct them or, more often, to monitor the self-corrections of inmates and students alike. She was available for consultation between sessions, and she was both practically and emotionally supportive of the students, particularly in the early days. From the beginning, she saw the potential for collaborative theatrical exploration to support the therapeutic goals of her program.

Keith Smith, a treatment specialist in the Axis 2 program, supported and facilitated the partnership. In addition to his philosophical support of the theater project, Smith provided continuous and often invisible practical support, helping us to wade through the enormous amount of paperwork and other security measures that might well have overwhelmed us.

Another key difference in the project is the particular inmate population encountered. To describe the inmates as a group is difficult. Consider this description borrowed from the introduction to Trounstine's book *Shakespeare Behind Bars*:

> I came to realize that most women in prison are not dangerous. The majority do not engage in physical assaults or sit in cells making weapons. Female inmates may form alliances against one another, and certainly they can be ruthless, but what characterizes them more than anything else is their heartache. Instead of frightening me they seemed lost, with tragic lives—lives like those of Shakespeare's characters, complete with flaws, comic mishaps, and ironic endings.[5]

This is *not* an accurate description of the inmates with whom we worked. Not that the inmates of Axis 2 are overtly frightening; but they are absolutely dangerous to others and especially to themselves. (Many of the Axis 2 inmates were at far greater risk of self-mutilation than of harming anyone else.) And they are all the more dangerous because they wear neither heartache nor anger on their sleeves.

The behavior of the inmates in Axis 2 was uniquely difficult to manage. The essential feature of their disorder is "a pervasive pattern of instability of self-image, interpersonal relationships, and mood."[6] Keith Smith describes the challenges of the symptomology this way:

> Most people automatically assume that someone is psychotic if they harm themselves or have dramatic mood swings. They throw medications at them just like they do with hyper kids in school with Ritalin. As they soon discover, however, personality disorders don't respond to medications, and they get frustrated. Our inmates tend to be very needy and attention-seeking. When you have a person with this combination, most people just want them out of their institution.

If these inmates were uniquely difficult, they were also uniquely charming. They were very ingratiating, easygoing, and welcoming to strangers. But their motives were not simple. Yes, they were sad and lonely. But they were also full of rage, prone to despair, confused about their sense of self, and eager to get out. Nonetheless, the inmates became our friends and our teachers. And, through these relationships, we were offered the rare opportunity to see performance with a peculiar clarity.

The most important difference in the project, however, was the participation of the college students. The inmates were stunned and excited that a group of young people wanted to go behind locked doors and spend time with them. They wanted to know why the students wanted to be with them and what the students got out of it. When I visited alone, as I did a few times, the inmates were visibly disappointed. In a free write that I asked the inmates to do at the beginning of one of these solo sessions, one of the inmates volunteered to read a piece that began with his foremost thought, "This sure isn't as fun as when the students are here."

For their part, the students had an opportunity to facilitate theater for social change in a social institution that is badly in need of it. Although some fine teachers of Boal's techniques in college settings are "determined not to use oppressed people as 'guinea pigs' for student learning," as Bruce McConachie contends,[7] I have found that, in practice, there is really nothing to be lost through such an exchange. I was there to offer gentle correctives when games went astray—reminding players, students and inmates alike, for example, that "freeze" means "freeze" or that asking questions in an improvisation is unfair to your partner because he/she doesn't know the answer—but such input was rarely necessary. The students facilitated the games in a spirit of mutual learning. They were keenly aware of all the inmates had to teach them and eager to revise games according to inmates' suggestions. In the second year of the program, some returning inmates became cofacilitators, sharing their expertise with new participants, students and inmates alike.

Furthermore, as McConachie acknowledges, only through interaction with populations outside academies of learning can students "begin to come to terms with their social isolation and privilege and also discover possibilities for cross-class (also cross-gender and cross-race) coalitions."[8] Similarly, this work breaks down the extreme social isolation of the prisoners in a way that no single visitor could. The value of an exchange between these two different communities is more than just one person could ever give the inmates or the students. Here, then, are three specific gifts that this work seemed to offer to all participants.

The Gift of Fear

Art is made from fear, like a vaccine.
—Aaron Freeman, "Art and Fear," *All Things Considered*

The first great gift performance gives is the gift of fear.

In the weeks of preparation preceding our first theater workshop at the prison, the eight students involved in the original project felt afraid. One did not have to look hard for outward signs of this. One student cried during our tour. Two others held hands as they approached the unit in which we would be working. Others were unusually sweaty or stiff.

As expressed in their journals, their fears fell into two categories: fear of physical danger and fear of emotional vulnerability. In the former category, they wrote, "This is one of the most dangerous situations I can think of" or, masking fear with humor, "Note to self: call mom and tell her you love her." One student said that the only comparable danger he could imagine was a course in skydiving. In the latter category, one student wrote, "They will laugh and yell at me. Scared scared scared." Another wrote, "I just feel completely strung out and vulnerable." The students were clearly afraid.

More tellingly, the inmates were also afraid. They were afraid, they later recalled, that the students would look down on them because of who they were, would have unreasonable expectations of them (such as requiring them to memorize long passages of text), or would make them look ridiculous.

And, of course, I was afraid, too. I had never worked in a prison environment, nor had I ever worked specifically with people with borderline personalities. I had trained students to lead theater workshops before but never in a situation where there was so much difference in background and experience between my students and their students. And although on some level I believed my safety would probably never be better protected than in this environment, when I first looked at the inmates, I empathized with the feelings of all the students and particularly with one, Melanie.[9]

Melanie

Melanie is a shy, pretty girl with short red hair and a sturdy frame. She wears jeans and solid Oxford shirts. She takes big strides forward, but every time she does so, it seems her feet are scurrying frantically backward across her mind, like a cartoon. Her nervous laugh is hearty, boisterous, not thin. At the beginning of our tour through the prison, Melanie folds her lips in and presses down on them hard to stop something from coming out—a cry? A scream? After a few minutes of walking, we are taken to a staff break room to receive instructions about basic rules and behaviors. The psychologist, Dr. Ashlock, says that the prisoners will stare at us, check us out. This is normal. She also warns that they will be very charming and that we will probably feel quite comfortable with them. But remember, she says, these guys are not in here for stealing some candy from a 7–11. They have committed murder, rape. At the word rape, *Melanie bursts into tears. "Oh, what's the matter, honey, am I scaring you?" the psychologist asks. Melanie nods vigorously, lips mashed, face wet and red. A few choppy breaths, a few choked sobs. Then, stiffening her arms and pressing her hands parallel to the floor, she composes herself. I try to touch her shoulder in the hallway but she doesn't want any more comforting. She will do this on her own now.*

The exercise that alleviated our fear was so simple it seems impossible that it did so. It was Give-and-Take, a game of abstract sounds and movements, a game about impulse. The students were skeptical about the whole undertaking of the theater workshops, and they were particularly skeptical about Give-and-Take as an opening exercise in the prison setting. It was not their favorite game, and it was not how they wanted to begin. One of my brightest students worried aloud that the inmates would find this game silly and that it would make them feel exposed. Her worry worried me. On my more tired and serious days, I, too, felt silly playing Give-and-Take. I longed for less abstract tasks and more interplay with language. Give-and-Take was primal and primary, completely uncerebral, but something told me this might be a good place to begin.

In Give-and-Take, the players walk around the room, and a leader calls "Freeze!" to begin the game. Once all the players are "frozen," someone spontaneously initiates an improvised sound and movement and travels alone around the room.

> Wooooo-cha! Woooo-cha! Woooo-cha! Woooo-cha! Woooo.

When ready, the traveler stands directly in front of another player and "gives" the space to that player, who responds on impulse with his/her own sound and motion.

Pinglingpinglingpinglingpinglingpinglingpinglingpinglingpingling.
Bezoink! Gubbagubba Bezoink! Gubbagubba Bezoink! Gubba!
Reeeveee, Reeeveee, Reeeveee, Reeeveee.

The game is played in this way for a while, and then the element of "take" is introduced. Now, a player no longer has to wait to be given the space but can "take" it at any time by erupting with his/her own sound and motion.

Wooo-cha! Wooo-cha! Woo—
Bezoink! Bezoink!
Pinglingpinglingpinglingpingling—-
Reeeveee . . . Reeeveee . . . Reeeveee.
Bezoink!

Finally, the two phases are combined into the complete game of Give-and-Take (see appendix C for a fuller description of Give-and-Take).

To our relief and great surprise, the inmates played this game with extraordinary proficiency. Although often players, even children, have to be coached not to think too much about the sound and movement they make but simply to respond on impulse, here no such coaching was necessary. (Here impulsiveness, a symptom of BPD, worked to the inmates' advantage.) The room became wildly alive with bold, guttural sounds and abandoned motion. An impulsive response of fear counted here in this game but no more and no less than an impulsive response of surprise, delight, suspicion, or silliness. Suddenly, fear was just one of a varied palette of possible responses.

The students could scarcely keep up with the inmates. The noise from the game drew other inmates from the ward to the window to watch. As the weeks went on, the excitement of the game only heightened. By the third week, I was no longer surprised, when Give-and-Take concluded, to find six or ten inmates' noses pressed against the glass or to find those inside the room, students and inmates alike, dripping with sweat and laughter.

Dude

One of the inmates we quickly came to love was a huge, squat man with thin brown hair down to the middle of his back whom everyone called Dude. When we entered the workshop room, Dude was always there, restless, pacing, waiting for us. Dude's voice was raspy, his large arms were completely covered in blue-faded tattoos, and he regularly flashed a wide, toothless grin. He introduced himself, "'To be or not to be / that is the question.' I know the whole thing, too." He was good at every game. On our second or third visit to the Fed Med, I was using the opening, walking phase of Give-and-Take to say hello to everyone and to pass on some information about what we were going to do that day.

Suddenly, in midsentence, I heard from across the room, "FREEZE!" It was Dude, eager to get on with the game.

In *The Gift of Fear,* Gavin De Becker dramatizes the value of fear as a signal from human intuition, "a brilliant internal guardian that stands ready to warn you of hazards and guide you through risky situations."[10] For De Becker, our intuitions about fear are "the cornerstone of safety."[11] Participants used fear in this way a number of times throughout the workshops.

A pool of a dozen students began the class, but only eight chose to participate in the project. A few of the students were simply too afraid, and I encouraged them to listen to that feeling. Others were philosophically opposed to helping criminals. I was disappointed in this attitude from students of performance whom I hoped would believe, if anyone would, that transformation is possible, but I accepted it.

Similarly, some of the inmates opted out of the theater project altogether. Others felt up for it or not depending on the week. Still others consistently attended the theater workshops but always declined to participate.

Across two cycles of the project, only one situation had the potential to become truly dangerous. It began with poems, and, therefore, I represent it in poetic form.

Becca and Jackson

Becca fell in love with Jackson's poems.
When the light shone through the crumpled page
he gave her and told her to keep
she thought she could read his soul.

Becca's hair was yellow;
Jackson had one gold tooth.
They joked with ease, outraged
Over who got cut last night
From "American Idol."
("I know, what's up with that?")

Then she learned that inmates write in code
That drugs can hide in paper
That a gift might be a hit,
she an accomplice.

Becca who was always happy
Becca who never stopped smiling cried then
partly out of fear at the danger

She'd so easily embraced, but more because
She didn't want to be like that:
Wary, suspicious, mistrusting.
She didn't want to look at him as if he were
essentially different.

It was all right, though.
She was all right.
She was an actress.
She would try to act normal, and, after all
She did still care.

But what of Jackson?
Would he sense that something was different between them?
Would he be suspicious?
Would he be angry?

The next week,
Becca took a deep breath and
came back for her visit.
She scanned the faces anxiously,
hopefully.
Jackson wasn't there.

When Dr. Ashlock told me that Jackson had developed a crush on Becca, I felt naïve for not anticipating it. When Dr. Ashlock catalogued the subtle ways in which inmates use personal relationships for criminal activities—posting messages to each other through poetry on the Web, hiding drugs in a piece of paper—I felt stupid. When she reminded me that for patients with BPD, interpersonal relationships are usually unstable and intense and can be characterized by alternation of overidealization and devaluation,[12] I felt worried. And when she told me that Becca had promised to write to Jackson over the summer, I felt frightened.

Becca had been on the verge of giving Jackson her home address. Might Jackson have used this information for criminal activities? To involve Becca? Or, when his idealization of her became devaluation, to harm her? A student had been near danger, and I had not seen it. This was certainly a lapse in my oversight as a teacher. But it had implications for me personally as well: would I have seen it if I had been in her place?

Dr. Ashlock told a visibly shaken Becca that it was her choice as to whether or not to pen pal with Jackson but that the doctor would strongly advise against it and that if Becca chose to write to Jackson, prison rules would prevent her from participating in future workshops. Becca, having no desire to put herself in grave physical danger, told Dr. Ashlock that she would not do so. Given the emotional danger, which is to say the extreme vulnerability, she was now in (Jackson had not shown up for class the next week, but perhaps he would return the following week or the week after), I told Becca that the decision was hers as to whether or not to complete the rest of the workshops.

Becca's fear of physical danger was compounded by a sudden threat to her sense of her own identity. She didn't want to be someone who viewed the inmates with suspicion; and she didn't want to put herself in danger. Dr. Ashlock urged Becca to read *The Gift of Fear* as a way of helping herself respect her own sense of danger. She did so and ultimately chose to continue to participate in the project. She also became one of three students who participated again the following semester.

Contrary to the beliefs espoused by some schools of training, I believe that the actor, not the teacher/director, must be the ultimate arbiter of what risks, both physical and emotional, he/she will take and what risks are simply too dangerous. Teaching the student how to evaluate these risks should be part of the responsibility of trainers. The actor needs to know that protecting him/herself from physical harm is his/her responsibility, and the actor needs to develop sophisticated tools for doing so. The actor's fear must become the cornerstone of his/her safety.

It is not unusual for a performer to be afraid. Fear of public speaking (or performance) is one of the most pervasive fears in our culture. De Becker explains that the fear of death and the fear of public speaking are not as different from each other as they may seem. The latter, he says,

> is linked to the fear of being perceived as incompetent, which is linked to the fear of loss of employment, loss of home, loss of family, your ability to contribute to society, your value, in short, your *identity and your life*. . . . Linking an unwarranted fear to its ultimate terrible destination usually helps alleviate that fear. Though you may find that public speaking can link to death, you'll see that it would be a long and unlikely trip. (emphasis added)[13]

In the theater, however, apparently paradoxically, fear can often be most valuable as a predictor of artistic promise. Whereas others seek to solidify their identities through public performance, actors seek to make our identities more fluid. Of course, our identities are not endlessly fluid, though the masters give us hope and joy by creating the illusion that this is so. But each genuinely new experience in the theater offers the promise of expanding who we are.

Artistic performance is, I think, unique in its ability to provide this promising fear. (Perhaps professional athletes, too, experience it.) Although I have on rare occasions used feelings of fear to link experiences in the theater to outcomes of physical or emotional danger and, therefore, to opt out of participation, usually fear sends me a different message. Usually, I am afraid not for my life but for my identity. I have learned to recognize this kind of fear as performance gold. Whether in the role of director, teacher, or performer, if I am afraid at the beginning of a project I know that I have chosen the right project. Where I fear going is where I must go. I try to pass this two-part message on to my students in the opposite order from the one I have rehearsed here: Fear can indicate an experience of value ahead. But *you're the one in charge.*

Being in charge is not just wonderful—it is also damned scary. It is scary because if we fail to expand who we are, we can come to question our identities as actors. On the other hand, if we succeed, the success can disorient us, usually temporarily, about who we are.[14] This identity experimentation can be particularly frightening for teenagers and young adults.

Of course, risking one's identity is not the same thing as risking one's bodily health or psychological well-being. If I *were* offering the students a course in skydiving, given my credentials and training, I'd advise them to run. For that matter, if I were offering to choreograph a stage fight, I'd advise students to look into my credentials and training—and then in my case to run. In the realm of the psyche, creative artists often talk about the need for an emotionally safe space in which to experiment and explore. One cannot explore or experiment if one fears being judged, intimidated, or ignored.

For all of my students, one new fear of the prison-theater workshops was the fear of artistic leadership. Of his feeling of fear in anticipation of the first prison workshop, one student wrote, "Prisoners will be cold, quiet, insecure, unwilling to try, and distant. I will be scared, and I will not know what to tell them. They will be quiet and I will stand in front of them fishing for things to say." Another wrote, "I have this horrible vision of the four of us being as enthusiastic as physically possible and getting absolutely nothing back. Furthermore, I couldn't be more skeptical about the idea that I can teach these guys anything that will have any lasting impact." Although the students were afraid of this new role, their willingness to participate suggests an intuitive sense that the experiment held the possibility, however remote, of lasting value.

For the inmates, the new role theater challenged them to play was an unfamiliar one: themselves. One of the key symptoms of borderline personality disorder is an unstable image—or lack of image—of self. The prison environment exacerbates this problem, because one of the primary tools of survival for inmates is to suppress feeling. As former inmate Delbert Tibbs said in an interview for the documentary play *The Exonerated*, "[T]he main adjustment was just learning to feel again. You know, when you're in prison, you can't allow yourself to feel too much. So when you get out, you've gotta practice. I had to practice a bunch to be human again. To remind me."[15] The workshops were optional, and many of the inmates arrived at them deeply skeptical or visibly nervous. Nonetheless, like the students, they came.

Give-and-Take is perhaps the purest exercise in spontaneity in the theater games repertoire. In her book *Improvisation for the Theater,* Spolin describes the value of spontaneity.

> Through spontaneity, we are re-formed into ourselves. It creates an explosion that for the moment frees us from handed down frames of reference, memory choked with old facts and information and undigested theories and techniques of other people's findings. Spontaneity is the moment of personal freedom when we are faced with a reality and see it, explore it and act accordingly. In this reality the bits and pieces of ourselves function as an organic whole.[16]

In Give-and-Take, the inmates were to respond to the sound and movement they were given not as the murderer, the rapist, the robber, or even the tough guy they performed every day in prison but as themselves. The games required them to work from honest, creative impulses. The challenge was to notice their own responses to another player's behavior and, instead of stifling them, find a way to use them. This, the prisoners felt, was preparation to face the greatest fear that many of them will face: getting out. "You showed us we don't have to be who we ain't," Dude said in our final session. "When we get out there, if we just be ourselves, we'll be all right."

Both groups of participants spoke, in the end, of the courage the workshops had given them. The students found the courage to use their performance skills to help people and, more generally, the courage to move actively into the "real world" they would face after their imminent graduation. The inmates found or at least began to find the courage to enter a new world of their own.

The gift of fear is really the gift of courage.

The Gift of Yes

The second great gift performance gives is the gift of yes.

Great theater is not always about democracy. At the Yale summer drama program in 1988, playwright Terrence McNally told a story about Edward

Albee congratulating him on an award after McNally made an acceptance speech that focused on his collaborators.

"You really believe in all that collaboration stuff, don't you?" Albee said.

"Yes, I really do," McNally responded. "And you really don't, do you?"

"No," Albee responded, "I really don't."

Beckett, too, infamously declined (to put it euphemistically) input from actors, directors, and designers. Many of our greatest artists have been autocrats.

But in theatrical improvisation, the cardinal rule is simple: say "yes." Say yes to a collaborator's offering, no matter what it is. The consequences of doing otherwise are easily demonstrated to students by an exchange such as the following:

IMPROVISER 1: Dad, you've got to tell me where Faye is so we can stop her from eating those poisoned bologna sandwiches!
IMPROVISER 2: I'm not your father.

Instant death, of course, not only to poor Faye but to the performers on stage. If the goal is to create a fertile environment for theatrical collaboration—or, in the case of Boal-style theater for social change, for community dialogue—the way to get there is yes.

Another game at which the prisoners excelled was a warm-up called Yes. (Although Spolin strongly emphasizes the importance of agreement and although a number of her games involve the building of improvised stories through the use of the word *yes*, this particular yes game does not come from her work. I cannot remember where I learned it.) Here, the structure is looser and the guidelines are simpler than those for Give-and-Take (see appendix C for a fuller description of Yes). In Yes, a player suggests a simple activity that can be accomplished by everyone in the room, such as tapping feet or snapping fingers. The group responds to this idea as if it were the invention of the light bulb, with five enthusiastic cries of "yes!" Then, all the players perform the suggested activity until the next suggestion is made.

> Hey, everybody! I have an idea! Let's all try to touch our tongues with our noses!
> Yes, yes, yes, yes, yes!! (*Everyone does until—*)
> Hey, everybody! I have an idea! Let's all get into pretend canoes and row them!
> Yes, yes, yes, yes, yes!! (*Everyone does until—*)
> Hey, everybody!

Although I tend to feel that this game expends more energy than it generates, college students adore it, and, it turned out, so did the inmates.

Reviewing one workshop, a student wrote, "Next came the Yes yes yes yes yes game. And the only thing better than the Yes yes yes yes yes game is a Yes yes yes yes yes game that I get to lead." By saying yes, we do much more than give value to a single idea; we welcome someone into an artistic community. Particularly for young student performers, nothing is more important. The game—and the concept—of Yes are invaluable not just for those who are at key moments in their artistic development but for anyone to whom society has consistently said "no." And no one is told no more persistently and more forcefully than a federal prisoner. Yes is also of special value to those whose communities of belonging are unstable, in flux. This is something that theater artists, college students, and prisoners have in common.

Dr. Ashlock marveled at the unique power of Yes for inmates. One week, just back from a national conference of prison psychologists, she spoke of her renewed awareness of what she called the "sad state" of the prison system: "I was just sitting there thinking, wouldn't it be great to get all these guys who are out there stabbing each other to play the Yes game?" Although her statement embodies a kind of wishful, even playful naïveté about solving the problems of the prison system, Yes can be a tremendous tool for transforming individuals and, through those individuals, whole communities.

Through rehearsal exercises and theater games, we say yes in the theater in many more ways than we are even aware. Any game that involves imitation, mirroring, or following is a way of saying yes to another's creative input. Even giving one's full attention as an audience member is a form of yes. Danny was a performer who commanded our attention.

Danny

Danny was intense. Even his fleeting glance was a stare. He had ice-blue eyes that seemed etched in their sockets. His voice sounded like a smoker's, wheezing impatiently through breaths; he had chronic asthma. Every time we left the prison, Danny wanted to shake hands with each of us, to thank us personally for the session and to tell us he would be there next time. When the game involved sound and movement, Danny always chose movements relating to dogs and the single syllable "woof!" We came to expect that Danny's input would involve barking sounds and/or pawing gestures and to enjoy the link between this person and these behaviors. It was only on the very last day of the workshop that we learned that there was a therapeutic reason for this link, that the pawing gesture served to remind Danny to stay in control. Danny told us this. Although this was very interesting, the choice to accept the nature of Danny's contributions had long ago been made. And, despite his eager vocal contributions, Danny's favorite game was silent sculpting. When we hadn't sculpted for a week or two, Danny always reminded us that it was time.

In evaluating the workshops, Danny said that it was the first time in his life that he'd ever had "fun *fun.*" *I suspect that this new sense of joy was also a new sense of belonging.*

Sculpting, the primary technique of Boal's image theater, is a nonverbal way of saying yes. Without speaking, participant "sculptors" must mold participant "clay" into an image representing an idea or issue at work in their community. What, for example, does violence look like in a community? What does family look like? Sculptors mold their fellow participants one at a time. For each sculpture, several players contribute possible interpretations, simply stating what they see in the image. Then, reminding the group that they are looking at one of a great many possible images of the central idea, the facilitator encourages a new sculptor to enter the process (see appendix C for a fuller description of the game Sculpting).

The work can initially be confusing to participants who are accustomed to exercises with more clearly defined structures and endpoints. The only rules in sculpting are that anyone can sculpt, that the image-making occurs in silence, and that, as Michael Rohd emphatically reminds group leaders, "THERE ARE NO WRONG ANSWERS OR IMAGES! It doesn't have to have a 'meaning' the sculptor wants to communicate. It can come from a gut response, thoughts, or just a feeling."[17] The idea is to proliferate possibilities, not to arrive at a single image. In this way, a group develops a repertoire of ideas that every member has participated in creating.

In addition to its direct benefits, sculpting teaches concepts that are transferable to other games, other contexts. I suspect, for example, that the sculpting work we did as a group enabled the inmates to improve on the game of Yes by incorporating each other's suggestions into their own, as the sculpting activity had encouraged them to do. The game Yes typically consists of a series of unrelated whimsical suggestions and corresponding activities, but this is not how the inmates played. Rather, as one student wrote, "They came up with the best ideas. We rowed a boat, fished, fell out of the boat . . . we played for quite some time and were hot and sweaty by the time we were done." While affirming others' ideas is a way of saying yes, an even more sophisticated way of saying yes is to build on those ideas. The inmates made the yes of the game active by not merely affirming but building on each other's ideas.

The gift of yes is really the gift of belonging.

THE GIFT OF ESCAPE

> *Having lost his mother, father, brother, and grandfather, his beloved teacher Bernard Kornblum, his city, his history—his home—the usual charge leveled against comic books, that they offered merely an easy escape from*

> *reality, seemed to Joe actually to be a powerful argument on their behalf. . . . That was magic—not the apparent magic of the silk-hatted card-palmer, or the bold, brute trickery of the escape artist, but the genuine magic of art. It was a mark of how fucked-up and broken was the world—the reality—that had swallowed his home and his family that such a feat of escape, by no means easy to pull off, should remain so universally despised.*
>
> —Michael Chabon, *The Amazing Adventures of Kavalier and Clay*

The third great gift performance gives is the gift of escape.

Three of the nine major symptoms of borderline personality disorder have to do with an inability to regulate one's emotions. Many of the Axis 2 inmates, therefore, used illegal drugs to try to manage their intense mood swings. The theater workshops helped them experience other ways to regulate their emotions. Olsen, an inmate who, like many others, had an extensive history of illegal drug use, frequently noted the "natural high" the workshops provided. Several other inmates told the students that they talked together about the workshops not only long into the night but throughout the week. "Friday's coming!" they told each other. Keith Smith told the students that the workshops had helped avert crises when the staff threatened to prohibit participation. He told us, "A man with nothing to lose is a very dangerous man." The workshop gave the inmates something to lose. Most eloquent in expressing the value of the escape performance offered was an inmate named Ritter: "I tend to be depressed a lot in here, and the laughter seemed to help me. I seemed to have good days after you all came."

Tour of a Place is an exercise directly connected to the idea of physical and, therefore, emotional travel. Players work in pairs. One at a time, they take each other on a physical tour of a place that is meaningful to them, not only describing the space but leading their partner through it. They must use all of the allotted time to provide the tour (five to fifteen minutes, depending on time available), so if they finish early, they must retrace their steps, adding physical details (see appendix C for a fuller description of Tour of a Place). Sometimes a partner's place can be eerily familiar.

Olsen and Deirdre

Olsen and Deirdre were a good pair. Both were tall and thin, though Olsen was taller and thinner—he towered over the rest of us and seemed almost two-dimensional in his girth. Both had long, brown hair and delicate features. Both were soft-spoken. Deirdre smiled more, but Olsen gave of himself in other ways, such as drawing tattoos for the other inmates and crafting spinning tops for the students out of paper clips. ("This one spins slower, but it'll stay up longer. See?") Deirdre was an actress of uncommon intelligence. Both were artists, the kind who were more comfortable expressing themselves indirectly.

Olsen wanted to do the exercises correctly. At the beginning of his Tour of a Place exercise, he said to Deirdre, "I hope I ain't gonna mess this up or nothin.'" Deirdre assured him that there was no way he could mess it up, because "it's all about something you know." For Olsen, the Tour of a Place was about going to a place where he was the absolute authority: his memory. He was the second person in his pair to do the exercise, and he picked a place that was similar to the outdoor childhood sanctuary Deirdre had described, probably out of a concern for "doing it right." But when he became truly involved in the exercise, he became an expert on the particularities of his place. The following is excerpted from Deirdre's journal.

OLSEN: There was a stream in our woods, too, and we put a bridge across it, or sometimes we'd just wade through it.

DEIRDRE: How wide was your stream?

OLSEN: Oh, about like this: from here to here (*about a ten-foot width*).

DEIRDRE: So yours really was wide; ours was actually really small, like about only two or three feet.

OLSEN: Not ours, it was pretty big, so we needed that branch across it. But my favorite part of the place was the secret hideout we built. We dug a hole pretty deep down into the ground, and we used to hang out down there. We'd hide things in it, too, and when we weren't in it, we made this top for it out of branches and leaves, so if you didn't know it was there, you wouldn't ever see it.

DEIRDRE: So it was like a clubhouse for your friends?

OLSEN: Yeah, exactly, and we didn't tell anybody else about it. It was a big secret if you knew where it was and how to find it, and it was only for a few of us to know.

In addition to the gift of escape to a place so unlike the prison, a place in which he is the authority of his world, Olsen gave Deirdre a profound gift of yes by including her in his big secret.

In addition to allowing us to escape *from* our emotional and physical prisons, theater also allows us to escape *to* worlds completely unknown to us. Schultz, an ex-paratrooper, gave me this gift by taking me on a tour of the clouds. Here is a small part of what he said as he led me through the empty space.

> You're in a C141 plane, it's very noisy. And you're sitting on this bench that's made of webbing. When the light goes from red to amber, you need to stand up and don your mask for depressurization. You got gloves on, too, 'cause it's less than twenty degrees up here. And when the light turns from amber to green, the gate comes down. You're four abreast. You take a running start. When you jump off of that plane, you see the world. It's

> moist and wet in here. You feel the rustle of air in your ears. You've got your helmet on, but you can still feel it through the holes in your helmet. You don't know what's on the other side, but it's a good feeling.

It's a good feeling to be invited into another world. It's a good feeling to be there and to be welcomed there with open arms.

Director and teacher Zelda Fichandler links play with the conditions of creativity and freedom: "Creativity is born out of the capacity to play, and it's the very capacity for meaningful play that defines us as human beings. . . . The notion of play is indissolubly connected to the idea of freedom."[18] Curiously, the inmate who spoke most eloquently about this connection was a man who didn't participate in our play—or did he? Ritter came to every session, but despite the group's hearty efforts to get him on his feet, he declined. Nonetheless, he told the students, "I'm gonna think back on these days when I'm free. This program has been good for me. Y'all really made me feel free."

And let us not imagine that inmates are the only people who need freeing. Foucault underscores the similarities between the prison and the walls that contain the rest of us.

> How could the prison not be immediately accepted when, by locking up, restraining, and rendering docile, it merely reproduces, with a little more emphasis, all the mechanisms that are to be found in the social body? The prison is like a rather disciplined barracks, a strict school, a dark workshop, but not qualitatively different.[19]

Foucault suggests that the methods for social discipline in the world at large are even more insidious than those of the prison system.

Linda, an unusually quiet student, wrote to me months after the prison project concluded.

> The reason I did this was a very selfish one that connects to my past, and I think in a way it is about dealing with loss through theater. My father worked as an undercover FBI agent; for four solid years he lived two lives. As newspapers would later report, he had exposed a huge ring of unlawful trading at the mercantile stock exchange.
>
> Dad came back into our lives angry and hurt. Much of that anger was taken out on my mother and myself. Many years later as a young woman, I have confronted him and asked him why he had acted out on us and where did the anger come from. He said that he felt he was a traitor; he befriended men who truly cared about him, he got them to a point of vulnerability and then turned on them. He destroyed them.
>
> How could someone care so much for a criminal that the guilt eventually tore him and our family apart?

> I needed an answer, and I found it in a prison. The men we worked with touched me in so many ways. I could hardly believe that these criminals were so gentle, intelligent, weak, and grateful to have us there just for a few hours a week. I know these guys aren't saints. But I have learned that true humanity is brought out in us at our lowest, darkest moments. Once you see that simpler part of a person, I can understand how hard it could be to betray them. And in a way I can sort of understand my father and maybe even forgive him.
>
> I think I received far more then I gave. I am definitely a more compassionate person. I'm more optimistic, I see joy in unlikely places. And I am even more convicted that theater has the power to change the world, or at least some people.

In a meaningful double entendre that connects her both to the prisoners and to a higher power, this student became "convicted" of the power of performance to gain release from the losses of her past (see appendix D for some thoughts about pedagogy and the performer's grief).

Here, then, is the most precious gift of the theater, the one that keeps us connected to wonder and awe: The gift of escape is really the gift of freedom.

What made it possible for both the students and the inmates to experience courage, belonging, and freedom was the liminal space of performance, a space of play, and, unexpectedly, of joy. Danny, an inmate, said, "I've never had *fun* fun," and Linda, a student, commented, "I see joy in unlikely places." In this space, neither the prisoners working toward release nor the students working toward graduation had to feel afraid of the outside world. In this space, every idea, no matter how silly or how mundane, was embraced with wild enthusiasm. And in this space, for a short time, no one had to live anywhere more confining than their own imaginations.

At the end of the first year of the project, Olsen made a large drawing on cardstock to give to the students as a thank-you gift (see fig. 7.1). On the front were colorful, apt caricatures of each of the inmates—including Danny with a speech bubble that said "woof!" The cartoon characters wore black and white striped prison uniforms (costumes that no longer exist in the prison system) and their characteristic expressions, some very eagerly participating, others staying back to watch. Inside the card, each of the inmates wrote a personal note to the students. Each signed the note with his name and, to our surprise, his prison identification number. Although they had made at least a provisional space for joy through performance, each still instinctively answered to this lifeless, institutional name. Or did they hope, by providing us with this information, to give us a way to hold on to them?

Figure 7.1. On their final visit to the Fed Med, Missouri State University students were presented a cartoon of prisoners drawn by Olsen. Names are changed for the sake of privacy.

In either case, it is important not to be too sanguine about the reach of such efforts, at least in the short term. For example, despite his positive experiences and active participation in both the treatment program generally and the theater workshops, Olsen was removed from the program shortly after our departure for chronic drug use.

If theatrical performance creates a safe space for dialogue apart from everyday life, improvisatory theater creates a space that is even more secure. It does this, above all, by eliminating the audience. In improvisatory performance, even group members who are not directly involved in an exercise are considered participants. Boal encapsulates this philosophy in the notion of the "spect-actor." Spolin advised that "the teacher-director should see to it that each individual participates in some facet of the activity at every moment, even if this means nothing more than 'standing by for curtain.'"[20]

In addition to the elimination of the audience, the ground rules of improvisational performance protect the players' emotional and social safety. In Spolin's workshops, "All words that shut doors, have emotional content or implication, attack the student-actor's personality, or keep a student slavishly dependent on a teacher's judgment are to be avoided."[21] In Boal's games, many of which involve a discussion phase, everything said and done in the room remains confidential among the spect-actors. And all improvisation demands, through the cardinal rule of Yes, that participants accept and build upon the contributions of others.

Further, while encouraging risk and demonstrating its rewards, improvisatory performance designates each player as the ultimate arbiter of which activities are safe and which are not. Rohd refers to this ground rule as the "right to pass" when an activity is uncomfortable, without being interrogated as to why.[22]

Improvisatory theater deemphasizes reasoned and intellectual responses. Games such as Give-and-Take and exercises such as sculpting teach performers to value impulse, nonverbal communication, visualization, movement, and fragmented and abstract thought. They also teach performers to value play, what Danny called "*fun* fun." Improvisatory performance *does things* with these invaluable human resources that no theatrical performance and few everyday life performances can do.

Finally, improvisation is total collaboration, not just between multiple minds but between multiple bodies and imaginations, multiple selves. While formal community dialogues can also be valuable, the experimental, playful form of collaboration created through improvisation enables communities to come together in ways we might otherwise never have imagined.

8. Loss, Performance, and the Future

PERFORMANCE PROCEEDS BY WAY OF PRACTICE. Yet, performers often devalue rehearsal and revision. Amateurs and preprofessionals in particular tend to think about rehearsal as what one has to do when one is not yet good enough or experienced enough to present one's work to an audience, as in the old joke: "Excuse me, sir, can you tell me how to get to Carnegie Hall?" "Practice!" Or the Mel Brooks psychiatrist routine: "Doctor, can you tell me how long you've been practicing?" "I never practice, I'm very good at it." More sophisticated performers, however, tend to view even public performances as rehearsals, through which their practice continues to evolve.

Practice is both a conceptual lens or perspective and a process through which we may come to better understand and respond to loss. Certain embodied practices, writing practices, and practices in reading an expansive range of "texts," from everyday behaviors to live performances to literary fiction, can provide much-needed models for collective action in a culture that still tells us to keep our grief to ourselves.

In her 1976 poem "One Art," Elisabeth Bishop describes how hard it can be to practice "the art of losing," both in life and in language.

> The art of losing isn't hard to master;
> so many things seem filled with the intent
> to be lost that their loss is no disaster.
>
> Lose something every day. Accept the fluster
> of lost door keys, the hour badly spent.
> The art of losing isn't hard to master.

Then practice losing farther, losing faster:
places, and names, and where it was you meant
to travel. None of these will bring disaster.

I lost my mother's watch. And look! My last
or next-to-last of three loved houses went.
The art of losing isn't hard to master.

I lost two cities, lovely ones, and, vaster,
some realms I owned, two rivers, a continent.
I miss them, but it wasn't a disaster.

—Even losing you (the joking voice, a gesture
I love) I shan't have lied. It's evident
The art of losing's not too hard to master
though it may look like (*Write* it!) like disaster.

Bishop's refrain "The art of losing isn't hard to master" is ironic. The speaker protests too much, undermining any illusion of mastery through her obsessive repetition of the claim, much as Jamaica Kincaid undermines her refusal to love her brother by her multiple insistences that she does not love him. The poem, through repetition and through an accumulation of ever more irreplaceable objects (first, generally, places, names, and "where it was you meant to travel," then more specifically, a watch, a house, a city, and finally, a loved one) demonstrates the extent to which the art of losing *is* hard, indeed, impossible to master.

The speaker's instruction to practice losing, however, is sincere and even urgent. Inspired by Bishop's anxiety over the anticipated loss of Alice Methfessel, the friend with whom she shared the last decade of her life, "One Art" describes two intimately related arts—that of losing and that of representing loss. The speaker practices losing through a range of everyday behaviors but, ultimately and most importantly, through writing itself.

To perform "disaster" in writing, the poem suggests, is to practice the particular kind of control in the face of chaos that writing affords; by naming "disaster" in language, the speaker gains authority, however qualified, over her experiences of loss. The poem as a whole is an act of technical "mastery," a villanelle conforming to the complex structural requirements of the form, which involve only two rhymes over six stanzas, recurring in a strictly alternating pattern. But, even for an accomplished poet like Bishop, such a form is difficult to master; the poem was the result of no less than seventeen drafts of "practice."[1] "One Art," then, is not merely about loss; it is a rehearsal of loss, of the practice of losing. As such, it is testament to both the difficulty and the value of such practices in keeping us "one" with our own feelings, actions, destinations, and most cherished relationships.

Not all losses are, to borrow Judith Viorst's title, necessary losses. Indeed, many of the losses described in this book are decidedly unnecessary ones. It is not necessary to leave large groups of citizens' voices unheard or to leave their experiences out of our national histories. Crushing poverty in the underdeveloped world is not necessary, nor is it necessary for powerful nations to systematically oppress or exploit weaker ones. The spread of AIDS is not necessary, and a terrorist act need not necessarily lead to a permanent state of war. It is not necessary for people to commit crimes against others or to be dehumanized for doing so.

But while not all losses are necessary, it is increasingly necessary to know how to respond to loss in our communities, our countries, and our world. Western culture is diverse and rapidly diversifying. Ethnic demographics that have remained relatively stable for a century are undergoing radical shifts. (The 2005 U.S. Census states that Hispanics are the largest and fastest-growing ethnic group in the United States and that one in every three U.S. residents is part of a group other than white.) These shifts will produce new alliances, new relations of power, and, inevitably, both new gains and new losses.

Our diversity is not yet making us stronger. At the beginning of the twenty-first century, the adverse consequences of a culture of radical individualism, particularly in the American context, were even more evident than they were in the 1980s, often dubbed the "me" generation.[2] Yet, in the first decade of the new century, it has become clearer than ever before that a mature understanding of both the losses we suffer and those we inflict, consciously or unconsciously, on others is a matter of life and death. In such a climate, creating space for diverse responses to loss is not only a moral imperative but a matter of cultural and political survival.

Models and Methods

Throughout this book, I have explored both models and methods for diversifying our collective responses to loss through performance.

Performance theorists have provided some of these models and methods. Beyond their specific substantive contributions to thinking about loss and performance, scholars such as Joseph Roach, Peggy Phelan, Diana Taylor, and Della Pollock have provided models for expanding the range of texts that can be considered as performances of loss. Phelan has expanded the purview of performance to include visual media, Taylor and Roach to "hemispheric" analyses of diverse cultural exchanges, and Pollock to include the world of personal narrative and history. A propos of Renato Rosaldo's appeal, they have also expanded the possibilities for how scholars might write about such issues, employing methods of performative writing that are both deliberately experimental in form and resolutely personal in content.

Other models and methods spring from performances of loss in everyday life. Although both of the hospice patients who served as key informants for my own ethnographic work around death and dying were actively grieving their own mortality, they rehearsed their grief in sharply contrasting ways. One's practice of losing followed a highly theatrical performance model, replete with gestural flourishes and broad vocal dynamics. The other's practice more closely resembled the performance-efficiency model embodied in the workplace by "performance reviews" of employees.[3] Her streamlined enactment of grief eschewed every excessive word or gesture, every enactment that smacked of "trivia." The diverse methods of devising theatrical performance can help to broaden the dissemination of such models, generating community dialogue around loss, grief, and mourning.

Characters in literature and drama can provide powerful models for performing loss differently. In *My Brother*, Kincaid models an anger that cannot be relegated to her own "scalded psyche" but demands an answer and will not stop reiterating itself until it gets one. Drawing parallels between her brother's AIDS-ravaged body and the landscape of Antigua, ravaged by abuse and neglect, she also models a determination to work for justice on behalf of those whom race and class discrimination have left behind. By contrast, Tony Kushner's Homebody in *Homebody/Kabul* performs mourning through an act of radical empathy with and even possession by the racial and economic other, an act that eventually launches her out of her titular isolation. Through the Homebody, Kushner models an intimate, empathic, and embodied interpretation of others' losses against American rhetoric and policies that pit a monolithic "us" against a demonized "them" for whom we are not responsible.

The writers themselves offer diverse methodologies for performing loss. The adaptation of literature for the stage is a valuable method of practicing the necessary psychological adaptations involved in performing loss. In addition, adapting a novel such as Jose Saramago's *Blindness,* in which loss is a principal subject, can yield new ways of staging such stories. In *My Brother*, Kincaid uses the method of performative writing to insist upon connections between a personal loss and a global one. For Kincaid, the act of writing is by definition performative, because it defies the expectation that her own life would be ravaged by illiteracy and poverty. Through *The America Play*, Suzan-Lori Parks "jokes with history," an approach to mourning that finds its power in creativity and, especially, in humor. Specifically, Parks finds compensation for historical losses by modeling the playful repetition and revision of historical narratives. And through the process of publicly reworking *Homebody/Kabul*, Kushner demonstrates perhaps less a methodology than an ethic of contemplation, interpretation, and revision that has the power to simultaneously humble and embolden us in our efforts to perform loss.

The model that one adopts for representing national tragedy may depend on how the tragedy is constituted. Two contrasting models for representing the events of September 11 arose from two different understandings of what constituted the tragedy. The first model, which I attempted to follow in my own writing, responded to the enormous loss of human life on that day by deliberately preserving a space that exceeds interpretation, acknowledging the mystery of catastrophic—and in this case violent—loss. The second model, responding to the loss of democratic ideals represented by the American response to the terrorist attacks, rejects indeterminacy in order to recover an alternate practice of making community. By responding in a deliberately representational way, with portraits of historical figures bearing their words, painter Robert Shetterly acted against the obfuscating governmental response to the tragedy then and still in circulation.

Finally, theatrical practices themselves can yield models for performing loss. In the U.S. Medical Center for Federal Prisoners, college students and inmates used improvisational theater work to create joy amid many layers of personal and interpersonal loss, including the loss of physical freedom, the loss of identity, and the loss of engagement with the world outside the prison. Although playful, pleasurable responses to loss may seem anachronistic, such practices may enable individuals to move from fear to courage, isolation to belonging, paralysis to collective action. The diverse methods of theatrical improvisation can help participants develop skills to negotiate their losses and become, against all odds, a community.

Metaphors

In addition to directly demonstrating a more diverse range of possibilities for "doing" or performing loss in everyday life, the various performance texts examined here expand the range of metaphors available for making sense of and, ultimately, for acting in the face of loss. One unique way that performance and other forms of artistic representation allow us to practice our responses to loss is through metaphor. If both loss and writing are, as Bishop's ironic protest to the contrary implies, hard to master, it is also true that to write "disaster" is to preserve the productive failures of writing to name reality. Losing may "look like (*Write* it!) like disaster," but in the literary distance of that simile, that *like*, is life itself. Losing may look like disaster, but the terms are not simple equivalents. Loss is many-named, many-voiced, and it is only in the articulation of the relationship as metaphor that the writer can make this inequality known to him/herself.

The word *metaphor* is often qualified by the word *mere*, dismissed as a conceit of literature or other forms of high culture. But artists and many other students of human cultures know that this is not so. For the anthropologist Victor Turner, metaphor consists of

> a certain kind of polarization of meaning in which the subsidiary subject is really a depth world of prophetic, half-glimpsed images, and the principal subject, the visible, fully known (or thought to be fully known component), at the opposite pole to it, acquires new and surprising contours and valences from its dark companion.[4]

The symbolic language of performance is a "depth world of prophetic, half-glimpsed images" from which human behavior, relationships, and experiences acquire "new and surprising contours."

Metaphor does in miniature what art does: It sheds light by way of darkness, making the familiar strange. There is, of course, that ecstatic moment in performance in which the metaphor seems to vanish. But, most of the time, performance proceeds by way of what the great acting teacher Konstantin Stanislavsky called the "magic if." Performance itself, as Phelan's work makes so vividly clear, is a metaphor for loss, because performance disappears before our eyes, refusing to be saved or kept.

How necessary metaphor is to understanding the problem of loss becomes particularly clear when we consider our own deaths. As a child, I remember being absolutely stymied by the problem of imagining my own death. Indeed, I was a child insomniac. What kept me awake, mostly, was my inability to reconcile myself with unconsciousness, which was, for me, the same as death. I'd lie awake at night and try to imagine: *Once I'm asleep, I won't be able to think. But I won't be able to think about the fact that I'm not able to think. I wouldn't even be able to have this thought I'm having right now about how I'm not able to think about not thinking* . . . It was a long childhood.

To negotiate loss, we simply must have recourse to metaphor; it is too difficult to understand our losses directly. The site of metaphor, the human imagination, is, as Hayden White argues, indispensable in the enterprise of "making sense of necessity"—in particular, the necessity of endings.

Literary adaptation is a metaphor for mourning insofar as it demonstrates that loss is the necessary condition of transformation. The purposeful manipulation of scale, space, light and sound can produce visual metaphors for the myriad feelings that make up the "mise en scene" of grief.

Viewed through the lens of adaptation for performance, everyday speech becomes ripe with metaphors for practicing mourning. In the context of the hospice performance *Not Quite Through*, these metaphors included an emotional cup in need of continual replenishment; a string that connects the "five stages of grief" at the same time that it binds the mourner to the lost object; the bifurcation of speech demonstrating the complex and even self-contradictory nature of grief; and the inanimate objects that stand in so powerfully for many human relationships.

Kincaid uses monuments as metaphors for the losses produced by historical oppression. The national library of Antigua, which has been in complete disrepair for decades, serves as a metaphor for the self-neglect of an impoverished and undereducated people. A monument to an Antiguan slave, ironically surrounded by a locked steel fence, is a metaphor for an international community that continues to enslave its former colonies, even as it professes to celebrate their freedom. Most of all, Kincaid uses her brother's waste, decay, and death as a metaphor for the waste, decay, and death that characterizes the social and political landscape of her homeland.

Certain metaphors are so powerful that they become reanimated again and again over the history of a nation or even, following Taylor's language, a hemisphere. The metaphor of the hole, for example, seems to resonate particularly strongly on the contemporary American stage, in the context of America's notoriously selective ways of writing and performing history. In the plays by Suzan-Lori Parks and Tony Kushner analyzed here, the hole stands in for a variety of conversations not had, stories not told, relationships not acknowledged, and voices not heard. What Parks calls the "Great Hole of History"—which is, in reality, many holes—is best approached with empathy, humor, and a keen awareness that although it can be marked and even compensated for, it cannot ever be filled.

In my own effort to create a metaphorical response to the losses of September 11, 2001, I found that large, abstract nouns such as *love* and *freedom* failed to communicate poetically because of their generality, while smaller and more specific nouns such as the objects left behind by the victims failed, as metonymies, to stand in for the enormity of the whole. Ultimately, I found only two words that seemed to have metaphorical power to illuminate this historical loss. The first, *again*, an adverb without a verb, approximated the impulse toward repair and recovery in the aftermath of the attack. The second, *we*, a subject accompanied by a wide range of verbs, approximated the struggle for a sense of community in the face of devastating loss.

The struggle to repair the American community inspired Shetterly to reject metaphor in favor of concrete historical examples. But it was the metaphor of the performing body standing in for—surrogating, as Joseph Roach would have it—these historical presences that he felt helped communicate to audiences the possibilities for realizing such a community today.

Theatrical improvisation also provides a metaphorical language for negotiating losses that may be too powerful to address directly. In the context of working with federal prisoners suffering from mental illness, the cultivation of physical and vocal impulse served as a metaphor for courageous intervention in the world, the improvisational rule of Yes served as a metaphor for social acceptance, and imaginative exploration served as a metaphor for freedom. For the inmates, nothing was "mere" about these metaphors.

Understanding our responses to loss as performances and those performances as evolving practices can enable us to recognize, create, build upon, and diversify a range of meaningful responses to loss. "Practice losing" can save us from responses that perpetuate violence and oppression. It can also help us hold on, in the largest sense, to "where it was we meant to travel."

A central effort of this book has been to move beyond a kind of hegemonic uniformity in the way many Western cultures command performances surrounding loss and to locate diverse spaces for radically diverse practices. To make of losing not one art but many.

It is the future. I am lying in bed. On the bedside table is a vase of irises, fresh, just beginning to open. Beside me sits my oldest son. He will be forty years old next week. His wife and children have planned a celebration. Right now, they are sitting quietly in the next room.

"Tell me one last story," my son asks me.

"I don't know if I can tell you a story," I say. "I'm too sad."

"Tell me a story about feeling sad, then."

"I don't know, honey. It doesn't seem important right now. It seems trivial."

"Stories are never trivial."

"Why don't you tell me a story, then?"

A long pause.

"I can't think of a story," he says.

"It doesn't have to be anything special," I assure him. "Tell me a very ordinary story."

"I can't think of a story," he says again.

"Me, neither."

A very long pause.

"I really hate this," he says.

"Me, too. I really really hate this, too."

Another very long pause. Then my son straightens up in his chair a bit. He clears his throat.

"The outlook wasn't brilliant," he begins.

We laugh. It is the opening line of "Casey at the Bat," a poem I used to read to him at bedtime, a poem about a seemingly indomitable baseball star who loses his final game. My son never cared about baseball; even as a kid, he was a math geek. But he loved the poem for its melodrama of losing and, above all, because it was the longest one in the book. Like his mother, he never wanted it to be time to go to sleep.

"The outlook wasn't brilliant for the Mudville Nine that day . . . "

My son continues to recite the poem. I am struck by the clearness of his voice, like a laser entering my brain. Several decades ago, when I was in training to become a hospice volunteer, they told me that hearing was the final sense to go. They were right.

As I continue to listen, I notice that something has happened. Slowly, almost imperceptibly, the voice I am hearing has changed register; it doesn't sound like my son anymore. The voice is unmistakably my father's. I am no longer lying in this bed, in this room. I have traveled back to the house of my childhood, not as someone who lives there but as a visitor on a final tour. I stand in the front hall, from where I can survey as much of the space as possible.

"Oh, somewhere in this favored land the sun is shining bright / The band is playing somewhere, and somewhere hearts are light . . . "

It is a good house. Like all the houses in which I have lived, it has its comforts. Like all of them, it has its leaky faucets and rickety stairs, its badly lit corridors and spotted ceilings. Still, as I lie there listening, I try to memorize the place—its colors, its smells. I try to hold it all inside my memory. Soon, I know, very soon, I will have to be going.

Appendixes
Notes
References
Index

Appendix A. Devised Performance Assignments

Generation of Sources

Purpose

To encourage students to think broadly about the genres and voices they might include in their performance texts.

Instructions

Bring to class a list of ten possible textual sources for your performance. Some of these should be directly related to the subject of your performance; some should be further afield. For example, if you are creating a piece about the 2000 presidential election, directly related texts would include candidates' speeches, statements by key public officials (e.g. Katherine Harris, Florida's secretary of state), and the text of the U.S. Supreme Court decision that finalized the results. But you might also include on your list an excerpt from the Gettysburg Address, the Yale *Wiffenpoof Song*, a dictionary definition of the word *chad*, and instructions for basting a turkey (because the issue was still undecided at Thanksgiving that year).

Guidelines

Wherever appropriate, bibliographic information for sources should be provided in MLA format.

Living History Interview

Purpose

To provide students with a structure for conducting a successful interview and to begin shaping the resulting source text for performance.

Instructions

Conduct a thirty-minute in-person interview with someone who has lived in or studied a time or place that interests you. Create a performance of approximately five carefully chosen minutes of the interview. Although you are required to provide a partial transcript of the interview, you should not use this transcript directly in your performance. Instead, concentrate on communicating the essence of the exchange, whether this means core ideas or core feelings. You may use material from other texts if you wish.

Guidelines

Balance of preparation. As a matter of both efficiency and respect, you must have conducted basic historical research on events or issues relevant to the conversation. You do not want to ask a Vietnam veteran when the war took place or what it was about. You do not want to ask an earth scientist what global warming is. You want to be prepared with a plan and a series of questions and willing to diverge from both.[1] Allow the interviewee to *guide* and *affect* the flow of conversation but not to *control* it. And the same goes for you! Also be prepared to ask interviewees to perform specific memories and imagine future scenarios. Interviews are creative spaces.

Schedule your interview in a generous block of time. Don't squeeze it into a free hour. You want to allow time for the conversation to extend and also for note-taking immediately afterward.

Tell the interviewee (both in scheduling and again at the beginning of the interview) that you want to talk to him or her for about thirty minutes. If the interviewee carries the conversation beyond that time period, allow that to happen, and ask follow-up questions as appropriate, but keep it focused. After forty-five minutes, you should be actively wrapping up the conversation. You don't want to tire your interviewee out or impose.

Label the tape with interviewee's name and date of interview. Load and test the tape recorder before you go to the interview. At the beginning of the interview, either ask permission to record and begin recording, or (this is what I prefer) ask if it's okay if you turn it on once the conversation gets started. I like to tell the interviewee that I'm recording so that I don't have to take too many notes and that the tape will remain confidential. A few minutes after you start the recorder, check it visually to make sure it's working. Take notes as a backup—you never know what's going to happen—and make sure to remove the tabs from the tape and as soon afterwards as possible (definitely the same day).

Suggestions on what to write down during the interview.

- facts that you are likely to forget—names, dates, places. You may well change all of these in the final script, but you want to have them in writing for future reference.
- a bare-bones topic outline. How did the conversation flow, from what general topic to what general topic?
- perfect sentences. Probably at least once in your interview, the interviewee will say something so beautiful that you will want to remember it exactly. It's okay to ask once or twice if he or she would mind holding for a moment (though obviously you don't want to do this all the time).

Level of probe. Ask questions without apologies or qualifications. Your interviewee will tell you if he or she does not wish to answer the question, and you will assure the interviewee that that's fine. But don't foreclose the possibility of an answer as you ask the question.

Balance of sharing. The interview should be an exchange, with the focus on the interviewee. If the interviewee asks you questions, be generous (but not long-winded) in answering them. If something said moves you to share your experience, do so. You should be careful to frame your experiences as related (or different) but never as the same. Good: "I have a little sister, too, so I can imagine . . ." Bad: "I know exactly how you feel." You do not know exactly how anyone feels, even if you have been through a very similar experience.

Patience with silence. Enormously productive things can come out of long periods of silence. When a question engages your interviewee, let him or her spend as long as he or she wants to spend reflecting before answering. Don't prompt or helpfully extrapolate.

Body language.

- Your hair is not interesting. Your clothes are not interesting. Don't wear either in a way that encourages you to pay it any attention.
- Dress respectfully. Avoid ratty shoes, t-shirts and sweatshirts, holey jeans.
- Be open and alert physically. Keep your weight from sinking backward and your arms from covering your torso.
- Allow yourself to naturally signal interest vocally, facially, and verbally.

Suggestions on what to write down after the interview. Everything you possibly can. What did the room smell like? How did the interviewee use his or her hands? What scenes were mentioned? What surprises you or makes you curious? How specifically can you remember what was said?

Ending the interview. Ask whether there's anything the interviewee wants to discuss that you haven't asked about. Tell him or her, too, that if he or she thinks of anything later to add to please let you know. Ask whether the interviewee would mind if you followed up if you thought of additional questions. For this to work, obviously, you'll need to exchange contact information. Remind the interviewee that you'll be doing a performance based on a group of interviews and that you'll invite him or her to come and see the performance once the dates are set. Be sure to thank the interviewee, and express how much you appreciate him or her taking the time to talk with you.

At some point during the interview, you'll need to ask the interviewee to sign a form that gives you permission to conduct the interview. You should cover the background information on the sheet in the initial conversation in which you set up the interview. Personally, I'd ask for a signature at the end of the interview so the interviewee knows what information he or she is agreeing to share, though you could also do it at the beginning. Just make sure it gets done.

Personal Narrative Writing Exercises

Purpose

To help students develop a personal narrative performance that is compelling and that contains multiple perspectives.

Instructions

To identify the story you wish to tell, make a list of all the areas in which you are an expert. These can include skills such as playing an instrument or a sport, activities such as juggling, or roles such as "being an older sister."

In a free write of five to seven minutes, tell a story connected to one of these areas of expertise from the point of view of someone else:.

- another character in the story.
- a particular outsider to the story, real or imagined, such as, the main character's grandmother, a celebrity, etc.
- your older self
- your younger self
- a celebrity
- your fantasy self
- your nightmare self

Genre twist. In a free write of five to seven minutes, tell the story in a different genre than you are currently using, for example, as a detective story, a fairy tale, a reality-television show, etc.

Fictionalized biography. Invent a fictional version of yourself, one better suited to comment on a particular event than the real you. If you were a seven-year-old, a convict, an anthropologist, what would you want to talk about? What would you have to say? How would you say it? To whom? Create a monologue or scene in which this other you gets to have his/her say.

Object narrative. Pick an object you own or have owned that either once belonged to or is strongly associated with someone precious to you. Tell the object's story.

Personal Narrative Performance

Purpose

To encourage students to incorporate public concerns into performances of personal narratives.

Instructions

Perform a story from your life in which you were at risk, either intentionally or unintentionally. This should be something that affected you and of which you therefore have a strong memory. In scripting the performance, you must use a minimum of three sources, as explained in the Mystory handout and workshop (Mystory is by Bowman and Bowman).

Guidelines

In selecting your sources, consider three areas of focus:

- personal importance. Why is this story important to you? Is the answer in the piece, ideally in an indirect but locatable manner?

- audiences. To what social, political, cultural, or other identity groups might this story matter? How does your language address and/or challenge these groups?
- structure. How will you provide both structure and surprise in both the script and the performance? How will you balance the narrative strategies of summary, scene, and description?

Historical Narrative Performance

Purpose

To create a performance text based on historical materials.

Instructions

Perform a historical moment in which a common idea about "culture" was challenged. This could be, for example, a scene from the life of a marginal or radical historical figure or an encounter between representatives of two countries. The central performance materials must be historical—such as, newspaper articles, biographies, letters, speeches, etc. You must document the use of at least three sources.

Structural Experimentation

Purpose

To let students experiment with various models for structuring a devised performance.

Instructions

Part 1. Choose excerpts of one to two pages from each of three sources you have decided to work with in devising your performance. Label the excerpts *A*, *B*, and *C*. You will need to divide each of these texts into sections for some of the tasks below. (You may change which is which for different parts of the assignment as you see fit.)

Part 2. Create a script draft in which two of the texts are interwoven and the third appears uninterrupted. For example: ABABCBA or ABABABC.

Part 3. Create a script draft in which one of the texts appears repeatedly as a structural "refrain." For example, ABACA.

Part 4. Create a script in which a repeated gesture or physical activity provides the structure.

Part 5. Create a script in which a design element (sound, lighting, set, etc.) provides the structure, either through repetition or through a gradual visual movement.

Staging with Anne Bogart's Viewpoints

Purpose

To provide focus to students staging their own work and to develop a range of staging styles and emphases across an ensemble or classroom.

Instructions

Group 1. Create a performance around three changes in tempo, a behavioral gesture that is repeated, and two expressive gestures.

Group 2. Create a performance around four changes in spatial relationship and at least three kinesthetic responses. Also include one movement of extremely long duration and two movements of extremely short duration.

Group 3. Create a performance in which the topography and tempo change as the text does. For ideas about strategies for exploring topography, see Dixon and Smith, *Anne Bogart*, 23.

Group 4. Create a performance that explores the physical space in which you are working in relation to the text through the use of external repetition and kinesthetic responses to elements of the architecture, particularly mass (walls, floors, windows, etc.) and light (sources of light, shadows).

Appendix B. Adaptation of Literature Assignments

Orchestrating an Adaptation

Purpose

To experiment with techniques for shaping prose in performance.

Instructions

Select any two pages from the text, and orchestrate them using at least three of the following techniques:

- refrain
- choral speech
- serial speech
- echo
- dissemination of narration among multiple storytellers

Bifurcating Narration

Purpose

To discover and dramatize multiple voices in a single narrator in prose fiction.

Instructions

Select a passage of approximately one page from the text. Create a script in which the narration is spoken by two different kinds of narrators named for their salient characteristics. For example, Old Narrator and Young Narrator or Optimistic Narrator and Cynical Narrator.

Guidelines

Choose a passage in which narration plays a central role. If you think it advisable, divide the narration among more than two voices.

Performing the Novel

Purpose

To adapt a fictional text to the stage without eliminating the narrator or the narrative perspective.

Instructions

Select a chapter from the novel to perform. The script will be an adapted excerpt from the novel that incorporates approximately two to three pages of material.

You may use material from various parts of your chapter, from elsewhere in the novel, and/or from secondary texts, but however you design your script, it should include at least two pages of your assigned chapter. You may condense the narration in your selection, but you should not eliminate it altogether.

Guidelines

You may work individually or in pairs. If you work in pairs, you should adapt a longer excerpt. Each person should have no less than five minutes of material to perform.

In crafting your performance, you should not assume that other members of the class are familiar with your text.

Your performance should be not much shorter than four and no longer than seven minutes. If your performance is longer than seven minutes, although it will kill me to do it, I will cut you off. To avoid this, simply time your rehearsal. Your set-up/takedown can be no longer than three minutes. I will assign you a rehearsal partner. Part of that person's job will be to help you make your setup and takedown efficient. Also, you are welcome to incorporate media into your performance—sound, lights, slides, television, videocassette player, DVD player, computers, etc. Just make sure that either you have reliable equipment or you tell me at least one class period in advance what you need. Also, make sure to rehearse with the equipment. If your performance fails because you've relied on equipment that doesn't work or isn't there, this will be your responsibility.

Adaptation Workshop

Purpose

To use a classmate to help you develop the form and content of your adaptation.

Guidelines

For each performer in your pair, spend at least ten minutes brainstorming answers to the following questions.

Instructions

Write answers to the following questions.

Dramatic situation: creating movement.

- What is the tone or primary speaker's attitude at the beginning of your selection?
- How does that tone change?

Visual elements of the performance.

- How can your use of space help you to communicate the dramatic situation?
- How can configuration of the audience/performer spatial relationship help you to communicate the dramatic situation?

- How can you use performance tools—lights, sound, costume, props—to help you communicate the dramatic situation?

Performing multiple characters.

- What distinguishes each of the characters in your selection vocally?
- What distinguishes each of the characters in your selection physically?
- How else can you make distinctions in characters? (locus, posture, movement, use of key props, etc.)

Soundscape Performance

Purpose

To heighten students' awareness of the aural elements of language including sound repetition and rhythm.

Instructions

Create a performance of a poem that highlights its sounds and rhythms. Use the medium of performance to help the audience hear what's important about the poem's sound patterns and how its sounds/rhythms contribute to its meaning.

Guidelines

Scripting. The original order of the poem's words, lines, and stanzas should be part of the performance. This does not mean that you need to restrict your impulses towards play, experimentation, arrangement, etc. It only means that if you are going to dramatically reorder the text, you should also include a reading of the original text somewhere in the performance. Please turn in one copy of your script on the day of your performance.

Memorization. The poem need not be memorized but you should know it well.

Length. Maximum time = six minutes, including setup and takedown.

Visual component. Although the focus of the performance is sound, you should also plan what you are going to do on stage. Visually, the performance may be very simple, but it should be organized and rehearsed.

Participation. Each group member must be actively involved in the live performance.

Image-Based Performance

Purpose

To communicate something important about your poem through the creation of a central image.

Source

Adapted from a class assignment by Mary Zimmerman at Northwestern University

Instructions

Use design elements and/or your body to create an image that is either

- contained in the text (e.g., for Poe's "The Tell-Tale Heart," an image of a heart) or
- metaphorically related to the text (e.g., for Perkins's "The Yellow Wallpaper," an image of a flower coming apart, petal by petal—perhaps with something unexpected inside!)

Guidelines

At least part of the text must be present in the performance in some way.

Time: four minutes, empty stage to empty stage. If you would like to go first to give yourself extra set-up time or last to give yourself extra takedown time, let me know at least one day before the performance.

Devise some way of letting us know when your performance begins and ends.

Appendix C: Improvisation Exercises

NOTE: All of the exercises below work best if led and coached by a facilitator. Viola Spolin, Augusto Boal, and Michael Rohd each provide model scripts for coaching their exercises. Spolin and Boal both have enormous repertoires of improvisational exercises, of which only a very few are indicated here.

Give-and-Take

Purpose

To respond on impulse and to develop awareness of the group.

Source

Viola Spolin, *Improvisation for the Theater: A Handbook of Teaching and Directing Techniques*, 3rd ed. (Evanston: Northwestern UP, 1999).

Instructions

Give. Players are distributed evenly across the space and are "frozen" in place. One player spontaneously begins by moving through the space with a strong vocal sound and physical movement. This player moves until he/she stands facing another player to whom he/she "gives." Player 2 should respond immediately on impulse with his/her own sound and movement, repeating them until he/she "gives" to a third player. Play continues in this manner. There should ideally be no silence/stillness between the end of one player's sound and movement and the beginning of the next.

Take. Again, players are distributed evenly across the space and "frozen." Again, one player begins with a sound and movement. This time, however, the initiating player must continue the sound and movement until another player from somewhere else in the room "takes" with a strong sound and movement. This player then continues until a third player "takes" the space. It is critical that the sound and movement be strong as the player in motion will likely not be facing the one who takes.

Give and take. After playing each approach separately, they are now combined. Players can choose whether to give or take the space. If a player gives, the player given to must take. If a player takes, the player in motion must freeze.

Guidelines

Each of the first two phases should be played for two to five minutes before they are combined. Players must be very aware of their own movement as any movement may "take." Also, players should be encouraged to vary the pace, volume, and rhythm of sounds as well as the height, fluidity, and rhythm of movement.

Yes

Purpose

To create a playful atmosphere, one of mutual support, and one in which all possibilities are explored.

Source

Unknown

Instructions

Players are distributed evenly throughout the room. One player initiates the game with the script, "Hey everybody, let's ______." The player fills in an action that can be easily accomplished by everyone, for example, "Hey, everybody, let's all hop on one foot." Immediately following the suggestion, the group responds in unison: "Yes, yes, yes, yes, yes!" Then, everyone in the group performs the suggested action until another player initiates a new activity. The game is finished when every player has made one suggestion.

Guidelines

No matter what the suggestion is, the group should respond to it with the enthusiasm that would greet a major scientific breakthrough. Suggestions should follow each other as quickly as possible, so that the entire game is finished in the shortest possible amount of time.

Tour of a Place

Purpose

To explore sense memory and to build a detailed environment. Also to explore the ways in which place is linked to character and plot.

Source

Unknown. Previously documented in Michael Rohd, *Theatre for Community, Conflict, and Dialogue*

Instructions

Each player selects a place that is meaningful to him/her. In pairs, partners take turns giving each other seven-minute imaginary tours of these real places, showing the space in as much physical detail as possible. The full group then discusses the experience for two to four minutes.

Guidelines

The tour must be physically active. Tour givers should not share stories connected to details of the place until asked by tour takers. If a player finishes giving a tour before the time is up, he/she must go back and fill in more physical details of the place.

Complete the Image

Purpose

To create awareness of oneself and others in space. Also, to explore how images can create a conversation about feelings, relationships, and ideas.

Source

Augusto Boal, *Games for Actors and Non-Actors*

Instructions

In partners, players shake hands and "freeze" in the image of the handshake. Player A remains frozen while player B steps out of the image to observe. Player B then reenters the space in a different physical and spatial relationship to A, creating a new image. Once this image is created, player A steps out to observe and reenter, creating a third image. Play continues in this way, alternating players who remain in the image and players who complete the image.

Guidelines

This game requires silence. Players may create images out of narrative ideas or simply in response to the shape and quality of the image before them. They should take in the image and then respond so that they complete the image if not exactly on impulse then at least from a gut reaction. The leader of the exercise may call out a word or theme and ask players to allow this to influence, though not restrict, their play.

Sculpting

Purpose

To collaboratively explore relationships issues, and ideas without words

Source

Augusto Boal, *Games for Actors and Non-Actors*; for an excellent description of the basic exercise and a number of variations, see Michael Rohd, *Theatre for Community, Conflict, and Dialogue*

Instructions

The facilitator calls out in a single word a theme, idea, or issue to be explored. Working in pairs, partner A molds partner B into an image. The group has now created a range of responses to a single word. Players go around the room and look at the images. The sculptures relax and become the sculptors.

Guidelines

This is a silent game. As with Complete the Image, images may be narrative or abstract in nature.

Appendix D. A Pedagogical Note on the Performer's Grief

Teachers of theater and performance traffic all the time in the manufacturing of powerful emotional events, yet they lack the training that would enable them to help an actor negotiate such emotions in real life. Director and scholar Suzanne Burgoyne[1] has studied what she calls "boundary blurring," in which an actor takes on the behavior and attitudes of a character with which he/she has been living. This can create any number of challenges both in and well beyond the rehearsal period, one of which is that the actor's real emotional responses may rise to the surface. In the case of performing loss, what is a teacher or director to do when the process of representation gives way to real grief, real rage, real tears?

The four suggestions below are simple, and some may be rather obvious. I share them because I believe they are important, I have seen them not implemented too many times, and I have failed to implement some of them myself. I share them, too, because the issue of how a teacher negotiates a performer's grief arose in every one of the performance projects described here.

Realize that you can neither know the cause of a performer's grief nor anticipate its appearance.

Two brief examples from the same student may be instructive. This student was involved in the making of *Not Quite Through*. Early in the process, she told me that her uncle had recently committed suicide. She chose to write a piece about this experience, one that the cast, including the student, ultimately decided did not belong in the final script. Despite what would appear to be highly emotionally charged subject matter, neither the writing of this piece nor the exclusion of it from the performance was notably emotionally difficult for the student.

Several years later, the student was cast in *Blindness*. During the rehearsal of the rape scene, an abstract movement sequence performed behind a scrim, she suddenly burst into tears. I assumed both that the rehearsal triggered traumatic memories for her and that I had compounded the issue through insensitivity in the rehearsal process. Both assumptions were wrong. Several years after the production, I asked the student, now an alumna, if she remembered that night of rehearsal. She remembered being frustrated by a discussion about the lighting of the scene. But, summarizing the rehearsal of what she remembered as a "sensitive" scene, she said, "I remember it going pretty well over all." I reminded her of her tears and told her what I thought or feared might have caused them.

She was surprised by my memory. She said, "I don't have any negative memories at all—especially the crying part."

We cannot know exactly where emotional land mines lie, what will cause them to detonate, or how capable a particular performer is of negotiating the detonation. We cannot even know if what appears to be a land mine is, in fact, a land mine. We can only respond more or less productively once grief appears.

Delay staging violent, sexual, or otherwise highly emotionally charged material.

Staging such content early in the rehearsal process is a mistake. We should not stage such scenes in the first week of rehearsal or worse, use them, as one misguided former colleague did, as audition material. In their study of debriefing as a psychological and aesthetic aid in the rehearsal process, Burgoyne, Karen Poulin, and Christopher R. Hodson discovered that even providing educational resources for understanding these highly charged situations at the beginning of the rehearsal process can be frightening to actors.

When grief does come into a rehearsal, give it some space.

This does not mean that we should allow an emotional reaction to hijack the rehearsal process. It does mean that if anyone besides a mental health professional should treat a strong emotional reaction as valuable information, it should be actors, directors, and teachers of theater.

The most disturbing moment in my graduate training was one in which a professor attempted to "save" a student performer from her own emotional reaction to some ethnographic material she was developing into a performance. Fluttering manically onto the stage, he pretended her response wasn't happening and cheerfully hurried on to the next performance. In doing so, he stopped both the student and the community (that is, the class) from gleaning critical information about both the material and themselves. What about the text might have tapped into the performer's social and/or cultural reality so strongly? What in the process of representation might have brought the performer into contact with the social and/or cultural reality of the text? How could the production encourage these connections in the experience of the audience?

More importantly, the response of the professor framed the student's reaction of grief as shameful, something to be covered up and sped past. Surely, this is not a message teachers want to give to students of human behavior. Instead, we want to give students space to have, notice, and analyze their own responses, either publicly if they are comfortable doing so or privately by marking them as valuable places to return to.

Be prepared to provide outside resources to students experiencing grief in rehearsal.

This resource may be as simple as a friend in the cast who can listen during a break or as sophisticated as a psychologist with expertise in the relevant issue area. Burgoyne, for example, enlisted a counseling psychologist and a PhD intern in counseling psychology to work with her cast before, during, and after her production of Karen Malpede's *Beekeeper's Daughter*, a play that deals with rape as a war crime. One advantage of this innovative approach is that it signals clearly to the performers the acceptability of a grief response and provides them with a tool to manage the response both as a group and as individuals.

One disadvantage may be that enlisting such a person as a participant sets up an expectation of a high level of emotional response. Cast members who do not have such a powerful emotional response may feel that they have disappointed the director, the cast, or themselves. And while cast members who do have such a response have a resource for managing it, it may not be the right resource or the right context for using that resource for a particular performer.

Another disadvantage, as Burgoyne notes, is the time involved in formal debriefing. Taking an hour away from the rehearsal process every week, as she did, to debrief can be difficult when rehearsal time is short. Having a professional's name and contact information on hand or even several such people and putting the information in the production contact list would be a simpler and more private way of making this kind of resource available. As teachers of theater, we rarely consider and almost never take this simple step.

Notes

1. Loss, Performance, and Contemporary Culture

1. Della Pollock, *Telling Bodies Performing Birth* (New York: Columbia University Press, 1999), 180.

2. John Skow, "Family Ties." *Time*, November 10, 1997, http://www.time.com/time/magazine/article/0,9171,987341,00.html?promoid=googlep.

3. Robert N. Bellah, Richard Madsen, William M. Sullivan, Ann Swidler, and Steven M. Tipton, *Habits of the Heart: Individualism and Commitment in American Life* (Berkeley: University of California Press, 1996), viii.

4. Richard Schechner, *Performance Studies: An Introduction* (London: Routledge, 2002), 32.

5. See, respectively, Terri Kapsalis, *Public Privates: Performing Gynecology from Both Ends of the Speculum* (Durham: Duke University Press, 1997); Peggy Phelan, analysis of Operation Rescue in *Unmarked* (London: Routledge, 1993); and anthropologist Greg Sarris's prologue to *Keeping Slug Woman Alive: A Holistic Approach to American Indian Texts* (Berkeley: University of California Press, 1993).

6. Judith Butler, *Bodies That Matter: On the Discursive Limits of "Sex"* (New York: Routledge, 1993), 234.

7. Philippe Ariès, *Western Attitudes toward Death: From the Middle Ages to the Present*, 4th ed., Johns Hopkins Symposia in Comparative History (Baltimore: Johns Hopkins University Press, 1974), 56.

8. Ariès, *Western Attitudes toward Death*, 67.

9. Phillippe Ariès, *Hour of Our Death*, 1st American ed. (New York: Knopf, 1981), 560.

10. Ariès, *Hour of Our Death*, 580.

11. Ariès, *Hour of Our Death*, 580.

12. Ariès, *Hour of Our Death*, 118.

13. Michael R. Leming and George E. Dickinson, "The American Ways of Death," in *The Unknown Country: Death in Australia, Britain, and the U.S.A.*, ed. Kathy Charmaz, Glennys Howarth, and Allan Hellehear (New York: St. Martin's Press, 1997), 169.

14. Leming and Dickinson, "The American Ways of Death," 169.

15. Jessica Mitford, *American Way of Death* (New York: Simon Schuster, 1963), 43.

16. Jenny Hockey, "Women in Grief: Cultural Representation and Social Practice," in *Death, Gender, and Ethnicity*, ed. David Field, Hockey, and Neil Small (London: Routledge, 1997), 93.

17. Neil Small, "Death and Difference," in *Death, Gender, and Ethnicity*, ed. David Field, Jenny Hockey, and Small (London: Routledge, 1997), 206.

18. Glennys Howarth, "Is There a British Way of Death?" in *The Unknown Country: Death in Australia, Britain and the U.S.A.*, ed. Kathy Charmaz, Howarth, and Allan Hellehear (New York: St. Martin's Press, 1997), 93.

19. Leming and Dickinson, "The American Ways of Death," 169.

20. See, for example: Kathy Charmaz, "Grief and Loss of Self," in *The Unknown Country: Death in Australia, Britain, and the U.S.A.*, ed. Charmaz, Glennys Howarth, and Allan Hellehear (New York: St. Martin's Press, 1997) and/or Pamela A. Boker, *The Grief Taboo in American Literature: Loss and Prolonged Adolescence in Twain, Melville, and Hemingway*, Literature and Psychoanalysis 8 (New York: New York University Press, 1996).

21. Donald P. Irish, Kathleen F. Lundquist, and Vivian Jenkins Nelsen, *Ethnic Variations in Dying, Death, and Grief: Diversity in Universality*, (Washington, DC: Taylor and Francis, 1993), 244.

22. See, for example: Joseph Roach, *Cities of the Dead: Circum-Atlantic Performance* (New York: Columbia University Press, 1996), Jessica Mitford, *American Way of Death Revisited*, rev. ed. (New York: Knopf, 1998), and/or Glennys Howarth, "Is There a British Way of Death?" in *The Unknown Country: Death in Australia, Britain, and the U.S.A.*, ed. Kathy Charmaz, Glennys Howarth, and Allan Hellehear (New York: St. Martin's Press, 1997).

23. Howarth, "Is There a British Way of Death?" 95.

24. Elizabeth Bronfen, *Over Her Dead Body: Death, Femininity, and the Aesthetic* (New York: Routledge, 1992), 14.

25. Hockey, "Women in Grief," 90.

26. Jessica Mitford, *The American Way of Death* (New York: Simon and Schuster, 1963), 43.

27. Aries, *Hour of Our Death*, 599.

28. Daniel Callahan, *The Troubled Dream of Life: In Search of a Peaceful Death* (New York: Simon and Schuster, 1993), 24.

29. Elaine Scarry, *The Body in Pain* (New York: Oxford University Press, 1985), 4.

30. Scarry, *Body in Pain*, 11.

31. John Horn, "You Start from a Different Place," *Los Angeles Times*, March 28, 2007, E1 (home edition).

32. Renato Rosaldo, *Culture and Truth: The Remaking of Social Analysis* (Boston: Beacon Press, 1993), 12.

33. Jacques Derrida, *Aporias: Dying—Awaiting (One Another at) the "Limits of Truth"* (Mourir—S'attendre Aux "Limites De La Vâeritâe") (Stanford: Stanford University Press, 1993), 20.

34. Derrida, *Aporias*, 20.

35. Derrida, *Aporias*, 21.

36. J. L. Austin, *How to Do Things with Words* (Oxford: Clarendon Press, 1962), 6–7.

37. Geoffrey Bennington and Jacques Derrida, *Jacques Derrida* (Chicago: University of Chicago Press, 1993), 22–23.

38. Bennington and Derrida, *Jacques Derrida*, 33.

39. Hélène Cixous and Mireille Calle-Gruber, *Rootprints: Memory and Life Writing* (London: Routledge, 1997), 201.

40. Della Pollock, "Performing Writing," *The Ends of Performance*, ed. Peggy Phelan and Jill Lane (New York: New York University Press, 1998), 94.

41. Bertolt Brecht, "The Street Scene," *Modern Drama*, 1938, ed. W. B. Worthen (Fort Worth: Harcourt Brace, 1995), 398.

42. See, for example, most books on theater of the oppressed by Augusto Boal and others. Despite their widespread use by psychologists and social workers around the world, these texts often explicitly disavow "therapy" as part of their work.

43. Della Pollock, "Marking New Directions in Performance Ethnography," *Text and Performance Quarterly* 26.4 (2006): 327.

44. See especially Paul Edwards's monograph, "Unstoried: Teaching Literature in the Age of Performance Studies," *Theatre Annual* 52 (1999).

45. Dwight Conquergood, "Rethinking Elocution: The Trope of the Talking Book and Other Figures of Speech," *Text and Performance Quarterly* 20.4 (2000): 326.

46. Shannon Jackson, "Why Modern Plays Are Not Culture: Disciplinary Blind Spots," *Modern Drama: Defining the Field*, ed. Richard Paul Knowles, Joanne Tompkins, and W. B. Worthen (Toronto: University of Toronto P, 2003), 32.

47. Martha Nussbaum, *Poetic Justice: The Literary Imagination and Public Life* (Boston: Beacon Press, 1995), 7.

48. Hayden White, *Content of the Form: Narrative Discourse and Historical Representation* (Baltimore: Johns Hopkins University Press, 1987), 181.

49. White, *Content of the Form*, 24.

50. White, *Content of the Form*, 180.

51. White, *Content of the Form*, 181.

52. Joseph Roach, *Cities of the Dead: Circum-Atlantic Performance* (New York: Columbia University Press, 1996), 19.

53. Roach, *Cities of the Dead*, 19.

54. Roach, *Cities of the Dead*, 2.

55. Maya Wiley, "Hurricane Katrina Exposed the Face of Poverty," in *The State of Black America 2006* (New York: National Urban League 2006), 143.

56. David Abram, *The Spell of the Sensuous* (New York: Vintage Books, 1996), 94.

57. Donna Brazile, "New Orleans: Next Steps on the Road to Recovery," in *The State of Black America 2006* (New York: National Urban League, 2006), 233.

58. I want to add here that I have also benefited from Della Pollock's work more directly as her student at the University of North Carolina at Chapel Hill. I owe much to her living example of how to listen, read, and act as a performance scholar.

59. Pollock, *Telling Bodies Performing Birth*, 4.

60. Pollock, *Telling Bodies Performing Birth*, 32.

61. Pollock, *Telling Bodies Performing Birth*, 32.

62. Pollock, *Telling Bodies Performing Birth*, 39.

63. Pollock, "Performing Writing," 85–86.

64. Della Pollock, *Exceptional Spaces: Essays in Performance and History* (Chapel Hill: University of North Carolina Press, 1998), 12.

65. Pollock, *Exceptional Spaces*, 20.

66. Diana Taylor, *The Archive and The Repertoire: Performing Cultural Memory in the Americas* (Durham, NC: Duke University Press, 2003), 19.

67. Taylor, *Archive and the Repertoire*, 28.

68. Taylor, *Archive and the Repertoire*, 197.

69. Taylor, *Archive and the Repertoire*, 199.

70. Peggy Phelan, *Mourning Sex: Performing Public Memories* (London: Routledge, 1997), 153.

71. Peggy Phelan, *Unmarked* (London: Routledge, 1993), 19.

72. Phelan, *Unmarked*, 2.

73. Phelan, *Unmarked*, 11.

74. Phelan, *Unmarked*, 27.

75. Phelan, *Mourning Sex*, 15.

76. Peggy Phelan, "To Suffer a Sea Change," *Georgia Review* 155.3 (Fall 1991): 523.

77. Phelan, *Unmarked*, 14.

78. Phelan, *Unmarked*, 68.

79. Phelan, *Unmarked*, 148.

80. Patraka, *Spectacular Suffering* (Bloomington: Indiana University Press, 1999).

81. Phelan, *Unmarked*, 140.

82. Phelan, *Unmarked*, 152.

83. Sigmund Freud, "Mourning and Melancholia," in *A General Selection from the Works of Sigmund Freud*, ed. John Rickman (New York: Doubleday, 1957), 125.

84. Sigmund Freud, "The Ego and the Id," in *A General Selection from the Works of Sigmund Freud*, ed. John Rickman (New York: Doubleday, 1957), 217.

85. Gillian Rose, *Mourning Becomes the Law: Philosophy and Representation* (Cambridge: Cambridge University Press, 1996), 11.

86. Rose, *Mourning Becomes the Law*, 70.

87. See, for example, Jacques Derrida, Pascale-Anne Brault, and Michael Naas, *The Work of Mourning* (Chicago: University of Chicago Press, 2001).

88. José Esteban Muñoz, *Disidentifications: Queers of Color and the Performance of Politics*, vol. 2 (Minneapolis: University of Minnesota Press, 1997), 74.

89. Jane Hamilton, *Map of the World* (New York: Doubleday, 1994), 386.

90. Jill Dolan, "Geographies of Learning: Theatre Studies, Performance, and the 'Performative,'" *Theatre Journal* 45 (1993): 419–20.

2. Practicing Grief: Devising Scenes of Living and Dying

1. Cicely M. Saunders and Robert Kastenbaum, *Hospice Care on the International Scene* (New York: Springer, 1997), 6.

2. Lucy B. McBee and Maureen Mason, "The Volunteer as Team Member," *Hospice: Complete Care for the Terminally Ill*, ed. James M. Zimmerman (Baltimore: Urban and Schwarzenberg, 1986), 129.

3. McBee and Mason, "The Volunteer as Team Member," 130.

4. Crystal Brian, "Devising Community," *Theatre Topics* 15.1 (March 2005): 3.

5. Joni L. Jones, "Why Devise? Why Now? Riffing on the Syllabus," *Theatre Topics* 15.1 (March 2005): 50.

6. Stacy Klein, "Why Devise? Why Now? Creating the Impossible," *Theatre Topics* 15.1 (March 2005): 70.

7. The notable exception is so-called "at risk" children, for whom violent death can be a part of everyday life. See Alex Kotlowitz's remarkable book *There Are No Children Here* (New York: Anchor Books, 1992).

8. In this chapter, all names, with the exceptions of Virginia Holtmann and Bradley Fisher, have been changed.

9. Jon McKenzie, *Perform or Else: From Discipline to Performance* (London: Routledge, 2001), 5.

10. Phelan, *Mourning Sex*, 161. Phelan explores this relationship between awareness of death and an intensified present extensively and specifically throughout her reading of the film *Silverlake Life* (*Mourning* 153–73).

11. Volunteer hours and writing assignments—including a project journal—were completed outside of class, with class sessions devoted to shaping and staging the performance text. The course was designated as a service learning course, and students received credit for it as such.

12. This was the criterion for the hospice program with which we worked. It is a common but by no means universal standard. Hospices are above all characterized by their diversity of practice, responding as they do to the needs and resources of the individual community.

13. See for example Michael S. Bowman and Ruth Laurion Bowman, "Performing the Mystory: A Textshop in Autoperformance," in *Teaching Performance Studies*, ed. Nathan Stucky and Cynthia Wimmer (Carbondale: Southern Illinois University Press, 2002), 161–74; Robert S. Breen, *Chamber Theatre* (Englewood Cliffs, NJ: Prentice-Hall, 1978); and/or Anna Deavere Smith, *Fires in the Mirror: Crown Heights, Brooklyn, and Other Identities* (New York: Anchor Books/Doubleday, 1993).

14. For *Fires in the Mirror*, Smith interviewed more than one hundred people about the rioting that erupted August 1991 between Jews and African Americans in Crown Heights, Brooklyn. Some of her interviewees were celebrities but most were ordinary people. Some were directly involved in the events, others were not.

15. McBee and Mason, "The Volunteer as Team Member," 130.

16. For a vivid example of how this can work in the adaptation of interview material, see Michael Frisch and Dorothy Larson, "Oral History and Class Consciousness: *The New York Times* vs. the Buffalo Unemployed" in *A Shared Authority: Essays on the Craft and Meaning of Oral and Public History* (Albany: State University of New York Press, 1990), 59–80.

17. Dwight Conquergood, "Performing as a Moral Act: Ethical Dimensions of the Ethnography of Performance," *Literature in Performance* 5.2 (1985): 5–6.

18. Adaptor/director Mary Zimmerman once told an audience that her favorite moment in a play was the one in which the narrator says, "and then she had a remarkable dream"—because, of course, in performance, we are already in one.

19. See for example Elisabeth Kubler-Ross and Ira Byock.

20. Anna Deavere Smith, *Fires in the Mirror*, xxxi.

21. Michael Bigelow Dixon and Joel A. Smith, *Anne Bogart: Viewpoints* (Lyme, NH: Smith and Kraus, 1994), 20.

22. Dixon and Smith, *Anne Bogart*, 22–23.

23. See Dixon and Smith, *Anne Bogart*.

24. When we decided that we would like to use this poem in the performance, I contacted the poet through her agent, and she generously gave us permission to use the poem in this context.

25. Cathy Caruth, *Unclaimed Experience: Trauma, Narrative, and History* (Baltimore: Johns Hopkins University Press, 1996), 91.

26. Dixon and Smith, *Anne Bogart*, 23.

27. Breen, *Chamber Theatre*, 4.

28. For Bakhtin's description of dialogism, see Bakhtin and Michael Holquist, *The Dialogic Imagination* (Austin: University of Texas, 1981). For an excellent exploration of how Bakhtin's ideas might be used to expand theory and practice in theatrical adaptation, see Michael S. Bowman, "'Novelizing' the Stage: Chamber Theatre after Breen and Bakhtin," *Text and Performance Quarterly* 15.1 (January 1995): 1–19.

29. Breen, *Chamber Theatre*, 26.

30. It was critical to the success of this experiment that the stories the students were telling came from their own lives. If the students had invented object stories, they would not have earned the trust of the audience members in the same way.

31. For an example of how this creativity functions on both levels, see Barbara Myerhoff, *Number Our Days* (New York: Touchstone, 1978).

3. Practicing Adaptation: Losses and Gains in Staging *Blindness*

1. Breen, *Chamber Theatre*, 86.

2. Breen, *Chamber Theatre*, 86.

3. The two major narrative strategies I refer to here are description and dialogue or scene. Sometimes, literary critics identify a third narrative strategy, summary, but for the purpose of this discussion, summary belongs to the category of description, because it is delivered through the voice of the narrator.

4. Leon Rubin, *The Nicholas Nickleby Story* (London: Penguin Books, 1981), 116.

5. Rubin, *The Nicholas Nickleby Story*, 116.

6. Rubin, *The Nicholas Nickleby Story*, 18.

7. An even more dramatic example of autonomous adaptation is the Spike Jonze and Charlie Kaufman film *Adaptation*, the story of a writer's unsuccessful attempt to adapt a work of nonfiction literature to the screen. The film includes the story of the work *The Orchid Thief*, a real story lived and constructed by real writer Susan Orlean (played in the film by Meryl Streep), but this is not the central story of the film.

8. Breen, *Chamber Theatre*, 6.

9. Bowman notes that in Britain, following the enormous success of the Royal Shakespeare Company with David Edgar's *Nicholas Nickleby*, the number of adaptations in the British theater skyrocketed. Most notable among American adaptor/directors are Frank Galati, who won the Tony award in 1990 for direction and play, and Mary Zimmerman, who won the 2002 Tony for direction, both for narrative adaptations.

10. Taussig says, "If I am correct in making this analogy with what I take to be the

magician's art of reproduction, then the model, if it works, gains through its sensuous fidelity something of the power and personality of that of which it is a model" (16). See his book *Mimesis and Alterity: A Particular History of the Senses* (New York: Routledge, 1993) for an extended discussion of this concept.

11. Derek Goldman, personal interview, August 22, 2006.

12. Michael S. Bowman, "'Novelizing' the Stage: Chamber Theatre after Breen and Bahktin," *Text and Performance Quarterly* 15.1 (January 1995): 3.

13. Julie Jackson, "Theatrical Space and Place in the Presentational Aesthetic of Director Frank Joseph Galati," *Theatre Topics* 15.2 (September 2005): 144.

14. Leslie Norris, "Blackberries," in *Sudden Fiction International*, ed. Robert Shapard and James Thomas (New York: Norton, 1989), 43.

15. Anton Chekhov, "The Lady with the Pet Dog," in *The Compact Bedford Introduction to Literature*, ed. Michael Meyer, 5th ed. (Boston: Bedford/St. Martin's, 2000), 176.

16. Jose Saramago, *Blindness*, trans. Giovanni Pontiero (San Diego: Harcourt, 1997), 265.

17. Goldman, August 22, 2006.

18. See Brecht.

19. Bowman, "Performing the Mystory," 5.

20. Robert E. Scholes, *Protocols of Reading* (New Haven: Yale University Press, 1989), 151–52.

21. Breen, *Chamber Theatre*, 33.

22. Saramago, *Blindness*, 2.

23. Saramago, *Blindness*, 131.

24. Saramago, *Blindness*, 177.

25. Saramago, *Blindness*, 153.

26. Saramago, *Blindness*, 209.

27. Saramago, *Blindness*, 217.

28. Saramago, *Blindness*, 18.

29. Saramago, *Blindness*, 173.

30. Mary Zimmerman, *The Arabian Nights: A Play* (Evanston, IL: Northwestern University Press, 2005), xv.

31. Rubin, *Nicholas Nickleby Story*, 41.

32. Rubin, *Nicholas Nickleby Story*, 79.

33. Saramago, *Blindness*, 43–44.

34. Saramago, *Blindness*, 176.

4. Practicing Community: Representing National Tragedy

1. This and all the following quotations are from Graham's speech on September 14, 2001, at the National Cathedral on the occasion of the National Day of Prayer and Remembrance. The full text of Graham's speech may be read and heard at http://www.americanrhetoric.com/speeches/billygraham911memorial.htm.

2. Phelan, *Unmarked*, 7.

3. Richard F. Ward, "Speaking of God: Performance Pedagogy in the Theological School," in *Teaching Performance Studies*, ed. Nathan Stucky and Cynthia Wimmer Stucky (Carbondale: Southern Illinois University Press, 2002), 64.

4. Pollock, "Performing Writing," 82–83.

5. Alan Shapiro, *Vigil* (Chicago: University of Chicago Press, 1997), 81.

6. E. E. Cummings, "since feeling is first," in *The Compact Bedford Introduction to Literature*, ed. Michael Mayer (Boston: Bedford, 2000), 880–81.

7. Fredric Jameson, "The Dialectics of Disaster," *South Atlantic Quarterly* 101.2 (2002): 298.

8. See Butler's introduction to *Bodies That Matter*, (see chap. 1, n. 6).

9. Bellah et al., *Habits of the Heart*, xxxii–xxxiii (see chap. 1, n. 4).

10. Nancy Fraser, "False Antitheses," *Feminist Contentions*, ed. Seyla Benhabib, Judith Butler, Drucilla Cornell, and Nancy Fraser (New York: Routledge, 1995), 68.

11. George W. Bush, "Address to a Joint Session of Congress and the American People," United States Capitol, Washington, DC, September 20, 2001, http://www.whitehouse.gov/news/releases/2001/09/20010920-8.html.

12. Martin Marty, "The Sin of Pride," *Newsweek* 141.10 (2003): 32.

13. Taylor, *The Archive and the Repertoire*, 150 (see chap. 1, n. 68).

14. Taylor, *The Archive and the Repertoire*, 245 (see chap. 1, n. 68).

15. Pollock, "Performing Writing," 91 (see chap 1, n. 39).

16. Robert Shetterly, phone interview, July 13, 2006.

17. Bush, "Address."

18. Taylor, *The Archive and the Repertoire*, 245 (see chap. 1, n. 68).

19. Taylor, *The Archive and the Repertoire*, 258 (see chap. 1, n. 68).

20. Colin Powell, "U.S. Secretary of State Colin Powell Addresses the U.N. Security Council," February 5, 2003, http://www.whitehouse.gov/news/releases/2003/02/20030205-1.html.

21. Shetterly, July 13, 2006.

22. Shetterly, July 13, 2006.

23. Walt Whitman, *Leaves of Grass* (New York: Penguin Books, 2005), 11.

24. Shetterly, July 13, 2006.

25. Shetterly, July 13, 2006.

26. Shetterly, July 13, 2006.

27. Shetterly, July 13, 2006.

28. Whitman, *Leaves*, 14.

29. Shetterly, July 13, 2006.

30. Alan Dershowitz, "Hate-America Lies for Kids," FrontPageMagazine.com, July 21, 2005, http://frontpagemag.com/Articles/ReadArticle.asp?ID=18850 for kids.

31. Robert Shetterly, "Dershowitz's Name-Calling," FrontPageMagazine.com, August 5, 2005, http://www.frontpagemag.com/Articles/ReadArticle.asp?ID=19060.

32. Christina Drale and Cheryl Hellman, "Truth Be Told," (working title), forthcoming.

33. Shetterly, July 13, 2006.

34. Shetterly, July 13, 2006.

5. Practicing Responsibility: Race, Class, and Specters of Justice

1. Gail Holst-Warhaft, *Dangerous Voices: Women's Laments and Greek Literature* (London: Routledge, 1992), 114–21.

2. Judith Viorst, *Necessary Losses* (New York: Free Press, 1986), 16.

3. bell hooks, *Teaching to Transgress* (New York: Routledge, 1994), 178.

4. Taylor, *The Archive and the Repertoire*, 193 (see chap. 1, n. 68).

5. *My Brother*, the only memoir in this study, is also the only one of the narratives that critics evaluated on the ground of how well the author mourned.

6. Skow, "Family Ties," (see chap 1, n. 2).

7. White, *Content of the Form*, 5 (see chap. 1, n. 47).

8. Taylor, *The Archive and the Repertoire*, 208 (see chap. 1, n. 68).

9. Jamaica Kincaid, *My Brother* (New York: Farrar, Straus, and Giroux, 1997), 76.

10. Kincaid, *My Brother*, 165.

11. Kincaid, *My Brother*, 82.

12. Kincaid, *My Brother*, 197–98.

13. Taylor, *The Archive and the Repertoire*, 208 (see chap. 1, n. 68).

14. Toni Morrison, *Playing in the Dark: Whiteness and the Literary Imagination* (New York: Vintage, 1993), 11.

15. Susan Sontag, *AIDS and Its Metaphors* (New York: Farrar, Straus, and Giroux, 1989), 9.

16. Jamaica Kincaid, "The Flowers of Empire," *Harper's Magazine* 292.1751 (1996): 28.

17. Kincaid, *My Brother*, 91.

18. Kincaid, *My Brother*, 19–20.

19. Kincaid, *My Brother*, 82.

20. Kincaid, *My Brother*, 87.

21. Kincaid, *My Brother*, 148.

22. Kincaid, *My Brother*, 137.

23. Kincaid, *My Brother*, 193.

24. Kincaid, *My Brother*, 128.

25. Kincaid, *My Brother*, 131.

26. Jamaica Kincaid, *A Small Place* (New York: Farrar, Straus, and Giroux, 1988), 8–9.

27. Kincaid, *A Small Place*, 43.

28. Kincaid, *My Brother*, 198.

29. Kincaid, *My Brother*, 197–98.

30. Kincaid, *My Brother*, 197.

31. Kincaid, *My Brother*, 76.

32. Pollock, "Performing Writing," 80 (see chap. 1, n. 39).

33. Kincaid, *My Brother*, 91.

34. Kincaid, *My Brother*, 196.

35. Caruth, *Unclaimed Experience*, 106 (see chap 2, n. 24).

36. Caruth, *Unclaimed Experience*, 105.

37. Kincaid, *My Brother*, 30.

38. Kincaid, *My Brother*, 180–81.
39. Kincaid, *My Brother*, 167.
40. Kincaid, *My Brother*, 96.
41. Kincaid, *My Brother*, 5–6.
42. Kincaid, *My Brother*, 6.
43. Kincaid, *My Brother*, 88.
44. Kincaid, *My Brother*, 96.
45. Kincaid, *My Brother*, 83.
46. Kincaid, *My Brother*, 181.
47. Kincaid, *My Brother*, 100.
48. Kincaid, *My Brother*, 144.
49. Kincaid, *My Brother*, 108.
50. Kincaid, *My Brother*, 99.
51. Kincaid, *My Brother*, 102.
52. Kincaid, *My Brother*, 195.
53. Kincaid, *My Brother*, 58.
54. Kincaid, *My Brother*, 20.
55. Kincaid, *My Brother*, 141.
56. Kincaid, *My Brother*, 106.
57. Kincaid, *My Brother*, 51.
58. Kincaid, *My Brother*, 159.
59. Kincaid, *My Brother*, 156.
60. Kincaid, *My Brother*, 149.
61. Kincaid, *My Brother*, 50.
62. Kincaid, *My Brother*, 149.
63. Paul Gilroy, *The Black Atlantic: Modernity and Double Consciousness* (Cambridge, MA: Harvard University Press, 1993), 81.
64. Gilroy, *Black Atlantic*, 80.
65. Kincaid, *My Brother*, 24.
66. Kincaid, *My Brother*, 24.
67. Kincaid, *A Small Place*, 34–35.
68. Kincaid, *My Brother*, 79.
69. Kincaid, *My Brother*, 11.
70. Kincaid, *My Brother*, 50.
71. Kincaid, *My Brother*, 49.
72. Kincaid, *My Brother*, 39.
73. Kincaid, *My Brother*, 195.
74. Kincaid, *My Brother*, 191.
75. Kincaid, *My Brother*, 192.
76. Kincaid, *My Brother*, 42.
77. Kincaid, *My Brother*, 31.
78. Kincaid, *My Brother*, 37.
79. Edwin Cameron, "Opening Address, AIDS in Context Conference, University of the Witwatersrand, Johannesburg," *Connect* 3 (2001): 18.

80. Kincaid, *My Brother,* 95.

81. Kincaid, *My Brother,* 59.

82. Kenneth J. Doka, *Disenfranchised Grief: Recognizing Hidden Sorrow* (Lexington, MA: Lexington, 1989), 303.

83. Neil Small, "The Public Construction of AIDS Deaths in the United Kingdom," in *The Unknown Country: Death in Australia, Britain, and the U.S.A.*, ed. Kathy Charmaz, Glennys Howarth, and Allan Hellehear (New York: St. Martin's, 1997), 159.

84. Small, "The Public Construction of AIDS," 160.

85. Small, "The Public Construction, of AIDS" 157.

86. Kincaid, *My Brother,* 125.

87. Kincaid, *My Brother,* 162.

88. Kincaid, *My Brother,* 168.

89. Kincaid, *My Brother,* 176.

90. Kincaid, *My Brother,* 9.

6. Practicing Compensation: Filling the Great Holes of History

1. Taylor, *The Archive and the Repertoire,* 28 (see chap. 1, n. 68).

2. Taylor, *The Archive and the Repertoire,* 33 (see chap. 1, n. 68).

3. I have, unfortunately, only seen video documentation of *The America Play,* a play far less seldom performed than it deserves. As I discuss below, many of the play's most important ideas, however, are communicated in unperformable footnotes.

4. Dolan, "Geographies of Learning," 420 (see chap. 1, n. 91).

5. Pollock, *Exceptional Spaces,* 15 (see chap 1, n. 66).

6. Morrison, *Playing in the Dark,* 8 (see chap. 5, n. 14).

7. Morrison, *Playing in the Dark,* 9–10.

8. Suzan-Lori Parks, *The America Play and Other Works* (New York: Theatre Communications Group, 1995), 4.

9. Parks, *The America Play,* 4–5.

10. Parks, *The America Play,* 17.

11. Parks, *The America Play,* 158. This stage direction is one of many examples of clever ideas in Parks's plays that are actually lost in production but preserved in private or public readings of the text.

12. Parks, *The America Play,* 159.

13. Parks, *The America Play,* 163.

14. Parks, *The America Play,* 95.

15. Pollock, *Exceptional Spaces,* 5.

16. Parks, *The America Play,* 164.

17. Parks, *The America Play,* 163.

18. Parks, *The America Play,* 160.

19. Parks, *The America Play,* 175.

20. Parks, *The America Play,* 187.

21. Michele Pearce, "Alien Nation: An Interview with the Playwright," *American Theatre* (March 1994): 26.

22. Parks, *The America Play,* 164.

23. Parks, *The America Play*, 164.

24. Parks, *The America Play*, 166–67.

25. Parks does not specify whether the visitors should be played by black actors or by white actors. Either way, however, the victim of the violence is black.

26. Parks, *The America Play*, 161.

27. Parks, *The America Play*, 163.

28. Parks, *The America Play*, 179.

29. Parks, *The America Play*, 180.

30. Parks, *The America Play*, 168.

31. Steven Drukman, "Suzan-Lori Parks and Liz Diamond," *Drama Review* 39 (1995): 73.

32. Parks, *The America Play*, 9.

33. Butler, *Bodies That Matter*, 237 (see chap. 1, n. 6).

34. Parks, *The America Play*, 19.

35. Shawn-Marie Garrett, "The Possession of Suzan-Lori Parks," *American Theatre On Line* 17 (October 2000), http://www.tcg.org/publications/at/2000/parks.cfm.

36. Parks, *The America Play*, 162.

37. Parks, *The America Play*, 166.

38. Parks, *The America Play*, 199.

39. For a longer discussion of this anxiety, see the section on Kincaid's *My Brother* in chapter 6 in this volume.

40. Parks, *The America Play*, 184.

41. Parks, *The America Play*, 185.

42. Parks, *The America Play*, 189.

43. Parks, *The America Play*, 162.

44. Gilroy, *The Black Atlantic*, 79 (see chap. 5, n. 63).

45. Parks, *The America Play*, 199.

46. Alisa Solomon, "'Signifying on the Signifyin': The Plays of Suzan-Lori Parks," *Theatre* 21.3 (1990): 73–79.

47. Parks, *The America Play*, 186.

48. Parks, *The America Play*, 16.

49. A play like *The America Play* encourages us to think with some particularity about the relationship between race and nation. At the same time, we must be careful not to associate these two categories too exclusively, as Paul Gilroy has argued forcefully in *The Black Atlantic*.

50. Tony Kushner, *Homebody/Kabul* (New York: Theatre Communications Group, 2002), 9.

51. Kushner, *Homebody/Kabul*, 24.

52. Kushner, *Homebody/Kabul*, 143.

53. Kushner, *Homebody/Kabul*, 24.

54. Kushner, *Homebody/Kabul*, 11.

55. Kushner, *Homebody/Kabul*, 9.

56. Kushner, *Homebody/Kabul*, 10.

57. Kushner, *Homebody/Kabul*, 5.

58. Kushner, *Homebody/Kabul*, 25.
59. Kushner, *Homebody/Kabul*, 26.
60. Kushner, *Homebody/Kabul*, 143.
61. Kushner, *Homebody/Kabul*, 144.
62. Kushner, *Homebody/Kabul*, 144.
63. Scholes, *Textual Power*, 22 (see chap. 3, n. 19).
64. Marty, "The Sin of Pride," 32 (see chap. 4, n. 10).
65. Kushner, *Homebody/Kabul*, 13.
66. Kushner, *Homebody/Kabul*, 23–24.
67. Tony Kushner, *Thinking about the Longstanding Problems of Virtue and Happiness* (New York: Theatre Communications Group, 1995), 44–45.
68. Kushner, *Homebody/Kabul*, viii.

7. Practicing Joy: Improvisation in a Federal Prison

1. Viktor Emil Frankl, *Man's Search for Meaning: An Introduction to Logotherapy*, 4th ed. (Boston: Beacon Press, 1992), 80.
2. Bellah et al. point out that genuine communities are characterized not only by stories of exemplary achievements and individuals but by stories of shared suffering and "if the community is completely honest," by stories of suffering they have inflicted (153). In the case of the inmates, only these last two types of stories are available.
3. Michel Foucault, "The Body of the Condemned (from *Discipline and Punish*)," in *The Foucault Reader*, 1977, trans. Alan Sheridan, ed. Paul Rabinow (New York: Pantheon, 1984), 170.
4. It should be emphasized here that not all or even many patients with a diagnosis of BPD commit crimes. Indeed, according to the Diagnostic and Statistical Manual of Mental Disorders published by the American Psychiatric Association, BPD is a common diagnosis.
5. Jean Trounstine, *Shakespeare behind Bars: The Power of Drama in a Women's Prison* (New York: St. Martin's, 2001), 2.
6. *Diagnostic and Statistical Manual of Mental Disorders*, Robert L. Spitzer, chair, Work Group to Revise DSM-III, text ed, Janet B. W. Williams, 3rd. ed. (Washington, DC: American Psychiatric Association, 1987), 346.
7. Bruce McConachie, "Theatre of the Oppressed with Students of Privilege," in *Teaching Performance Studies*, ed. Nathan Stucky and Cynthia Wimmer (Carbondale: Southern Illinois University Press, 2002), 249.
8. McConachie, "Theatre of the Oppressed," 249.
9. In this chapter, the names of students and inmates have been changed.
10. Gavin De Becker, *Gift of Fear: Survival Signals That Protect Us from Violence* (Boston: Little, Brown, 1997), 7.
11. De Becker, *Gift of Fear*, 27.
12. *Diagnostic and Statistical Manual*, 364.
13. De Becker, *Gift of Fear*, 342–43.
14. For more on this, see Suzanne Burgoyne's work on "boundary blurring" in acting, published in several issues of *Theatre Topics* including 9.2 (September 1999). For

a more evocative treatment, see Kurt Vonnegut's funny and chilling short story "Who Am I This Time?" in *Welcome to the Monkeyhouse* (New York: Delacorte, 1968).

15. Jessica Blank and Erik Jensen, *The Exonerated: A Play* (New York: Faber and Faber, 2004), 67.

16. Viola Spolin, *Improvisation for the Theater: A Handbook of Teaching and Directing Techniques*, 3rd ed. (Evanston, IL: Northwestern University Press, 1999), 4.

17. Michael Rohd, *Theatre for Community, Conflict, and Dialogue* (Portsmouth, NH: Heinemann, 1998), 62–63.

18. Zelda Fichandler, "Whither (or Wither) Art?" *American Theatre* 20.5 (2003): 68.

19. Foucault, "The Body of the Condemned," 216.

20. Spolin, *Improvisation for the Theater*, 279.

21. Spolin, *Improvisation for the Theater*, 8.

22. Rohd, *Theatre for Community, Conflict, and Dialogue*, 131.

8. Loss, Performance, and the Future

1. Anne Stevenson, *Five Looks at Elizabeth Bishop* (London: Bellew, 1998), 155.

2. Bellah et al., *Habits of the Heart*, xi (see chap. 1, n. 4).

3. See Jon McKenzie's *Perform or Else* for a thorough examination of this model.

4. Victor Turner, *Dramas, Fields, and Metaphors* (Ithaca, NY: Cornell University Press, 1974), 51.

Appendix A. Devised Performance Assignments

1. For detailed guidelines on how to formulating good questions, see Hugo Slim and Paul Thomson, *Listening for a Change: Oral Testimony and Community Development* (Philadelphia: New Society, 1995).

Appendix D. A Pedagogical Note on the Performer's Grief

1. Suzanne Burgoyne and Karen Poulin, with Ashley Rearden, "The Impact of Acting on Student Actors: Boundary Blurring, Growth, and Emotional Distress," *Theatre Topics* 9.2 (September 1999): 157–79.

References

Abram, David. *The Spell of the Sensuous.* New York: Vintage, 1996.

Ariès, Philippe. *The Hour of Our Death.* New York: Knopf, 1981.

———. *Western Attitudes toward Death: From the Middle Ages to the Present.* Johns Hopkins Symposia in Comparative History. 4th ed. Baltimore: Johns Hopkins University Press, 1974.

Austin, J. L. *How to Do Things with Words.* Oxford: Clarendon, 1962.

Bakhtin, M. M., and Michael Holquist. *The Dialogic Imagination: Four Essays.* University of Texas Press Slavic Series 1. Austin: University of Texas Press, 1981.

Bellah, Robert N., Richard Madsen, William M. Sullivan, Ann Swidler, and Steven M. Tipton. *Habits of the Heart: Individualism and Commitment in American Life.* Berkeley: University of California Press, 1996.

Bennington, Geoffrey, and Jacques Derrida. *Jacques Derrida.* Religion and Postmodernism. Chicago: University of Chicago Press, 1993.

Bishop, Elizabeth. "One Art." In *The Vintage Book of Contemporary American Poetry,* edited by J. D. McClatchy, 39. New York: Vintage, 1990.

Blank, Jessica, and Erik Jensen. *The Exonerated: A Play.* New York: Faber and Faber, 2004.

Boal, Augusto. *Games for Actors and Non-Actors.* 2nd ed. New York: Routledge, 2002.

Boker, Pamela A. *The Grief Taboo in American Literature: Loss and Prolonged Adolescence in Twain, Melville, and Hemingway.* Literature and Psychoanalysis, 8. New York: New York University Press, 1996.

Bowman, Michael S. "'Novelizing' the Stage: Chamber Theatre after Breen and Bahktin." *Text and Performance Quarterly* 15.1 (January 1995): 1–19.

Bowman, Michael S., and Ruth Laurion Bowman. "Performing the Mystory: A Textshop in Autoperformance." In Stucky and Wimmer, *Teaching Performance Studies,* 161–74.

Brazile, Donna. "New Orleans: Next Steps on the Road to Recovery." In *The State of Black America 2006,* 233–37. New York: National Urban League, 2006.

Brecht, Bertolt. "The Street Scene." In *Modern Drama,* edited by W. B. Worthen, 396–401. Fort Worth: Harcourt, Brace, 1995.

Breen, Robert S. *Chamber Theatre.* Englewood Cliffs, NJ: Prentice-Hall, 1978.

Brian, Crystal. "Devising Community." *Theatre Topics* 15.1 (March 2005): 1–13.

Bronfen, Elisabeth. *Over Her Dead Body: Death, Femininity, and the Aesthetic.* New York: Routledge, 1992.

Burgoyne, Suzanne, Karen Poulin, and Christopher R. Hodson. "Debriefing Theatre Rehearsals: A Grounded Theory Study." *Journal of the Research Institute for Integrated Brain Studies* 1 (March 2005): 79–91.

Burgoyne, Suzanne, and Karen Poulin, with Ashley Rearden. "The Impact of Acting on Student Actors: Boundary Blurring, Growth, and Emotional Distress." *Theatre Topics* 9.2 (September 1999): 157–79.

Bush, George W. "Address to a Joint Session of Congress and the American People." United States Capitol, Washington, DC, September 20, 2001. http://www.whitehouse.gov/news/releases/2001/09/20010920-8.html.

Butler, Judith. *Bodies That Matter: On the Discursive Limits of "Sex."* New York: Routledge, 1993.

Byock, Ira. *Dying Well: The Prospect for Growth at the End of Life.* New York: Riverhead, 1997.

Callahan, Daniel. *The Troubled Dream of Life: In Search of a Peaceful Death.* New York: Simon and Schuster, 1993.

Cameron, Edwin. "Opening Address, AIDS in Context Conference, University of the Witwatersrand, Johannesburg." *Connect* 3 (2001): 17–22.

Caruth, Cathy. *Unclaimed Experience: Trauma, Narrative, and History.* Baltimore: Johns Hopkins University Press, 1996.

Charmaz, Kathy. "Grief and Loss of Self." In Charmaz, Howarth, and Hellehear, *Unknown Country,* 229–41.

Charmaz, Kathy, Glennys Howarth, and Allan Hellehear, eds. *The Unknown Country: Death in Australia, Britain, and the U.S.A.* New York: St. Martin's, 1997.

Chekhov, Anton. "The Lady with the Pet Dog." In *The Compact Bedford Introduction to Literature,* edited by Michael Meyer, 165–76. 5th ed. Boston: Bedford/St. Martin's, 2000.

Cixous, Hélène, and Mireille Calle-Gruber. *Rootprints: Memory and Life Writing.* London: Routledge, 1997.

Conquergood, Dwight. "Performing as a Moral Act: Ethical Dimensions of the Ethnography of Performance." *Literature in Performance* 5.2 (1985): 1–13.

———. "Rethinking Elocution: The Trope of the Talking Book and Other Figures of Speech." *Text and Performance Quarterly* 20.4 (2000): 325–41.

Cummings, E. E. "since feeling is first." In *The Compact Bedford Introduction to Literature.* Ed. Michael Mayer, 880–81. Boston: Bedford/St. Martin's, 2000.

De Becker, Gavin. *The Gift of Fear: Survival Signals That Protect Us from Violence.* Boston: Little, Brown, 1997.

Derrida, Jacques. *Aporias: Dying—Awaiting (One Another at) the "Limits of Truth" (Mourir—S'attendre Aux "Limites De La Vâeritâe").* Translated by Thomas Dutoit. Stanford: Stanford University Press, 1993.

———. *Specters of Marx: The State of the Debt, the Work of Mourning, and the New International.* Translated by Peggy Kamuf. New York: Routledge, 1994.

———. "The Theatre of Cruelty and the Closure of Representation." In *Mimesis, Masochism, and Mime,* edited by Timothy Murray, 40–62. Ann Arbor: University of Michigan Press, 1997.

Derrida, Jacques, Pascale-Anne Brault, and Michael Naas. *The Work of Mourning.* Chicago: University of Chicago Press, 2001.

Dershowitz, Alan. "Hate-America Lies for Kids." FrontPageMagazine.com (July 21, 2005). http://frontpagemag.com/Articles/ReadArticle.asp?ID=18850.

Diagnostic and Statistical Manual of Mental Disorders. Robert L. Spitzer, chair, Work Group to Revise DSM-III. Text edited by Janet B. W. Williams. 3rd ed. Washington, DC: American Psychiatric Association, 1987.

Dickens, Charles. *The Life and Adventures of Nicholas Nickleby.* Adapted by David Edgar. Garden City, NY: Nelson Doubleday, 1982.

Dixon, Michael Bigelow, and Joel A. Smith. *Anne Bogart: Viewpoints.* Career Development Series. Lyme, NH: Smith and Kraus, 1994.

Doka, Kenneth J. *Disenfranchised Grief: New Directions, Challenges, and Strategies for Practice.* Champaign, IL: Research, 2002.

———. *Disenfranchised Grief: Recognizing Hidden Sorrow.* Lexington, MA: Lexington, 1989.

Dolan, Jill. "Geographies of Learning: Theatre Studies, Performance, and the 'Performative.'" *Theatre Journal* 45 (1993): 417–41.

Drale, Christina, and Cheryl Hellman. "Truth Be Told" (working title). Forthcoming.

Drukman, Steven. "Suzan-Lori Parks and Liz Diamond." *Drama Review* 39 (1995): 56–75.

Easthope, Anthony, and Kate McGowan, eds. *A Critical and Cultural Theory Reader.* Toronto: University of Toronto Press, 1992.

Edwards, Paul. "Unstoried: Teaching Literature in the Age of Performance Studies." *Theatre Annual* 52 (1999).

Eng, David L., and David Kazanjian. *Loss: The Politics of Mourning.* Berkeley: University of California Press, 2003.

Ensler, Eve, et al. *What I Want My Words to Do to You: Voices from a Maximum Security Women's Prison.* United States: Borrowed Light, 2003.

Fichandler, Zelda. "Whither (or Wither) Art?" *American Theatre* 20.5 (2003): 28–73.

Field, David, Jenny Hockey, and Neil Small, eds. *Death, Gender, and Ethnicity.* London: Routledge, 1997.

Foucault, Michel. "The Body of the Condemned (from *Discipline and Punish*)." In *The Foucault Reader*, edited by Paul Rabinow, translated by Alan Sheridan, 170–78. New York: Pantheon, 1984.

Fraden, Rena. *Imagining Medea: Rhodessa Jones and Theatre for Incarcerated Women.* Chapel Hill: University of North Carolina Press, 2001.

Frank, Arthur. *The Wounded Storyteller: Body, Illness, and Ethics.* Chicago: University of Chicago Press, 1995.

Frankl, Viktor Emil. *Man's Search for Meaning: An Introduction to Logotherapy.* 4th ed. Boston: Beacon, 1992.

Fraser, Nancy. "False Antitheses." In *Feminist Contentions*, edited by Seyla Benhabib, Judith Butler, Drucilla Cornell, and Fraser, 59–74. New York: Routledge, 1995.

Freud, Sigmund. "The Ego and the Id." In Freud, *A General Selection*, 210–35.

———. *A General Selection from the Works of Sigmund Freud.* Edited by John Rickman. New York: Doubleday, 1957.

———. "Mourning and Melancholia." Freud, *A General Selection*, 124–40.

Garrett, Shawn-Marie. "The Possession of Suzan-Lori Parks." *American Theatre Online* 17 (October 2000). http://www.tcg.org/publications/at/2000/parks.cfm.

Gilroy, Paul. *The Black Atlantic: Modernity and Double Consciousness.* Cambridge, MA: Harvard University Press, 1993.

Graham, Billy. "Billy Graham: Address at the Episcopal National Cathedral." September 14, 2001. http://www.americanrhetoric.com/speeches/billygraham911memorial.htm.

Gray, Paul H., and James Van Oosting. *Performance in Life and Literature.* Boston: Allyn and Bacon, 1996.

Hamilton, Jane. *A Map of the World.* New York: Doubleday, 1994.

Hauerwas, Stanley. "September 11, 2001: A Pacifist Response." *South Atlantic Quarterly* 101.2 (2002): 425–33.

Hockey, Jenny. "Women in Grief: Cultural Representation and Social Practice." In Field, Hockey, and Small, *Death, Gender, and Ethnicity*, 89–107.

Holst-Warhaft, Gail. *Dangerous Voices: Women's Laments and Greek Literature.* London: Routledge, 1992.

hooks, bell. *Teaching to Transgress.* New York: Routledge, 1994.

Horn, John. "You Start from a Different Place." *Los Angeles Times*, March 28, 2007, E1 (home edition).

Howarth, Glennys. "Is There a British Way of Death?" In Charmaz, Howarth, and Hellehear, *Unknown Country*, 84–97.

Irish, Donald P., Kathleen F. Lundquist, and Vivian Jenkins Nelsen. *Ethnic Variations in Dying, Death, and Grief: Diversity in Universality.* Series in Death Education, Aging, and Health Care. Washington, DC: Taylor and Francis, 1993.

Jackson, Julie. "Theatrical Space and Place in the Presentational Aesthetic of Director Frank Joseph Galati." *Theatre Topics* 15.2 (September 2005): 131–48.

Jackson, Shannon. "Why Modern Plays Are Not Culture: Disciplinary Blind Spots." In Knowles, Tompkins, and Worthen, *Modern Drama*, 31–51.

Jameson, Fredric. "The Dialectics of Disaster." *South Atlantic Quarterly* 101.2 (2002): 297–304.

Jones, Joni L. "Why Devise? Why Now? Riffing on the Syllabus." *Theatre Topics* 15.1 (March 2005): 49–50.

Kessler, Glenn. "Powell Expresses Doubts about Basis for Iraqi Weapons Claim." *Washington Post* (April 3, 2004): A19.

Kincaid, Jamaica. "The Flowers of Empire." *Harper's Magazine* 292.1751 (1996): 28–31.

———. *My Brother.* New York: Farrar, Straus, and Giroux, 1997.

———. *My Garden (Book).* New York: Farrar, Straus, and Giroux, 1999.

———. *A Small Place.* New York: Farrar, Straus, and Giroux 1988.

Klein, Stacy. "Why Devise? Why Now? Creating the Impossible." *Theatre Topics* 15.1 (March 2005): 69–72.

Knowles, Ric, Joanne Tompkins, and W. B. Worthen, eds. *Modern Drama: Defining the Field.* Toronto: University of Toronto Press, 2003.

Kubler-Ross, Elisabeth. *On Death and Dying.* New York: Macmillan, 1969.

Kushner, Tony. *Homebody/Kabul.* New York: Theatre Communications Group, 2002.

———. *Thinking about the Longstanding Problems of Virtue and Happiness.* New York: Theatre Communications Group, 1995.

Leming, Michael R., and George E. Dickinson. "The American Ways of Death." In Charmaz, Howarth, and Hellehear, *Unknown Country,* 169–83.

Lentricchia, Frank, and Jody McAuliffe. "Groundzeroland." *South Atlantic Quarterly* 101.2 (2002): 349–60.

Long, Beverly Whitaker. "Evaluating Performed Literature." In *Performing Literature: An Introduction,* edited by Long and Mary Frances HopKins, 147–58. Dubuque, IA: Kendall/Hunt, 1997.

Marty, Martin. "The Sin of Pride." *Newsweek* 141.10 (2003): 32.

McBee, Lucy B., and Maureen Mason. "The Volunteer as Team Member." In *Hospice: Complete Care for the Terminally Ill,* edited by James M. Zimmerman, 129–32. Baltimore: Urban and Schwarzenberg, 1986.

McConachie, Bruce. "Theatre of the Oppressed with Students of Privilege." In Stucky and Wimmer, *Teaching Performance Studies,* 247–60.

McKenzie, Jon. *Perform or Else: From Discipline to Performance.* London: Routledge, 2001.

McManners, John. *Death and the Enlightenment: Changing Attitudes to Death among Christians and Unbelievers in Eighteenth-Century France.* Oxford: Oxford University Press, 1985.

Minh-ha, Trinh T. "Grandma's Story." In *The Woman That I Am: The Literature and Culture of Contemporary Women of Color,* edited by D. Soyini Madison, 462–85. New York: St. Martin's, 1994.

Mitford, Jessica. *The American Way of Death.* New York: Simon and Schuster, 1963.

———. *The American Way of Death Revisited.* Rev. ed. New York: Alfred A. Knopf, 1998.

Morrison, Toni. *Playing in the Dark: Whiteness and the Literary Imagination.* New York: Vintage, 1993.

Muñoz, José Esteban. *Disidentifications: Queers of Color and the Performance of Politics.* Cultural Studies of the Americas 2. Minneapolis: University of Minnesota Press, 1999.

Myerhoff, Barbara. *Number Our Days.* New York: Touchstone, 1978.

Norris, Leslie. "Blackberries." In *Sudden Fiction International,* edited by Robert Shapard and James Thomas, 39–44. New York: Norton, 1989.

Nussbaum, Martha. *Poetic Justice: The Literary Imagination and Public Life.* Boston: Beacon, 1995.

Parks, Suzan-Lori. *The America Play and Other Works.* New York: Theatre Communications Group, 1995.

Pastan, Linda. *The Five Stages of Grief: Poems.* New York: Norton, 1978.

Patraka, Vivian. *Spectacular Suffering: Theatre, Fascism, and the Holocaust.* Bloomington: Indiana University Press, 1999.

Pearce, Michele. "Alien Nation: An Interview with the Playwright." *American Theatre* (March 1994): 26.

Phelan, Peggy. *Mourning Sex: Performing Public Memories.* London: New York: Routledge, 1997.

———. "To Suffer a Sea Change." *Georgia Review* 155.3 (Fall 1991): 507–25.

———. *Unmarked*. London: Routledge, 1993.

Pollock, Della, ed. *Exceptional Spaces: Essays in Performance and History*. Chapel Hill: University of North Carolina Press, 1998.

———. "Marking New Directions in Performance Ethnography." *Text and Performance Quarterly* 26.4 (2006): 325–29.

———. "Performing Writing." In *The Ends of Performance*, edited by Peggy Phelan and Jill Lane, 73–103. New York: New York University Press, 1998.

———. *Telling Bodies Performing Birth: Everyday Narratives of Childbirth*. Popular Cultures, Everyday Lives. New York: Columbia University Press, 1999.

Portraits 9/11/01: The Collected "Portraits of Grief" from the New York Times. New York: Times/Henry Holt, 2003.

Powell, Colin. "U.S. Secretary of State Colin Powell Addresses the U.N. Security Council." February 5, 2003. http://www.whitehouse.gov/news/releases/2003/02/20030205-1.html.

Roach, Joseph. *Cities of the Dead: Circum-Atlantic Performance*. New York: Columbia University Press, 1996.

Rohd, Michael. *Theatre for Community, Conflict, and Dialogue*. Portsmouth, NH: Heinemann, 1998.

Rosaldo, Renato. *Culture and Truth: The Remaking of Social Analysis*. With a new introduction. Boston: Beacon, 1993.

Rose, Gillian. *Mourning Becomes the Law: Philosophy and Representation*. Cambridge: Cambridge University Press, 1996.

Rubin, Leon. *The Nicholas Nickleby Story*. London: Penguin, 1981.

Saramago, Jose. *Blindness*. Translated by Giovanni Pontiero. San Diego: Harcourt, 1997.

Saunders, Cicely M., and Robert Kastenbaum. *Hospice Care on the International Scene*. Springer Series on Death and Suicide. New York: Springer, 1997.

Scarry, Elaine. *The Body in Pain*. New York: Oxford University Press, 1985.

Schechner, Richard. *Performance Studies: An Introduction*. London: Routledge, 2002.

Scholes, Robert E. *Protocols of Reading*. New Haven: Yale University Press, 1989.

———. *Textual Power: Literary Theory and the Teaching of English*. New Haven: Yale University Press, 1985.

Schraeger, Samuel. "What Is Social in Oral History?" *International Journal of Oral History* 4.2 (1983): 76–98.

Schultheis, Alexandra W. *Regenerative Fictions: Postcolonialism, Psychoanalysis, and the Nation as Family*. New York: Palgrave Macmillan, 2003.

Shapiro, Alan. *Vigil*. Chicago: University of Chicago Press, 1997.

Shetterly, Robert. "Dershowitz's Name-Calling." FrontPageMagazine.com, August 5, 2005. http://www.frontpagemag.com/Articles/ReadArticle.asp?ID=19060.

———. Phone interview. July 13, 2006.

Skow, John. "Family Ties." *Time*, November 10, 1997. http://www.time.com/time/magazine/article/0,9171,987341,00.html?promoid=googlep.

Small, Neil. "Death and Difference." In Field, Hockey, and Small, *Death, Gender, and Ethnicity*, 202–21.

———. "The Public Construction of AIDS Deaths in the United Kingdom." In Charmaz, Howarth, and Hellehear, *Unknown Country*, 155–68.

Smith, Anna Deavere. *Fires in the Mirror: Crown Heights, Brooklyn, and Other Identities.* New York: Anchor/Doubleday, 1993.

Solomon, Alisa. "'Signifying on the Signifyin': The Plays of Suzan-Lori Parks." *Theatre* 21.3 (1990): 73–79.

Sontag, Susan. *AIDS and Its Metaphors.* New York: Farrar, Straus, and Giroux, 1989.

Spolin, Viola. *Improvisation for the Theater: A Handbook of Teaching and Directing Techniques.* 3rd ed. Evanston: Northwestern University Press, 1999.

Steinbeck, John. *The Grapes of Wrath.* Adapted by Frank Galati. London: Chappell Plays, 1991.

Stern, Carol Simpson, and Bruce Henderson. *Performance: Texts and Contexts.* White Plains, NY: Longman, 1993.

Stevenson, Anne. *Five Looks at Elizabeth Bishop.* London: Bellew, 1998.

Stucky, Nathan, and Cynthia Wimmer, eds. *Teaching Performance Studies.* Carbondale: Southern Illinois University Press, 2002.

Taussig, Michael. *Mimesis and Alterity: A Particular History of the Senses.* New York: Routledge, Chapman, and Hall, 1993.

Taylor, Diana. *The Archive and the Repertoire: Performing Cultural Memory in the Americas.* Durham, NC: Duke University Press, 2003.

———. "Dancing with Diana: A Study in Hauntology." *Drama Review* 43.1 (1999): 59–78.

———. *Disappearing Acts: Spectacles of Gender and Nationalism in Argentina's "Dirty War."* Durham, NC: Duke University Press, 1997.

Trounstine, Jean. *Shakespeare behind Bars: The Power of Drama in a Women's Prison.* New York: St. Martin's, 2001.

Turner, Victor. *Dramas, Fields, and Metaphors.* Ithaca, NY: Cornell University Press, 1974.

Viorst, Judith. *Necessary Losses.* New York: Free Press, 1986.

Walter, Tony. "Emotional Reserve and the English Way of Grief." In Charmaz, Howarth, and Hellehear, *Unknown Country*, 127–40.

Ward, Richard F. "Speaking of God: Performance Pedagogy in the Theological School." In Stucky and Wimmer, *Teaching Performance Studies*, 55–67.

White, Hayden. *The Content of the Form: Narrative Discourse and Historical Representation.* Baltimore: Johns Hopkins University Press, 1987.

Whitman, Walt. *Leaves of Grass.* New York: Penguin, 2005.

Wiley, Maya. "Hurricane Katrina Exposed the Face of Poverty." In *The State of Black America*, 143–53. New York: National Urban League, 2006.

Williams, Rowan. *Writing in the Dust.* Grand Rapids, MI: Eerdmans, 2002.

Wolfe, Thomas. *The Lost Boy.* Adapted by Matthew Spangler. Unpublished. 1999.

Zimmerman, James M. *Hospice: Complete Care for the Terminally Ill.* Baltimore: Urban and Schwarzenberg, 1986.

Zimmerman, Mary. *The Arabian Nights: A Play.* Evanston, IL: Northwestern University Press, 2005.
———. *Metamorphoses: A Play.* Evanston, IL: Northwestern University Press, 2002.

Index

Page numbers in italics indicate illustrations.

JODI KANTER is an associate professor of theater and dance at George Washington University. Her work focuses on performance, loss, and adaptation. Her essays have appeared in *Text and Performance Quarterly*, *Theatre Annual*, *Cultural Studies/Critical Methodologies*, and *Women and Language*.

Theater in the Americas

The goal of the series is to publish a wide range of scholarship on theater and performance, defining theater in its broadest terms and including subjects that encompass all of the Americas.

The series focuses on the performance and production of theater and theater artists and practitioners but welcomes studies of dramatic literature as well. Meant to be inclusive, the series invites studies of traditional, experimental, and ethnic forms of theater; celebrations, festivals, and rituals that perform culture; and acts of civil disobedience that are performative in nature. We publish studies of theater and performance activities of all cultural groups within the Americas, including biographies of individuals, histories of theater companies, studies of cultural traditions, and collections of plays.